deathland

Vampire State book three

Kevin Dickson

Vonsson Press

For Heather Taylor
the heart of my heart

Contents

Chapter One

Learning the difference between alone and lonely was proving to be a bitter lesson for Sara. For centuries, she had lived alone, and frequently, after dealing with the complex entanglements of governing her Lock, she wanted nothing more than to be left alone. Invariably, her alone time would be interrupted by a phone call, a letter or a text from a woman somewhere in the world seeking her guidance on a matter. At times, she felt like she could never be alone enough to satisfy her need for personal peace.

But in the immediate wreckage of her boyfriend Silas's departure, however noble his intentions, Sara was inundated by unfamiliar, ugly emotions. Her shock became fear became anger became abandonment, which led to the realization that she felt lonely, for the first time in her life. And it was nothing like being alone. Being alone was comfortable, rich with potential, exciting in its indulgence. Lonely was overwhelming, incapacitating and inescapably cold. Silas's absence became a presence in Sara's heart and gut, a black center of emotional antimatter that weakened her and forced her to stare it down. She had woven the tapestry of her new life with Silas in every thread, and now, all color drained from the tapestry, and she felt... lonely.

After crying herself to sleep provided too many tears and little sleep, an escape hatch appeared like a vision. Her old apartment. When Sara lived in that apartment, her world had been contained and safe. To her, it represented something more than a home, and now, for the first time, she realized the reason she had resisted moving to another apartment was that she saw that space as a talisman, somewhere she could be both alone and secure. In the darkest hour before dawn, a winter storm rattling against her windows, Sara decided to move home.

Now, hours later, the trauma still ricocheted through Sara's body, stealthy, explosive and omnipresent. Age-old insecurities and secrets hiding in sinews and dreamscapes, corrosive even in their quiet times, bounced around her subconscious, gaining momentum until they surfaced, not always legibly, in tears that came and went like summer storms, and now, in the raspberry violet of a bruise.

The bruise on Sara's arm stopped her in her tracks. Mainly to take her mind off things, and even though she absolutely knew what would happen next, she paused and watched the life cycle of the bruise. Almost as soon as its colors peaked, they began to fade as the virus in her system reclaimed the blood from beneath the surface of her skin. Distracted and absent, she watched as the colors desaturated, first to an olive mauve, then a yellow gray, and finally, a barely visible irregular mark on her even skin. She knew that that spot would remain visible for some time, as evidenced by the scores of matching discolored spots she was sporting up the front of both of her legs, and along both arms.

Sweating and shivering against the cold, Sara shoved the source of the bruise, her leather couch, roughly back into place, in the center of the living room of her old apartment, resisting the urge to flop down onto its firm yet worn cushions. A wave of angry exhaustion washed over her, and she blinked it away, heading into the kitchen and pulling a blood bag from the fridge. It hadn't cooled too much yet. She'd only turned the fridge back on an hour or two earlier. Testing the blood bag against her lips, it was only slightly colder than room temperature, and she could probably get away with drinking it without warming. Another wave of tiredness convinced her that it was worth a shot, and she unceremoniously twisted off the end of the drip tube and popped it in her mouth, drawing the blood into her mouth, slowly at first. The blood made her gag. Angrily, she pinched her nose and returned the straw to her mouth, sucking down the nauseating coppery liquid as quickly as she could, relishing the strength that immediately pulsed in her veins, her heart beating loudly as the bag emptied.

She tossed the empty bag onto the countertop where it joined five equally empty bags, the remnants of an angry, confused morning. She hated these new blood bags, the ones arranged by Silas. They reminded her of juice boxes, and she felt vaguely stupid every time she opened one.

They also reminded her of Silas, which was enough reason to hate them right now.

Patting her pants pockets for her phone, she groaned. She'd left it in the other apartment, the one she she'd shared with Silas until what? She had no idea of the time, but a glance out the windows told her it was around midday, the weak winter sun at its peak. So she did the math. She began hauling her stuff back to her old apartment once she had stopped crying. The sun had been up. By her calculations she'd been moving out of that apartment for six hours. And it had been at least an hour since she checked her phone. She knew she needed to go and get it, but she simply did not want to.

Forever feels a lot longer when you're dealing with an ex. She'd said these exact words to countless sisters, and here she was, paying the price for thinking the advice she'd given for centuries did not apply to her.

Spying his all-too-brief farewell note on the coffee table, she picked it up to read it for maybe the fiftieth time, as if it could give more information. This time it hit different. She felt needy and weak and dependent, on top of everything else. Angrily, she crumpled it into a ball with both hands and then tossed it at the kitchen trash can. The new blood in her system made her stronger, and the ball of wadded paper overshot the trashcan and landed in the cold, soapy water in the sink.

If something happened to Silas on his hare-brained trip to confront Desdemona, that was the last note she'd ever receive from him. With a grunt, she pushed herself from the couch and fished the note from the water. As she shook droplets of water from the paper, the tears resumed and the black hole inside her grew larger. She felt as if she was hollow, and the space was filling with black, liquid pain. A maelstrom of emotions swirled through her, and she allowed herself to feel them while she tried to identify them.

She was terrified.

Of losing the man she loved.

And she missed him. She'd never missed anyone like this. Not even when Teddie went to live in Paris for a decade, a century ago. Missing Silas so acutely was the generator that powered her loneliness. .

Why hadn't he called her?

Making her way clumsily to the couch, arms and legs stiff and disobedient, she sat, her face pressed into her hands as her tears subsided, but nothing could dispel the abject grief at her core. She tried to fire up some anger, but she understood exactly why he had chosen to leave. He wanted to stop their nemesis Desdemona from creating any more men cursed with their vampire virus. But he didn't need to go alone. Sara would have gone with him. But she wasn't asked. Suddenly, Sara wanted Silas to feel as abandoned she felt right now, but she knew that he would be missing her as much as she missed him, with an added layer of guilt. Smoothing out the wet sheet of paper against the arm of the couch, she couldn't tell if the words were smudged or if she had cried herself beyond being able to focus her eyes.

'What if Silas has landed?' her mind nagged at her. 'What if he is calling with information?'

Hating how badly she wanted to talk to him, she drew a shaky breath and moved to the rear door of the apartment, padding silently along the darkened corridor that led to her now-old apartment, feeling the familiar ghosts of centuries swirl around her, a solitary woman inside a vast stone complex, almost everyone that she loved flung to the corners of the earth. She was a single point in the universe, one star among billions.

Her feet heavy, she entered the apartment, its previous order now destroyed, furniture out of place, clothing and linens strewn on the floor, and yet, above it all, she still sensed Silas. She needed to get out quickly. She snatched her phone from the coffee table, careful to not look at the screen. Back in her old flat, she moved Silas's note, choosing the mantelpiece, beside her bluetooth speaker, as the safest space for it. The sight of the speaker suddenly made the silence in the room feel oppressive, and without thinking, Sara flipped her phone to connect it and before she could undo the damage, she saw the screed of notifications on her home screen, mostly texted variations on PICK UP!! and CALL ME!! from Crina and Heather, and lastly, a text from Imani.

> You okay guv? Spoke to Heather.

As much as she really didn't want to engage, she knew that once acknowledged, she'd not be able to rest until she tore off the bandaid. She paired her phone with the speaker, selected Dorothy Ashby, and the air filled with notes of sparkling harp that shrank the darkness inside her, just a little bit. After warming a mason jar of blood she plopped onto the couch, texted Imani that she'd call her in a half hour, then scrolled through all the texts from Crina and Heather, only absorbing the fact that there was nothing from Silas. As much as she didn't want to, she knew she had to call Crina. Sighing, she hit the call button, silencing the music.

"Sara my love," Crina answered before the phone could even ring.

"Hey mom," Sara said, her voice much less nonchalant than planned.

"How are you doing?"

Tired, Sara wanted to say. I'm tired and not just because I haven't slept. I'm tired of life.

"I'm good," she said instead.

"I spoke to Silas," Crina said, before pausing infuriatingly, and Sara knew instantly that Crina was going to cover for Silas. She wanted to hang up. "Sara, are you there?"

Sara took a long sip on her drink before answering.

"What? Yes, sorry, I'm in the middle of a million things."

"Sara," Crina's voice was stern. "I know Silas left without telling you and I just wanted to check in and see how you're doing?"

"Did you tell him to go?"

The brief hesitation in her reply told Sara all she needed to know.

"He's an adult, Sara," Crina said evasively. "He's taking steps to mitigate the damage he feels responsible for."

"Right," Sara said. "So what can I do for you? I have to get back to my prisoner."

"He's fine," Crina said. "Embla has been taking care of him while you slept."

"Right," Sara said.

"You didn't sleep did you?"

"Yep. Just woke up."

"Oh good," Crina said, her voice tinged with sarcasm. "I'd hate to think you stayed up doing something stupidly dramatic."

Sara literally counted to ten while she sipped at her blood.

"Nope, I was exhausted," she said. "There was nothing else I could do so I went to sleep."

"Well good," Crina said, and Sara was grateful she didn't push it. "And you haven't heard from our boy yet?"

"Not yet, no," Sara said, her voice neutral.

"I just talked to Stef, she's on her way to Budapest to meet him."

Budapest? Sara was confused but refused to show it.

"And are you still in the Reykjavik house with Heather?"

"What?" Crina seemed surprised by the question. "No, I'm at the airport."

"Oh right, the airport. The one airport."

"Don't be a brat," Crina said. "I'm at the airport in Iceland headed to Spain."

"Okay well fly safe and text me when you land."

Sara hung up. Music resumed pouring from the speaker. She cast her mind back, as she had done many times recently, over centuries of Crina and her mysterious behavior, still undecided as to whether Crina was manipulative, deceptive or just secretive. Whichever it was, the way that Crina selectively shared information was beginning to wear her out. She let herself ponder Crina's reasons for going to Spain for a moment, then pushed it out of her mind. Sara refused to spend any more time pondering Crina's actions. She'd learned long ago that it was pointless.

Now that she had a destination for Silas, she spent a few minutes googling and located his flight, which left JFK seven hours earlier, and still had an hour in the air. She fought an urge to see if the flight offered in-flight Wi-Fi, then hated herself for needing the reassurance. Silas could have texted her from the airport, or at any point after leaving the building, but he did not, so why would he text from a plane? Glancing at the clock, she knew that once she talked to Imani she'd need to go downstairs and see what was up with the Romanian, and only then, she could sleep. The bruise was no longer visible on her arm. Unsatisfied, she prodded the area with a fingertip. No pain. A wave of sad loneliness rolled through her and she wished her heart was as impervious as her skin.

On the couch, her phone lit up with an incoming call from a No ID number, and her heart leapt in her chest. Tipping the remaining blood down her throat, she set the empty jar on the floor and grabbed the phone.

"Hello?" she hated the eager sound of her voice.

"Sara?" Desdemona's deep voice sounded surprised, and Sara's stomach sank.

"What the fuck do you want? Of course it's me."

"You sounded almost happy," Desdemona said. "Which is why I didn't think it was you."

"I'm giving you thirty seconds," Sara said. "Make it good."

"My gift arrived, I presume," Desdemona said. "He's such a lovely addition to your collection of vampire men."

"Twenty seconds."

"Dios mio, you're tiresome," Desdemona said. "I only wanted us to get onto the same page. You know what I want. And we both know that it will take Yukari more than a week to find a counteragent to the vaccine in my system."

"Especially without a sample of your blood," Sara said angrily.

"Another purpose of this call. There will be a delivery for her today, seven vials of my blood. That should speed her up."

"You do realize we can also just wait you out?"

Desdemona inhaled sharply, and Sara knew she'd landed a hit.

"If you do that, Sara, I will flood New York City with infected men. And women. And children."

Pressing a finger to her temple, Sara inhaled slowly.

"Des," she said finally, "did you ever take our rules seriously?"

"Pinche puta," Desdemona spat. "From you, that's insulting *and* hilarious."

"I've never broken a rule," Sara said. "I didn't make Silas a vampire, I just didn't kill him."

"That's breaking a rule."

"You infected a man and sent him out to kill," Sara said. "You've got me beat."

"And once again, you've let him live. If Silas wasn't there, you would have already fucked him too. I bet one of your other sluts is probably fucking him right now."

"God, I hope so," Sara said with a laugh. "From the sound of you, you would have benefited from a little fucking yourself, Des. I'm guessing it's been a while."

"Even when the threat is this serious, you make jokes," Desdemona said.

"I've never taken you seriously," Sara said, waiting for the explosion.

"When your beloved city becomes the epicenter of a vampire outbreak, you'll take me very seriously."

"Doubtful," Sara said. "And even though we could talk for hours, I need to warn you that I'm about to hang up, so if you've not said whatever you called to say, I'd start talking."

"Next Friday," Desdemona said tersely. "The next infected man will arrive in New York. Unless Yukari has a medicine for me. Contact details will be included with the blood samples arriving today. Let's stay in touch, Sara, if you want to save your town."

"It's a city, Desdemona," Sara said wearily. "Why don't you just come here yourself, we can shoot the shit, challenge each other to a duel and sort this out in your beloved old ways?"

"I've wanted to kill you in a duel since the day we met."

"And I've gone decades without even thinking of you," Sara said, and the line went dead.

Once again, the music restarted, and Sara felt it swirling around her, its surging beauty contrasting against her messy, disorganized apartment. The thought of Desdemona sending an unchecked number of infected to New York hit her like a boulder. It would be impossibly dark, for the whole world. Now was not the time to fall apart, she told herself as she felt her edges fraying. This wasn't a job just for her, she reminded herself. Not any more. Under the new structure, she was just a cog in a wheel of the machine that would battle Desdemona.

All machines need a driver, she thought irritably, and she needed to blame someone, anyone, for this. The easiest target was Silas, so she focused on blaming him and instead, her eyes welled with tears, irritating her even more. On her lap, her phone buzzed as a call came in. Teddie. She swiped at the screen and raised the phone, gulping away tears.

"Mom," Teddie sounded concerned. "What's going on?"

"What do you mean?"

"We were supposed to talk this morning, I got worried when I didn't hear from you."

"Nice try," Sara sniffed. "Who have you talked to?"

"Okay, fine, busted. I talked to Crina, so don't try to play me."

"I wasn't going to, Ted," Sara said. "I was going to call you and then..."

"Sure you were, mom," Teddie said. "Is Silas really gone?"

"Yeah," Sara exhaled. "He's gone off to be our knight in shining armor."

"Bless him," Teddie said sarcastically. "And how do you feel about this?"

"Pretty fucking awful," Sara said, her throat constricting around the words.

"And what can I do to help you?"

Sara paused, biting down on the answer that sprang to her lips, and then thinking fuck it and letting it rip.

"I would really like you to come home," Sara said, her voice naked. "I... uh... Ted, don't make me say it."

"I won't, mom," Teddie's voice was soft. "You gots yourself some boy troubles huh?"

"Seems like," Sara said. "I *gots* other troubles too."

"Oh yeah," Teddie said. "Apart from your new Romanian prisoner?"

Suddenly very tired of Crina's meddling, Sara got testy.

"Let me see if there's anything Crina hasn't told you already," she said passive aggressively. "Oh wait, yes, you didn't ask about the reason why I didn't get to call you yet."

"Are you gonna make me ask?"

"Well," Sara's voice was churlish. "You know, in case Crina's got my apartment bugged, you might already know."

"Hooooo boy, you're in full on sulk mode," Teddie said with a gentle laugh. "Mom, what happened that prevented you from calling me?"

"I had a fun phone call from your favorite auntie!"

"Oh, was it Yfke? Did she talk your ear off?"

"No, my child. The other favorite. Desdemona called me with her plans to destroy New York."

"Bitch!" Teddie was aghast. "Start with that. Always start with that. Mom, sit tight. I'll leave right now. There'll be traffic for sure, but just hang in there, and tonight, we can have a girls' night and talk about how shit Silas is."

"Don't go speeding," Sara said. "What would you like for dinner?"

"Nope," Teddie said dismissively. "It's my turn to be the mom. I'll bring dinner. See you tonight."

As the music resumed again, another wave of tears took shape, and Sara cut it off dead, relieved that she was able to. It was time to disassociate and save her city.

Chapter Two

The knock at Sara's door startled her mid-sip on a fresh mug of blood, and she set it on the counter.

"Hello?"

"It's me, love, Imani."

Stepping over a pile of clothing, Sara fumbled with the locks before finally pulling the door open to reveal Imani holding a bunch of flowers and a Fairway bag, a bemused expression on her face.

"Happy housewarming," she said, thrusting the flowers at Sara. Stepping into the apartment, Imani stopped in front of Sara and rubbed a thumb across Sara's chin.

"You missed a spot," she said, holding up her thumb to display a smudge of ruby blood.

"Sorry, I was halfway through a juice box," Sara said, making Imani laugh. Sara took the flowers and set them on her kitchen counter, then gathered all the empty blood bags in one hand, waving it in the air as evidence.

"Ah, I see," Imani said as she hoisted the groceries onto the counter beside the flowers. "I love what you've done with the place," she said with a smirk. "It's giving first apartment out of high school vibes."

"It was either that or smash stuff," Sara said bluntly before pushing the blood bags to the bottom of her trash. "Imani, I've never been so angry at anyone."

"That's what happens when you fall in love, guv," said said, patting Sara gently on the shoulder. "You want to control the wind."

"Right and that's impossible yada yada yada," Sara said, wondering what was in the Fairway bag. She was starving.

"So, to update you," Imani sat on the couch and patted the cushion beside her, "we've moved our new houseguest into Marguerite's old apartment."

Sara jerked around from inspecting the Fairway bag's contents. "Oh?"

"Yeah, Embla and I visited him this morning and he wasn't happy in the old panic room. Marguerite's has bars on the windows and we disabled the locks on the inside. Anyway, he seemed happier there."

"Thanks for taking care of that," Sara said. "Imani, I'm starving, do you mind if I...?"

"Forgive my manners," Imani sprung up from the couch and took Sara by the shoulders, leading her to the couch. "We have sandwiches and bagels, what do you feel like?"

"Not making decisions," Sara said. "That's what I feel like."

"Sandwiches it is," Imani said without missing a beat. As Sara watched, Imani pulled wrapped packages out of the plastic bag and set them on the counter. "Don't bite my head off, but did plates make the great migration?"

Sara shook her head wanly.

"Not to worry, we can brown bag it," Imani laughed, bringing two wrapped sandwiches and sitting beside Sara. "Italian or roast beef?"

"Surprise me," Sara said. "Still avoiding decisions."

Chuckling, Imani handed her a sandwich, and in silence they unwrapped and ate for several minutes.

"Do you want to talk about what happened?"

"Sure," Sara said around a mouthful. "When I can get through a sentence without crying, I'll let you know."

"I'll be waiting," Imani said, and they finished their sandwiches without another word.

"Wanna come talk to our new friend?" Imani gathered the trash and went to the kitchen, gasping when she lifted the lid on the trash can. "Sara! How much blood have you had today?"

"Well I'm out now so it doesn't matter," Sara sniffed. "I guess the answer is all of it. I had all of it."

"No shade, love" Imani dumped the lunch wrappers into the trash and closed the lid. "You feeling presentable for our guest? I have a bagel or two for him."

"You tell me," Sara said, standing and glancing at all the clothes she needed to put away.

Imani tore a paper towel from a roll on the counter and came to stand in front of Sara. She dabbed the towel over several spots on Sara's face, tousled Sara's hair with her free hand, then nodded in satisfaction.

"You're right as rain," she said. "Let's go, we don't have to stay long."

"Let's go via the back way," Sara said, leading the way to the door at the rear of her apartment, and holding it open until Imani had walked past. They continued in silence to the elevator, dropped down two floors and then made their way to an unoccupied apartment and through to the hallway outside Marguerite's old flat. A flash of memories, Marguerite's destroyed body, April Veronica's horrified, blood covered face, sent a shiver of revulsion through her as Imani knocked on the door.

"Uber eats," she called out.

"Let yourself in," came Toma's deep, accented voice. "You're going to anyway."

"Step back into the living room," Imani said as she pressed her finger against the security pad.

"I'm on the couch," Toma called, his voice indicating distance. "I'm not getting up for anyone."

Kicking the door open with her foot, Imani quickly took in the empty hallway and nodded to Sara, who stepped inside first and walked along the short, dark corridor, consciously banishing memories with every step until she reached the living room, where Toma, now clad in cargo shorts and a blue button down, sat on the sofa, his wide handsome face glaring at her suspiciously.

"Oh, it's you," he said when he saw Sara. "Pardon me for not getting up. I don't know the correct manners for greeting your jailer."

"Hi Toma," Sara said. Imani appeared beside her and tossed the Fairway bag to Toma who caught it effortlessly.

"You have options," Imani said. "There's a bunch of bagels with various fillings. Help yourself."

"Three stars," Toma said with an almost smile, giving the contents of the bag a quick inspection. "No tip. I ordered hours ago."

"Like I said," Imani's voice was playful. "Be nice to your mama and she'll be nice to you."

Toma fully smiled at Imani and Sara rolled her eyes.

"So, Toma, how are you?"

Shrugging, he sat back in the couch. "Is it meal time or question time?"

"You can eat while we talk," Sara said. "Up to you."

"I'll wait," he said.

"As you wish," Sara said.

"Take a seat," Toma waved at the empty spaces on the couch.

"Thanks, I'll stand," Sara said, and Imani, who'd taken a step forward, stopped.

"Yep. Me too," she said. "Standing. We're standing."

"Toma," Sara's voice was commanding. "Can you tell me everything you know about the location of the cave where you found the infected bats?"

"I already told her," he nodded at Imani. "Don't you guys talk to each other?"

"Sorry guv," Imani said. "Stef talked to him hours ago. We have directions to all the caves he visited with Des."

"Right," Sara said, trying to keep the irritation out of her voice. "Since I don't want to repeat myself, is there anything you haven't told us yet that might help us all out?"

"Sure," Toma's tone was playful. "Can you tell me what right you have to lock me up like this?"

"I can," Sara matched his tone. "We have absolutely no right to do this to you."

"So you'll let me go?"

"Sure, why not?" Sara stared into his eyes. "Where would you go?"

"Oh you know," he smiled. "Times Square, catch a play, then maybe get a horse carriage around Central Park, then I'd like to go to a taping of SNL and catch a Knicks game."

"Original," Sara quipped. "And where are you going to get the blood you need to survive?"

Toma's head jerked up, and anger flashed behind his eyes.

"Well?"

"Look, Toma," Sara deliberately softened her tone. "You don't want to hurt anyone, and until we can make you better, it's not safe to let you go out into the City."

"I know," he said, his shoulders slumping. "Look, sorry, I'm really jetlagged and every time I wake up I think that all of this will go away like a dream, but it doesn't. I... I uh... don't know what's going on, I just wanted to do what that woman asked so my brother would be safe."

"If we find Desdemona, we find your brother," Sara said. "We will do everything we can to help him."

"And until then, I stay here?"

"A lot of people would kill for a free apartment in New York," Sara said.

"I'm not a lot of people," Toma countered. "I don't like being locked up."

"And I apologize, but right now, it's the best we can do."

Toma glared at Imani. "You said she would let me go."

"Don't play me like that, mate," Imani scofffed. "I said she's the only one who can, not that she would."

"I will let you go," Sara said. "As soon as it's safe for you, and us. Until then we will take very good care of you. But first, to be fully transparent, I had a phone call from Desdemona just now..."

Sara saw Imani's head jerk in her direction and it made her happy.

"...and she is sending another infected man to New York this Friday."

"Is it my brother?"

"She did not say, I'm sorry, but Toma, anything you can tell us about where she might send him will be massively helpful," Sara said. "Central Park is very large and anything you can tell us that helps us narrow down our search area will possibly save a lot of time... and lives."

"She gave me your address, that's all I had," Toma said. "Wait, is there a place called North Woods? I heard her talking about a place called North Woods, she was originally going to send me there. Do you know that place?"

"It's the whole northwest corner of Central Park," Sara explained. "It's very overgrown and there are lots of small paths."

"Then maybe try ordering an Uber and seeing where it drops you? Because she will send the person by her Uber account. That's what I did."

Sara felt a glimmer of victory.

"Where is your phone?" she asked, and Toma nodded sullenly at Imani.

"She took it," he said. "By whose authority, I don't know, but I don't have my phone any more."

"Right, sorry, and I'm sure you understand," Sara said. "Thank you for your help, that's a great idea."

"Hello?" Liz's voice came floating in from the hallway and Sara cursed herself for not closing the door. "What's going on? Why are you in here?"

Before Sara could do anything, she heard Liz's footsteps in the hallway, turning just in time to see Liz's eyes widen at the sight of Toma.

"What the actual fuck is going on in here?" she asked, panic edging her voice as her blue eyes widened.

"Long story," Sara said. "Let's leave and I'll explain everything."

"Yeah right," Liz was defiant. "So much for honesty, I mean, come on, why is there a guy in Marguerite's apartment?"

"Who is Marguerite?" Toma asked, clearly entertained.

"Who the fuck are you?" Liz yelled at Toma, who stood and extended his hand.

"My name is Toma," he said cordially. "Would you like to join me for a bagel?"

Imani stepped between Toma and Liz.

"Not. Now." she hissed.

"Oh don't even fucking try it," Liz snarled. "I have so many questions."

"And I have answers," Toma called as he settled back onto the couch. "Wait, I also have a question. How are all of you so beautiful?"

"For fuck's sake," Sara snapped. "You two, outside, now." She pointed at the door, and Liz and Imani skulked down the hallway. "And you," she returned to facing Toma. "I'm sorry for all of this, but it's only for a day or two."

"And I'm expected to believe you?"

Switching to Romanian, she gazed into his eyes.

"It's too soon for either of us to engage in trust."

After pulling the door closed, Sara turned to see Liz and Imani standing stiffly against the wall in the hallway.

"You two look like kids who got in trouble in school," she chuckled.

"Fuck that," Liz snapped, pushing away from the wall. "Tell me what's going on. We are supposed to be doing the whole transparency thing and once again, I walk into some bullshit secret plot and what now? You guys have another Cursed man and he's your prisoner?"

"As of 4am this morning, yes," Sara refused to be baited. "Long story short, Desdemona has found a new source of the virus, and she has sent him here as proof." Liz went to speak and Sara raised a finger. "Yes, he's infected but I'm not done. It's Desdemona so of course there's an ultimatum. If Yukari doesn't come up with a workaround for the vaccine we gave Des, she's going to send more infected men to New York."

"Fuck," Liz said. "Wait, can I speak now?" Sara nodded.

"She's mad because you let Silas into the Lock?"

"That would be a guess," Sara said, glancing at Imani. "A good one, probably, but Des has not said."

"She's aging," Imani said. "My guess would be that she's entirely in self-pity land at the moment."

"Don't get me wrong," Liz met Sara's eyes. "I like Silas, I really do, but I knew all along that we were poking the bear by letting him be part of the Lock."

"Well, good news for you then," Sara's voice rose with each word. "Because Silas took off this morning to go poke the bear in person."

"What the hell..."

"Imani, can you walk me back to my apartment? Bye Liz, it was nice to see you."

Without another word, Sara spun on her heel and walked along the hallway, then realized that she would need to take the stairs down to the street and reenter her building from the front door unless she wanted to go back to where Liz was standing. Reaching the front door, she held it open for Imani.

"I love a good storming off," Imani laughed as she stepped through. "Even if we do have to go the long way."

"Totally worth it," Sara said, following her down to the sidewalk. Winter dusk was already gathering and rain had plastered the street with the last of the season's fallen leaves, a slippery carpet of rust and gold. The cold wind bit through her track pants and light sweater.

"Quick, before we freeze to death," Sara darted down two steps to a metal grille door, opening it with her fingertip, repeating the process on the solid steel door behind it, and rushing them both inside.

"This is really the long way now," Imani said. "But so worth it. Did you see Liz's face?"

"I did and I'm not proud," Sara said. "She tries to fit in but-"

"You still don't trust her, me neither."

"It's not exactly that," Sara said, leading the way to the elevator that would take them to her place. "I actually just don't think of her when I'm strategizing."

"That's even worse," Imani said. "If you want my ten cents worth, I don't trust her."

"I can't really think that way," Sara said. "Whether she's good or bad or just opportunistic, it doesn't matter to me. I simply don't think she will be there when I need her, so I've never given her a chance to prove herself."

"Or to disappoint you."

"Oh, she's already done that," Sara said as they stepped into the elevator and rode up to the fifth floor. When they reached the rear entrance to Sara's apartment, Imani threw an arm across the door.

"Just quickly," she said conspiratorially, "I don't want you to be mad at me if you don't like this."

"Imani," Sara gritted her teeth. "What have you done?"

Pressing her finger into the keypad, Sara pushed against the door and as it opened, the hallway flooded with music and laughter. Fran, Embla and April Veronica all froze mid-chore once they saw her.

"Oh shit," Fran pulled her phone out and turned the music down. "Hey Sara, welcome to your new home."

Glancing around the room, a smile played on Sara's lips. The piles of clothing were already gone, and the apartment looked almost like it did before she left for Iceland.

"I feel like Cinderella," she said. "Thanks, you guys."

April Veronica and Embla, both wearing pink rubber cleaning gloves, rushed over and gave her air kisses.

"We wanted you to have a calm space," April Veronica said.

"Yes, neutral territory is key right now," Embla said. "And so is self-care. I'm happy you made this decision."

"How was our prisoner?" Fran hauled a very full laundry basket to the front door. "Tell me before I run this down to the laundry room."

"He was fine til bloody Liz stumbled in and hit on him," Imani said, and Fran gave her a high five.

"Did that really happen?" Embla asked.

"Course it bloody did," Imani continued. Sara gave Imani a quizzical look, bemused at how quickly Imani had staked a claim on their guest, whom Liz absolutely had not tried to hit on.

"Okay, well you guys, I'm gonna go check on Liz after I get your new clean sheets started," Fran said. "I'll fill her in, make her feel like she's part of the team."

"You're a good one, Frannie," Sara wrapped her in a hug. "And also, you don't need to do my laundry."

"Last thing you need is sheets that remind you of the man you want to forget," Fran quipped, wriggling out of Sara's embrace and dragging the laundry basket to the front door. "I won't be long at Liz's. If I think she needs it, is it okay if I bring her back up here with me?"

"It's the fair thing to do," Embla said, and Sara nodded. Holding the door open with her foot, Fran saluted them and left.

"You guys didn't have to do this," Sara said.

"We needed somewhere nice and clean where we can get good and drunk tonight," April Veronica said. "Oh yeah, there will be a rather sizable delivery from the liquor store arriving in about forty five minutes, so let them in when they buzz."

"I'm hosting a party?"

"Nobody likes being alone when they're sad," Embla said, coming close to Sara. "Are you sad?"

Sara nodded and rested her head against Embla's chest. "Sad and lonely, which is new for me. Worried too, which isn't."

"Stef has already met him at the airport," Embla said. "I understand your worry, but have you ever fought him?"

Sara shook her head again.

"He trained me, and he is a spectacular warrior," Embla said. "If he's with Stef, there's nothing to worry about."

"It's Desdemona," Sara countered. "With her, there's always something to worry about. It won't matter how good he fights if she brings a gun to a knife fight."

April Veronica appeared on Sara's other side. "You think that Silas is walking into a trap that Des has set?"

Sara nodded. "Sure, maybe, but that's just basic worrying. Des doesn't know him well enough to bait a trap for him. Turns out, I don't either. As recently as this morning, I didn't think he'd do anything like this."

"It didn't surprise me," Embla said. "He's a weird man, he readily accepts blame and rushes into the protector role."

"I knew those things," Sara chuckled.

"He's hypersensitive to the danger he has brought upon this Lock," Embla said. "We have talked about it many times, he is stubborn. And I promise you he will be back before the next Cursed man arrives in New York."

"He's going to be so confused by the new living situation," April Veronica said. "It'll be much cozier living here."

"I don't think I want him to live here," Sara said.

"Oh" Embla said, and silence fell.

"You guys, come on," Sara pressed herself off Embla's chest. "We moved way too fast, we don't need to move fast, and this is what I get. He didn't ask me. We didn't talk about this."

Embla theatrically gazed around the apartment, then returned her gaze to Sara.

"It looks like both of you may have overreacted in the heat of the moment," she said, her voice kind. "This is what happens when strong willed people think they know the solution to a problem."

"Do you ever lose your temper?" Sara said with a smile.

"No," Embla said. "Anger is a distraction. I spent most of my early life as an angry person. It never helped me. These days, I rely on two things – common sense and the knowledge that everything works out if you let it."

"You're an... wait, what's the word? You're an inspo!"

"Okay grandma," April Veronica said. "Enough of this chit-chat, we need to get this place party-ready."

"Teddie and Yukari are about two hours out," Embla said. "We have time."

In Sara's pants pocket, her phone began to ring. Pulling it out, she saw Silas's name and photo on the homescreen. She held her phone aloft, showing the girls who both made cartoony shock faces. Flipping them off, she retreated to the bedroom and pulled the door closed behind her.

"Hello?"

"Sara? Is that you?"

"Yes, Silas, it's me."

"You sounded different."

"Nope, it's me."

"Look, Sara, I'm sorry we didn't talk about it, and I knew that if we did, you'd ask me to stay and I can't say no to you."

"I would have asked you to stay because we have enough crises here for all of us."

"And I will be back for them all," Silas's voice was reassuring and Sara strengthened herself against it. "I promise."

"You can't promise, Silas. You don't know what you're rushing into."

"Me and Stef will find the caves where the bats live, then we will kill all the bats and I'll be back."

"You remember that region? There are tons of caves."

"All the caves were walking distance from a single campsite," Silas said, and Sara rolled her eyes. Once again everyone was talking to each other and not to her. She felt like Liz. "Toma told her pretty much exactly where it was."

"We have Stef, your mother, Heather, Yfke and even fucking Eleanor still over there. You didn't have to be such a man about it."

"Ouch," Silas said. "Sara, a cave system full of the virus is too great of a threat, to the whole world. I can neutralize it in a couple days."

"Like I said," Sara's voice was cold, "Stef could have handled it."

"And like I said, I'm deeply sorry."

"Did you sleep on the flight?"

"I did not, and please, Sara, don't shut down on me."

"Desdemona called me this afternoon," Sara, desperate to shut down, said.

"Ah shit, what was her deal?"

"She's committed to the bit," Sara said. "We have six days until another man arrives. Yukari and Teddie are on their way back to the city right now."

"Are you having a big meeting tonight?"

"No, judging by the order April Veronica placed at the liquor store, we are having a party."

"A drink before the war?" he said with a chuckle that irritated Sara instantly.

"No, a *girl's* night,"

"Ouch, again," he said. "Listen, Stef is just grabbing supplies and we will be off. I just wanted to-"

"Apologize, yep, got that," Sara said. "Noted. I have to go get ready for the party. Have a good night."

She hung up, catching herself as soon as she felt a lone tear spill from her eye.

Chapter Three

S tepping back into the living room just in time to see April Veronica struggling with a large box of alcohol, Sara kept her head down and slipped into the bathroom, pulling the door closed behind her. The mirror revealed what she already knew, her eyes were red from crying, and her tears were a thick, watery red from her morning blood binge. She needed to cover up both. Grabbing a tissue, she wiped her face dry, then sat on the edge of the tub while she got her breathing under control.

Through the door, she heard Embla and April Veronica laughing as they unpacked the alcohol, and Imani singing along to a reggae song she didn't recognize. In any other part of the world, these were the sounds of a party taking shape, a night dedicated to fun, but to Sara's ears they felt like the headiest of denials. The game that she'd been playing for five centuries had ceased to be predictable, and now, with Desdemona's plan feeling inexorably imminent, she didn't even know the rules.

One of Heather's old sayings played in her mind. "Sadness is inevitable but misery is optional." Casting her mind back, Sara saw that she'd been a misery for years, increasingly so, and Silas hadn't changed that, he'd just given her misery a pretty party frock to wear for a while and now that he was gone, it was back to being its ugly, undermining self. Instead of compartmentalizing her feelings, Sara decided to banish the misery and let her hair down and enjoy the party. And the first step was... what? She decided to call Heather, who of course answered before it rang.

"Greetings from Iceland," Heather said. "How are you doing, pet?"

"Hmmmm, let's see. My abandonment issues are in full swing. Imani is flirting with our prisoner, Embla's decided to throw me a party and I had a charming phone call from Desdemona."

"Thank heavens I just poured a wine," Heather tittered. "Where are you? It sounds like you're in an echo chamber."

"I'm hiding out in the bathroom, I just talked to Silas and Heather, I was a bitch."

"Course you were," Heather said. "Not a dig. But you're hurt and he hurt you. Be a bitch."

"I need him here, Heather."

"Why? So you can keep him safe? He's doing a very smart thing, Sara. You'll have more than enough muscle for if and when Des sends the next infected man."

"It's not an if, it's happening on Friday."

"Well, by then, I'll be back, and so will Fan and Ama."

"Not Crina?" Sara was surprised.

"Maybe, maybe not," Heather said. "She left this morning."

"Silas didn't mention that she was joining him."

"She's not, she's off on another quest to find some of the elders or something. She was pretty vague when I talked to her."

"Wait, I thought you two were together?"

"No, I was up in Akureyri until this morning. Stef left in such a hurry, I had to lock everything up for winter. Who knows how long it'll be til we can come back? Then I drove down here. I just finished in the greenhouse and while I was at it I did all the laundry."

"It's not a vacation rental," Sara laughed.

"You'd never guess by the way you lot left it," Heather sniffed. "Anyway, I'm flying back tomorrow."

"Good, I miss you, and you've been gone long enough."

"I miss you too, now get out and enjoy your party, I still have a couple loads of laundry to get through."

Standing in front of the mirror, Sara blinked rapidly as if that would dispel the puffiness around her eyes. It didn't. She sighed. It was time to face the music. She opened the door to a flood of music and laughter. Fran and Liz were holding hands and dancing circles around Imani, and suddenly, Embla was beside her thrusting a cocktail into her hand.

"It's a French 75," she said conspiratorially. "I've already had one!"

"Thanks, I'll catch you up real quick."

Taking the drink, Sara retreated to the far wall, her back against the cool brick. She'd gotten used to the gatherings in the other apartment, the Silas apartment, but it was jarring to see a party happening in her old apartment. At most, she'd host Teddie and Heather for wine. She watched as Liz let go of Fran's hands, winked at her then scooped up a wrapped present and skipped over to her.

"Sorry about earlier," Liz said. "My paranoia kicked in before I could get the leash on it."

"Don't worry about it," Sara said. "I'm sure it looked kinda sus. I'm sorry, Liz, but I honestly figured you all just talked and you already knew."

"I was just getting home," Liz admitted sheepishly. "And my phone battery was dead."

"Good night then?"

"Let's just say it was what I needed."

"Well good," Sara said. "We're good then?"

"Yeah, sorry I'm so high maintenance."

They both stood there in silence while Sara wracked her brain for the appropriate response. Thankfully, Liz didn't make her wait.

"I got you something," she said, thrusting a gift wrapped in Bluey wrapping paper at Sara. "Please don't think I'm a weirdo."

Steeling herself, Sara took the gift and gently tore at the paper, revealing a box with a lot of Japanese words on it, Flipping it over in her hands, she saw that it was some sort of sex toy.

"Is that a housewarming present?" April Veronica bounced over to see what was going on.

"No," Liz said proudly. "It's a my boyfriend left suddenly present!"

"Embla," April Veronica winked at Sara as she called out. "Come look! Liz got Sara a dildo!"

At least the blush that was burning her cheeks was also obscuring the red around her eyes, Sara thought as she pasted a smile onto her face.

"Thank you, Liz," she said, throwing her arms around Liz's shoulders, clearly taking her by surprise. Was this the first time she had ever hugged Liz? Survey said most probably, and it took Liz several seconds to respond. When they separated, Liz took the box from Sara's hands and removed the rest of the wrapping paper.

"It's not a dildo," she said to April Veronica. "The girl at the adult toy store said it has so many settings, you'll never miss a man."

Taking that as her cue, Sara moved over to where Fran and Imani were standing with their arms folded, bemused smirks on their faces.

"I hope you enjoyed that," Sara said.

"Not as much as you're going to," Imani said, ducking as Sara took a swipe at her.

"You know what?" Sara put her hands on her hips. "I don't even know where my trusty friend ended up."

Wincing, she realized that Crina had probably included it in the care package she sent to Iceland.

"Never mind," Fran said. "There's a new kid in town."

"Okay, enough you two," Sara stomped over to where Liz was still extolling the virtues of her gift to Embla and April Veronica. "I'll take this off your hands Liz!"

Snatching the box and not making eye contact with anyone, Sara headed for her bedroom at the same time as the front door opened revealing Teddie and Yukari, their arms full of bunches of flowers.

"Mom, happy housewarming," Teddie yelled, rushing towards her. "Wait, what's that?"

"Ooooh Sara," Yukari was grinning cheekily as she read the box in Sara's hands. "They are saying some very big claims on the box."

"It was a gift from Liz."

"We got you flowers," Yukari said. "Nobody told us this was sex toy party."

"Okay stop," Sara opened her bedroom door and tossed the box onto her bed, pulling the door closed. "It's not a sex toy party. It is now a welcome home Teddie and Yukari party!"

Snatching the bunches of flowers from the arms of her friends, Sara quickly took them to the kitchen and laid them atop the liquor bottles that now occupied all of her limited counter space, and before she could turn around she felt Teddie's arms encircle her from behind and she relaxed back against her.

"So how you doing mom?"

"Better now that you're here."

"Well don't be mad at me when I disappear in a few minutes to ah... in case you wondered where your vases were... they're in my place."

"I *was* wondering, thanks, I'll need them, you guys brought half a florist in with you. I had to use a big jar for the flowers Imani gave me earlier."

"Flowers are a lot cheaper outside of New York City, as it turns out."

"I bet vases are too," Sara said, spinning and kissing Teddie on the nose.

"He really hurt you, huh?"

"I'm still unpacking it," Sara said honestly. "I think I hurt myself."

"Huh?"

"I mean, it's not his job to be obedient to me..."

"Not sure I follow, mom."

"He's been so goddamn accommodating," Sara said. "He's been like the perfect boyfriend, in terms of meeting my needs, and this just felt like... he did something I did not want him to do and he didn't think how it would affect me."

"Well, there's that," Teddie said. "But none of us know how to navigate what you two are doing. And it's not like he needs your permission to handle his own shit."

"It's not just his shit," Sara snapped. "It's all of our shit."

"True, but we all get to react to it in our own ways," Teddie said. "Don't bite my head off, but it sounds like this is more about your control issues than his obedience issues."

"Probably a good time for you to go and get the vases you stole, Theodora!"

Sara turned and walked over to where Imani was sitting, joining her on the couch without a backward glance. She hated being a bitch to Teddie but wasn't there some code that made Teddie's support of another woman compulsory? As her anger prickled and burbled beneath her skin, she suddenly wondered if Silas had called Teddie, and that made her feel worse.

"I think I ruined my housewarming party," she said to Imani.

"It's your party," Imani wrapped her arms around Sara. "Burn it to the ground if you want to."

"Tempting," Sara said. "Imani, I just feel so rootless."

"Not something you often hear from a five hundred year old woman."

Chuckling, Sara nestled against Imani's chest. "This whole thing," she flapped a hand at her living room, "it's not going to work. I'm chasing the past and we both know that never works. I should have stayed in the other apartment."

"But then we wouldn't all be getting blasted and dancing."

"We are doing neither."

"The night is young, love."

"But do you hear what I'm saying?"

"Oh, loud and clear," Imani gave her a squeeze. "But you just did a lot of things that you haven't done, maybe ever. And now your feelings are hurt and you want some familiar comfort. I say you did the right thing, definitely in the short term. Self care, yo. It's not something you've ever indulged in. We all need it, Sara, and right now, I need a strong-ass cocktail. You sit right there, and I'll go mix us up something that will chase the blues away and get us dancing."

"I love you Imani."

Imani wrinkled up her face in joyous pleasure. "I love it when you're schmaltzy," she said, before heading to the kitchen. Immediately, her place on the couch was taken by Yukari.

"Sara I know you're busy with sex toy party," pausing, Yukari tittered, "but I have to say something that is upsetting me."

Sara nodded.

"It is impossible to make the medicine that Desdemona needs before Friday."

"I know, Yuka, but do you want to know a secret?"

Yukari nodded, and Sara took her hands.

"I don't want you to make a vaccine that cures her, she doesn't deserve this life."

Yukari's head jerked up in surprise.

"But she will risk all of New York!"

"She will do that anyway," Sara said. "So, let's get samples from our guy downstairs and get ready for that eventuality. If she sends men, and you have a vaccine that works, we can literally hit them with a blow dart and be done with it."

"But sooner or later, she will do something worse."

"Yes, but we can lure her here."

"You're willing to kill her?"

Sara nodded slowly.

"Of all the things that I fucked up in recent times, letting her go was so stupid of me, so capricious."

"It was also noble, and just," Yukari took her hands from Sara's and pushed a lock of Sara's hair behind her ear. "I was so proud of your solution, we stood above our beginnings, and you showed a way forward that was much more in line with how we feel as humans."

"But now innocent people are becoming collateral damage."

"We will be able to save them," Yukari said firmly. "I want to get blood from this new guy immediately. We don't even know whether it's the same virus that we have or something slightly different."

"It's similar enough that Desdemona's blood is immune to it."

"Yeah, because I cooked up that mRNA vaccine in five minutes and it is scorched earth," Yukari said. "It attacks binding proteins on a blanket scale. Frankly I was worried that the vaccine would kill her."

"You never told me that."

"I was ashamed, but we needed it in a hurry and that vaccine was something I'd worked on and abandoned, but I knew it would definitely stop the virus. I wouldn't have given it to any of us."

"Nothing to be ashamed of, Yuka," Sara said. "And you'll have a bunch of Desdemona's blood to work on, she's sending you a care package right now."

Yukari's eyes widened as she grinned. "That is excellent news," she whispered. "Thank you."

Imani returned with two very full glasses.

"Shit, Yuka," Imani said handing her a drink. "I didn't mean to leave you out. Take this and I'll be right back."

"I have to work tonight," Yukari protested. "I need to go see the new guy."

"He's very handsome," Imani said with a wink. "You'll need a drink under your belt."

"He really is," Liz said, appearing at Imani's side.

Yukari's lips pursed and she glanced at Sara for confirmation.

"He's okay I guess," Sara said, watching as Imani shot daggers at Liz. "I haven't really been in checking him out mode, what with the whole panic stations and boyfriend vanishing thing."

"Don't listen to her," Imani said, before chugging half of the other cocktail she was holding then handing the rest to Sara. "He's got floppy black hair, sexy full lips and he scowls a lot."

"He's a bloody prisoner and he's scared to death," Sara said. "And how come you drank half my drink?"

"We're sharing," Imani sniffed. "Now before you move apartments again, I'll go make us fresh ones. And Yuka, seriously, if you're seeing him tonight, you'll need a couple more of these."

Imani returned to the kitchen, Liz at her side.

"She's so bad," Yukari said. "And I can't tell when she's serious."

"She's serious," Sara said. "I think that her and Liz are going to get in a catfight. They both like him."

"Now you're making me really nervous."

Embla sidled up to the couch. "Can I join the nervous party? I love a nervous party."

Yukari nodded and patted the cushion beside her, and Embla sat down.

"Is something bothering you?" Yukari put a hand on Embla's leg.

"Yeah, but I don't think a party is the right venue for the discussion," Embla said. "I just wanted to see if you'll have time for a chat tomorrow?"

"Honestly, I'd rather we talked now, if that's okay," Yukari said. "I'm feeling a lot of pressure, and as soon as I get that guy's blood sample, I know I won't sleep til I understand what's going on."

"No, then no, let's not, it's not important."

"Embla, I insist."

Sara took in Embla's concerned appearance, then glanced over to where April Veronica was standing, on the other side of the room in a conversation with Fran and Liz. She was clearly not paying attention to the women, her eyes were fixed on Embla, and Sara felt worried.

"Fine," Embla sighed. "It's pretty simple. I'm aging faster than before."

Embla bowed her head to Yukari and separated her long brown hair with her fingers.

"See all the gray hairs?" she asked. "I used to find one, maybe two, a year. Then, like three or four years ago, they started coming in thicker. I didn't want to worry mom... I mean Stef... so I went and got it dyed, but I got distracted when I moved here, and now April is worried."

"How old are you?"

"It's sixty one years since I was born," Embla said.

"And have you noticed any new wrinkles or changes in your skin?"

"I'm Icelandic," Embla said. "We don't get a lot of sun. I guess I have some new crow's feet."

"And did you ever drink blood, or has it always been synthetic?"

"I had some human blood for a few years after I *transitioned*," Embla said with a chuckle. "But I switched to synthetic pretty quickly. I haven't had real blood in twenty eight years."

"Interesting," Yukari said. "I"m sorry this is stressing you out."

"It's actually stressing April Veronica out more than it's stressing me. I've approached this whole thing as an experiment, I've talked about it so much with Fan and Ama and with mum too. I never set out to live five hundred years, I just wanted to see what I could achieve as a vegan."

"And now?"

"Well," Embla looked at the floor, her feet moving nervously. "Let's just say I have an interest in a long shared future with someone."

"Don't!" Sara yelled theatrically. "They just lure you in and then you're vulnerable when the shit hits the fan."

"That's what I'm signing up for, one hundred per cent," Embla said with a laugh. "So Yukari, I just wanted to sort of put it on your radar..."

"You want to know if you're going to have to drink blood to get the full benefits of the virus?"

Embla nodded sheepishly. "Yeah, something like that. And I don't want to risk triggering any suppressed gender shit, I'm just scared of it."

"For years," Yukari's voice was stronger than usual, "we have sourced our blood very ethically. For my research purposes, we pay donors very well. The stuff we stole from hospitals was also taken voluntarily from patients. It's not the same as killing an animal for food."

"Right, yeah," Embla muttered nervously. "It's the cisgender issue more than that."

"Well, once we get past this whole Desdemona drama, I'm happy to work with you on this."

"Thank you, Yuka," Embla had tears in her eyes. "I just want to explore the world with my girl for as long as we want to. I look at Fan and Ama and they inspire me, think about it, they've been a couple longer than anyone on this planet, in history, and they're so vibrant and fresh and in love. I want to have a chance at that."

Before Sara could jump into the conversation, her phone buzzed in her pocket and she pulled it out, sure it would be Silas. Instead, it was a text from Ama. After reading it, she slipped it back into her pocket just as Imani plopped into the last space on the couch, handing her a fresh cocktail.

"Speaking of Ama and Fan," she said, "I just got a text, we need to wrap this party up. They'll be arriving in the morning, and they want us all ready for some "intensive training" at noon."

"Wrap it up my arse," Imani said with mock indignation. "We're just getting started. If they want us, they can take us hungover."

Chapter Four

———————————————

The sound of something rapping against her door woke Sara, and she had a split second of clarity before her consciousness was set upon by the greasy claws of a spectacular hangover. Groaning aloud while wishing the knocking would stop, Sara attempted to twist herself free of her bedding but each movement only mummified her more tightly. Groaning as the pounding in her head synced to the banging on her door, Sara fell back against her pillows and opened her eyes to best figure out her escape strategy from her bedding.

"Okay you can quit knocking," she called out, wincing at the volume of her own voice inside her skull.

"It's me guv," came Imani's voice. "Don't get up, I'll let meself in."

The sound of the door unlocking echoed around the living room, and Sara made a mental note to have Heather reset the access to her apartment. Imani's face appeared in the doorway.

"You look like I feel," she said, before stepping into the doorway, revealing two huge bloody marys and some sandwiches on a tray in her hands.

"I am stuck," was all Sara could manage, and with a nod, Imani set the tray on the bottom of the bed and began tugging at the tangle of comforter and sheet until Sara was able to wriggle free.

"You're bloody lucky I came along when I did," Imani chuckled as she unwound the comforter from around Sara's shoulders. "You got yourself fully trapped you did. Anyway, first things first, a toast."

Sara groaned as she watched Imani twist and grab the two cocktails, tomato red in tall curvy glasses, brimming with garnishes, celery stalks and olives on skewers. Their scent hit Sara's nose and her stomach contracted.

"I don't think I can, Imani."

"You're going to have to," Imani said with faux severity. "Fan and Ama turned up an hour ago and they're getting set up for a training session on the roof deck."

"Using literally in its least hyperbolic sense," Sara said with a chuckle, "I literally cannot do any fight training right now."

"They have a dog with them."

Sara's head cocked and a smile crossed her face.

"They got us a puppy?"

"No," Imani said, setting the bloody marys on the floor and pulling a blood bag from the pocket of her floor length chocolate suede coat. "Here, this will settle your stomach for the booze."

After blowing Imani a kiss, Sara took the blood bag, twisted it open and put the tube into her mouth.

"Drink your juice, Shelby," Imani said, causing Sara to sputter a spray of red across her comforter. "Gonna need to soak that in cold water"

Finishing her blood in silence, Sara welcomed the swoon, mainly because it temporarily blocked out the throbbing in her head. When she came to and opened her eyes, all she could see was the bright green celery leaves of the cocktail Imani was holding in front of her face. Gingerly she took the glass from her old friend.

"Thanks, I think," she said, and they cheersed in silence. The first sip went down easier than Sara expected, and almost instantly her hangover began to fade.

"Wait, is there a puppy or not?"

"There's a dog," Imani said with a theatrical eye roll. "But it's not ours to keep. They rented a bloody scent dog. You know how much they love weapons and gadgets. They probably also have a trained beluga on call in the Hudson."

Sara laughed, nodding her head in agreement. She marveled at the tenacity of Fan and Ama, the way they never took their eyes off the target. She needed to get out of the full training session, though. She couldn't let them see just how rusty she was. Every time she tried to initiate sparring practice with Silas, it devolved into sex. She could hear their reactions in her head already.

"I'm not gonna go," Sara said, taking a defiant sip of her cocktail.

"I don't think you have that option," Imani said. "They came knocking on my door after they couldn't find you at your other place. I told them that you'd gone for a run."

Turning to her bedroom windows, Sara pulled the curtains back and a shaft of weak November sunlight spilled across her blood spattered covers.

"Nice day for a run," she said.

"It's never a nice day for a run," Imani laughed. "Now let's finish these dranks and get you showered, because honey, you smell like a dive bar."

A short while later, Sara took a deep, calming breath as she pushed open the heavy door from her upstairs loft out onto the roof.

"They won't bite," Imani said from behind her.

"They're more likely to bite than the dog," Sara said, her voice stern. "I am still getting over the loss of my full day in bed ahead of an all-new crisis."

"When aren't we in crisis?"

"Fair," Sara said, turning to face Imani. "Thanks for getting me up and at 'em."

"You've done the same for me, so many times. It was the least I could do."

Before Sara could answer, a pair of arms wrapped around her waist and squeezed.

"Sara Sara Sara!" Fan yelled into her shoulderblades as she hugged Sara from behind. "Come meet Mr Handsome."

After making panicked eye contact with Imani, Sara fell back into Fan's arms. Without skipping a beat, Fan caught her and dragged her backwards, her heels bouncing over the roof's bumpy brickwork. Suddenly grateful for the calming effects of the bloody mary, Sara went limp and enjoyed the ride, watching the pale gray sky through passing olive branches until Fan stopped suddenly and bounced her effortlessly to an upright position, right in front of Ama, an expectant smirk on her face.

"Delivery for Ama Singh."

"Oooh, spicy Romanian goulash," Ama said, wrapping her arms around Sara. "Just what the doctor ordered."

"I'm glad you're here," Sara said. "I talked to Des. We're gonna need your... muscle."

Ama shook her head and stepped back from the hug, taking Sara's hands in hers. "We-" she paused, waving an arm around the roof deck, empty except for Fan and Imani, who waved feebly, "-we got this."

"Great. The four of us. Shouldn't be a problem."

"Five!" Fan said, clapping her hands. "Mr Handsome? Where's Mr Handsome?"

As if on cue, a brindle Aussie cattledog scampered out from behind one of the raised garden beds.

"Here he is," Ama yelled. "The man of the hour!"

"I thought we were going to do fight training," Sara began, and Ama burst out laughing.

"Fuck no," she said. "That's on you guys. Everyone should be keeping up with their training."

"But we don't think there'll be any fighting this week," Fan said, wrapping her arms around Ama. "We're gonna use Mr Handsome to find the infected guy. We rented him but I already want to keep him."

Bending, Fan scratched Mr Handsome behind the ear and he rose up, licking her face. In a gale of giggles, Fan threw herself on the ground and began to wrestle with the dog, squealing when he licked her.

"Horizontally, you're about the same size," Sara said, making Ama laugh.

"Hey," Fan called out, "you're already short-shaming me?"

A rustle of voices from the far corner of the roof caused Sara to look up and see Fran, Embla and April Veronica flanking Toma, all walking in their direction.

"Oh shit," Ama said conspiratorially. "Don't say anything about Mr Handsome's job. For now, he's just our new puppy okay?"

Confused, but knowing better than to ask questions, Sara just nodded and waved to the newcomers as Imani appeared at her side.

"Tell me that's not one fine man," Imani said.

"I'm presently anti-men," Sara said.

"I'm anti war but I can still appreciate a nice weapon," Imani said, clucking her tongue. "Thank you, I'll be here all week."

Sara was still laughing when the newcomers arrived.

"Toma, hi," Sara said, waving at the man, who smiled and waved back.

"Hi Sara," Toma paused, then moved his attention to Imani. "And you, Imani, it's very good to see you."

Sara watched as Imani's eyes twinkled and she did a little bow, and she was grateful when Fan bounced up to Toma.

"Hey, new guy," she said, presenting her palm. "I'm Fan, sorry we weren't here when you arrived but look! We got a new puppy! This is Mr Handsome."

"A very accurate name," Toma said as he surveyed the dog waiting expectantly beside Fan. Kneeling, he gently extended a closed fist and the dog inched forward, first sniffing and then licking the back of Toma's hand.

"I knew it," Ama said. "He likes men better than women. Good thing we have you staying with us. I'm Ama."

After shaking her hand, still kneeling, Toma returned his attention to the dog, and within seconds the pair were rolling around on the ground. After a minute, Toma glanced embarrassed at the women and pushed himself to his feet, wiping his hands on the front of his pants.

"I'm sorry, I have a dog at home and I miss her very much," he said.

"Nothing to apologize for," Imani said. "I'm sure she misses you too."

Immediately, Toma's face was stricken.

"I don't know if she's okay," he said. "I would like to get back to her as soon as I can."

"That's the plan," Sara said. "Give us the address where your dog is and we will make sure she's taken care of."

"Thank you," Toma said, a genuine smile softening his eyes. "Have you talked to the other man today?"

"Not today," Sara said.

"Actually," Ama raised her hand as if she was in class. "Can I request that we all get updated at once? Can we schedule a meeting, for every-one?"

"You can do whatever you want," Embla said. "Remember?"

"Excellent," Ama smiled. "Let's have a meeting up here in the pent-house at what? Four? We have a lot to update each other on, but until then," she smiled at Toma, "those who want to can join me and this guy here for a puppy playdate."

Immediately, Imani fell to her knees and started calling Mr Hand-some, and Sara joined Embla and April Veronica in a group eyeroll.

"Okay, well if you're not a dog lover," Fan stared into Sara's eyes, "can the rest of us all try to talk to whoever is out in the field so we have a comprehensive picture of what's going on by this evening?"

Sara nodded and began walking back to her apartment door, her mind already consumed with the fact that they wanted her to talk to Silas, something she very much did not want to do.

"Hey, April Veronica, Embla," she called out. "Wanna keep an old woman company?"

Instantly, the couple began to walk briskly in her direction.

"Thanks for getting us out of that," Embla said. "I don't understand the whole dog thing."

"That was the only thing wrong with Iceland," April Veronica said with a cheeky grin. "Dogs were illegal there or something."

"We've been through this," Embla began, and April Veronica cut her off.

"Yes, and unless you want a puppy for Christmas..."

"I agree with you, Sara," Embla said. "Being in a relationship is annoying."

"That it is," Sara said, holding open the door to her loft and ushering them inside. "And full disclosure, that's why you're here. I have to call Silas and I'd rather it be a group effort."

"So you're using us as buffers?" Embla's voice was full of mock offense as she carefully made her way down the spiral staircase to the living room.

"I'll pay you in wine... oh wait, that's right that's an old lady thing."

"You're never going to let me live that down," April Veronica groaned as she took a seat on the couch. "You're stressed. If it makes you feel better we can all have a wine."

Smiling, Sara went into the kitchen and looked through the wreckage from the night before. The counter was littered with liquor bottles in various states of fullness, and the simple math of making a cocktail was too complicated for her to process.

"I'm sorry you guys I'm kind of melting down here," she said, feeling weird about being so publicly vulnerable. "Can one of you come in and create the cocktails while I set us up to talk to my ex?"

Embla leapt from the couch and wrapped her in a hug, and Sara relaxed into her grip.

"He's not your ex, and we are here to bartend for you," Embla said.

"For right now, it's easier for me to pretend that he is," Sara said. "On top of the whole Desdemona might kill him thing, I'm starting to feel like I did rush into this and I also don't need a distraction right now."

April Veronica appeared at their side.

"Au contraire mon frère," she whispered. "Right now, us being in love, us being happy, that's the one thing Desdemona can't fuck with."

"But I'm not happy," Sara began.

"You were forty eight hours ago," April Veronica said. "Right now, you're dealing with abandonment issues, that's all."

"That's all?" Sara scoffed. "That's ALL?"

"Okay, okay," April Veronica inserted herself into the hug and pried Sara out of Embla's arms, leading her to the sofa. "Sorry, I didn't take your feelings into account, I'm sure it feels huge and horrible. Embla, honey, can you please make something, anything, as long as its strong?"

"On it queen," Embla called, and Sara heard glass clinking as she flopped onto the couch.

"Where is your phone?"

Sara reached into the pocket of her pants and pulled it out, wincing when she saw a bunch of missed calls from Silas.

"Do you want voice or video?" April asked as she took the phone from Sara's hand, and a wave of panic rushed through Sara. Silas couldn't find out about this apartment, not like this.

"Just voice," she said quietly.

"I made Negronis," Embla said, setting three drinks on the coffee table. The pungent aroma of Negronis made her stomach twist, so she held her nose, and downed her drink in one gulp, sputtering when it was done.

"You could have just asked for something else," Embla sniffed, cheersing April Veronica.

"Call him," Sara said, and April obeyed. Silas answered immediately.

"Sara? Sara? Are you okay?"

"Sorry, Silas, yes, I'm fine, sorry we've been training with Fan and Ama?"

"With the dog? Is he cute?"

"Sure, he's cute I guess, he's just a rental, let's not get too attached," Sara said as she felt the liquor hit her system.

"Sara, are you okay? You're still mad at me, aren't you?"

"I'm here with Embla and April Veronica," Sara said, and a moment of silence fell on the line.

"Oh hi guys," Silas said eventually.

"Everyone is carrying on as if that dog is a baby," Embla said.

"Welcome to America," Silas said.

"Fan and Ama need a progress report," April Veronica said. "We have to get back up to the roof deck for a meeting and they've instructed us to get your updates."

"Ah, so Fan and Ama asked you to call me huh?" The disappointment in Silas's voice hurt Sara's heart briefly, then was replaced by anger.

When nobody replied, Silas continued.

"Okay, Stef and I located the cave that Toma sent us to. We've spent the last day sealing that cave and all the caves near it and then we lit a fire inside. We've suffocated all the bats inside those caves, but you guys, there are so many caves in the mountains."

"Right," Sara interjected, her voice firm. "So it's a bigger job and you won't be back in time for the arrival of the next infected man on Friday."

"Was that a statement or a question, Sara?" Silas was getting bristly too, and Sara watched as her companions exchanged wide-eyed glances.

"Well are you going to try to kill all the bats? Because that won't happen in one day."

"You're right, it won't," Silas said, his voice steel. "But for now, Desdemona would have to find new caves. The caves she knew about have been contained. We have collected dead bats from each of the caves and we need to return to Bucharest and ship them, then we can return."

"It's Wednesday," April Veronica said. "I think it's safest to assume you won't make it in time."

"I'll do my best," Silas began and Sara cut him off.

"Do you know where your mother is?"

"She is trying to meet us in Bucharest," he said. "She's wrapping up in Madrid."

"Wrapping up what exactly? Why is she in Madrid?"

"Your guess is as good as mine," Silas said. "You know her. She tells you after the fact."

"That's not how we should be working right now," Sara said.

"Then I suggest you take it up with her," Silas snipped.

"If she was answering her phone," Embla interrupted, "we would."

"I'm sorry," Silas's voice softened. "Peanut? Embers? Can I get a second alone with Sara?"

Sara shook her head, but the women beside her stood and let themselves out of her front door.

"They're gone," Sara said.

"Sara, did I fuck up?"

After indulging in a long sigh, mainly to buy herself time, Sara replied.

"I don't know," she said, her voice tiny. "Either you did or we did or I did."

"Let me rephrase the question then. Sara, did I hurt you?"

Her silence was her answer.

She heard Silas exhale, then swallow.

"I will be there as soon as I can," he said. "But until then, Sara, please, please know that I love you more than I've ever loved anyone or anything on earth. After I talked to Toma, I called Stef and the plan snowballed so quickly, and I did a stupid thing."

"Which was?"

"Sara, I confused your strength with what you needed in the moment," he said plainly. "I forgot that you need to protect me as powerfully as I need to protect you."

"I'd say you forgot that you were part of a couple," she said, her voice bitter. "That's what it felt like."

"I'm not going to make excuses," Silas said. "What's done is done and we can add it to the long list of things I'll be apologizing for for eternity, but at the end of the day, I did what I did because I ferociously want you to be happy, and have a hassle free life, and this fucking bitch is getting in the way of what I want."

"She's been doing it to all of us for so long," Sara said, her anger being replaced by a clammy sadness. "Look, Silas, we can talk when you get home. What you're doing is valuable, you're very right. I'm just not used to..."

"...to getting hurt?"

Even though he couldn't see her, Sara shrugged, unwilling to answer any further.

"I have to get back upstairs," Sara said. "I'll see you when you get..." She paused, unable to say 'home.' "When you get back."

"I love you, Sara."

She hung up, and the pain in her heart reached a new level.

"You guys can come back inside," she called out, and the door opened, and within seconds she was engulfed in a four-armed hug. "This couples shit is exhausting," she mumbled into Embla's ear.

Chapter Five

When they got to the roof, they were disappointed to find it empty, a near-freezing light rain hanging in the air like mist, the trunks on the bare fruit trees glistening like ice.

"Can we be your therapy dog?" April Veronica asked. "We'll do anything to cheer you up."

"Make it all make sense," Sara said before they both wrapped her in another hug. "Love, life and leaving. You guys, this is the first time I've ever missed someone. That was rough."

"Course it was," Embla said. "But we are here now and he will be back soon."

"That's the problem," Sara said with a small laugh. "When he gets back, he sees the mess I made of our life."

"Say the word and we will move your stuff back to the other apartment," April Veronica said enthusiastically.

"Ohh good idea," Embla said.

Sara rolled the question around in her mind, her arms pulled up to her chest inside a warm cocoon of women.

"No," she said eventually. "No. I like that space, so no matter what happens, I think I'll keep something for me."

Embla went to speak, and then caught herself. Pushing herself out of the group hug, Sara looked her in the eye.

"What were you going to say?"

"I'd rather not say it," Embla smiled. "That's why I didn't say it."

"I can take it," Sara said. "Please."

"Silas will be..." Embla paused, "...hurt. Your actions will hurt him."

"There's a lot of that going around," Sara said with a shrug. "Right now, I need to at least give myself the illusion that I have something that's just mine."

"Nothing is truly ours," Embla said, kissing the top of Sara's head. April Veronica broke up the hug and led Sara in the direction of the roof deck house, giving Embla a cross-eyed death stare.

"We can be early to the meeting," April Veronica said. "You've completed your assignment. And it's warm in there."

"I have to tell you something," Sara whispered, and both women leaned in close. "I miss the old meetings."

"There's nothing stopping you from structuring a meeting any way you want," Embla said.

"Right, but the old way means me being the boss and I don't want to do that any more."

"Old habits die hard, but they mutate beautifully," April Veronica said. "Let's regroup after this and see if we can't modernize the old meeting structure into something that works for you. "

"You guys take such good care of me," Sara said, taking a hand from each of them and squeezing it. "Thank you."

"I don't feel like doing mushy stuff right now," Embla said, blinking away a tear. "I want to get a good seat for the Liz and Imani show."

A full-throated laugh escaped Sara's lips, and she nodded.

"Me too, let's go."

The sight of all the thrones arranged into an inward facing circle set Sara's nerves on edge.

"It feels like an AA meeting," she whispered to April Veronica, jumping when Fan popped up from behind the bar.

"I heard that," she squealed, only her head and shoulders visible above the bar top.

"Calm down, child bartender," Embla called out. "Do you want me to get you a booster seat?"

"New York has made someone unbearably sassy," Ama said, emerging from the small bathroom at the back of the space. "I think I preferred gloomy emo Embla."

Sara smiled as a blush rose on Embla's pale cheeks, and a cheeky glint appeared in April Veronica's eyes.

"You didn't like that version of me," Embla snarled at Ama, fairly shoving Sara down onto her throne.

"You were emo?" April Veronica was bouncing with energy.

"I was a gender dysphoric genius living on a farm in Northern Iceland," Embla said dismissively. "What else could I be?"

Fan leaped over the bar, landing beside April Veronica. "You shoulda seen her back then," she crowed. "Dyed black hair in a big swoop, one eye covered by it, black lipstick, Doc Martens, crazy designs on her clothing."

"Sounds hot to me," April Veronica laughed. "I wanna see photos."

Embla went quiet, suddenly busy swiping dust off the arm of her throne.

"There are none," she said, resignation in her voice. "At least none that we can get our hands on."

Sara watched as Fan and Ama exchanged knowing glances, and Ama changed the subject.

"So Liz asked me if Toma could come to the meeting..."

Sara was glad that Liz hadn't called her.

"She said no," Fan added. "Liz doesn't like hearing no."

"Actually," Sara said, "it might not be a bad idea to have him here for some of it. He should hear the reports from Romania, he might have input."

"I just hate letting Liz have her way," Ama said, as the door opened in Imani hurried in, shivering, followed by Teddie and Yukari. Excitedly, Sara patted the cushion on Teddie's throne, right beside her, and Teddie rushed over, kissing the top of Sara's head on her way down.

"What's this," Imani mugged. "A fucking encounter group?"

"I told you they hate change," Fan said to Ama.

"I don't hate change," Imani said. "In moderation. How am I gonna sit and scroll on my phone during the boring bits?"

"Easy," Fan laughed. "Our meetings don't have boring bits. But if I was you, Sara, I'd be so offended right now."

Sara glanced at Yukari, her face pale and drawn, dark circles below her almond eyes.

"You okay, Yuka?"

Yukari barely made eye contact with her before nodding wanly and taking her seat, directly opposite Sara. Making a note to circle back with her later, Sara blew her a kiss. Yukari merely nodded to her and then whipped out her phone, immediately lost in its contents.

Heather and Fran arrived, arm in arm and laughing. Sara, surprised that Heather hadn't texted her to let her know she was back, waved at them as they took their seats.

"I'm not waiting for Liz," Ama said, moving to the center of the room while Fan returned to the bar and noisily began to move warmed goblets of blood onto a serving tray. "So if we are all in agreement, we will go get Toma for the second part of the meeting." A round of shrugs met Ama's statement. "I suppose that's a yes. Anyway, Fan, if you can give out everyone's drinks, we can start by asking Heather for her update."

Sara glanced at Heather, in her winter uniform of a tartan skirt, cable sweater, black tights and lace up boots, her face paler than usual and slightly pinched. She watched carefully, as Heather fussed with a strand of her long chestnut hair, eventually shoving it angrily behind an ear before she looked up at the group.

"I'll cut to the chase," Heather said bluntly. "Something's up. And I don't know what it is."

Everyone started talking at once, but Sara kept her gaze fixed on her friend. A noise at the door told her that Liz had arrived, but something about Heather was setting off alarms inside Sara. She heard Liz begin to complain, only to stop suddenly and take her seat.

"Heather, sorry," Fan said handing her a goblet of blood. "Please, continue."

"I don't want to repeat myself," Heather said. "So has anyone here been talking to Eleanor?"

"I have," Liz said, "but she hasn't said anything important."

"Elle and I agreed that this was an in-person talk," Heather said. "When I left New York, I met up with her, and we traveled to Edinburgh..." Pausing, Heather downed her entire goblet, gently setting the empty vessel on the floor, her tongue dealing with a small trickle of blood at the corner of her mouth. "It was the worst thing I have ever seen."

Silence fell in the room. A faraway siren keened. Sara did not take her eyes off Heather, who was inhaling deeply and raggedly.

"It was as if Desdemona just left as soon as... it... was done," she said eventually. "She just locked the door and left them all where they lay. I won't ever speak of what we saw, but me and Eleanor, we opened the windows and took care of them. They're all laid to rest now."

Out of the corner of her eye, Sara saw Ama signal to Fan to bring Heather more blood.

After a shaky breath, Heather continued. "After what we saw in Edinburgh, she and I traveled to Helsinki and Warsaw. Exactly the same story, you guys."

"I'm curious," Liz's voice was mildly antagonistic. "What was Eleanor's excuse for treating dead sisters so poorly?"

"Wait," Teddie leapt in before Sara could even take a breath. "I'm assuming she was just following Desdemona's instructions at that point. Just like you were."

Liz, already irritable, went to stand. Fan, en route to deliver fresh blood to Sara, paused to push Liz back into her throne, then handed Heather her drink.

"Thanks, pet. And Liz, no amount of blame will make up for what I saw in those Locks. What I will say is that we got lucky. Very lucky. With nobody coming or going from the buildings, the doorways were full of junk. Unhoused people had taken up residence in front of Edinburgh and Warsaw. There was trash and flyers and junk mail and all sorts of shit just littering up the place. We are so lucky that nobody broke in or called the police and asked them to investigate. We would have never been able to talk our way out of that one."

"I'm sure that was part of Desdemona's plan," Fran said.

"I'm not so sure there was a plan," Heather said. "It's worth talking to Eleanor. She was with Desdemona during this whole thing."

"Then why doesn't she come home?" Liz's voice was still snotty.

"She's deeply embarrassed," Heather said. "Like you should be, Liz. She's also badly scarred, physically. She wears a face covering at all times, but you guys, they beat her almost to death. The virus healed her, but it could only do so much. She's missing some teeth, her nose looks like a boxer's and her lips healed crooked. She is very self-conscious."

"And you're sure she's on our side now?" Sara tried to make eye contact with Heather, but her old friend refused to look her way as she nodded.

"Yes, she's back to being the Eleanor we all know and love."

"Heather," Sara spoke directly to her. "It feels like there's something else."

Heather finally looked her way, and Sara saw weary new lines around her mouth and eyes.

"Yes," she said quietly. "There's more but I was hoping to have an answer instead of just a bunch of clues. For the past month or so I've been talking to the girls in London and Paris, the ones that didn't come from Spain, and I've been monitoring what the Madrid girls have been up to since they took possession of the buildings and assets of those Locks, and the answer is, they've not been up to much at all. But the reason I came home is, a few days ago, they all disappeared."

Sara's head jerked up.

"What do you mean?"

"I mean what I said, love," Heather said. "With no warning, all the Madrid transfers have left their Locks."

"So is that where Crina has gone?" Imani said, waving her empty goblet at Fan. "She's gone to Spain to deal with them?"

"No," Heather replied. "She went to Madrid, but so far, none of the missing women showed up there. She has the place staked out, but it's not looking like that will be their destination. We don't know where they've gone, but we presume they've gone to meet up with Des."

"Wait," Teddie leaned forward. "Is Madrid fully staffed? Is everyone there?"

"We are waiting for Crina to confirm," Heather said.

"Didn't you just talk to her? Sara's tone was terse. She felt certain that Heather was covering for Crina.

"I tried to," Heather said. "And lassie, don't start with me. While you've all been playing happy families, I've been dismembering and burning the bodies of women I loved. I'm not feeling cheery or generous at the minute."

"I apologize," Sara said.

"Anyway, I don't have an update from Crina. But if anyone sees any activity from the Madrid sisters, please do let me know."

A round of murmured agreements ended in deafening silence.

"Yukari," Fan said eventually, "you look tired, and I think there's too much on your plate right now. Is there anything we can do to help you?"

Yukari lifted her face and Sara was shocked at just how dark the circles beneath her eyes were.

"I don't have any answers," she said, her voice breaking. "I don't have the equipment to do the kind of work-around vaccine that Desdemona needs, and this timetable is impossible. Every time I try to sleep, I come up with another solution, but so far, none of them work."

"We've been unfair," Sara said gently. "You're so talented, we just assume that it's easy, but of course it's not. I am volunteering to work with you until this is done."

"Us too," Embla said, her arm around April Veronica.

"And me," Imani said.

"Thank you," Yukari's head dropped. "That still won't be enough. I'm grateful and it will help, but what we need is time. Sara?"

Yukari raised her eyes to meet Sara's.

"Yes?"

"Can you talk to Desdemona and just ask for time?"

"I will ask next time she calls," Sara said.

"Actually," Ama interrupted. "Let's get Toma up here."

"Oh good," Liz piped up. "Let's give the prisoner some freedom."

Ama rolled her eyes and continued.

"Sara, did you talk to Silas?" Ama turned to her and Sara nodded. "Well, let's update the Romanian bat situation with him, but then, and I want you all to be as deceptive," she paused, glaring at Liz, "as manipulative, as you can be. We need to find out one thing that might help here, which is, how rapidly is Desdemona aging? If it's not something that he noticed, then she might be aging slowly, which might make her more amenable to extending our deadline."

Fan stood and walked to the door. "I'll go get him," she said. "Hang tight."

While she was gone, the room fell into silence, but for once, only Liz reached for her phone and began to scroll. Everyone else just gazed around the room, eyes moving on quickly when they connected with another human. The sound of footsteps approaching brought everyone back to attention, and they all turned to face the door, which Fan opened, standing aside to let Toma in.

"Is this an AA meeting?" he asked, confusion on his face, and Imani laughed loudly.

"That's what I said guv," she said, standing. "Lemme get you a seat." Imani went to the back of the room and picked up Eleanor's throne, carrying it over her head, using her hips to push her own throne sideways to make room for it.

"Thanks, Imani," Toma said, watching as Imani patted the upholstered seat. Sara couldn't resist watching Liz's face darken as the events unfolded, and she rushed to speak before Liz could say anything nasty.

"Toma, thanks for joining us," Sara said. "I wanted you to know that I talked to Silas, the other Romanian man, and he said that all the bats in the caves you sent him to have been killed."

Strangely, Toma's face did not register surprise at the news. His dark eyes bored into Sara's as if he was expecting her to say something more. After waiting for him to speak, Sara continued.

"So, thank you for your help in that matter, it seems that we've been successful."

"There are hundreds of caves," he said. "Hundreds."

"We will neutralize them eventually," Sara said. "But for now, the caves that Desdemona knows about are not a threat."

"And what about Friday?" Toma's tone was sullen and defiant. "Will there be another one like me?"

"We haven't heard otherwise," Sara said.

"Will I be... permitted... to assist in locating the newcomer?"

Shrugging, Sara looked around the room for support, glaring at Fan when she noticed Liz preparing to speak.

"No, Toma," Fan said kindly. "It's going to be crazy enough, and there's nothing to stop you from running away."

"Like I keep on saying," he said, threat in his voice, "there shouldn't be anything to stop me from running away."

"Exactly," Liz hissed.

"And that's where we have differing opinions," Fan continued. "We've talked about this Toma, and as soon as it's safe, you'll be returned to wherever you'd like to go."

"It's safe," he said snottily. "I'd like to go now, to Bucharest. This house arrest is bullshit."

"It will be more bullshit if we have to drug you," Fan said with a sweet smile. "I've spent a lot of time with you today and this wasn't what you said to me an hour ago."

"You guys!" Liz yelled, leaping to her feet. "Can't you see that he's terrified? He's a human being. I'm sorry Toma, I'll sort this out."

Imani leaned in close to Toma and whispered in his ear. Sara watched as his eyes darted in Liz's direction as he listened, nodding his head slowly in understanding.

"Are you kidding me?" Liz's face was reddening. "What the fuck is she saying to you?"

Toma gestured for Liz to sit down.

"Imani is right, I am sorry," he said. "But, Liz, you are right too. This is very scary to me. I don't see a solution where you let me go, and I get to live. Imani swears to me that she will protect me and I have no choice but to believe her."

"Fuck this shit," Liz said before standing and letting herself out of the room. Sara was not disappointed by the slamming of the door.

"Ignore it," Imani said to Toma. "She's always like this."

"She reminds me of Desdemona," Fan said, "always throwing a tantrum like a child."

"Desdemona was very volatile," Toma said. "I didn't think you knew her very well?"

"Some of us know her well," Fan said. "Some of us have known her for years. You were only with her, what? A month?"

"Closer to two," he said.

"Gawd, two months of that bitch," Imani said with a laugh. "I can't even imagine her in the outdoors. A bug would set her off, I bet."

"She was always angry," Toma said. "One day she found a gray hair, and she had an anger like I've never seen."

"Yeah, that's not a big deal," Imani said. "Right?"

"She just needed to go and buy more hair dye," Toma said. "Because a week later, most of her hair was gray, and I said to her that I could get some dye sent to where we were, and she hit me. It was later that night that they... you know, they did what they did to me. I think what I said to her made me a target for her."

"Brother," Fran said, nodding sagely in his direction, "we will make it right, and we will never hurt you. You just need to give us a little time. We will keep you comfortable and as soon as we can we will cure you of this disease."

"I don't want a fucking cure," Toma said. "She said that I can live forever. Isn't that what you're all doing?"

"That's not exactly accurate," Yukari said, her voice louder than usual but still barely audible. "I have infected a baby rat with your virus and it is aging naturally."

"Please don't assume that I trust anything that any of you say," Toma said. "She told me that you would all lie to me."

"I'm not lying to you," Yukari said. "I can prove it to you, quite easily."

"Save your breath," Toma said. "It's one thing to hold me against my will, but I will fight to the death to prevent you from vaccinating me."

"Men are so tiresome," Embla said, standing and towering over Toma. "Listen, if you want to get ahead in this situation, please refrain from being so alpha. It just won't work, okay?"

Sighing deeply, Toma bowed his head.

"I am sorry," he said quietly. "You've all treated me well, and I'm trying to understand how I can get out of this alive."

"I'm a newcomer too," Embla said with a smile. "But I can tell you one thing. These women will not hurt you and they won't deceive you."

"She's speaking the truth," Imani said. "I promise you."

"Now you, I trust," Toma said with a wan smile. Sara watched as Imani grinned and looked at her hands in her lap. "I mean it," he continued. Then, to Sara's surprise, he reached over and took Imani's hand, causing her head to jerk up, but not, Sara noticed, to pull her hand away. "You've been very good to me and I'm grateful for you."

Imani inhaled to speak, but a round of various alert sounds dinged and rang, echoing around the room. Nervously, Sara turned her phone face-up and read the message on her screen. It was from an unknown number, a +380 country code she didn't recognize.

"Your next infected man will be in your neighborhood in twelve hours," Teddie read aloud. "Happy hunting."

"Okay girls," Ama said loudly. "That means an early start. If he's hitting the North Woods at five a.m. we need to be there by four. I will have updated maps to you all inside the hour, with your positions noted. We will search in grid formation. Phones, walkie talkies, tasers and a flask of blood laced with sedatives for each of us. Fran, you'll be circling in the car. We've been training Mr Handsome with Toma's backpack, so hopefully that will be enough of a scent. Let me just say one thing. This could be a trap. This isn't just a hunting party. If we find the guy, we have to neutralize him rapidly and get the hell out. If we see anything unusual, anything threatening, we bail. The object of the mission is to remain invisible."

"That area code is Ukraine," Fran said. "Same as my hacker girl."

"Doesn't mean anything," Ama said. "If anything it means she's not in Ukraine."

"It doesn't matter," Teddie said. "We can't go following her red herrings, we'll go crazy. We have a plan, we will stick to it."

"It makes me so angry," Toma said. "I wish you'd let me come with you, I will be able to recognize if it's one of the expedition crew."

"He's right," Imani said, still holding his hand. "And I think that I'm willing to take the risk. I want him with me."

A volley of meaningful stares bounced from woman to woman, around the room. Finally, Fan shrugged.

"His escape would be your responsibility," she said firmly, and Imani nodded.

"These men are my friends," Toma said. "I don't want them to be as afraid as I was."

"I already said yes," Fan said, and another ding rang out in the room. Sara looked at her phone. It was Silas, with flight details. He was landing the following day, at noon.

She would be facing the new arrival without him.

Chapter Six

Standing on the peak of a curved stone bridge, the pre-dawn air chilling her nostrils, Sara scoured the paths and barren forest of her beloved North Woods with an eagle's eye. Behind her, Teddie, in full burka and head wrap, was doing the same thing. She had requested this little square of the park as the area she and Teddie would surveil because she knew it well and loved it deeply. She remembered the first time she ventured into these woods, before the roads, before the bridges. She had felt immediately at home in this facsimile of the Romanian forests of her childhood, and she would bring Teddie here and teach her about herbs and the changes that each season brought. Together they found a place where they could be peaceful.

"Hey Ted," she called out, not turning around. "Remember when we led the charge against those fools who wanted to put the zoo here?"

"Hell yes," Teddie said. "It's still one of my favorite memories, you in your stupid, heavy nun outfit, at those town halls. You said you'd get a letter from the Vatican if you had to."

"Oh shit, that's right," Sara laughed, turning to see Teddie gazing through binoculars directly at her. "I did write to the Vatican, we got that letter back, they told us to bless the land and declare it a site of worship."

"I still have that letter," Teddie said, not dropping the binoculars.

"What are you doing? Inspecting my pores?"

Teddie finally dropped the binoculars, letting them swing on the cord around her neck. The face mask that Teddie had to wear outside the compound hid whether she was smiling or not.

"It was just a new way to see you," Teddie said. "After all this time, a new perspective was nice. Also, your pores are literally frozen shut."

"Everything is," Sara laughed. "I definitely did not dress for standing around."

"I told you to wear your long coat," Teddie said. "But no. Someone needs to be dressed for running and hunting and catching."

"That's why we're here..."

"I'm as snug as a bug in a rug," Teddie sing-songed, modeling her purple full length parka, the furry hood framing her face. "Remember you used to say that to me when I was little?"

Sara walked across the bridge and wrapped the woman in a strong hug.

"Of course I do," she whispered. "That was the best saying I learned in London."

"Do you think we will be the ones to find him?"

"No," Sara said. "I think that Fan and Ama plus scent dog is an unbeatable combination. They'll catch our guy."

"Maybe Liz can flirt with this one," Teddie said with a chuckle.

"I was not ready for that madness," Sara said, unzipping Teddie's parka and wriggling her arms inside it. Teddie pulled it closed behind Sara's back and warmth caressed her immediately.

"Oh come the fuck on," Teddie chided. "Behind your back everybody is low-key jealous you got a Cursed man. Everyone knows that Cursed sex is legendary AF."

"We don't even know what kind of cursed Toma is," Sara said. "The jury is still out. Actually, what has Yukari been saying?"

"It's too early, that's what she says," Teddie replied. "But she's actually been doing some animal testing, which you know she doesn't do, which means that she doesn't think it's a threat to the animals."

"I was surprised she infected rats."

"Rat. Singular." Teddie laughed. "It's Yukari, remember? And like she says, she doesn't need an army of immortal, blood hungry rodents to deal with."

Sara shuddered at the thought.

"Anyway," Teddie continued, "she gave it to a pinkie and it's growing normally, it got fur yesterday, so she thinks it will age normally."

"She needs to kill that thing," Sara said. "You know what a disaster that would be for New York?"

"I do. She does. We do," Teddie said. "I think that she'll keep it alive for observation. Don't tell her I told you, she already is worried that you'll want to kill it."

"I don't have that kind of jurisdiction any more," Sara said. "She can do whatever she wants, it's just risky is all I'm saying."

"She knows, mom," Teddie kissed the top of Sara's head. "I've never seen her so stressed."

"There's too much pressure on her," Sara said. "Now listen, this new man could have walked right past us and we wouldn't have noticed. Let's do our job."

"You're right," Teddie laughed, evicting her from the parka. "Once you said that we wouldn't be the ones to find him, I checked out."

Laughing, Sara snuck in one last hug before she broke away. Since her return to New York, Sara's love for Teddie had changed into something concrete, something tangible that accompanied her through every day. Even on days when she was just hanging out with Silas, she had a need to see Teddie and it had already become a joke between them. When Teddie decided to accompany Yukari to the lake house,

Sara strongly considered following, but Teddie refused to permit it. "No mom," she'd said. "Now's the time for you to be in love. Stay." Sara had leaned into daily – sometimes hourly – video calls, until Teddie told her she'd preferred Checked Out Sara to Smothering Sara. Still, she never told Teddie that she checked for her on Find My Friends hourly.

"Let's head north and do a perimeter check," Sara said, smiling when Teddie's gloved hand wrapped around hers, and they set off along the trail, both of them wrapped in memories of the hundreds, no thousands, of times they'd walked this path together, as the sun rose around them and the park came to life. They circled the North Woods for hours, only speaking when someone in their earpieces asked for an update, and even those had grown infrequent.

"How long since you heard from anybody?"

Teddie's voice yanked Sara out of a lengthy reverie about how to deal with Silas's return, and she was grateful. Pulling her phone out of her pants pocket, she was surprised to see that it was just after ten. They'd been meandering on and off trails for over five hours, and she was jonesing for a coffee and fighting an urge to pee. There hadn't even been any new texts for almost half an hour.

"It's gone so quiet," she said, jumping when her phone rang in her hand, startling her.

"It's a New York number," she said to Teddie, turning the phone to her so she could see.

"Right, cool," Teddie laughed. "Why don't you answer it?"

Nervously, mainly because she thought it might be Silas, Sara pressed the phone to her ear.

"Hello?"

"Hello," said a male voice. "Is this the Sisters Of Holy Silence?"

"Yes," Sara said, confused as she scrambled to remember her current nun name. "This is Sister Bernadetta speaking."

"Oh good," the man said. "Sorry to bother you so early but I have a bit of a problem."

"Yes?"

"When I came to open the museum, there was a young man waiting at the entrance. He doesn't speak much English but he's been saying that someone from your order will find him."

Sara's stomach dropped and she fought to keep her voice steady.

"How curious," she said. "And you're sure he's asking for us?"

"Yes, definitely," the man replied. "I'm sorry to bother you, I got your number from Father Jacob, he also apologizes for bothering you."

"Oh, of course," Sara said, waving wildly at Teddie who stared at her uncomprehendingly. "What is your name, child?"

"I'm Joey, sister," the man said. "And I'm sorry to say this, I... uh... I think this guy might be on something, you know."

"We don't turn anybody away, Joey," Sara said. "Now, I'm sorry but I missed where you're calling from."

"Oh sorry, sister, I'm a bit flustered," Joey said. "I'm a docent at the Cloisters."

A bolt of anger rattled Sara. Desdemona had led them all on a goose chase and then sent the man to a place that she knew Sara cherished. Counting to ten rapidly to still her voice, she continued.

"Joey, I'm actually out jogging with another sister right now, so I must ask if it's okay with you if we come straight to you? It's very improper for us to be seen without our robes, but time is of the essence."

"I understand completely sister," Joey said. "I'll bring him inside and get him some coffee."

"Thank you, my child," Sara said, desperate to get off the phone. "But please also remember to put yourself first here, and don't get too close if you think he's agitated. I'd hate for you to get hurt."

"Don't you worry, sister," the man said with a laugh. "I could snap this kid like a twig."

"Well good," Sara said officiously. "We should be there in around twenty minutes. I"ll see you then and thank you."

"She fucking sent the guy to the Cloisters," she said after she hung up, grabbing Teddie's hand and beginning to run to the park's western edge.

"Oh shit," Teddie said. " Hang on, let me text the others."

"NO!" Sara yelled. "We don't need us all descending on The Cloisters, we can handle this."

Forced into silence for the duration of the taxi ride uptown, Sara and Teddie spent the time texting each other potential strategies for their arrival at the museum. In between checking her phone and replying to Teddie, Sara stared out her window, watching the street numbers click upward with infuriating slowness until at some point in the 170s, Teddie let out a gasp.

"I'm sorry," she said immediately, then glared at Sara's phone and tapped out a text which arrived immediately.

> Imani hooked up with Toma in the park!!!!!!!

Sara raised a palm and shook her head, before replying furiously:

> Not now. Focus.

They completed the rest of the drive in silence. Sara fought to keep her mind on what to do once they reached the Cloisters. Under the new rules, Imani could do whatever she wanted, but this would definitely create new tensions within the Lock. Finally, the taxi pulled to a stop in front of the Cloisters and Sara rushed out, leaving Teddie to pay.

Racing past the bare trees into the darkened entryway, Sara scanned for anyone lurking in the shadows, but saw nothing. To her left, a large Italian man emerged from the shadows.

"Sister Bernadetta?"

"Joey!" Sara ran over to him. "I'm sorry it took so long to get here, I hope there's been no trouble."

"Nothing a cup of coffee and a heater couldn't fix," the man said, shuffling from foot to foot.

"Bless you my child," Sara said, feeling stupid and anxious in her winter athletic wear. When she wore a nun's habit, it somehow made the pretense easier. "Where is the man?"

"In my office," Joey said, ushering her past the stanchion and inside the museum's dark atrium. He led her to a door and opened it for her, and Sara gasped before she could stop herself. Seated on a small couch was a tall, gangly youth, his thick black hair matted, his eyes wild, rimmed in tell-tale dark circles. She doubted that he was twenty years old. Furious at Desdemona, she turned to Joey.

"Please leave us to get acquainted," she said gently. "There will be a second sister arriving, please send her in."

Stepping into the room, she pulled the door closed behind her, the man on the couch's eyes wide and following her every move.

"You asked for me," Sara said quietly.

"You are who?" the young man said in thickly accented English. Sara switched to Romanian.

"I am from the Sisters Of Holy Silence," she said.

"You don't look like a nun."

"Do you think we exercise in our robes?"

The guy shrugged and remained silent.

"What do you want from me?"

"She told me to find you," he said. "She said you would take care of me."

"What else did she tell you?"

"She said that you were a killer."

"Then why did you ask them to call me?"

"The pain," he said, groaning as if to illustrate his point. "I eat but I starve, my head hurts like I have a hangover, and she tells me that you alone can help me."

"I'm sorry for your pain," Sara said. A gentle knock at the door made her turn as Teddie came in. The guy on the couch flinched and pressed himself back against the cushions, his eyes fearful again.

"Do not worry, she is a sister like me," Sara said, turning to take in Teddie's raised eyebrows above her sunglasses. Sara pointed at Teddie, then smiled and pointed at her own face. Teddie smiled. "We are not killers."

"Hello, I'm Sister Anita," she said, and the man mumbled a hello back.

"Would you like to come with us?" Sara continued in her native tongue, and the man nodded slowly. "Do you have a suitcase?"

He shook his head, and Sara took in his clothing: dirty jeans, worn sneakers and a threadbare coat over a patterned sweater. He must have been freezing, and she marveled at Desdemona's intentional cruelty. She took two steps closer to the man and extended her hand.

"Come with us, we will help you," she said as he took her hand and she pulled him to standing. "What is your name?"

"I am Andrei, from Bucharest," the man said.

"And how old are you, Andrei?"

"I am nineteen," he said, his answer like a knife in her heart. It was an unspoken agreement that nobody under twenty eight could be converted. Converting one so young was definitely designed to get under Sara's skin. She fought to keep it from getting to her.

"Give him your coat," she said to Teddie. "Let's get him out of here."

"He's a fucking child" Sara bellowed, tears in her eyes, as Fran and Heather looked on. They were inside an empty studio apartment on the inside of the building, fourth floor, one window opening to a long drop in the light well his only escape. Andrei was showering, with new clothing from Silas's wardrobe to change into when he was done.

"She did it to piss you off, sister." Fran was angrier than Sara had ever seen.

"I know," Sara said. "I know. And I know that we can probably vaccinate him and send him home and this will all just be a weird story for him."

"It's worse than that," Heather said. "I'm not saying we should kill them, you know I'm not saying that. But the flipside is, too many people have been inside this building. If we send them away, this building is now publicized. If they go to the police, for whatever reason, they'll come around here."

"I know," Sara said curtly. "I have been thinking this for a while. Our time in this building is drawing to a close."

They all sat in silence, Sara's words hanging in the air, until they heard the water shut off in the bathroom.

"Can we get Toma up here?" Heather asked. "I think it might help."

"Did you guys hear that Imani-"

"YES!" Fran and Heather said in unison, silencing Sara.

"Whatever," Sara continued. "Have Imani bring him here. Heather, I need to contact Desdemona. This is insanity. We can't deal with one of these every week. I'm going to beg her for time. Can you two handle whatever this is while I try to buy us more time?"

Heather nodded, and Fran flexed her biceps theatrically.

"Your goon squad at your bidding," she said with a laugh.

"I love you Frances," Sara said, before letting herself out. As she neared her apartment, her pulse quickened at the thought of confronting Desdemona, and she had her phone out before she even opened the door, hitting the call button before she sat down. She was surprised when Desdemona answered before it even rang.

"Don't you love him?"

"He seems nice," Sara said, refusing to be goaded. "Bit young."

"Mouthy little asshole," she quipped. "That's what he gets for saying I look old."

"I see your decision making process is as solid as ever," Sara said. "And it was nice of you to send him to the Cloisters, I hadn't been there in quite some time."

"You're welcome," Desdemona cooed. "Is there a reason for this call other than to congratulate me on a job well done?"

"I'd like to ask for a favor," Sara said.

"I'm not in the habit of granting favors."

"Oh, I know, but come on Des, you also know that there's no chance we can get the vaccine you need in such a short time."

"I don't know that," Desdemona said brusquely. "I know that Yukari made the filthy poison you put in me, so she can make an antidote. That's all I ask."

"Vaccines don't have antidotes," Sara said. "Don't play. You know this."

"Right. I also know that this new virus doesn't have the life extending properties of the original, but I figure that if I send enough human guinea pigs, she'll be able to create a new strain that can reinfect me."

"She's working day and night, Des," Sara tried to make her voice friendlier. "She just needs more time. Can you give us like four weeks?"

Desdemona erupted.

"She needs more time?" she spat. "The one thing I don't fucking have is time. Four weeks? You want me to wait four weeks?"

"Sure, send four guys in four weeks, if we don't have you fixed."

"Did you think this would be funny?"

"Actually no, I just thought you'd die," Sara said, abandoning friendly even though she knew it would cost her.

"Your biggest mistake was letting me go," Desdemona's voice was chilling. "I will not fucking rest until I have stolen from you as much as you've stolen from me."

"You'd better be careful, a woman of your age and delicate condition," Sara said. "How fast are you aging, anyway?"

"Slowly enough that I'll see you die first," Desdemona said. "Here's my counter offer: Four men next week."

And she was gone.

Angry at herself, Sara fell back against the sofa, her head pounding with tension. She felt cornered by unsolvable problems. Her phone dinged in her hand. It was a text. From Silas.

Sara, I'm home. What the hell has happened? Where are you?

Chapter Seven

Sara stared at her phone, in complete stillness, for so long that vertigo began to blur her reality. Shaking her head to clear her vision, she sighed heavily. Just because someone sends a text doesn't mean you have to answer it immediately, she told herself. She was being a coward. You've been worse, she thought, making herself laugh. She knew she had to reply before Silas called around and found out where she was. She remembered some advice that she received from Embla that sounded useful at the time. "The best way to deal with any situation," Embla had told her, back in Iceland, "is to ask yourself what you want out of that situation."

Her options were to either ask Silas to come to her new apartment, or to face him in their old shared one. She reacted strongly against having him in her space. Something about him being in her newly reclaimed space made her uneasy. Or guilty. Yep. Definitely guilty. The thought of meeting in their old apartment made her heart pound with anxiety.

The roof deck it was.

As she picked up her phone to text him, it rang. Silas. Panicked, she swiped the call away and sent her text.

> I have some explaining to do. Meet me up on the roof in five minutes.

Without waiting for a reply, Sara hurriedly put a mason jar of blood into the warmer, then went to the bedroom and retrieved the ugly old long down coat she used to wear to work. Pausing briefly, she considered what message Silas would draw from the coat, because he would definitely recognize it. Angrily, she thrust one arm and then the other inside the coat, pulling it closed around her chest as she returned to the kitchen. A quick check of the time she sent the text told her that she could let the blood warm for another sixty seconds, so she increased the temperature, leaning against the counter, her fingernails tap tapping on the countertop.

She did not know what she was going to say to him.

And what would she do if he tried to kiss her.

What do you want out of the situation?

She had actively avoided the meditation that might have provided her with an answer. Silas already knew she was angry. No need to convey that. He also knew she'd set up a new home, without him. And he would be very sad. She'd never had to decide how transparent to be with a partner, since all of her previous relationships had been built upon lies. Should she be an open book, or should she play it cool? She didn't even know how to play anything cool. Panic fluttered inside her chest.

Now she had three minutes. A frantic dash to the mirror in the bathroom – and the sight of her make-up free face and ratty hair pulled back in an even rattier ponytail – told Sara that there wasn't enough time to right that particular ship. She would lean into frumpy. Because she didn't care, she tried to convince herself, and failed. She cared very much. Ditching her old work coat, she dragged a mystery hoodie from her dresser, hauled it over her head, quickly chugged the blood, wiped her mouth with her sleeve and ascended the spiral staircase to the loft. There, she paused, blinking to clear her mind, before shoving the roof door open with her shoulder and stepping out into the chilly afternoon.

"There you are!"

Silas was standing closer to the center of the rooftop, looking infuriatingly, effortlessly handsome in carpenter pants, work boots and a hoodie. A bunch of red roses hung forlornly from one hand. He walked over to her, a smile playing at the corners of his mouth.

"What is so funny?" she asked, regretting the words as soon as they hit the frosty air.

"People also smile when they're happy," he said as he reached her, stopping a few feet from her. "I'm happy to see you."

"Oh, right, okay," Sara began, then her mind went blank so she shuffled her feet and looked at the ground.

"I can see this is going to be a weird one," Silas said. "Is it better to sit or stand for weirdness?"

Since sitting offered more privacy, Sara nodded at the benches in the corner, shielded as they were by the hedges in their planter boxes. Without waiting, she walked over and sat on the frigid wood.

"We should have brought cushions," she said. "The bench is frozen."

"Do you want me to go get cushions?"

Sara shook her head.

"Okay," Silas said gently as he sat on the bench across from her. "Discomfort is the name of the game. And Sara, I know you're gonna let me have it, but first can I say one thing?"

Sara nodded, feeling like a recalcitrant teenager.

"Sara, if I had known how much it hurt you, of course I would never have left. I'm so sorry."

Expecting there to be more to his apology, Sara remained silent, slowly raising her face to his.

"There's no but?" she asked finally.

"Are you crazy? There's a ton of but, but the most important thing here is that I accept responsibility for hurting you, whatever my reasons were."

"Silas, you vanished and left me the world's shortest note," Sara's voice was incredulous and she reined it in. "Instead of a discussion, you basically left a post-it. It was the equivalent of breaking up over text message. A note. That's what you thought was the right way to let me know."

Silas mulled the words in silence, his head shaking slowly.

"I knew I was doing something you would prevent," he said. "I'm not going to lie. I knew you'd be angry. But in that moment, I'd talked to Stef, booked the ticket and called the car. I just needed to get out before you came back. Did I handle it well? Fuck no. Did I do what my heart said was right at the time? Sadly, yes."

In all of her panicked preparation for this meeting, she'd forgotten how charming he was, and also, how perfect he was. Feeling herself wanting to forgive him, she cast her mind back to their apartment, the moment she found the note, and the hollow ache of abandonment filled her chest.

"Thank you," she said, quietly.

"And I'm assuming you need space?"

She nodded, dropping her eyes so that she wouldn't see the blow land in his.

"Alrighty then," Silas clapped his hands together. "We need to make this brief, I need to go buy a bed."

Sara's head snapped up.

"Oh god, I'm so sorry," she said. "I didn't even think..."

"I'm just fucking with you," Silas said. "I still have my place downtown. I need to go there anyway."

The thought of him not being in the compound made Sara very uneasy, but she couldn't ask anything of him.

"Sara? Is there anything you want to say to me? I feel like I rushed this, making you talk right now. We don't have to talk right now, at least not about us. Like the us-us. And you probably don't even know if there still is an us, and that's your call, but if there's still even a glimmer of an us, I'm happy to take some time to get back to ussing around with you."

"There he is," Sara said, a faint smile appearing. "I was wondering where your nervous rambling was."

"It's never far away," Silas said. "But now that we're doing eye contact, would you like the download of the trip? I'm afraid it's not all good news."

"Did you talk to anyone here today?"

"I know that the latest capture is a young man," Silas's voice dripped scorn. "This is why we need to stop her. What if next time she sends us someone's actual kid?"

"I don't think he's part of a trend," Sara said. "And... well, I tried to buy us some time and I called Desdemona and asked for a four week break to give us a chance for Yukari to undo the vaccine."

"I'm gathering she wasn't receptive."

"Yeah no," Sara exhaled. "We can expect four men next Friday. Or four vampire children, if your instincts are right."

"It will be what it will be," Silas said angrily. "And this one wasn't even in the North Woods? She's toying with us."

"And you have more bad news?"

"It can wait," Silas said. "It's not timely, and right now, the most important thing is to locate Des. That's the information I'd rather share with you. Considering she wasn't from our area, she knew the location of a lot of the caves where they used to get the bats. I talked to people in the places where she stayed, she was throwing money around like crazy. She wasn't exactly inconspicuous. She told people that she was a scientist from Madrid who was working on preventing the next pandemic, so people wanted to help her. A silver lining of her behavior was that everyone over there is now terrified of both bats and going inside the caves. Nobody wants to be patient zero in a new pandemic. But the most important thing that I heard was how the locals constantly described her."

"Oh yeah?"

"Sara, each person referred to her as *o bătrână*!"

The Romanian word shocked Sara. It was a mean word used to describe a haggard old woman.

"Did you get a description?"

Silas nodded, his hands clasped in his lap.

"Sara it sounds like her hair has greyed, and her face is wrinkling."

"That's so fast," Sara said. "I mean, we had no idea what would happen, even Yukari could only guess, but she thought that the aging process might have just naturally restarted but now it seems like.."

"She's disintegrating," Silas said. "The first round of guides that she hired all quit because of the way she treated them. Impatient and unpleasant."

Sara laughed.

"She's always been like that with me," she said. "I wish I could have quit."

Chuckling, Silas stared into her eyes until Sara turned to the ground.

"Have you had any luck getting any info out of Toma?"

"Not really," Sara said. "He's hot shit and he's been busy playing tug of war with Imani and Liz, though from what I hear, that battle ended today."

"Sorry, I'm not following."

"Everyone's jealous of my vampire boyfriend, so when another one got delivered to our door, it caused a little bit of-"

"Rivalry?"

"Outright war," Sara smiled. "But I heard that Imani got some action in the North Woods today while she was supposed to be hunting for vampire men."

"Poor Liz," Silas said. "Really. But maybe we shouldn't worry, if Des does send four men next week, we can give Liz first pick and then see who else wants a cursed man?"

"Can you imagine?" Sara laughed then caught herself. "Actually, I don't want to. One cursed man has been more than enough for me."

"And here we are again," Silas said. In the silence that followed, Sara could almost tangibly feel how badly he wanted to sit next to her and warm her, but she clung to her resentment, not ready to let herself feel that way again.

"I'm sorry, that was a low blow."

"It's how you feel," Silas said. "And I appreciate it that-"

"Oh for fuck's sake, can you just stop?" Anger brought Sara to her feet. "Silas, I've been a difficult whiny baby ever since we started doing... this... and I really need you stop being so endlessly accommodating. Can't you just tell me to fuck off or grow up or quit my shit?"

"Sure," his voice didn't change. "If that was how I felt, then that's what I would say to you. But it's not. I'm not angry, I'm... well you know how I am feeling and this isn't about how I feel. I've done a stupid thing. I made you feel vulnerable and I know that's your least comfortable place."

"Okay we can stop," Sara said, unsure whether to sit or remain standing. "No need to drag my deepest and darkest out into the light. Silas, I haven't been meditating, I haven't been doing any of the things that got me through the past five hundred years. I'm a cliché, a care-taker who never addressed her own needs. I hid behind it. And now I don't even know what I want out of this situation."

"Oh you've been talking to Embla," he said. "She trained me on that one too."

"Do you ask yourself that question?"

Silas clasped his hands together and gazed into her eyes.

"It's why I went off script in your practice," he said. "What I wanted out of that situation was to work on our chemistry, see if we might be... you know... something more."

"So this is all Embla's fault," Sara said with an awkward laugh that hung in the air like cobwebs.

"No, it's mine," Silas's earnestness was his most reliable and annoy-ing feature, Sara thought.

Standing slowly, Silas slid his hands into the pocket of his coat.

"I'm gonna head out," he said. "Sara, please, if anything happens, call me. I'll come back tomorrow, if that's okay with you. I need to talk to Toma."

Sara's heart heaved inside her chest, painful and sharp.

"Wait," she said suddenly. "What was it you wanted to talk about ? The news that can wait?"

Looking down, Silas shook his head.

"It's not for right now," he said, sadness in his voice. "Take this the right way, just as facts, not manipulation, but in my head I pictured us as having all night to discuss it, and it's not something I can dump on you and then just leave. It's also just a hunch, a weirdness that I want to discuss, but it's not timely."

"Then tell me now," Sara's voice was imperious and as soon as she heard herself, she realized just how much she had been accustomed to getting her way forever. She raised a palm. "Sorry, I sound like a bossy old bitch. Of course you don't have to tell me anything. Is it something we can discuss tomorrow?"

Silas continued to stare at his dirty boots, eventually nodding non-committally.

"You have a lot on your plate," he said quietly. "Let me talk to Ama, Heather, Fan, maybe even Embla."

Now Sara was definitely feeling like she was being deliberately frozen out, and she fought to bite her tongue.

"Well as long as nobody is going to die," she began and he cut her off.

"Sara, I'm not playing twenty questions with you on this." Silas's voice was firm in a way she rarely heard it, and she knew she couldn't push it any further.

"Gotcha," she said, mainly because he'd told her once that he hated the expression, and he looked at her knowingly.

Doffing an imaginary cap, he turned and walked off in the direction of the doorway that led down to the abandoned apartment that Crina usually stayed in. Sara watched him move away from her, drifting between the planters. Before he reached the door, he paused, and Sara's heart fluttered expectantly, irritating her.

"Hey," he called out. "Did the new kid have a phone or any luggage?"

"Nope, just the clothes on his back."

"Thanks," Silas turned and pulled open the door. "Sara, can I ask one favor?"

"Sure."

"Don't go out at night, please," Silas turned back, his eyes pleading. "I don't want to sound paranoid, but we shouldn't assume that infected men are the only thing Desdemona is sending our way."

Chapter Eight

Seeing Silas in person completely wrecked what Sara's apartment was meant to be. Her self-care safe-space felt crowded with floral arrangements and his absence. Most of the women had gone out, despite her protests, to something in Williamsburg, and Teddie, still very much a prisoner in the compound, had taken an edible and was too drowsy for a late-night phone call. Since it was still too early in the European morning to bug Yfke or Christine, Sara had found herself on Heather's Peloton bike in an unoccupied apartment at one a.m. tackling an hour long class that left her sweaty and drained, but not sleepy.

Still awake at four a.m., she cursed Silas for pointing out the obvious. They'd all presumed that the newcomers had come directly from the airport, fresh off flights from Romania. Silas raised an excellent point, which was the lack of any travel documentation on the kid. Toma had been carrying his passport. Her mind whirring with possibilities, Sara sought out a small bottle of April Veronica's new blood and weed elixir, and, despite knowing how strong it was, she did two shots of it, in bed, and the swoon that followed was enough to actually send her off to slumber.

Now, fresh out of the shower, her phone was dinging like a wind chime on a ship in a rough sea, irregular, frenetic and impossible to ignore. Ditching her towel, she clambered onto the bed, digging around until she found the phone. The most recent text was from Heather, inviting her to "a rather spectacular brunch" in her apartment, at which the food was "already getting cold." At the thought of food, her stomach grumbled, but getting dressed felt like a complicated matter and she wished she still had her Care Bears onesie, making a note to get a new one at a Walgreens later that day. Since Iceland, she'd become a fan of a floor clothes day, so she snatched up a pile of clothing from beside her bed, fishing around until she had some workout pants, a long sweater and some stripy socks which she augmented with some sheepskin slippers. Jamming a knit cap on her still-damp hair, she let herself out the rear door of her apartment, stopping instantly at the sight of a large bunch of gerber daisies, electric pinks, lavenders and oranges. There was a note.

Happy housewarming – Silas x

Hurriedly scooping up the flowers, Sara decided she had no room for them, and would regift them to Heather. She made her way along and down to Heather's rear door, hearing voices before she even knocked. Heather answered the door immediately, a comical look on her face.

"Got dressed in a hurry did ye pet?"

"Good morning to you too," Sara said, pressing the flowers into Heather's hands.

"It's afternoon, and your jumper's inside out," Heather tutted, spinning on her heel and heading down the hallway. With a loud huff, Sara whipped her sweater up over her head, pulling it right-side out in the cold hallway.

"I can see Sara's boobies," April Veronica called from inside the apartment as Sara hurriedly pulled the sweater back over her head, covering herself.

"It's not a party til someone gets their boobies out," Fran called, and Sara smiled, walking along the corridor, the scents of baked goods, coffee and bacon luring her on until she reached the living room, her heart leaping when she saw Silas, in the kitchen with his back to her. He would be crushed that she didn't keep his flowers.

"You're serving bag lady today," Embla laughed.

"And I'll be serving cunt if there's not a coffee in my hand in-"

With lightning speed, Silas darted from the kitchen, slipping a very hot take-out cup into her waiting hands.

"No serving the c-word on my watch," he laughed, returning to the kitchen without making eye contact. Looking around the room, Sara noted that it was just the seven of them. Heather had set the flowers on a sideboard, and Sara wondered if she could sneak them to Heather's bedroom without being caught.

"Where's everybody else?"

Heather, kneeling at the coffee table and about to dig into a break-fast burrito, looked up.

"Yukari just went to sleep a while ago, poor thing," she said. "Fan and Ama are grilling the kid. Liz is not answering her phone, and, shocker, Imani spent the night in Toma's-"

"Arms," April Veronica yelled.

On the sofa, Teddie patted the cushion beside her, and Sara obliged, sitting so close she was almost on her lap.

"Hey mom," Teddie said with a chuckle. "Are you baked?"

"I was," Sara said. "I couldn't sleep, so I took drastic measures."

"And more than one shot of our elixir," Embla said. "Not accusing, just observing."

"Do you have the munchies? Silas called from the kitchen.

"I'm hungry, yes," Sara replied tersely, and within seconds, Silas had plated a burrito for her and set it on the coffee table, once again leaving before making eye contact.

"Why couldn't you sleep mom?"

Sipping on her coffee, Sara gave Teddie some side eye and shrugged.

"There's a lot going on," she said eventually. "Have you guys been talking? Care to catch me up?"

"Lots of theories, not a lot of facts," Fran said, looking up from a leafy salad. "It doesn't look like the new kid can give us concrete proof that he flew in and came straight here."

"This is why I couldn't sleep," Sara said, starting work on her burrito. Silas appeared in front of her again, this time depositing a mason jar of blood on the coffee table before returning to the kitchen.

"You two are acting weird," Heather said. "Silas, come sit, she won't bite."

Shooting Heather a death glare, Sara snatched up the jar of blood and chugged it down, even though she would now have to wait to finish her coffee or risk some serious nausea, forcing her eyes to stay open until the surge passed. She watched Silas slink into the room and sit on the floor beside Fran.

"My name is Heather and never have I yada yada yada" Heather looked around the room, a cheeky smile on her face. "There, Sara, does that make it feel more normal?"

On the couch, struggling to keep her eyes open, Sara wondered why Heather was coming for her. Feeling Teddie's hand give her knee a squeeze reassured her.

Ever the peacekeeper, Fran took up the slack.

"We were pretty dumb to believe Toma," she said. "No shade, no blame, but we might have missed out on some valuable time to search out a hiding place if these guys are already in the City."

"Is there any weight to these new rumors," Sara looked directly at Fran, "or is it just an uninvestigated possibility?"

"Andrei arrived pretty much empty handed," Teddie said. "We were both so upset by his age that we didn't stop to think that it was weird, that he had no luggage."

"I watched over him off and on last night," Fran said. "His English is pretty bad, but I went out and got him new clothes this morning and I offered to wash his old stuff and there was nothing in the pockets. Not so much as a boarding pass."

"How does he seem?" Sara kept her attention on Fran.

"You know," Fran said, her fingers nervously twirling a strand of gray hair, "that's what got me wondering in the first place. He didn't seem as... I dunno, as perturbed as one might be after getting infected with a weird virus and flying halfway around the world. He had a really strange air of calm around him."

Sara nodded, her mind racing as she tried to figure out if Fran gave Silas the idea or vice versa. As much as she didn't want to, she needed to address Silas.

"Silas, have you talked to him or Toma yet today?"

Silas shook his head, finally meeting her gaze.

"I'm going to visit them both, after this delicious brunch," he said. "I already texted Imani and told her to get herself out of Toma's apartment before I got there." Glancing at his Apple watch, he continued. "I told her I'd be there at one, so I have fifteen more minutes. Sara, would you like to be with me during either conversation?"

"Well, who else is going?" she asked, looking around.

"Nobody else speaks Romanian," Embla said.

"And we don't want to crowd either of them," Heather said as her phone dinged in her pocket. She pulled it out and read the message, her eyebrows raising slightly. "Crina just landed at JFK," she said, surprise in her voice. "Silas, did you know she was headed back?"

Sara had been stealing a look at Silas while he was looking at Heather, and she saw shock pass across his features before he could catch himself. He clearly didn't know.

"No," he said, his voice tight. "Actually, Sara, would you mind coming with me to see the Romanians now?"

"Sure," she said with a nod and a shrug. "Is there a problem?"

"I just want to talk to them before the Crina show blows into town," he said, pushing himself up to standing. Sara could tell that he was lying. Suddenly intrigued, she snatched up her coffee, kissed Teddie on the cheek and made her way to the rear door without looking back.

As soon as the door closed and they were alone in the hallway, she spun to face Silas.

"Okay, out with it."

"Honestly, Sara, I'd rather not," Silas said, as he began to walk in the direction of the elevator. "Not now. I might be wrong. For now, can we just talk to these guys and see what they say?"

"It just feels like you're punishing me," Sara said,.

Silas didn't stop walking. He reached the elevator and pressed the button.

"I'm not the one who gave away the flowers I left for her," he said quietly as she caught up to him, and the elevator doors opened and he stepped inside. "I'm not punishing you. What I want to talk about is a discussion, I just don't know the full picture and it's sensitive and it's vague enough to add a lot to your plate, possibly unnecessarily"

"You have a hunch," Sara said, taking the opposite corner of the small elevator car.

"I have a lot of them," Silas said. "But right now, we need to find out if the next wave of men is already in New York. Once I have that answer, I can tell you the rest, but right now I'm..."

"You're what?"

The elevator stopped at the second floor.

"I'm just hoping that I'm wrong."

With that, Silas exited the elevator and didn't pause or look back until he was at the door to the small panic room where they'd held Desdemona only a few months earlier.

"Did we fuck up, Si?" Sara asked as she drew near. "By not killing Des, I mean. None of this would be happening now if we'd just killed her outright."

"That's not who we are," Silas said, not facing her. "Becoming a killer should not be an option, and Sara?"

"Yes?"

"I'm glad we didn't make that decision, it will always mean that we are better, smarter and more human than Desdemona ever was or will be."

"Okay," Sara said. "Will you still feel the same way if she ends up infecting all of New York City with whatever virus these guys have?"

"I'd rather not let it get to that point," he said, pressing his finger into the keypad, the sound of the door unlocking effectively ending the discussion.

"Andrei?" Silas called out, then switched to Romanian. "My name is Silas, I'm here to help you."

The boy stepped into the doorway between the two small rooms, a heartbreaking look of hope on his face.

"Can you get me out of here?"

Silas nodded. "Yes, that's why I'm here. Are you hungry?"

Andrei shook his head. "Just scared," he said.

"I'm sorry," Silas said, not moving any closer. "I have heard of the woman who sent you here, she is crazy."

Andrei's head jerked up, but he remained silent.

"She hates our religion," Silas continued. "She is always trying to make trouble."

Andrei shrugged.

"I am going to take you back to Romania as soon as we can get tickets," Silas said. "Do you have your passport?"

Andrei shook his head.

"Andrei, I can't book your ticket without your passport."

"Well, I do not have it."

Glancing at Sara, Silas gestured for her to join in.

"Andrei, it is me, sorry I am out of my religious robes, but sometimes it is better for us to be informal."

Another shrug.

"I'm wondering if there is anything you'd like to tell me, about how you got here? We want to get you home."

Andrei grimaced, then shook his head.

"Why can you not talk to me? I am a nun, my life is dedicated to helping the lord's charges."

"That's not what she said," Andrei barked. "She said you would lie to me and confuse me, and then kill me. She said you're not a nun, you're a killer."

"Like my friend said, she is a crazy woman," Sara said, her voice calm. "Can you tell me where you hid your belongings? I will go and retrieve them and Silas will then take you home to Bucharest."

"I do not live in Bucharest," Andrei muttered.

"We will return you to wherever you wish to live," Silas said.

"It doesn't matter," Andrei said. "because I do not have my passport so I cannot travel."

"Okay," Silas nodded. "I will contact the embassy to see what we can do, and I will call the police in Bucharest. Can you give me a phone number for your parents perhaps?"

"NO!" Andrei yelled. "NO. Do not do those things or she will kill my parents. I beg you. Just keep me here forever. I don't care."

Silas raised both palms. "Do not worry," he said. "We need to leave you now, but I will come back for your information so I can get you a passport. Is there anything else you need?"

"Can I have a television, or a screen?" The boy's eyes were pleading. "A PS5 and some games? It is hard to be alone in here with my thoughts, it's like jail."

Sara looked at the floor, certain that Silas would have the kid gaming by mid-afternoon.

"I'll be back in an hour or two with something for you," Silas said. "For now, be patient and do not worry."

Dejected, Andrei slunk back into the room where Sara had faced Desdemona, just months ago.

"Let's go," Silas said, turning and leaving the room. Again, Silas did not wait for her, his long legs striding down the hall to the rear door to Marguerite's apartment. He knocked on the door twice, then called out in Romanian.

"Toma, it's me, Silas, we met on the night you got here."

"Come in," the man called out, and Silas pressed his finger into the security pad by the door handle.

"His voice sounded like he's in the living room," Sara whispered. "But be careful."

Opening the door gently, Silas quickly ascertained that the hallway was empty.

"Show yourself," he called out, and Toma, in Silas's old clothes, appeared at the end of the hall, waving a solitary finger at them.

"I am back from the motherland," Silas said. "I have some questions."

"And if I answer them will you let me go?"

"We're going to let you go very soon," Silas said. "That's what we are here to talk about."

Silas, followed by Sara, entered the living room. Toma moved back to the couch but remained standing, his arms folded. Silas and Sara stood across the room from him.

"Have you talked to Yukari?" Silas asked. Toma nodded. "And did she tell you that this virus that you have, it will not give you a long life?"

"She took so much of my blood," the man replied sullenly. "She only said she didn't think that was an option but also she wants to give me a vaccine so I will never know."

"Right," Silas said. "So that's the plan. To vaccinate you and let you go."

"I will tell everyone your secrets," Toma said. "If I don't leave here with the same virus that you have, then I will make sure you are uncovered."

"Do you want us to kill you?" Silas took a step in his direction. Toma didn't budge.

"You do not kill here," he said. "This much I am certain of."

"Correction," Silas said. "They do not kill, but I am not a member of this..." he paused, waving his arm around, "this organization. I can kill."

Toma's veneer cracked a little, and Silas took another step forward.

"So, let's reset this," Silas kept his voice light. "I was in the forests and I found the caves, thanks to you. They are no longer a threat, the bats are all dead."

"There are thousands of caves," he said. "The bats live in barns and houses and just everywhere."

Silas nodded sagely. "I know, but for now, I've done what I can do. But I did not find it easy to get to Bucharest from New York, and I was wondering about the flights that brought you here. Did you go to Paris to get here?"

Toma nodded. "Yes, how did you know?"

"Oh, that's the same way I had to come home, I just assumed," Silas said. "And where would you like to be returned to? We will be happy to pay for your silence, you will be able to live anywhere you want to."

Toma's face lit up.

"I would like to return to London," he said. "Is this a genuine offer?"

Silas nodded.

"I just have a few more questions," he continued. "Did you know Andrei before he arrived here?"

Toma shook his head.

"No, he is not known to me before now."

"Okay, we are going to go and talk to him now," Silas said, and Toma seemed surprised by the brevity of their visit.

"Is that all?"

"Sure," Silas kept it light. "Anyway, thanks for your help finding the bats, it was very good to be back in the old country, she is still very beautiful."

"Bye," Sara said, waving and moving to the hallway, confusion roiling her mind. When she reached the door, she turned to see Silas blocking the hallway. He nodded for her to proceed and she unlocked the door with her fingertip and held it open for him. Once the door was locked behind them, Silas put a finger to his lips then pointed to the end of the hallway, and began to walk. When he reached the elevator, he called it, the doors opening instantly. As soon as the doors closed, he turned to Sara, panic on his face.

"Okay, this is the bad thing that I didn't tell you but we have to move fast. Crina is here to kill them both."

Uncomprehending, Sara stared into Silas's eyes.

"Sara, I don't know how to tell you this, but uh... my mother, she's not who and what we think she is."

"Silas, I don't understand."

"Sara, I'm pretty certain she killed all the women in Madrid, she killed them the same way Desdemona killed those other sisters, In cold blood and with no mercy," Silas paused, a pained expression on is face. "And Sara, she's killed before."

Chapter Nine

Sara felt her reality shimmer as Silas's words sank in. Gripping the small handrail in the elevator to anchor herself, she became painfully aware that the ground beneath her feet was the tiled floor of a elevator, and below that, a dark, empty shaft. Crina could not be killing people, it went against every ounce of her fiber to even process information like this. Leaning back against the elevator wall as it rattled upward, her eyes closed, Sara forced herself to inhale deeply as too many questions swirled in her mind. A million miles away she heard Silas speak, and she slowly raised a hand to buy herself some time, a reprieve from any new information while she struggled to parse what she'd just heard.

Reaching its destination, the elevator doors slid open, and so did her eyes. Silas stood in front of her, his hand holding the elevator door open, his face pale with concern, dark circles below his eyes.

"Do you want to stay in the elevator?" he asked, and she shook her head, surprised that she had been able to answer him.

"Are you comfortable with me coming to your new place, or would you rather go to our old place?" The care in his voice was heartbreaking. "Or somewhere else, but it has to be private."

"Let's go to our old place," she said, her voice raspy and weak, and she felt an arm circle her shoulders, a strong human connection that guided her off the wall, then all the way to the brick door to the old apartment. Once they were inside, Silas led her to a pile of cushions in the corner, arranged them into a seating area, and held her hands as she lowered down.

"I'm sorry Sara, but I really need some blood," he said. "There's a lot that I need to tell you and I'm getting scratchy."

Releasing her hands, Silas moved to the kitchen and inspected the fridge.

"The larder is bare," he said with a half-smile. "Is there blood at your place?"

Sara nodded, then groaned when she remembered that she'd instructed Heather to not give Silas keypad access to that apartment.

"Be right back," she mumbled, forcing herself to her feet and stumbling blindly along the corridor.

"Please do," Silas called after her.

Alone in the hallway, the import of Silas's words hit her like a truck, and nausea bloomed deep in her gut. Crina was her maker, her teacher, her mother, her friend and her spiritual ally.

Or so she thought.

Back in her apartment, she quickly emptied three full blood bags into two large mason jars, placing them in the warmer and texting Silas that she'd be there as soon as it was drinkable. Suddenly, her trust issues flared up, with a dash of paranoia. Who else knew this? Clearly Silas was as shocked as she was, which was a huge silver lining, but what of Stefanya? Fan and Ama? Was Heather covering for Crina?

The suspicions raced through her mind, the ripples too numerous and too complicated for her to grasp. And if Crina was indeed headed this way to dispatch the Romanian men, she needed to work quickly. She texted Heather, demanding that she disable all access to the street entrances and Toma and Stefan's rooms temporarily, and that she'd explain as soon as she could. The warmer dinged and she grabbed the two jars and carefully made her way back to the other apartment, kicking at the door with her shoe for Silas to let her in.

"Glad you came back," he said, taking both jars from her and returning to the cluster of floor pillows. Once Sara was seated, he handed one to her, then remained standing while he downed his jar in a single chug, then waited patiently to take Sara's empty from her, burping loudly when he bent to get it, which made her smile. He was wobbly on his feet as he walked the short distance to the small kitchen and back, concern on his face, a trickle of blood at the corner of his mouth.

"This is what you wanted to talk about last night," Sara said, and he nodded as he crossed his legs and sank onto a pillow beside her.

"It's not like I could drop that bombshell and just leave," he said. "And I was already in the middle of dealing with..." his voice trailed off and he waved an arm at the wreckage of the apartment.

"Right," Sara said. "Do you want questions or do you just need to get it out?"

"Either or," Silas said. "I can start, and you can question, but I don't know everything. I'll do my best. I... uh... Stefanya, that's who told me."

"She thought you'd be okay with the news that your mother is a killer?"

"No, she was hammered," he said with a laugh. "She forgot how strong Pálinka is. We'd been killing bats all day and we were tired and filthy when we got back to the hotel, and she grabbed two bottles from the bar and we went to her room to plan the next day. Cut to, she pretty much finished one bottle by herself."

"Oof," Sara said, wrinkling her nose at the memory of Pálinka, a fruity brandy that was as potent as it was sweet.

"Right," Silas continued. "So then I got the whole Stefanya show. She got very careless, and at some point, I mentioned my mother and how we all needed to get back to New York ahead of the men, and Stef said something like, oh she'll kill them on sight. Sara, I freaked but I bit my tongue and put on my poker face. I didn't react. Then I said that it might not be the worst thing, you know, to kill them, just to give Stef more rope, and she went for it."

"She said, what else were we supposed to do with all those whores in Madrid? Fan and Ama liberated most of the halflings, but some wanted to stay, they'd developed a loyalty to Des or something, and my mom swooped in and killed them all. Then, she got into the Madrid headquarters, and did the same thing there. Stef said that there were only two or three sisters there when she got inside."

"Silas, I know you feel the same way... wait, let's check in on that – how do you feel about this?"

"I'm fucking disgusted," he spat. "This is the opposite of how I was raised and it's so opposite that I can't even really get my head around it. And I know you feel the same way. Wait... Sara, for one second did you even suspect that I might be okay with this?"

"Hi my name is Sara and I feel like trusting people isn't in my best interest at the moment," she said. "Of course I considered it, because why wouldn't I? Silas, when you left, yes, I had a bit of a meltdown. You could call it a tantrum, it just seems so stupid."

"I'm sorry in advance for what I'm about to say," Silas said, something new and disarming in his voice. "I get that it's hard to break centuries of mistrust, I really do, but come on, Sara. I did what I did for us, but also, I did what needed to be done. And," he paused, his eyes boring into hers. "I did the right fucking thing. And I think for right now, we need to pause the relationship talk before I say or do something I'll regret."

Sara was suddenly itching for a fight, increasingly aware that Silas's constant passivity had been driving her crazy.

"Go ahead," she said coolly. "Speak your piece."

"I don't need to," Silas said, infuriating her further. "Your actions are saying it for me. Again."

"This is a trap," Sara said angrily. "No matter what I do here, you've cast such a wide net that anything I do will be the wrong thing."

"Would it kill you, just once, to realize that you've been playing the misunderstood victim since we met?" Silas's voice remained firm. "If my mother had gotten you to Iceland fifty years ago, we wouldn't be in this predicament. You weren't fighting to save this Lock, you were building walls around it, for your own safety, not anyone else's."

"Like you said," Sara said, her voice tight with anger. "You weren't here."

"In every other Lock except Madrid and New York, the women switched Mothers every ten or twenty years. Imani has been a mother, Heather has been a mother a couple times. They did it and they moved on. You got stuck. Because you liked being stuck And the thing I don't want to say is, you liked having everyone do what you told them to do. And Sara, that's not what a boyfriend is, and the fact that you burned our little life to the ground because I acted out of my own conscience says it all."

"You're so far off the track," Sara said.

"I disobeyed you and you broke up with me," Silas said.

"I never once said we were broken up," Sara said.

"No, you just needed to create a space in which you always get your way," Silas countered, a rueful chuckle a brutal punctuation mark. "You didn't consider us, you considered yourself, and that's the difference here. You're mad at me for doing something that was entirely for the benefit of both of us, and you reacted by doing something that was beneficial only to yourself. And here we are, and you know what Sara? I'm okay with it."

"Oh sure you are."

"I can't do the hand-holding any more," Silas said. "Which means, most likely, that our..." he shrugged, glancing around the decimated apartment, "...our thing together is at an end."

Sara realized that in all of this, she never once considered that Silas could leave her.

She had mistaken his passivity for submissiveness.

When she didn't reply, Silas continued.

"Sara, you talk about trust the way I talk about freedom," he said. "My freedom is under threat right now. The easiest thing for me to do is to vanish. I have lost Iceland, it's not a secret any more, but it's also not my only bolthole. I've been a member of this Lock for a millisecond out of my entire life, and leaving it would be so easy."

"So you're leaving?"

Silas gave her an infuriating nod/shrug combination.

"Ultimately, yes," he said. "I need some time alone to figure that part out, but right now, I have to decide what to do with the Cursed men, because that clock is ticking fast and we are the only people who know how much danger they're in."

"This is the weirdest breakup in human history," Sara said, her voice neutral. "I also need some time alone."

"That's all I needed to hear," Silas pushed himself to his feet. "I'll deal with my mother by myself. Goodbye, Sara. I'm..." his voice thickened. "...I'm really sorry."

"NO!" she leapt to her feet. "She is my mother too."

Silas chuckled again. "*Now* it's the weirdest breakup in human history."

"She is though," Sara said. "She's been mothering us both for five centuries."

"Of course that's what you'd say," Silas said, anger tinging his words. "Because she did mother you. I got very different treatment, because she wanted this Cursed life so badly." Silas said. "She dumped me with a farmer for a decade, then had me fostered at a bunch of convents and seminaries. In the fifteen hundreds. Do you even have an inkling of what that was like?"

Once again, Sara was reminded that she didn't know even the smallest percentage about Silas's actual life, but she remembered the cruelty, hypocrisy and misery of a lot of the local religious orders all too well.

"I can get the broad strokes," she said softly. "And I'm sorry, no matter what we are or what we become, I really need to just sit and hear your whole life story."

"Don't," he spat angrily "Not now. I don't like talking about it, for obvious reasons," Silas said. "I need to say something. You keep on saying you want to hear all my secrets, and Sara, that bothers me because it feels like you believe you're entitled to know all this stuff. I've been alive as long as you have. I have kept confidences, and I plan to continue to keep them. Some stuff, I'll tell you when the time is right. However, some things are not mine to tell you, and as long as they pose you no danger, I will not speak of them. The world I lived in for most of my life was not your world." Silas paused, catching himself. "Shit. I need to stop talking. Please, can we get back on track?"

Confused by the weird turn the conversation had taken, Sara blinked and shook her head, then nodded.

"Sure," she said, biting her tongue to prevent herself from saying anything she'd regret. "Crina. Let's get back to Crina."

"Thank you," Silas said. "Right now, I just need you to see my mother as I see her. She's my mother, yes, but also, she's incredibly selfish and driven. The most surprising thing about her is that she actually came back and got me from the farm. I had already started calling that farmer woman "mama" and I considered the other children to be my siblings."

"Fucking hell, Silas," Sara took his hand. "This is the stuff I'm talking about in your past. Why didn't you ever tell me any of this stuff?"

"Because it's so insanely complicated, and I mean, come on, it's hard enough for regular people to talk about their pasts," he paused and looked away, and she wondered if he was crying. "We have five hundred years of intertwined existence, and I just can't lightly go telling you something because I'm afraid it will impact you in some way, and," he paused again. "Sara, this is literally the thing I was afraid of, that we'd be talking lightly and together our stories would reveal something terrible that we never suspected."

"Exactly this," she said. "Exactly this. Silas, this will cause Teddie to actually explode."

"That's how I felt when Stef told me," Silas said. "She kept on talking for a while and then fell asleep, and I sat there feeling like that bit in Alien where she's hit the autodestruct button on the spaceship. I felt like I was counting down to obliteration."

"Why didn't you call me?"

"It's not news to deliver to an angry girlfriend," he said, finally turning his face back to hers. "Additionally, I had an opportunity so I used it."

"Oh yeah?"

"Did you know you can use a sleeping face to open an iPhone?"

"Oh shit," Sara smacked her forehead with her palm. "Bet you got more than you bargained for."

"Yeah, I went into her encrypted chats, and I will say this, Stef and Ama tried to talk her out of it, but apparently neither of them could talk her down and also, their attempts were pretty half-assed."

"I mean, for those elders, it's not like they've been quiet about you know, hoping that our numbers would reduce."

"Sara, another thing that has always annoyed me, not just about you, about all you Lock ladies, is that you have this weird picture of the Elders as this other thing."

"You didn't even mention a first thing that was annoying and now we have another thing?"

Silas rolled his eyes.

"We are elders, Sara," he said, as if he was explaining physics. "I'm twenty eight years younger than my mother. You, me, Fan, Ama, Yfke, we're all pretty close in age. Just because we didn't go into the castle and fight the original Cursed men doesn't mean we're super different. The Elders are just a clique of bossy bitches who use their cache to fuck off and do whatever they want. That's why they are willing to let it all burn, as long as they get to protect their little lifestyles."

Sara pressed her back against the cold brick wall, her eyes closed.

"Sara, at a certain point, the parent/child dynamic becomes invalid," Silas continued. "Crina is my mother. Crina has never really performed a traditional mother role. In you, she saw someone reliable, someone good, and she needed that, because she wasn't either of those things. You softened her, you also kept her in line. But she hid a lot of things from you, and I'm not playing bait and switch here, I'll tell you, in time. But right now, we need to figure out what to do with these men."

"Do you really think she'd just waltz in here and slaughter them?"

"That I can't tell you," Silas rubbed his temples. "I mean, she could. What would the fallout be? What recourse would any of us have?

Devil's advocate, in the long run it would be easiest, if we didn't have a conscience."

"Can we take them to your upstate place?"

"We could, short-term," he said. "But it's the first place she'd look."

"We don't have long," Sara said. "We'll have to bring Imani."

"There's no we here," Silas said. "This is another me on my own thing. You have to stay here and find the next men."

A knot of hurt and confusion and anger formed in Sara's chest, and she stared at Silas, her eyes pleading words that she couldn't bring her mouth to say.

"We don't have time for this," Silas said. As he began to turn away, his phone rang in his pocket. Looking at it, his face fell.

"It's my mom," he said.

"Answer it on speaker," Sara whispered, and Silas complied.

"Hi mom!" he said with ersatz cheeriness.

"Si, why the hell is my fingerprint not working? Come let me in, I'm downstairs."

Chapter Ten

Shoving the rooftop room door open with her shoulder, Sara blinked to adjust her eyes to the darkness after the whiteout glare of a sky full of steam-white clouds.

"Come sit by me," April Veronica called out. Sara was surprised that someone had beaten her to the meeting, given that she'd only sent the text ten minutes ago, while Silas went down to get Crina from the street. As the room took shape in her vision, she saw April hauling Sara's heavy throne backwards to where she had been sitting, her muscles not yet strong enough to lift it overhead.

"Here, let me," she said, stepping in and, handing her Stanley cup to April Veronica, effortlessly lifting the heavy chair over her head, then setting it in the space beside where April had been sitting. As she sat, she noticed that April was sitting in Rosa's old throne. "You know you can get a throne of your own? You don't have to sit in Rosa's."

"I know," April Veronica said cheerily. "But this is such a beautiful antique, the carving, the upholstery, it would be a shame to you know, ignore it because it was owned by a crazy person. Now it gets to enjoy being sat on by me for a few centuries."

"Fair," Sara said, glancing at the door.

"So what's the tea, sis?" April Veronica rested a palm on Sara's jacket sleeve. "Embla was in the shower, she'll be here in a minute, but your text freaked us both out. Is there a new Cursed man already?"

"No, that's still a few days away," Sara said, wondering how much to share before deciding that Old Sara would have kept it quiet and enjoyed the gasps of a big reveal. She needed to not do Old Sara things anymore. "It seems that Crina went and killed a bunch of Cursed women and she may or may not have returned to dispatch the men."

The shock on April Veronica's face almost made Sara wish she'd done it the old fashioned way.

"I just needed to get us all on the same page," Sara said, her eye still on the door, "before any more blood is spilled. Speaking of blood, did you feast before you came up here?"

April Veronica shook her head, and Sara passed the Stanley Cup back to her.

"Drink deep," she said. "It's full."

Obediently, April Veronica drew deeply on the straw, slipping back against the chair when the blood hit her system. The door opened, filling the air with bustle and chatter as Heather, Imani, Fran and Yukari entered.

"Where's the fire?" Imani called out. "Sara, you are interrupting a very good afternoon in my life."

"Spare me the details," Sara said with a laugh.

"So what's the dramurgency?" Teddie called out from the doorway. Before anyone could answer, she was joined by Liz, Fan and Ama. Everyone went directly to their thrones, except Fan and Ama who sat cross-legged on the dais, facing back at them all. Heather, Yukari and Fran were still whispering in a group until a cough from Sara silenced them and they took their seats.

Sara surveyed the room in silence, trying to figure out how to best monitor the reactions of people when she confronted Crina, then second-guessed that. Under this new freeform Lock structure, there was nothing but democracy. Crina could insist on killing the men, and then what? A vote? A physical battle? For an organization built on trust and conformity, this current crisis was a serious trial.

The door opened again, bright light temporarily blinding her.

"Sorry I'm late," Embla said, and Sara felt Embla's arms snake around her in an awkward hug. When her vision returned, she saw that Silas and Crina had entered at the same time as Embla, and Crina was looking at her with a big smile, waving her hand in greeting. Beside her, Silas was the complete opposite, glowering at her angrily. What? If he didn't need to tell her he was going to Romania, she sure as hell didn't need to tell him she was calling a meeting. She'd already decided that she would confront Crina, it wasn't fair to ask Silas to do it.

"Hey," she said, rising to her feet, "If we can all grab a seat, I'll get this started. I don't have any updates, I haven't talked to Desdemona since yesterday, but I do want to get us all onto the same page before we received a potential four new males this Friday."

"What page?" Imani said incredulously. "There's one page. Find the fuckers as fast as we can and get them here."

The reactions in the room told Sara all she needed to know. Righteous nodding from all of the regular New York members, with the exception of Heather, who stared ahead, her eyes fixed on the wall behind Sara, her lips pursed. Sara realized that since her return to New York, Heather had still not reached out to her at all. Fan and Ama exchanged glances, and Crina was examining her fingernails very intently. Silas's eyes were downcast.

"Wait..." Imani continued. "Is there another page? Sara, is there a solution that I don't know about?" A note of mild panic crept into Imani's voice.

"Of course not," Sara said. "But some things have come to my attention, and I want to clear the air right here, and right now."

"Oh, for fuck's sake," Crina said, her eyes lifting slowly to meet Sara's. "Spare us the bullshit, Sara. We are not running a dog shelter, we are in the middle of a crisis the likes of which we've never seen before. And you guys, I know what she's getting at so I'll beat her to it. I went and ran cleanup on Madrid."

"Cleanup?" Fran's eyes narrowed as she spoke. "Can you clarify that for us?"

"There were loose ends," Crina said, leaning forward in her throne. "There are no loose ends now."

"I didn't ask for a fucking riddle," Fran said. "What exactly did you do, Crina?"

Standing, Crina approached the dais but did not step up onto it. With deliberate slowness she turned her back on Sara and faced the room.

"We are at war," she said, her voice strong. "And we are very close to losing the war, just purely on a numbers basis."

"Crina," Fran's voice was steel. "What did you do?"

With an exasperated sigh, Crina faced Fran directly.

"Any halflings, as you called them, that refused to return to their hometowns, I killed them."

A round of gasps filled the air, then silence fell.

"Then, I went to Madrid, and I took care of all of the sisters who were still there. I deactivated Desdemona's nerve center."

With that, chaos erupted in the room. Sara kept her eyes on Silas, hunched forward, his head clasped in his hands. Standing behind

Crina as she was, Sara could see the faces of everyone in the room, the disgust, the anger, the frustration, but she couldn't make out what anyone was yelling at Crina, the air was full of jagged, ugly voices all demanding further explanation. Crina's shoulders expanded as she inhaled deeply.

"Shut the fuck up!" she yelled, and silence fell. "Okay, fine, you don't kill. And if it makes it any easier, I resign from this Lock, so your rules don't apply to me."

"Oh great," Imani's voice dripped with sarcasm. "Well that settles that, you're James Bond now, is that it?"

"No, Imani, I'm the same woman who went in and killed a bunch of men because they were evil and killing them was literally the only solution."

"That was five hundred years ago," Imani said. "There are other options now."

"Such as?" Crina's voice was emotionless. "There are less than eighty of us now, worldwide, and of that number, around half have been indoctrinated by Desdemona. And just because she chose relatively peaceful ways to murder the other Locks, it was still murder. She's using your softness against you the same way she used it to slaughter the women of Helsinki, Warsaw and Edinburgh."

"What do you mean by 'took care of'?" Fran's voice trembled. "I presume you killed them. I'm asking how."

"Well, to be fair, they tried to trick me into a cell," Crina was defiant. "I was just-"

"Have you always been a liar?" Fran asked bluntly, and everyone's eyes turned to Crina, who was not fazed.

"All this because you think I'm a *liar*?"

"The worst women are women who lie," Fran said angrily. "Honest women are the greatest thing on Earth. It's the liars who fuck it up for all of us."

"There's a difference between lying and keeping your mouth shut," Crina said, her voice even. "I only speak when I have something I want to share. I don't want to sound defensive, because I have nothing to defend. My life's work has been to safeguard our kind, and to ensure that our lifestyle, no, our lives, get to continue. Over the years, as sisters chose Surrender or became complacent, the job fell to me, alone. Some," she paused, glancing at Fan, then Ama, "have known something of my actions, but nobody, not even Stefanya, has stood beside me in this role."

"You were always a member of this Lock," Sara stated. "You founded this Lock, you and I came up with the directives, that we would never kill, that we would always aspire to peace. Did you mean any of it?"

"My child," Crina said, her voice honest, "I meant every word of it. It remains the goal of everything I do. But every person in this room knows that a rot set in, and each Lock independently moved in its own direction, and some of them became toxic."

"At what point did you decide to start murdering people?" Silas stood to face his mother.

"About two weeks ago," Crina said. "Until that point, I had not killed since the Purge."

Everyone began to speak at once, and Crina stood patiently, her hands clasped in front of her, until the hubbub subsided.

"There are things that I still refuse to speak of, secrets I intend to keep, for the good of us all-"

"Now is not the right time to be enigmatic!" Silas took a step closer to his mother, his voice cracking. "Because everything you're saying goes against the way you raised me, they way you guided all of us."

"All of us have secrets," Crina kept her voice soft. "Mine are potentially very destructive. I'm not being enigmatic. Quite the opposite, in fact, because I know that all of you feel some entitlement, that I should throw myself at your mercy, shed light on all my shadows. None of you would do that in my position, I assure you."

"What happened two weeks ago, Crina?" Imani leaned forward in her chair.

"It was a month ago," Crina said. "I heard that Desdemona was hunting for the virus in Romania, and so I knew I would have to do something. And seriously, you guys, I wanted to kill Desdemona while we had her in custody. And I caved, I went along with your plan, even though every fiber of my being wanted her dead and forgotten. My hope was that the vaccine would kill her before she could do any damage. And I'm not being facetious, your intentions were admirable, if somewhat crueler than you'll admit. But once I heard what she was up to, I knew I had to step in."

"And you didn't think to involve us?" Sara asked.

"Literally why would I?" Crina glared at Sara. "I didn't have time for death by committee, talking about the problem wouldn't solve it."

"It would have, though," Silas interjected.

"Did you ask your girlfriend for permission before you ran off to be a hero?" Crina's voice was surprisingly spiteful, and Sara flinched. Silas stood firm.

"Nice try Diddy," April Veronica said, making Embla snort laugh. "Killing a bunch of bats is not the same as killing a bunch of women. Don't be so disappointing."

"Don't go blaming Si," Imani chimed in. "At least one person in your family has been able to stick to our rules, guv. And it sure ain't you."

"I asked you before," Fran stood up. "How, exactly, did you kill these women?"

"As painlessly as possible," Crina said. "For the halflings, I fed a hose from an exhaust pipe into their building while they slept. The sisters in Madrid, I killed them traditionally. With a Slicer."

A loud sob burst from Embla's chest.

"Crina, I am heartbroken by your actions," Embla said through her tears, holding April Veronica's hand. "Do you know the stress that I live under? The crushing fear that one day I will have the urges of a man? My everyday life is filled with a terror that one day, I won't see murder as the worst thing a person can do to another human. And you know this. And you taught me that I could create my own destiny, my own world free of murder. Is Frances right? Were you lying the whole time?"

Crina made an expression somewhere between sympathy and frustration, and shrugged.

"No, I was encouraging your idealism," she said, and Sara watched Embla's eyes widen. "That world *can* exist for you. I want that world to exist for you so much that I will do anything to guarantee it."

"It's the anything part that's proving problematic," Fran said. "It's really discouraging that you can't see it."

"I see it, Frances," Crina said condescendingly. "I also see the bigger picture, I see human nature as flawed and violent and selfish and prone to insanity-"

"Except when it's you embodying all of those things," April Veronica said. "Crina, do you not see how *basic* you've been? How ridiculously out of touch, out of date and out of sync you've been with the progress that Sara has fought to realize?"

"Sara here has valued keeping her hands clean more than she values the safety of the rest of the world," Crina said. "As you'd say, no cap, no shade, but now we have a crisis. We have two men, infected with a form of our virus, living in this building, and four more arriving in four days. Even worse, Desdemona is somewhere out there, with the power to infect another army, like she did with those poor young women. I for one will not rest until she is dead, and I have burned her body and I'm dancing on the warm ashes."

"Here here," Liz yelled.

"Oh, Elizabeth," Crina turned to her. "Now you're okay killing the woman you trusted a few months back?"

LIz's mouth opened and closed as a hundred answers logjammed, and none of them came out.

"So the question is," Crina continued, "are those of us willing to do what it takes still welcome to stay here in the compound until the job is done?"

"Nope," Teddie raised a middle finger to Crina, her eyes narrowed in hatred. "You can get the fuck out right now."

"No offense, Ted," Crina began, and Sara clenched her fists, prepared to attack Crina if she went for her daughter. "But what is the hardest thing you've ever gone through?"

"I"m in the middle of it right now," Teddie spat.

"Then you've had a blessed life," Crina said. "Look, you all can be as evolved as you want, but Fan, Ama and I are going to save our kind, and we are going to save the world. It's that simple. And once it's done, I'm really happy to sit and talk with you guys and I will promise to try to not kill anyone else ever again, but right now, we don't have that freedom."

"Cool sermon," Imani said, rising to her feet. "But what about the men that are already here? You know, asking for a friend and all."

"Imani needs to protect her boyfriend," Liz teased in a sing-song voice. "Gets dick once and instantly becomes needy girlfriend."

"Don't think I won't smack you upside your stupid head," Imani spun to face Liz, her hands bunched into fists. In a flash, Embla stepped between them.

"I will also protect the men already in our custody," Embla said. "I would prefer not to use my fists."

"What, exactly, do you all propose we do with the men in our custody," Ama asked. "Because, fine, I'll just say it, Fan, Crina, Heather and I are all of the opinion that the only way forward is to kill them also."

Heather, whose head jerked up at the mention of her name, made eye contact briefly with Sara, then returned her gaze to the floor. Panicked, Sara wondered if Heather had been lying to her alongside Crina. Another bout of yelling erupted in the room, and Sara waited for it to subside before speaking.

"The one condition of belonging to this Lock is that we respect life," she said. "For those of you who are advocating killing, I'm gonna ask real politely for you to vacate the entire compound immediately."

"No," Crina said, finally turning to face her. "That won't be happening, not right away."

To Sara's surprise, Silas stood and pushed his way up to face his mother.

"It's going to happen, right now," he said, his voice raw.

"Not now, Silas," Crina said dismissively. "Stop trying to impress your girlfriend. We are under attack. We don't know where nine of the Madrid sisters are, and we don't know if there is already an army of infected men already in New York. The kid arrived with no luggage, no passport. He didn't come directly from the airport."

"We know all that," Silas said. "But like I said, the members of this Lock have chosen peace, and if you can't respect it, then you should leave."

Fan shot to her feet.

"Whether we live here or not, we plan to kill any future Cursed men that arrive in New York," she yelled at Silas. "Also any infected women from Madrid who are a threat. Don't you get it, Silas? All of you? What Desdemona is doing is waaaaaay more serious than the shit we saw in the first Purge. We don't know what this virus does, but we all know that we can't afford to have all of New York City infected with it."

"It does not seem to slow the aging process," Yukari said, barely audibly. "And I have already identified its binding protein in their version of the virus, so I can probably vaccinate the men here, safely, in the next week or two. We do not need to kill them."

"Oh good," Crina said condescendingly. "So once we get them cured we can just send them back to Romania and our secret is safe with them?"

"No, Crina," Sara said, the solemn tone of her voice making Crina turn to face her. "It would mean dissolving this Lock, abandoning this building."

A round of gasps lead to dead silence as the news sunk in.

"Or we kill them," Ama piped up, "and we get to keep our lovely home."

"That price is too high," April Veronica said. "At the end of the day, this is just a pile of bricks. It is not worth more than even one human life."

"I agree," said Fran, raising her hand as if someone was conducting a poll. In solidarity, Sara raised her hand, with Silas, Embla, Imani and April Veronica following suit. Teddie and Yukari, who had been deep in conversation, quietly stood and raised a hand.

"What's this bullshit?" Crina asked.

"It's seven to four," Sara said. "Against whatever you are trying to do. Heather? How do you vote?"

With a slow inhale, Heather stood.

"I'm sorry, pet, I really am, but if you'd seen what was left of Edinburgh, you'd be seeing things differently. I'll be siding with Crina on this. We can't pussyfoot around it any longer. There just aren't enough of us to contain the threat."

Disappointment flooded through Sara upon hearing Heather's words. She didn't know what to say.

"Well that settles it," Fran said to Heather. "Sorry to be a narc, Heath, but I'll need you off all security systems immediately."

"You're bloody joking," Heather protested, and Fran shook her head.

"Give me your iPad right now, please." Fran extended a hand, and Heather hesitated briefly before digging into her satchel and pulling out her tablet.

"Unlock it," Fran said, and Heather obeyed, then handed the tablet to her. Immediately, Fran returned to her seat and began tapping at the screen.

While they were all waiting for Fran to finish, Sara realized that Liz hadn't voted.

"Elizabeth," she said sternly, "I don't believe I saw how you voted in the proxy."

"Bitch, nobody even called a vote," Liz said snidely.

"How would you have voted if they did?"

Liz shrugged.

"If you don't assure us that you're in favor of not killing, I'm going to have to ask you to leave with the pro-death mob here."

"It's just so typical," Liz whined in her California twang. "We didn't even discuss this. I mean, did you even listen? Fucking Heather is siding with them. That means that they have a point, right?"

"I believe so," Heather said. "Good women have been murdered. I won't lose another."

"That's a noble sentiment," Teddie said. "But Heath, come on, you're endorsing murder."

"That's right, I am," Heather said brusquely. "We've been here before, we're here again. It's human nature and sometimes it's unavoidable."

"Nothing is unavoidable," Fran said, looking up from the iPad. "And as of right now, I've stripped Crina, Ama, Heather and Fan of their accesses in this compound. Lizzie, I need a vote from you real quick."

"Killing is bad," Liz said sarcastically. "Blah blah blah, I'm still a member of this Lock."

"For now," Embla said, and Liz whipped her head around to face off. "But I will be watching you. And Fran? While you're in there, can you strip Liz of any access to the hallways where the men are being held?"

"Already did," Fran said. "Sorry Lizzie, but murder isn't some wishy washy thing you don't really have a stance on."

"This place sucks," Liz said. "Fuck it, you all suck."

With that, Liz stood and stormed out, slamming the door behind her.

"At least she's reliable," Sara said once silence returned, "Anyway, I'd like to remind you four that we have jurisdiction over the city of New York, and-"

"Oh, Sara," Crina raised her voice. "Do fuck off, please. There is no jurisdiction, there is no authority, there is no magical territory that you have some feudal right to. This is just a fucking city and we are in the city at the same time as you and we will do whatever we want in this city."

Setting her face to stone against Crina's hurtful words, Sara faced down her maker.

"Get out of *my* home, right now."

"Sara, when will you ever understand?" Crina's voice was threatening. "You're powerless. The old ways are dead. The future is unwritten, and if none of you survive this, it'll be because you're stupid and you asked for it. You're handing a victory to Desdemona, and that doesn't seem to bother you," she paused. "I've never been so disappointed in you, not when you fed on a human, not when you seduced my son, not even when you failed not once but twice to step up and take a Slicer to Desdemona. You're just-'"

"SHUT UP!" Silas screamed at his mother. The effect was instant. Crina froze, her words hanging in the air. "Leave. Now. Not another word."

In shocked silence, after a round of shrugs and eye contact, Crina, Ama, Heather and Fan stood and exited.

"I'll need to walk you out," Fran called out, running after them with the iPad in her hands.

As the door closed behind them, Embla's tears became a torrent, and April Veronica wrapped her in a hug. Breathing heavily, Silas collapsed onto the closest throne, and Sara's heart ached for him, confusion coursing through her. Sara watched closely as tears rimmed his eyes and his chin trembled, but full tears never came. Teddie rose and embraced Sara in a tight hug."

"It will be okay, mom."

Kissing the top of her head, Sara hugged her back.

"I don't think it ever was," she said quietly.

Chapter Eleven

In the aftermath of the meeting, Sara and Teddie wandered the rooftop as the other sisters and Silas trickled away, disappearing into various doorways, the compound absorbing them like a tomb. The weak sun was losing a battle with a sheet of dishwater clouds, and the wind off the river had teeth. Sara dropped her arm from Teddie's shoulders and took her hand, and they walked in silence, a circuitous path around all the olive trees in their planter boxes.

"I'm getting a bit frosty," Teddie said, and Sara glanced at her thin lavender hoodie.

"Of course you are, Ted, you're not dressed for weather."

"I was working out when you sent the urgent text," Teddie led them in the direction of Sara's loft door. "And mom, I love it when you talk like it's the past."

"Shut your bone box," Sara said with a smile, causing Teddie to laugh out loud, the sound warming Sara's worried heart. "Hey, are you up for some hang time?"

"I did presume that's what we were doing."

Sara stopped walking, and Teddie faced her, puzzled.

"Let's go to yours then," Sara said. "Trust me, somebody will be knocking on my door every five seconds if we go there. I'd like some just-us time."

Pivoting without a word, Teddie walked back across the roof to the fire escape entrance that led to her floor, near darkness engulfing them inside the stairwell.

"I'm gonna warn you," she said as they neared her door. "I kind of went a bit nutso after your death, and then I was upstate with Yukari and, fuck it, I haven't really had time to redecorate."

Pushing the apartment door open with her shoulder, Teddie stood aside and let Sara pass her down the short hallway. Teddie's apartment, two stories above Marguerite's, had the exact same floor plan, though Teddie's was furnished differently, no television and all her couches and chairs facing windows, slivers of the Hudson visible between buildings. The normally tidy shelves and pretty much any flat surface were all covered with framed photos. Of Sara.

"Oh my, this is a lot of contraband," Sara joked around a rapidly forming lump in her throat. "Where did you get all these pictures?"

"I got ways and means," Teddie said, skipping into the kitchen. "And yes, I broke a rule. But who doesn't love a photo album?"

"I mean," Sara joked, "if you're gonna break a rule, this is the one to break."

"Amen," Teddie called out. "Blood or wine?"

"That doesn't have to be an 'or' statement," Sara said. "Let's do blood *and* wine."

While Teddie busied herself in the kitchen, Sara bent to inspect the framed photos, all of them candid. The largest one was an eight by ten black and white photo of Sara, in the mid sixties as evidenced by her bouffant short black bob and heavily made up eyes. In the photo, Sara smiled as she kissed a tiny duckling on the beak. She instantly remembered that moment from a weekend away at a farm up by Kingston. She heard Teddie enter the room behind her.

"Isn't that a great photo?" Teddie asked as she handed Sara a very full glass of pinot noir.

"It's bringing the entire day back to me," Sara said, "But how did you get it?"

"That girl I was dating at the time, the one whose commune it was, she was shooting film all weekend."

"I was so careful of that adorable little shutterbug," Sara said.

"Not careful enough, apparently," Teddie smiled, clinking her glass against Sara's. "But somehow all the negatives of that weekend went missing, remember?"

"Honestly, I didn't even remember that weekend until I saw that photo," Sara said, sipping her wine. "Wasn't that just after Fran got made?"

"Yeah, remember, we took her and they gave her LSD?"

"Oh hell, that's right, but I think it was the other way around. Fran had that whole bottle of LSD-25," Sara laughed, and Teddie gestured at the overstuffed brown sofa. Taking a seat, Sara patted the cushion beside her and Teddie sat, their thighs touching.

"There is an amazing shot of her dancing in front of one of them psychedelic light shows in a barn," Teddie said. "I'm gonna make a print for her birthday."

"That's great," Sara said, her eyes still drawn to the thirty or so images of herself, scattered in frames large and small across the shelves of the room. Over the centuries they'd all had photos made, daguerreotypes, tin type, plates, film and polaroids, enjoying the thick paper images for a brief time before burning them. She'd never seen anything like this though, a random sampling of moments she'd shared with Teddie, each one capable of unleashing a cavalcade of memories as rich and thick as the moment captured on thick shiny paper.

"Did everyone except me keep their photos?" she asked suddenly.

"I can't answer for anyone else," Teddie said softly. "But I already lost one mother, and I got nothing of her except a couple dresses and her shoes. I can see her in my mind, some times better than others."

"That's how it is for me with my mom," Sara said. "She's a feeling more than a recognizable face these days. I did have a really strong flash of memory while I was in Iceland, I remembered the faces of my siblings and my mom, as well as the smell of our little hut, the feel of it. It was intense."

"Oh wow, did it knock you over?"

Sara shook her head. "No, I was still too broken, too worried about you. I enjoyed it briefly and honestly, I didn't think of it again until now."

"I have memories like that all the time," Teddie said, leaning her head on Sara's shoulder. "They're all of you. You've been so good to me, I'm so lucky that my mom came to you for help."

"I wish we could have saved her too," Sara said. "It's one of my life's great regrets. But she was a person of faith and that was a rule and you know..."

"Mom," Teddie twisted suddenly, "do you think Crina ever believed in the rules?"

Accustomed to Teddie's curveballs, Sara wriggled around to face her.

"I've had maybe an hour longer than you to consider this," Sara said. "I think she believes in them, but also she sees herself as outside of them. It seems that once again, the rules were made by a few to control the many."

"And the few did whatever they wanted?"

Sara nodded. "It really feels like the end of our perfect little world."

"Don't say that," Teddie said quietly. "We'll figure out a way through this."

"Oh, there's a way through it," Sara said, swallowing the rest of her wine just as the timer on the warming oven signaled that their blood was ready. "It's Crina's way. It's to literally murder Desdemona, her followers, these infected men and whatever else people are around them. But at that point, is the price too high? Just so a very elite group of women can be immortal?"

Standing in one lithe motion, Teddie pressed two fingers into Sara's shoulder.

"Pause," she said. "I've paused you. Hold up. I'm getting more blood for this."

This time, Sara looked at the photos but they hit different. She saw photos spanning eighty years, and she wondered what she had done with this gift, this endless time on Earth, and she felt hollow. She'd been insular and tended an even more insular group of women while the seeds of social destruction took root around the world. Sure, they'd donated heartily to countless causes, but now, looking back, it was as if the New York Lock was a cruise ship and she'd spent most of her life at sea, only occasionally setting foot in a port and truly experiencing it.

"Uh oh, reverie face," Teddie said, jolting her back to reality as she slipped a rough earthenware mug into Sara's hands.

"Yeah, that one was rough," Sara said, turning to face Teddie as she sipped her blood. "Ted, Crina said some shit that shocked me."

"She was out of line," Teddie began, and Sara raised a hand.

"Do all of you think I'm kind of a crazy bitch?"

"That's not how I'd describe it, but let's just say that you became predictable and everyone took advantage of it."

"Including you?"

Teddie shook her head. "No, bitch, I told you everything and got in trouble for everything. I had my freedom, and I love the rules, and

I was raised in them so they don't feel restrictive. But people knew your routines and they knew your blindspots, so whether it was dating someone for eight or ten years or hitting the blood extra hard when we had plenty in stock, that was normal. It was more about getting out of responsibility. Look at Imani, she hasn't worked in so long until now. She just keeps on telling you that she's working on her fiftieth doctorate but she goes out and gets involved in worlds. Her research is all experiential. She knows you won't look too closely."

"Because I trust her," Sara said indignantly.

"Well, sure," Teddie began, then a knock at her door startled her. "Hang on."

Listening intently after the door creaked open, Sara was shocked to hear Heather's voice, then she heard Teddie invite her in. Sara glanced at the alter to herself, mortified that Heather would see it, only for a second, because then Heather was standing in front of her.

"Well that got heated," she said.

"It did," Sara said. "But I thought Fran marched all you murderers out."

"Yeah yeah yeah," Heather mugged while pointing at Sara's empty wine glass and then at her half-empty blood glass. "Pet, I'll take one of each if you don't mind."

"Wait," Sara said annoyed, "Did Fran kick you all out or not?"

"Well, she escorted us to the street, but she didn't ask for my key fob back, so here I am."

"And how did you know I was here?"

"Air Tag."

"Fucking hell, Heather," Sara felt her anger start to boil. "You picked a side and now you're just showing me how weak our security system is.."

"I don't care if you want to hear it or not, love," Heather crossed her legs and sat on the rug facing her. "If you keep playing this way, you're going to lose. You'll lose Teddie. You'll lose Silas-"

"I already did, thanks for asking," Sara snapped bitterly.

"He's still alive, isn't he?" Heather was defiant. "He won't be for long. And then, maybe, just maybe, you'll feel the way I do about taking extreme measures to protect the things and people that we love. I'd rather you came to that realization without his dead, limp body in your arms."

Teddie returned with a glass of wine for Heather, handed it to her and then sat beside Sara on the sofa.

"Where's me blood?"

"Ye can bloody wait," Teddie snapped in a perfect impersonation of Heather at her most brusque.

"Sara, Teddie, I hate that there's distance between us," Heather began. Beside her, Sara felt Teddie tense, about to say something, so she gently placed a palm on her thigh. "I know you're angry, and if it helps, I haven't killed anyone... at least not yet. I just wanted to clear the air with you, and then I'll be off."

"Fine," Sara said, "but if you're thinking that this conversation-"

"Or home invasion," Teddie said with a laugh.

"Or home invasion is going to convert me into a killer, you're going to leave disappointed."

"I know how you feel love, I do," Heather's voice was strangely shaky. "And I know you saw things, early on, terrible things, and you're devoted to never killing. What I saw in Edinburgh, or Helsinki or Warsaw... Those women didn't die theatrically, they didn't die in a metal coffin of spikes or have their veins torn open by a man with metal fangs..." Heather's voice began to crack and tears pooled in her eyes. "You two, those women were discarded, as if they were worthless. "

Heather paused for a sniff, then resumed. "That was the hardest thing. I realized that to Desdemona, they meant nothing. There were former Madrid sisters in amongst the dead, and she left them like trash. It was the most disgusting thing I've ever seen, and that was my tipping point. I'm not a killer but I am willing to do whatever it takes to stop Desdemona. And that means killing her. There's no safe alternative."

"That's your opinion," Sara began, and Heather waved an angry arm at her.

"Do you not see how badly we screwed up by not killing her?" Heather said. "How smug we were, giving her a vaccine and sending her on her way? She was ambitious and ruthless, and now she's got a time bomb ticking inside her. Isn't your conscience keeping you up at night because you had the chance to kill her and instead you chose a showy, unproven punishment that is presently blowing up in your face?"

"The vaccine thing was Crina's idea..."

"It was the only thing that Crina knew she could get you lot to accept."

Another loud knock at the door caused them all to jump, then they heard Fran.

"Heather, open up, I know you're in there."

"Fucking Air Tags," Heather said, sipping her wine, while Teddie went to answer the door.

Sara had never seen Fran so angry. Her face red, she raced into the room, her flat palm extended in front of Heather's face.

"You used a key fob to enter the basement trash disposal door," she said. "Hand it over."

Fran was livid. Heather pulled a keyring out of a pocket in her kilt, and wrestled a small plastic fob off it, placing it gently on Fran's palm. "Is that the only one?"

"It's the only one I have with me," Heather said. "There are some spares in my flat."

After she shoved the fob angrily into her jeans pocket, Fran looked at Sara.

"So what's going on here?"

"Well, Teddie and I were trying to have a catch up after Crina's delightful performance, and then this one rapped at the door and now she's trying to sell us on the whole murder thing. Pull up a seat, if you like."

"Sure," Fran said, folding herself into a lotus position on the floor, much closer to Sara than Heather. With a groan, Teddie got up and went to the kitchen.

"I'll take a beer," Fran called out. "You can skip the blood, I chugged some after the meeting."

"So," Sara said, "Heather here is telling me that I'm stupid for not killing Crina."

Before Fran could reply, Heather leapt to her feet.

"For fuck's sake, Sara, you fed on a human, so kiss my arse with this high road bullshit."

Sara recoiled as if Heather had slapped her, then she waited for an apology that never came.

"I'm serious, Sara," Heather's tone was imploring. "I love you so much, but even after you endured the worst thing that I can imagine, you retreated into the rules. You have said it yourself, our rules are nothing more than stop signs."

"It's not rules to respect human life." Fran said gently. "Heather, you're my friend, we've spent so many nights talking, I always thought we were kindred spirits."

"Frances," Heather took Fran's hand with her spare hand. "I love you. That's the thing. I love you, and I love you, Sara, and Teddie, you're like the niece I never had, the most inspiring thing in my world. And if I have to kill Desdemona to prevent you three from all ending up broken and rotten with, fuck it, okay, I'll say it. The rats had a field day, in each of those Locks. I've never seen such human wreckage, just broken at weird angles. She killed these women to make a point. She's a fucking psychopath. Let me ask you this – if you could kill Charles Manson before he got going, would you? And please don't make me play the Hitler card."

Silence descended in the room as all four of them sipped their drinks.

"Yes," Teddie said eventually, and Sara's head whipped around in shock. "I would kill Hitler, I would kill Charles Manson. I'd kill Mao Zedong and Trump and Stalin and Pol Pot and Reagan. There are a lot of crazy people, historically, whose early death would have saved immense suffering." She turned to Sara. "I'm sorry mom, but Heather has a point," she paused, pointing at Heather, "and don't you go getting excited, I'm not jumping ships here. But Desdemona, I'll admit that I'm disappointed that the vaccine didn't kill her, because she is spreading suffering. But Heather, there are victims in this story. Crina killed innocent women. We can't go killing those men. The second one is just a kid. And Toma, he seems decent, we could at least invest some time in him to see if he can work out as a Lock member."

"I hear you, lassie," Heather said, releasing Fran's hand. "I'm not all of a sudden a blood thirsty murder machine. I just want Desdemona dead. And we can all be as woke as we want and throw our arms up in the air and call Crina a pariah and, what is it? Cancel her, you guys want to cancel her, but right now, she's the only one playing this situation realistically. Instead of booting her out of the building, we should have tried to find common ground. She is capable of compromise, you know?

"I've actually never seen her compromise," Sara said. "I always thought it was her superpower but now I see that I was enabling a murderer."

"It's that kind of talk that makes you look stupid, Sara," Heather's tone was harsh. "You're the only one in this room who saw the events that shaped her, the brutality."

"Which is why I can never condone that kind of brutality. I've spent half a millennium convincing myself and others that we can live in peace."

"We can," Heather said. "Desdemona can't. We have to neutralize her."

"It's like telling someone to breathe underwater, I'm afraid," Sara said quietly. "Do you have any idea how haunted I am by feeding on that woman? And you guys? She was almost dead when I fed on her, I couldn't have saved her, and even that doesn't give me any peace."

"I'm sorry love, I can only guess how horrible that is for you," Heather's eyes were soft. "But I just think that we need to get Crina and the elders back in here, we need to be together, and we need to find a solution that works for all of us."

"Silas will never go for it," Sara said. "He's broken by these revelations."

"Do you have any idea how foolish it is to not have him locked away in this compound?" Heather said, anger returning. "You guys had a little fight because he wasn't an obedient lapdog and you're making him go live off-site? Has it not occurred to you that Desdemona might already be here? And how do you know that we aren't already under attack?"

"What have you heard?" Fran asked sharply.

"I've heard nothing," Heather replied, "but I'm looking at this situation from every vantage point, and she can do far more damage from a closer proximity."

"You're supposed to be monitoring her movements," Sara snapped.

"Sara, for the love of all that you hold dear, can you please pull your head out of your arse?" Heather's tone was harsher than Sara had ever been on the receiving end of. "Snap out of your weird victim parent role and be a fucking warrior. That's what we all need right now."

Sara felt sick to her stomach as she looked into the concerned faces of the women she'd protected and nurtured, all of them looking at her expectantly. As critical as sisters could get, they never stopped wanting her to mother them. Sara stared back at the women surrounding her, until her eyes locked on Teddie's, filled with love and pleading. She heard Embla's voice inside her head. What did she want out of this situation?

"Thanks for your Ted talk," she said, pounding her wine and heading for the door. "Gotta go."

She needed Silas to be safe. She needed Silas.

Chapter Twelve

The last time Sara had been in a taxi hurtling down the West Side Highway to Silas's place was also the end of her old life, she mused from her slippery seat in the back of a cab that smelled like lilac Fabuloso. After that ride, she found out that Silas was Cursed, and her world had split apart. Just like the last time, a light rain began to fall, drops whipping against the window turning the lights sparkling on the Hudson into a kaleidoscope of stars. She didn't even know if Silas was at his place, and she didn't want to text and find out. If he wasn't there, she'd walk home, in the rain, in a brand new coat that she'd buy on the spur of the moment in an expensive West Village boutique. She wanted to be irresponsible in a way that she'd never been, to be impetuous and romantic and above all, she wanted to be selfish. Shaking her head, she tried to focus on her breathing and get her shit together before she faced Silas. If he was home.

It was only when she was pressing the buzzer on the building on Washington Avenue that it occurred to her that he might not be alone, but by then, she laughed to herself, it was already too late.

"Yes," came his voice through the dilapidated intercom on the brick wall.

"Si, it's me, please let me up."

The buzzer sounded instantly, and Sara pushed her way in, then spun and pushed the door closed, certain she had put Silas in danger. She'd been stupid to come here, if Desdemona was in New York already, Silas may have been followed. As she bounded up the stairs to the top floor, she wondered about the building's security, confident that it was stronger than she knew. As she rounded the final corner and began the last eight steps, the door opened, revealing Silas in gray sweatpants and a t-shirt that told her he'd finished a charity 5k, a panicked expression on his face.

"Sara, is everything okay?"

At the doorway, she threw her arms around him and kissed him hard on the lips, pulling him so tight against her that she felt his back crackle a million miles away as she inhaled him deeply into her nostrils, a surge of relief when his arms wrapped around her. A fountain of red light shot through her, rising from her feet and out through the top of her head as his scent filled her and her sense of self blended into something scalding and undefined. Her hands dropped down his back, her palms following the curves and ridges of his muscles. As they were crossing the small of his back, he tensed and broke the kiss.

"Sara, wait'"

"No, I need you, keep going,"

"Sara," this time his voice had an authority, and she blinked to clear her vision. "Sara, no, please, what's going on?"

Her head was still too fuzzy, she couldn't separate the million strands of half-formed things she needed to say to him. Her breath shaky, Sara stepped back, noting with disappointment that there was no sign of an erection in his pants.

"Sara, what's going on?" Silas dropped his arms to his sides, his eyes boring into hers.

"I've... had an epiphany."

"Ah, okay," he said with a throaty chuckle. "Well that explains everything. Here, come inside, we don't want the neighbors to see."

"You don't have any neighbors," she teased, stepping inside and pulling the door closed behind her.

"Au contraire, ma Sare," Silas said. "Your mother and mine has moved in downstairs, thank you very much."

Sara made a cringe face and mouthed I'm sorry and Silas laughed out loud.

"She and Heather are staying two floors below us," he said. "Don't worry, she can't hear anything."

"And where are Fan and Ama?"

"Of course they decided to go live in Central Park," Silas said. "They went and spent a fortune at REI and by now I'd assume there's quite a command center somewhere in the North Woods."

"Is it okay I showed up, Silas?"

He shrugged. "Sure, I suppose," he said. "Now, are you going to tell me about this epiphany and if so, well actually, even if you're not going to tell me, would you like some wine to... calm you down?"

She considered asking for blood but quickly decided against it.

"Actually, can I get a whisky drink?" she said cockily. With a raised eyebrow, Silas turned and walked across the living room to the kitchen area. As she watched him, or more specifically, his ass in the gray sweatpants, walk away, Sara felt the rush of passion drain away leaving her feeling adrift and awkward, and she didn't know whether to stand or take a seat on the sofa.

"You want it neat?"

"Got any of them fancy freezer rocks?" Sara asked, aware that he had some in the freezer.

"Ah, so you did some snooping last time you were here."

"Looking in a man's freezer isn't exactly snooping."

"It also isn't exactly polite," Silas said as he opened the freezer and took out a little cotton bag containing said rocks. Dumping a handful of them into a glass, he poured a modest splash of whisky over them and returned to where she was standing. "You can sit, you know."

"Yes," Sara said, regretting the word as soon as she heard it aloud and clumsily plopping onto the sofa. Silas handed the drink to her and she took it, swirling the amber liquid around the small gray cubes. "So what were you up to?" Sara asked.

"Oh, you know," Silas sat at the opposite end of the couch. "I'm on a text chain with mom, Heather and the elders."

"Did you know I was coming then?" Sara said, mildly annoyed at Heather.

"Kinda," Silas said. "You don't really have many places to go after a dramatic storming out."

"It was not dramatic," Sara said, taking an overly large swig of her drink and coughing.

"Depends on who you ask apparently," Silas smiled. "Sara, I'm just going to say it. You hurt my feelings today. You've been hurting my feelings since I left for Bucharest. So, can you please tell me what's on your mind? I don't know what the hell is going on after a greeting like that..."

The look in his large orange and brown eyes broke her heart. He loved her, she knew that, and he had clearly been more patient than she could ever know.

"I need to apologize," Sara said plainly.

"For?"

"For being me," she said, raising a palm when he began to protest. "No, Si, hear me out. I'm old as fuck but..."

"But what?"

"I've never had my heart broken."

Silas blinked at her, repeatedly, as they sat in silence.

"I need a drink," he said eventually, springing from the couch and busying himself in the kitchen. While he worked, Sara replayed her words over in her mind, not liking what she heard.

"What I'm trying to say is," she called out to him, "I'm not saying you broke my heart. I broke it myself. I'm a caretaker. You took yourself out of my care and you went somewhere dangerous and you went with Stefanya and you've known her forever and it was just all too much."

"Hold up," he said, his back to her. "Were you jealous or angry or sad?"

"I was all of those things," Sara said quietly, "but the worst thing was that I felt vulnerable, in a way I've never felt before. And worse? I felt incapable. And it fried my circuits."

"Well, I'll start by saying I appreciate your honesty," he said, turning and walking back to the couch, "but I need to say something. Your fried circuits broke my heart too."

"I know," she said quietly. "And I'm sorry."

Sitting closer to her this time, Silas rested his free hand on her leg.

"I ran too," he said, pausing to sip his whisky. "I could have stayed in our old place. I just didn't want you to see how hurt and confused I was. I needed distance. It wasn't my first heartbreak, but it was my first in a very long time. Me no likey."

"Me sorry. Me likey you."

"What the hell has gotten into you tonight?" Silas gave her a wicked grin.

"Nothing, yet," Sara raised her glass to him.

"Sara!" Silas jerked as if she'd actually shocked him. She sipped her drink in silence, smiling because she'd forgotten how prudish he could be. The whisky was warming her heart and little by little her self-disgust began to fade.

"Okay, fine," she said. "So how much did Heather spill about her angry little home invasion?"

Silas laughed out loud. "Is that what it was?"

"Kinda?" Sara rested her free hand atop the hand he still had on her leg. "It began as Heather's pro-murder rally and ended with them all unloading on me because I've always been somewhat... uh... let's go with avoidant, shall we?"

"Don't beat yourself up for having a survival mechanism that worked," Silas said, his tone soft. "Okay, so you spent a quarter of your life lost in a job because you didn't want to what? Get hurt? Be vulnerable? People do that shit all the time."

His words washed over her like a blanket straight out of the dryer, and she felt deep love in her heart, and salty tears stung her eyes.

"Hey,' he panicked. "I didn't mean to make you cry."

Sara shook her head. "I'm not going to cry, my eyes are welling up because you literally just said the perfect thing," she paused. "The perfect Silas thing."

He shrugged and stared into his drink.

"What is it you said to me?" He raised his eyes to hers. "Regret is a toxic indulgence in a life as long as ours?"

"Don't quote me at me," she laughed. "One, regret is always a toxic indulgence, and two, regardless of how long we live, spending a century hiding out from heartbreak is a bit extreme."

"Depends who you ask," he said. "I got my heart destroyed in the 80s. Haven't let myself fall for anyone since. If you hadn't let me in, I'd be heading for the century mark too. If you're looking for someone to judge you, you're going to have to go back to Heather and Fran."

"Hey, they weren't judging me," Sara said indignantly. "Wait, have they been judging me?"

"No, they just want you to be happy, and they're happy that you're finally taking a chance on..."

"Love?"

"I was going to say me, but sure," he laughed, leaning forward and kissing the tip of her nose. When he didn't pull back, Sara lifted her face and brushed her lips across his, relieved again when he didn't pull back, Gingerly she kissed him again, lips soft, his stubble prickling her deliciously. Tentatively, she caressed his bottom lip with her tongue, and a tiny groan escaped his throat, and she felt his hand take her drink from her, breaking the kiss as he set the two drinks on the floor. Then their lips were together again, still slow but now hungry, and it was just them, no bloodlust, no intoxication, just their faces pressed together in the moment, flooded with chemistry and connection.

She registered his hands on her shoulders, then one traced her breast, her nipples coming alive beneath her clothing as he lightly trailed his fingertips across one and then then other, on repeat, as the kiss went on. Cloudily, she felt him fumbling with her jeans button, lifting her hips to help him get them off. They caught around one ankle and he left them there, hanging, while she threw the other leg over the back of the sofa and he pushed his sweatpants down just enough to get the job done. An "I love you" escaped her lips as he pushed inside her, and his arms encircled her shoulders, pulling her tight as she bucked against him. They'd never done it with clothes on, and something about it felt more intimate to her, more comfortable.

Raising her hands to his temples, she pushed his hair back and stared at his face, his closed eyes, his long lashes on his reddening cheeks. She curved herself upwards so she could kiss him, this time with abandon, their tongues dancing across each other, the taste of whisky adding something heady, new and they found a rhythm and stayed there timelessly. Her hands dropped to his shoulders, his lats like cables, a vein standing out on his neck was soon joined by another at his temple as his breathing began to catch. As he sped up his hips, Sara dropped her hands to the bare skin of his ass, grabbing his buttocks as hard as she could, pulling him impossibly closer with each thrust as she felt energy blooming between her legs, emanating up her spine and all through her stomach until it took over all of her and she sank her fingernails into the meat of his ass, and he kissed her again, deeply, while he shuddered to climax alongside her, holding the motion as long as he could, until she stopped whimpering and fell back against the sofa and he released her shoulders, laying on top of her.

"I love you too," he murmured into her hair, then kissed her neck, and she burrowed against him, his weight calming her, and they stayed like that, awake, silent, in tune, for a long time, neither of them wanting to break the spell until she tried to wriggle the jeans off her ankle and he popped out of her and they both laughed.

"Sorry I spoiled the moment," she whispered as she twisted her foot in an attempt to dislodge the jeans. With a wink, he leaned over and yanked them free, dropping them in a pile on the floor.

"That's my fault for not doing the job properly in the first place," he said, returning to lay on her, his eyes looking at her adoringly. In the past she would have found it uncomfortable to be stared at like that, even by him, but now it felt rich and real and somehow appropriate. Fuck, she thought to herself, she finally felt like she deserved to be looked at like that, like she deserved it, owned it, returned it.

"Why do you always take responsibility for everything?" she whispered.

"It's the easier option," he whispered back. "What are you going to do? Take it out of my allowance?"

She laughed and tried to pull herself up to sitting, which resulted in both of them having to adjust both their clothes and their positions on the couch, which suddenly felt very itchy and prickly on Sara's bare butt.

"Uh, Si, can I tell you something and can you promise not to overreact?"

"I'll do my best."

"I don't like your couch," she said. "It's so scratchy on my skin."

"Oh, no worries," he said. "I'll get rid of it and we can buy a new one together."

"That's what I meant by overreacting," she said with a laugh. "Or, you could, you know, buy a throw? Offer me your lap?"

"Mi lap es su lap," he laughed, rolling back so that he was sitting upright, his pants still around his thighs. Sara stood, turned, and sat on his lap, her back against his chest, her head back, their ears touching. She felt his dick start to harden against her bare ass and his fingers moved to her chest, and as much fun as a round two sounded, she suddenly very much wanted to be face to face with him.

"Can we move to the bed?"

Without a word, she felt his arms beneath her and he stood, carrying her to the bedroom in short truncated steps because his pants were still half on. When they got to the bedroom, it was exactly as she remembered it. He gently laid her on top of the bed, then shucked off his sweatpants.

"There, now we can both be Donald Ducking," he said as he snuggled against her, and she turned to face him.

"Before we get back to business, can we just stare into each other's eyes and talk?"

"Don't threaten me with a good time," he said, kissing her between the eyes. "What else do we need to talk about?

"Oh you know, the usual. The imminent arrival of a number of hungry vampires in a public place. Your position on what to do with said vampires, and the two we already have at home. How we deal with your psycho killer mother."

"Wait, so you want us to fight in between rounds of awesome sex?" Silas kept his tone playful and she was grateful. "Sure. Fire away."

"Do I have to become okay with killing?"

He pushed back, startled.

"Fuck no," he said emphatically. "Double triple fuck no. Sara, I'm a Cursed man. For me and Embla, this is our massive fear, the source of our anxiety. What if it's genetic? What if brutality comes easier to our birth gender? Even though Embla is on hormones, this fear is literally never far from the front of her mind. Even considering being okay with it feels like opening the door a crack to the weakness of being male. And for me, I've done five centuries of making sure this is never an okay option."

"But what if you're like me? Hiding behind a set of ancient rules and that somehow, as humans, we are animals and when things get serious, we murder?"

Silas propped himself on one elbow, consternation on his face.

"The only way we can live with ourselves is to constantly seek enlightenment," he said. "I could not and would not want to live like that. What was it that Gandalf said in Lord Of The Rings? Until we can give life we shouldn't be prepared to take life?"

"But we do give life," Sara said. "Your mother gave us both endless life."

"You know the difference," Silas said.

"I'm just trying to find a way forward," Sara said, shifting so that she too was on one elbow. "I just got told that everyone I know thinks I'm an obedient, avoidant robot, so I'm opening up the discussion."

"Fair enough," Silas said. "But the taking of a life is something I'll never do. I've never touched a gun. I studied Buddhism, what? A hundred years ago, in Goa."

"You never told me you were a Buddhist!"

"I'm not," Silas said. "Well, I can't be, technically because I need to consume animal products to live."

"But you don't kill to obtain them."

"Makes no difference to me," Silas said. "But I align closely with their precepts. Fan and Ama and I traveled there to study, it was really amazing to see Ama in that world."

"We have so much to catch up on," Sara said. "I want to spend the next hundred years hearing about your last five hundred years."

"That would be heaven," Silas said. "But we just need to get past this current... speedbump."

"And how do we get through it without killing?"

"Well it's not entirely up to us," he sighed. "I'm not avoiding responsibility, per your earlier comment, but I don't see any way to control my mother, or the elders."

"And they're out for blood?"

"No," Silas said firmly. "They're out for peace. Sara, these men, Desdemona is responsible for killing them, not us."

A wave of tiredness hit Sara suddenly, and all she wanted was to fall asleep here, on top of his covers, both of them pantsless.

"But we can technically still save them," she said with a little smile. "I need to sleep on that. In your arms. Any second now."

Silas pressed himself up onto his palms and leaned over her.

"Sure, but there's the matter of a round two that we need to address first," he said, climbing between her legs.

Sleep did not happen for quite some time.

Chapter Thirteen

The following morning, Sara awoke before dawn, a strange feeling of peace in her heart. Pressing her naked side against Silas's, she felt the rumbles of his gentle snoring in her chest. In the faint gray dawn light, her eyes trailed around his bedroom, and she wondered why he hadn't taken any of these belongings up to their shared apartment. The decor reminded her of his house in Connecticut, tidy, impersonal. He didn't connect with things, he'd told her that. She made a mental note to let him decorate their next place. The thought of a next place made her smile, and she lay there, content, almost meditating, until he stirred, hours later.

Once he moved, she reached for her phone.

"Anything I need to know about?" mumbled Silas beside her. Instead of replying, Sara tossed her phone into the folds of the comforter and burrowed her shoulder into Silas's armpit, her cheek resting on his furry chest while she snaked an arm beneath his back and wrapped him in a hug.

"I sure don't know," she whispered. "But whatever it is, there's a lot of it."

He wriggled around to face her, and she inhaled all of him deeply, his skin, his musk, even his morning breath, rusty and pungent from another round of late-night blood, whisky and sex, and his eyes peered into hers.

"Your eyes are extra orange this morning," she said softly.

"Yeah, that happens when I'm in love," he said, kissing her nose. "True facts. Watch. I'll show you."

Slowly, Silas closed his eyes, concentration lines forming between his brows. Sara watched as his eyelids moved in tandem with the eyeballs beneath them, after pressing his eyes closed tighter he then sprung them open, and sure enough, the orange flecks were indeed brighter, a kaleidoscope of chocolates and ambers.

"Pretty neat, huh?"

"So you can tell what color your eyes are?"

"Nope, but I know that if I feel a strong surge of love, then that's the effect it will have, and my love, that was one hell of a surge."

His arms encircled her and he kissed her, languidly and she pressed her stomach against his, warming to the idea of another all-day bed club before her conscience reminded her what day it was. She broke the kiss.

"We can't," she said. "I'm sorry, but it's Thursday. I'm sure that one of those texts was Amazon telling me that my order of four male vampires was scheduled for tomorrow."

"Well we could," Silas smirked, and she felt his erection against her thigh. "Like real quick?"

"You're such a dude," she laughed. "Where the hell is my phone?"

Silas kissed her again while his free arm searched the bedding.

"Voila," he said, breaking the kiss and rolling onto his back, glancing at the phone's screen before handing it over. "Yep. That's a lot of texts and also, it's after ten." The red dot on Sara's phone told her that she had 978 unread texts, meaning she'd been added to a bunch of text chains and she groaned in frustration. She hated group texts with a passion and had asked to never be included, but as usual nobody listened. Her attention was briefly distracted by Silas rolling off the bed and padding naked out of the room, and she took a moment to admire his muscly back and the way his curved butt bounced, just once, with every step. She heard the comforting clatter of glassware and the fridge being opened, followed by the espresso machine whirring to life, and smiling, she decided on the quickest solution. She called Teddie.

"Hey mom," Teddie answered immediately. Sara heard street noises in the background. "Let me guess, you just woke up and you want the Cliff's Notes?"

"Ding ding."

"Let me see," Teddie said, then the phone went muffled as she talked to someone else before returning. "Blah blah freakout what to do tomorrow. Blah blah Yukari has not made enough progress and needs help. Blah blah Liz wants us to have a meeting about whether we are no-kill or pro-kill, avoid that chain, it's frustrating. Oh, and the big one is the everybody chain that Fan and Ama started. Crina added you to it overnight. It's a doozy."

"Do I need to read it on an empty stomach?"

"No, mom, what would you like?"

"Who are you with?"

"I'm with the kids," Teddie said brightly. "Say hello to mom, you guys." Embla and April Veronica's garbled voices sounded in the background.

"I would absolutely love to see all three of you, with your arms full of breakfast food."

"Sure, which apartment are you in? Destroyed love nest or independent woman hideout?"

"Neither, I'm at Silas's but we can be home in half an hour. Bring something for Silas too please."

"Was already gonna."

"Okay, let's meet in the what was it? The independent woman hideout in thirty minutes."

The line went dead. Sara switched the ringer back on and tossed the phone back to its hiding place among the covers.

"If you want your quickie," she called out, "it better be right now."

"I was hoping you'd say that!"

Instantly, Silas appeared in the bedroom doorway, his erection bouncing beneath a tray carrying two large mason jars of blood and two demitasses of espresso.

"First things first," he said, smoothing the comforter beside Sara with one hand while balancing the tray on the other. "The coffee can wait, it's too hot," he added as he set the tray down then scampered around the bed, snuggling in beside her and handing her blood to her. They both drank quickly, in silence, his free hand now resting on her tummy, moving up and down gently, slightly lower each time, until the silence was broken by a low chime.

"Piss shit balls," Sara said, spraying blood onto the white bedding. "It's Des."

"Drink up then," Silas said, his hand now waiting for her empty glass. Obediently, she chugged it and answered the phone as the dark cobwebs invaded her consciousness.

"Hello?" Desdemona's voice was irritable. "Can you hear me."

"Yeah," Sara said. "I just don't see the point of pleasantries. What do you want?"

"An update? You pinche puta loca, or tomorrow's going to be the worst day of your life."

Sighing as her vision cleared, Sara pushed herself upright.

"You've set an impossible deadline and you've given me unbeatable odds," Sara fought to keep her voice even. "And tomorrow will be what it's going to be. If the point of this whole thing is for me to take you seriously, you've won."

"Perdón?"

"I'm taking you seriously Des. I am. You're willing to threaten the entire human race in exchange for your immortality. That's pretty fucking serious. But if you had shown that you were willing to even compromise a little, give Yukari a bit more time-"

"I AM OUT OF FUCKING TIME," Desdemona roared into her phone. Across the room, Silas's eyes widened as Desdemona's voice quietened and she continued. "This timetable is all your making."

"You do realize that we could have killed you? We should have killed you. Instead, we are giving you the one gift that none of our kind has ever had before, which is to know what it feels like to age, to taste the final chapter of every human life, except ours."

"Oh you can shove that right up your sanctimonious ass," Desdemona hissed. "Do you have any updates from Yukari?"

"You have her number."

"That little bitch hung up on me after saying she doesn't talk to murderers."

"Good for her," Sara said, thinking quickly. These conversations with Des, any conversation with Des over the last fifty years, had always degenerated into name calling, increasing volume and one of them hanging up mid sentence. She needed to try. "Des, is there another way? Where are you? What would it take for you to call off this madness? Cursed men! The one thing we agree on."

"Agreed," she spat. "Past tense. You're fucking one now, total abomination."

Biting down on countless inflammatory retorts, Sara pushed forward.

"Can we stick to the facts? Please? Silas was raised exactly the same as you and I, by the same person, and right now, dear sister, you're the one with the body count. So can we focus on keeping it from growing? Please."

A series of strange rustling sounds came through the phone, and then it pinged.

"Look at what I sent you," Desdemona whispered. Moving the phone away from her face, Sara clicked on the notification, barely able to suppress a gasp as the screen filled with a selfie of Desdemona, head and shoulders, her face now lined, wrinkles around her eyes, her cheeks hollower, her thick raven hair now shot with white. After seeing her look twenty six for five centuries, she presently looked like she was in her mid forties.

"We need to stop this, while I still can," Desdemona said.

"And we will," Sara said emphatically. "Yukari thinks she's onto it, but this pressure, it's too much for her. She needs a chance to get her head together. You're making it too hard for her to get actual thinking done."

"Oh please, let me hold some space for your poor little pampered scientist princess," Desdemona said sarcastically. "It's a shame her only real-world experience is in your fairyland where nobody cares if she ever gets any results or actually figures out how to do anything that works."

"She cured your ugly ass," Sara said, wincing as the words left her mouth before she could stop them.

"And here we are at the part where I hang up," Des said. "But first, I'll leave you with this. Four very hungry men. The North Woods. Four a.m."

The line went dead.

"I tried so hard," Sara said, and Silas handed her coffee to her. Now warm, she tipped it down her throat, and Silas resumed rubbing her tummy.

"Sorry soldier," she said. "Our sister is quite the lady boner killer. Can we rain check our sexy times and call a car?"

They'd barely gotten inside Sara's apartment when a knock rapped at the door. Modestly pointing at his revealing gray sweatpants, Silas pulled the bedroom door closed behind him. Sara went to open the door and was instantly smothered in hugs from all three visitors. Behind them, the bedroom door opened and Silas emerged, shirtless but still in the sweatpants.

"Uh," he said sheepishly, "I don't have any clothes here. I need to go to the other apartment."

"It's way too early for so much chest hair," Embla was laughing as she set a bunch of bags on the counter.

"Speak for yourself," Teddie crowed. "Damn, Silas, you fine."

"Hey, keep your eyes on your own paper," Sara said as April Veronica hugged her again before flitting back to the doorway.

"You guys, I'm not as strong as you, I'm gonna need some help!"

"Be right there, darlin'" Embla called, rushing to help her girlfriend.

"How much did you buy?" Sara asked, and Teddie made a weird face.

"Not us," she said. "There was a rather large delivery waiting for us in front of the main entrance. Luckily for you, we came up West End and saw it all. I'm surprised you didn't hear us hauling it all up the stairs."

"We came in the side entrance and up the back way. We were a bit late."

"Because of make up sex?" Embla called from the kitchen.

"Because I was on the phone with Desdemona," Sara said, stopping Teddie in her tracks. They both turned to see April Veronica and Embla pushing two stacks of large, obviously heavy brown boxes into the entryway. "Holy shit, what is all that?"

"The return address is a PO box, there's no name," April Veronica said as Silas handed her a butter knife and she sliced open the top box on her pile, her face falling as she saw the contents. "You guys, it's all weapons and tactical gear. I wonder who-"

Silas and Embla cut her off.

"Fan and Ama."

"I'll call them," Sara said. "Can we eat first?"

As if on cue, her phone rang. It was Fan. She held the screen up for them all to see.

Sara answered the phone on speaker.

"Good morning Fan."

"It's Ama, Fan's off running reconnaissance in the park."

"And she left her phone with you."

"We have comms," Ama said condescendingly. "I'm in her ear, she's in mine. Well, not now because I'm talking to you but anyway, good morning ladies and honorary ladies, or Silas."

"Wait, how did you know I was here?"

"I was staked out at your place last night," Ama said with a laugh. "I lost a bet, thanks Sara. You took longer to show up than I expected. Anyway, I see that you have the packages we sent you, and I wanted to run through what's going to happen tomorrow, that is, assuming you're all still willing to come to the forest and fight."

"Fight might not be the right word for what we are prepared to do," Sara said. "We want to capture the four men that Desdemona is sending."

"Right, right, slight difference of opinion, but I'm happy that we're all on the same page."

"We're not all on the same page, Ama," Silas said, his voice jovially belying the serious expression on his face.

"Oh hey, Si. That's enough from you right now. I have a lot to get through. Anyway, since we don't know what time to expect the men-"

"They'll be arriving at four a.m.," Sara said. "I just got off the phone with Des."

"Interesting but we can't trust her," Ama said. "But that will change up our plans slightly. So, first things first. We will be pairing up, so that each couple is evenly matched for weapons experience and strength training. Are you taking notes?"

"Yes, of course," Sara lied, waving her arms at Silas who pulled open Sara's everything drawer in the kitchen, returning with a pink highlighter and some unopened bills. "Go ahead."

"We want every one of us protected. That means bulletproof everything. There will be another round of boxes arriving with the vests and such. What you have there is weaponry and night vision goggles, as well as our communications earpieces. Fran will be networking them this evening. Also, we got you all some nice new tasers and cattle prods, a bunch of random shit, you guys can spend the afternoon shooting at the dummy in the basement."

"We don't have a dummy in the basement," Sara said.

"The biggest box contains your brand new dummy," Ama said like a game show announcer. "So, open your boxes and get training. We will all meet at midnight at Central Park West and 100th. You'll be assigned to your war buddy then! It's gonna be okay. We trained Mr Handsome with the scent of the new guy. We bought him. He's our baby now. He's great. So anyway, any questions?"

"I have a question," Silas said.

"Of course you do," Fan said in a bored voice. "Fire away."

"Ha ha," Silas deadpanned. "But of course you know what I'm going to ask. Will there be guns?"

"Not for any of you peaceful protesters," Ama said cheerily. "But yes, the four of us warriors will be packing heat. With silencers."

Sara felt confusion as she tried to imagine Heather with a gun.

"Also, don't be angry, April darling, but your fight training isn't up to scratch, so we're going to have you driving around the perimeter from midnight onward, to see if we can catch them arriving. If Des is in New York, she'll be the one dropping them off. If you see her, you're to follow her to wherever she goes, but do not engage."

Sara watched as Teddie, Embla and April Veronica exchanged resigned glances, and she wished that none of them needed to be involved. April certainly didn't have the training to face Desdemona. During their time in Paris, centuries ago, Sara had trained alongside Des, and she was a shrewd, dirty fighter.

"Also on the you're not coming list, obviously, we have Yukari and Fran," Ama continued. "Fran's got an army of hacker ladies deployed, all of them working to lighten Yukari's load and get some results on the vaccine front. Which seems like a lot of work to waste, because, I promise you, as soon as Desdemona is Cursed again, me and Fan will be taking a Slicer to her spine, but there you go."

"Good to know," Sara said. "I'll make sure to let Yukari know."

"Oh she already knows and she doesn't care," Ama said. "She said that she's grateful for the help, she's making some good breakthroughs, just not on the exact thing we need. But there's no such thing as bad research, right?"

A round of confused silence met her comment, so she continued.

"Look, you guys, I really regret the way things went yesterday, but the last thing we want is for any of these guys to infect a stranger, and we don't know what state they'll arrive in-"

"Oh shit," Sara said. "Sorry, well, actually not sorry, you haven't stopped talking for a second, but Desdemona did say that they'd be arriving hungry."

"Yep, that's exactly what we were expecting." Sara was annoyed by Ama's unflappable demeanor. "So that's why we will have guns. There weren't many ways that Desdemona could ratchet this up, we expected them to be starving. We will be leaving out some bowls of blood, just like trapping a feral cat."

"Well not exactly like that," Sara said.

"I've taken up enough of your time," Ama said, ignoring her completely. "I need to get back in contact with my darling so I'm gonna let you go. Oh, and to avoid any midnight drama from you, Sara, I'll tell you now. Crina requested that you and her get paired together."

Chapter Fourteen

The light rain hitting the leaves sounded like snowflakes hitting a cymbal. The vest that could potentially save her life was doing little by way of warmth. Sara hunkered down on her favorite rock on the edge of The Pool, the small lake in the North Woods, comfortable in the darkness because she usually visited this spot at night. Several yards away, Crina continued her theatrical surveying of the small lake, her night vision goggles obscuring the top half of her face as she turned this way and that, her arms akimbo as if she was watching virtual reality.

The little earpiece in her ear messed with her balance, and Sara alternated between wishing she could accidentally lose it and hoping for an update from Silas and Teddie, partnered together and presently scouring the dark from the roof of The Blockhouse, at the northern end of Central Park. Another glance at her watch told her that four a.m. was still twenty minutes away. At least Crina wasn't trying to talk to her.

"Are you going to say anything?" Crina asked, appearing beside her and making her jump. "And now is not the time for a reverie."

"I'm not in reverie, I'm focused," Sara lied, knowing Crina would spot the lie a mile off but still taking a child's delight in irritating a parent. "And please stop looking at me through those things, nobody looks good in night vision."

Crina pushed the goggles up onto her forehead and wiped her nose with the back of her sleeve.

"I should never have made you watch that Paris Hilton tape," she joked, her face falling when Sara didn't laugh.

"As much as that might be true," Sara said, "I don't feel like talking. We're here to do a job, let's do it."

"Well sitting on a rock and navel gazing wasn't on the job description either," Crina said.

"I've done a lot of great work on this rock over the past couple hundred years," Sara said, careful to not sound defensive. Crina loved to pounce on defensive.

"I know you have," her maker said, her voice gentle. "Sara, you know I love you, right?"

"Actually," Sara said, pushing herself upright, "I don't know what to believe any more, at least not from you. And before you leap in, hear this one thing: There's no point for you to defend yourself. Not to me."

"Okay, fine, I won't," Crina said. "And what I wanted to say was simply that. I love you. I've run through a million things to say in my head, and they all just sound like parental bullshit. I did this for you! You were the reason! Nobody ever buys that. So, simply, the one thing that you need to accept as true is that I love you."

"I liked it better when you were a silent high-tech meerkat," Sara said. "Go back to doing that."

Disappointment clouded Crina's face, and she slid the goggles back over her eyes and walked back to where she had been standing, resuming her irregular spinning, her head tilting, her arms stiffly away from her body. A crackle in her ear turned into April Veronica's voice.

"Checking in. Nothing to report. No cars have stopped, no people on the streets."

"Thanks April," came Fan's voice. "Keep cruising north and west borders. Report anything suspicious."

"Will do."

Silence returned, but now it felt oppressive, and her position on the rock felt suddenly vulnerable. Stepping down, Sara did a quick three-sixty, the night vision reducing the lake and the tall trees around it to shades of silver and green with no true black anywhere. Water streaked the lenses of her goggles and she needed to move. Without a word, she set off along the path around the lake.

"Where are you going?" Crina's voice appeared in her earpiece instantly.

"Perimeter," she replied tersely. "I won't be out of sight."

"All teams are to remain together," Fan said. "Please regroup."

Or what? Sara thought, continuing on her way, wondering if Crina would rat on her. She didn't, so Sara continued until she was on the opposite side of the lake. Pausing she turned to see Crina staring directly at her, her attention never wavering as Sara continued to walk, leaving Crina completely unguarded. Unsure if it was actual protectiveness or the height of passive aggression, Sara angrily walked faster.

When she completed her circuit, Sara returned to her perch on her rock, Crina still staring directly at her. Pulling off one of her gloves, she hit the mute button on her earpiece, gesturing for Crina to do the same.

"What the fuck was that about?" Sara asked angrily. "You left yourself completely vulnerable that whole time."

"Did you even look behind yourself once?" Crina's voice was angry. "No, you just went for a fucking stroll. You put us both in danger."

"Well I can't just sit here like a useless lump," Sara said. "I needed to do something."

"Well how about doing what we're supposed to do? Stand back to back, circle slowly, and listen?"

"It's not even four yet," Sara protested.

"And they're not going to arrive on time," Crina said. "They're walking in, from somewhere. They can just as easily be early as late. So please, stop being... for fuck's sake Sara, can you stop being you for just one second? Fine, it's a fucking job, let's just do it. Without talking, as you wish."

Mainly because she knew it would infuriate Crina, Sara stayed silent as she walked over to her and pressed her back against Crina's, and they began to circle. A slow gray and neon-green blur of trees, broken into tiny prisms by raindrops, revealed nothing, and after several spins, nausea pulsed at Sara's temples and she tapped Crina on the shoulder, then moved to face her again, tapping her earpiece mute.

"You know, it's just so hard to see you acting as if you're actually my mother," Sara said, anger firing her. "You're just some opportunistic bitch who needed a handmaiden. You didn't make me so that I could have a wonderful life, at the time you didn't even know what our future would be."

"Oh, here we go again," Crina said, her finger pressed to her earpiece. "We've been through this before, Sara. Every time you don't get your way, you scream that I'm not your mommy. And you're right. And even if I was, what of it? Who wants to mother another human for endless centuries? Even Silas, he hasn't needed me to be his mother for a very long time. We redefine roles, we create our own worlds. And in my world, I have maternal feelings for you. Sorry, but I do. I love you and I would die for you, and I think that qualifies me for the job."

"Then how can you think it's acceptable for you to raise us one way, under unbreakable rules, while at the same time you're being somewhat cavalier with the big ones?"

"Sara, it's not like I'm running around feeding on humans, I am doing cleanup on a mess that I made the second I took my eye off Desdemona."

"It's still killing," Sara said.

"I haven't killed anyone who wasn't already doomed," Crina explained, the rain getting heavier. "Trust me, I fought for a solution for the women in Madrid, but there was none. They're brainwashed. Sara, my love, trust me on this. I love the world you created, and that's why I did what I did. To give it a chance."

Frustration swirled in Sara, and a deeper confusion. She heard honesty in Crina's voice, but to her, Crina was justifying using violence to protect peace, and Sara wondered if her idealism only worked inside the walls of her compound. In a flash, she saw the damage that Desdemona had done, Marguerite's blood-soaked body, Teddie plastered all over the newspapers, the death-cult videos of the mass suicides in Warsaw and Helsinki all playing over a jerky black and green image of Crina's stricken face.

"Okay," she said quietly. "Alright. Now isn't the time, it's not, I can't process, but I hear you and I want you to know I'm hearing you."

"You've been spending too much time with April Veronica."

"Or not enough," Sara said with a smile. "Mom, can we pin this and get back to it if we make it through the next couple hours?"

Nodding, Crina stepped towards her, and they dropped their arms in preparation for a hug only to freeze as their muted earpieces screamed back to life, filled with the panicked cries of Teddie and Silas.

"Teddie has been shot," Silas screamed, freezing Sara and Crina on the spot. "She's down. I can't see the directional, it was an arrow, she went over the side. Fuck, another arrow, missed, hang on."

"I'm here, Silas," Teddie groaned. "South side by the grill, I crawled behind some bushes, there's a fucking arrow in my shoulder."

Sara stared into Crina's panicked eyes. Crina raised a calming palm, and they kept listening. All Sara wanted to do was run, at full speed, cover the thousand yards separating them, be there defending them.

"On our way," Fan's voice came over the airwaves. "Liz, speed up. Silas, I have your location locked, we're leaving West Drive now, taking pathways, we will be there in one minute. Get off the roof now, you're too exposed."

"Got it," Silas yelled, and then they heard him exhale loudly as he landed.

"Silas, I'm here," Teddie said, louder than she should have, and then they heard grunting.

"Everybody hold position," Ama said, and staring at Crina, Sara shook her head, she wanted to run. Crina grabbed her hand and forced her to stay. "We are under attack," Ama continued. "Vigilance stations, back to back, move slowly. If you have a gun, be prepared to use it."

"Teddie and I are behind the bushes to the left of the grill door," Silas whispered, and they heard Teddie groan in the background. Sara breathed deeply to still her adrenaline, her right leg already twitching with energy she needed to burn off or control, and she pressed her back against Crina's as they began to rotate slowly, scrutinizing every patch of darkness for movement. She felt Crina's hand squeeze her thigh, trying to ground her.

"Over there, to the right," Imani said suddenly.

"Guys, we have a visual," Ama said. "Lone male, on the southern edge of the Great Hill meadow. He's wearing all black."

"Fuck us," Imani spat. "He's got a gun."

"My love?" Fan asked, and Ama answered immediately.

"Take the shot."

An eternity of silence in her left ear made the raindrops in her right deafening as Sara held her breath.

"Man down," Ama said, no emotion in her voice. "One shot. Imani and I will clean up."

"I can see our shooter," Teddie said.

"I see him," Silas said.

"Stay there," Fan ordered.

"No, I can get him," Silas said, followed by sounds of brush moving, then the thud of steps and the sounds of two men colliding. Grunts and garbled Romanian filled their earpieces, and Sara's steps faltered, and Crina forced her to continue circling until the grunts stopped, suddenly replaced by a guttural scream from Silas and more sounds of a struggle, then another scream, not Silas, then some static. They stopped circling.

"I got him," said Teddie, clearly running. "Nope, he's up and running north, out of the park..."

"Silas," Crina spoke finally. "Silas, your condition?"

"The motherfucker stuck an arrow through my hand, into a tree," Silas said. "Teddie tased him and he's bolted."

"Teddie do not follow," Fan said. "I'll go for him. Liz has your position."

Crina suddenly pulled Sara around and muted her earpiece, motioning for Sara to do the same. Sara couldn't, not now, but Crina waved her other hand – and the gun it was holding – angrily, so she complied.

"We can't just stand here," Crina said. "We're a sitting target, they've been watching us all night. Follow me. Back to back, sideways."

"Teddie and Silas safe with me," Liz said. "Sorry Si, this might hurt-"

A snap sounded, then Silas groaned, and Sara's heart clenched painfully at the sound.

"Free," Liz continued. "Both of you, onto the scooter."

"Take them back to Central Park West. April, be prepared to pick them up and get them out of here."

"I'm there already, at a hundred and fifth," April Veronica said, her voice shaky. "And I just saw a guy sprint across 106th with a crossbow and some arrows."

"Let him go," said Heather. "You guys, we are being hunted. Two guys together. We can't see anything but we heard footsteps pass us twice. Embla and I are by the Loch Waterfall."

Tapping Crina on the shoulder, Sara mouthed "follow me" and left the path, rushing through the low scrub, gathering speed as she wove around trees before splashing into a shallow rocky creek and following it upstream, her arms flailing as she slipped on the uneven rocks beneath the icy surface.

"Hold tight, Heather, we're coming," Sara said.

"No, hold your position," Ama said.

"Too late, sorry," Sara said, and she unleashed her full adrenaline, her legs pumping, her feet moving so fast they barely had time to slip before she lifted them again. "Embla, your position."

Silence.

Sara's heart sank.

"Heather?"

"I've lost sight of Embla," Heather whispered over a wall of static. "I'm pressed against the back of the waterfall using the water to hide my heat signal."

"They don't have night vision," Ama said.

"You're certain are ye, pet?"

"Stay where you are!" Sara yelled. "One minute."

A loud splash sounded in her earpiece and Sara willed herself to pick up the pace, now using her hands to repel trees and boulders along the creek's edge, propelling her forward.

"She's got him," Heather yelled. "Embla's got him, they're wrestling in the water."

"Try to take him alive," Ama said. "On my way."

Breaking through a clearing, Sara saw the waterfall ahead of her, and frantic splashing in the pool below it. She saw Heather emerge from behind the veil of water, something in her hand, and she advanced on Embla and a man, wrestling in the pool. Sara saw Heather slam her fist into the side of the man's head, lifting his whole body out of the water and knocking Embla off balance. Quickly changing course, Sara launched herself at where Embla had fallen, reaching beneath the water and grabbing at cloth, lifting the limp woman up, relieved when Embla spluttered messily as her face broke the surface of the water. Without hesitation, Embla blindly hurled herself to where the man was floating in the water.

"You took your time," Heather said as she grabbed the man under the armpits and he groaned loudly.

"Let's get out of this fucking water," Crina said, arriving at Heather's side and lifting the man over her shoulder. When they were all out of the water, Embla examined the man's wound.

"He will live," she said bitterly.

"I speak the mothertongue," Crina said, in Romanian, and the man's eyes fluttered open.

"Help me, please," he said, "I am sick, so cold."

Sara moved closer.

"We will help you, but we need you to tell us, how many of you are there? One of you is dead already, another has run to freedom."

"That is all," the man said.

"You lie," Crina said. "We can leave you here, you'll freeze."

"Please, no," the man begged. "I swear, the fourth, he refused, she couldn't make him agree, he is not here."

Sara looked into Crina's eyes, then the man's.

"He lies," she said, still in Romanian. "Let the bastard freeze."

The man struggled to stand, and Crina effortlessly forced him back onto the cold earth, one hand on his chest.

"I give my word," he said. "We were just three, abandoned here last night."

Now it was Crina's turn to glare into Sara's eyes. She had been right, about how stupid Sara's behavior had been by the lake.

"Take him home," Crina said to Heather, "as agreed."

With a curt nod, Heather knelt beside the man and wrapped an arm around his neck, choking him out as his hands scrabbled and his feet kicked. Once he was unconscious, Heather stood, wiping her palms on her pants. Embla bent and lifted the man, throwing one of his arms around her neck, then the other around Heather's.

"Cleanup on aisle five," Heather said into the earpieces.

"Meet you on East Drive in two minutes," Ama said. "Is he heavy?"

"Not too bad," Embla said.

"Can I get some assistance?" Fan asked. "I was bringing the dead guy to The Pool but you've all bolted."

"Sorry, we'll head right back," Crina said. "Sara, you with me?"

Without a word, Heather and Embla turned and walked away, the man hanging limp between them, his feet dragging behind them as Embla stooped to accommodate Heather's lack of height and they vanished into the darkness. Facing Crina, Sara tapped her earpiece, muting it. Crina followed suit.

"Sorry but the fastest way is back along the stream," she whispered.

"I can't feel my feet," Crina said with a wan smile.

"I can't feel my anything," Sara said, extending a hand. As Crina reached to take Sara's hand, something large and shapeless flew out of the darkness and slammed into Crina, and she fell almost faster than Sara could see, images of shock on Crina's face flickering in microseconds until her head crashed against a rock and her arms and legs twisted at incorrect angles and she went still. The shape that hit her solidified into a man, taller and wider than Sara, his bald head glistening wet, murderous anger on his face as he lurched across the water, his fists swinging at her,

Turning rapidly, Sara leapt from the water. She knew she could outrun him but she couldn't leave Crina, so she halted and turned, throwing one leg behind her as support as the man advanced. His face registered brief surprise when she faced him, and he slowed his approach, and Sara cast her mind back to the earliest training, which was to let a man think he had an easy victory.

"Please, no," she said, in Romanian, as a cacophony of panicked voices rose in her earpiece which she quickly pinched from her ear and hurled into the darkness.

"What is your name?" the man asked. "Are you Sara?"

The shock of hearing her name in the stranger's mouth caused Sara to flinch involuntarily, telling the man everything he needed to know, and a sickening grin spread across his ugly face.

"She wants you alive," he said.

"I don't know what you're talking about," Sara said, stepping back as if she was frightened, her legs braced for battle with each step. "But please, don't hurt me."

The man advanced quickly, and she was ready, bobbing deftly beneath his grabbing arms when he threw himself at her. Spinning around, she saw him totter as he spun, his size and weight working against him on the slippery, muddy ground.

"She said that if I had to kill you, that was okay too," the man licked his lips and charged again, and through the falling rain, Sara saw Crina running up to him, blood streaming from a gash beneath her hair. In a split second, she leapt onto the man's shoulders, gripped his head between her hands, and snapped his neck as if it was made of tiny sticks, twisting his neck so severely that when he landed on his stomach, his face was turned upwards, rain filling his eye sockets, his eyes open in small pools of water while his immense body twitched.

With a grunt, Crina pulled her legs out from under his chest and stood over his lifeless body. Sara looked for the source of the blood running in watery rivulets down the side of her face.

"Are you okay?" Sara rushed to her side and caught her as she stumbled.

"This ain't my first concussion," Crina said, before she passed out in Sara's arms. Plucking the earpiece from Crina's ear and shoving it in hers, Sara collapsed to the ground, cold grabbing at her bones.

"It's Sara," she said. "I'm with Crina, just south of the waterfall, she needs assistance. We're gonna need a pretty big body bag."

Chapter Fifteen

H er whole body shivering uncontrollably, Sara stepped into the shower in her bathroom, recoiling instantly as the hot water scalded her shriveled, blue feet. Hurriedly, she turned the hot down and tried again. Still painful, but bearable, she slipped under the steam, the water hitting her freezing skin, the warmth not enough to still her shivering.

Turning up the heat gradually, she felt herself thawing, her hands drawn up under her chin as she inhaled steam to lungs that also felt frozen. Slowly, her shivering subsided, only to be replaced by sobbing as suppressed panic broke open inside her and all the fear and worry came to the surface. She welcomed the tears, letting them become moans escaping from her throat, the tension leaving her body in the notes of her voice.

She knew that Silas and Teddie were okay, somewhere else in the compound, being tended to by Imani and Liz, and they'd both be arriving at her apartment soon. As her internal temperature rose, images of the morning replayed, strobing black and green snapshots of death and hate, the most haunting being the dead eyes of her attacker as they filled with rainwater, sightless, no longer connected to anything. She had seen death before, but this was different. She'd seen the eyes narrowed in hateful anger, and it was the absence of that intensity mere moments later that was disturbing to her, it was like watching his soul drown as the life left his body. She wondered about him, whether he had a family in Bucharest, or if he was in love or a good or bad person, driven by whatever leverage Des was using over these men to make them into ruthless killers.

It didn't matter. He was dead now.

It did matter. It absolutely mattered. Somewhere in Romania, his family would never know what happened to him. The mystery of his disappearance would haunt his family for generations.

About to kill the water, Sara glanced down at her feet, shocked to see pink toes attached to blue feet. Sitting, she forcefully massaged both feet under the water, reaching up to turn the temperature even higher, her thumbs leaving pale streaks that pinkened slowly until she was satisfied that her slippers could complete the job. In her bedroom, she pulled on thermals, then added sweatpants and a cashmere sweater, then her vintage shearling slippers. As she was adjusting her thermostat, a soft knock sounded at her door and she ran to open it, revealing Teddie and Silas, and behind them, Imani.

A sob escaped her throat as she went to throw her arms around Teddie and Silas, but Imani caught her wrists in mid-air.

"Gotta be careful with the stitches, guv," she said, releasing Sara's wrists.

"Oh, shit, I'm sorry," she sniffed. "Come in."

"It wouldn'ta hurt, mom," Teddie mumbled as she shuffled to the couch and plopped down. "I'm high AF."

"Me too," smiled Silas, waving a left hand so heavily bandaged that it looked like a clown mitten. "They gave us the good stuff."

"How's Crina?" Sara asked as she guided Silas to the other end of the sofa and gently pushed him back.

"She's got a concussion and quite a gouge but it'll heal okay," Imani said. "I hope you don't mind but I made an executive decision and we are all under one roof tonight."

"That's where I want us," Sara said. "Imani, we were hunted tonight. At any point, she could have had them kill us."

"That's what I was thinking too," Imani said, wrapping Sara in a hug. "Why do you think she had them honor the four a.m. start time?"

"She needs us," Teddie said. "She needs Yukari to heal her and give her back her immortality. They were never going to kill us."

The image of the face of her attacker flashed before Sara's eyes and she blinked it away. There was murder in that man's eyes.

"You're right," she lied. "She just wanted to toy with us again."

"Sit down, Sara," Imani said, pointing to the couch, and she obeyed, pausing to survey the loves of her life. Teddie, her right arm in a sling, her eyes glassy with opiates, blew her a clumsy kiss. Silas patted the sofa beside him with his good hand, and she obeyed, snuggling hard against him.

"You guys," she said, turning to face one then the other, "I've never been so worried, never in my life."

"Sorry mom," Teddie said, taking her hand.

"Yeah, sorry sis," Silas said, making Teddie giggle, which made Sara smile and tear up at the same time and she watched as both of them reclined their heads, their eyes closing.

"I'm gonna make us all some blood and then we can let them sleep," Imani said from the kitchen.

"Need any help?

"No love," Imani turned and smiled. "I got this."

"Can you update me while you work?"

"Sure can. Fan lost sight of the arrow bloke up in Harlem somewhere, they'll go back with the dog in a little while, but the other guy, he's downstairs, he had a phone in his pocket. In fact, they all did."

"Where are the other two..."

"They're amazing, Fan and Ama," Imani said as the warming oven dinged and she juggled three very full jars of blood over to the couch. Sara took two, handing them to Silas and Teddie, who began sipping in silence, and then the one for herself. "They put them in moving boxes, in the park, and wheeled them all the way here on one of them dollies, just before it got light. Yukari is working with the... with them now, and then..." Her voice trailed off and Sara looked up to see Imani pull an orange from the pocket of her coat.

"I'm confused," Sara said.

"Oh this? Don't be," Imani laughed. "I just had a hankering for old fashioneds. I'm gonna make a pitcher, feels like a donkey's age since we've had a good catch-up, and Sara...?"

"Yes?"

"I don't want to be alone," she said. "I can't shake the vision of that man stalking us around the edge of the meadow. I fuckin' hate guns."

"I thought you were spending your nights with Toma?" Sara said with a wink.

"Fuck no, Sara, how stupid do you think I am? I visit him, I get what I need and I leave."

"Girl, look at you, gettin' it," Sara laughed. "I thought you were shacking up?"

"No, Sara, I was just bored, and he is fun, a bit of sweetness during wartime."

A thump from her left caught Sara's attention, and she saw Teddie's empty jar rolling on the rug. Glancing to her left, she saw Silas's empty jar begin to tilt and she snatched it from his loose fingers, then stood and picked up Teddie's.

"They're out," Imani said, setting a pitcher and two glasses filled with ice on the coffee table. "Trade ya?" She took the empty glasses back to the kitchen and then came and sat on the floor across the coffee table from Sara.

"It's good to see you," Sara said. "I feel like this new structure is kind of disconnecting, for me anyway."

Imani shrugged. "It is and it isn't," she said. "But it's up to us to shape it, and I suppose it's just like friendships out in the real world, you get out of it what you put into it. Things will change but I think we will be fine, you and me."

Imani poured two very full glasses of liquor, then mouthed "shit" and went back to the kitchen, returning with a saucer of small curls of orange peel, topping their drinks with one apiece, then handing one to Sara.

"To surviving," she said, and Sara clinked her glass against Imani's and sipped the fragrant mix, the citrus delighting her.

"I needed this," Sara said. "No cap, I thought I was a goner."

"It got real hairy, did it? Crina was characteristically evasive when I was treating her, pretending to be less conscious than she was."

"She tried to talk to me–"

"Course she did," Imani scoffed. "You got totally set up, you did."

As soon as she heard those words, a lightbulb went off in Sara's head.

"That fucking crafty bitch," she marveled.

"What? What fucking now?"

"I got double played," Sara said. "I bet she was the one who put Silas and Teddie together, she literally put all my eggs in one basket to prove a point."

"Paranoia isn't your color, love." Imani said, as her phone dinged in her pocket

"I'm gonna ask her."

"You can do that now if you like," Imani said, looking at her phone. "She's asking if she can come up."

"She's as irritating as a real mother," Sara said. "Fine, tell her fine." She looked at Teddie and Silas knocked out on the couch. "Can you help me get these two onto my bed? I'll sleep out here."

"Sure, guv," Imani pushed herself to her feet. "Now who's acting like a real mother?"

After flipping Imani off, Sara carefully crossed Silas's arms across his chest, slipped her arms beneath him and lifted him effortlessly, guiding him through the doorway and laying him on her bed.

"I'm gonna need some help," Imani said, "we can't put any pressure on her shoulder."

Sara whispered in Teddie's ear, and her eyes fluttered open.

"We're gonna move you to the bed, love," Sara said, and she and Imani lifted Teddie to standing by hoisting her butt, then supported her by her good arm into the bedroom, laying her on her back next to Silas, who was snoring already.

"Thanks mom," Teddie mumbled before passing out again.

"So much for our girls' night," Sara said as they returned to the couch, relieved when Imani sat beside her.

"We can raincheck it for tomorrow night," Imani said, "because right now, I gots a front row seat for a real vintage vampire smack down. You know I live for this kind of crap."

"That's nice dear," Sara said, her voice dripping with condescension. "Who's coming? Crina always travels in a pack when things get rocky."

"I would presume Heather," Imani said. "They're pretty tight these days."

"Yeah, it's a bit worrying," Sara said, refilling their glasses. "I didn't realize until this recent... brouhaha... how deeply I relied upon Heather, she was the most even-keeled of all of us."

"She still is, Sara," Imani raised her glass. "Put yourself in her shoes. She just disposed of the bodies of women she loved, you gotta keep that front and center. Of all of us, she's the one who keeps the global friendships going the most, she's always on group zooms and just, you know, texting and calling. For most of us, the deaths of all those women, it's like the pandemic, it's a terrible loss but you can't feel it as acutely, it's just a blanket awful grief. For Heather, her life changed. Women she laughed with, and shared secrets with, and loved in a real part of her daily life, they were killed. And she had to cut them up and burn them. Her life changed. You have to expect it will change her, make her angrier than you or I."

"God you're good," Sara said, clenching her eyes closed. "Hearing that makes me feel super selfish and shitty."

"Guv, your superpower has always been your deep focus on New York," Imani said softly. "Everybody can't do everything all the time."

A soft rap sounded on the door, and Imani set her drink on the coffee table, rising to answer it. Sara squared her shoulders, fully aware that she was expecting a battle, pleased to find none of her usual reluctance in confronting Crina. She heard footsteps and then Crina and Heather appeared, both in matching Peloton sweatsuits, brandishing bottles of wine and smiling. A bandage encircled Crina's head.

"We come in peace," Crina said as Imani took the wine from their hands and took it to the kitchen.

"Good," Sara rose to hug them. "Because this wartime bullshit is exhausting."

"Wait," Heather broke the hug, "do I smell Old Fashioneds?"

"You sure do," called Imani, "but I only brought a pitcher for me and Sara, and you brought wine so that's what you're getting."

"Fine," Heather took a seat on the couch. "Someone's tetchy."

"I'm not tetchy at all," Imani said. "I just know the damage you can do to a pitcher of Old Fashioneds, and Sara's been through it tonight."

Sara resumed her seat, with Crina predictably sitting next to her, a bit closer than she needed to, taking her hand.

"How are the kids?" she asked.

"Well my kid and your son are asleep in my bed," Sara said. "They'll be fine."

"I know," Crina said. "I was there when Yukari sewed them up."

"Yeah, so was I," Imani said, borderline snottily, as she handed very full glasses of wine to Crina and Heather and took her seat.

"Wow," Crina said. "I figured Sara was going to be the tricky one."

"I'm not being tricky," Imani said. "We all just went through a lot, and it doesn't excuse what you did, and you don't need to come in here bragging about stuff while you're still pretty much Vampire Enemy Number Two."

"I said we came in peace," Crina protested.

"Then start acting like it," Imani said. "You're basically out of this Lock, and the way things are, I may never see you again. I don't need to watch my p's and q's around you and right now, I'm fresh out of fucks."

"That's fair," Crina said, sipping her wine. Sara knew that silence would unsettle Crina, so she reached for her glass and took a languid sip, savoring the faint snoring coming from her bedroom and the rattle of raindrops against her windows. She looked at the bandage taped to Crina's temple, but stayed silent.

"I was worried sick," Heather said eventually, her voice breaking before her shoulders started to shake, and she began to cry. "I've lost so much, and Sara, I... just the... when I thought we'd lost the pair of you, I just couldn't.."

Sara snaked her arm along the couch behind Crina and squeezed Heather's shoulder, Heather's hand raising immediately and covering hers.

"I've lost so much," Heather continued between sobs. "Everything in my life is, I don't know, vanishing? I'm tired of being tough, I'm tired of the loss and I just need it all to stop."

Silence returned between them as Heather cried softly, pulling tissues from inside her sleeve and drying her eyes as the tears subsided.

"I'm sorry," she said. "I just can't front no more, the past year is worse than anything I've ever been through and we don't have an end in sight."

"You don't have to apologize, Heather," Sara said, wishing she was sitting beside her instead of navigating around Crina, who hadn't taken her eyes off Sara since she sat down. "I feel like a lot of it is my fault, and I apologize."

"Oh don't be silly pet, we've all melted down at one time or another," Heather said, draining her wine and holding out her glass to Imani. "To be fair, we can blame Des squarely for your crisis. I just hate her so much."

All three women turned to face Sara, but she had nothing to say.

"Are you okay?" Crina asked.

Sara nodded, closing her eyes.

"Just a lot to process," she mumbled, feeling Heather squeeze her hand. Opening her eyes, she saw Crina's concerned face, inches from hers, and she decided to go for it. "So, Crina, I have something to ask you, and I would appreciate an honest response."

"I'll try," Crina said. "You said you wanted honesty, and that's honest. I'll try."

Sara nodded. "How calculated was your decision to pair Teddie with Silas, that's part one," she paused, her eyes boring into Crina's. "And how much of that decision was made to teach me a lesson?"

"Oh that's easy," Crina said flippantly, moving away from Sara but never breaking their gaze. "It was entirely calculated, and I did it to teach you a lesson."

Crina pressed her back against the couch, drinking her wine, finally moving her focus from Sara to Imani and then back again.

"That's cold," Imani said.

"So let me get this straight," Sara said, her voice even. "You thought it so important to teach me some random lesson that you were willing to put two people in mortal danger? I don't care what their relationship is, you didn't think of their strengths or weaknesses or their fight history, you just needed to teach me a fucking lesson?"

"This will be easier if you can refrain from being dramatic," Crina said, and Sara had to force her jaws together to keep from replying, because her reply would be emotional, and Crina would dismiss her as theatrical. She'd been here before. "Of course not. Silas's fighting skills are better than mine, I knew that Teddie would be safe in his care. You know, because you've let her skills get, shall we say, a little rusty?"

"Right, right," Sara said, sitting as upright as she could. "Because she needs to be proficient at dodging fucking arrows on a night out in Bushwick? It's a different time, Crina. She's still a black belt in martial arts."

"I didn't mean to imply that their skills were imbalanced that greatly," Crina said, now trying to placate Sara. "I'm sorry if it came off that way. I did not think that trapping a bunch of recently infected weaklings would come to this. Clearly. But I wanted you to worry, I wanted you to see the scope of loss, the sheer weight of what I'm fighting to protect."

"Oh, that makes it all better," Sara struggled to rein in her anger. "Because I'm too what? Too stupid? Too shallow? To comprehend how much these people mean to me?"

"No, Sara," Crina said, very coolly, "I wanted you to find that thing inside you, that thing where you'd kill for them. I wanted you to really understand why "never pick a mother" is probably our most enduring rule. There is not a woman on this earth who would voluntarily sit back and watch her children age and then die when she could prevent it. Not one. But I have learned something else, and that is that once cursed, the stakes get even higher, and I will do anything, absolutely fucking anything, to protect my children."

"So you wanted me to be so terrified, just so I can condone your actions?"

Crina nodded with infuriating calmness.

"Precisely," she said. "Think of that moment, over the radio, when you knew Teddie was hurt and Silas was being hunted. If you were there, if you were closer, and your only option to save them was to kill that man, what would you have done? Where would your no-kill politics have gotten you in that instant?"

Sara looked down and shook her head.

"I do not know," she said finally. "I honestly do not know."

"Well I do," Crina said. "You would have killed him. And you could have done it with your bare hands. And it isn't the Curse, it's not something we do because of what we are. It's the most human response to that kind of terrible threat. It's motherhood. You would have flown to that man and torn his arms from his shoulders, his head from his neck, and in that moment, you would have been right."

"You're veering into drama," Sara whispered. "If I'm not allowed to, neither are you."

Sara heard Crina exhale, angrily and slowly, and she knew that she was driving her crazy. It felt good, but also, she wasn't letting herself go into that moment, to feel whether she would in fact have killed that man.

"Sara, I know how stubborn you are," Crina's voice was soft again. "I worship at your stubbornness, your certainty of your world, but it needs to crack if we are to survive. And I want to open your mind a little more. It's so long since I gave birth to Silas that his biological connection to me is almost conceptual, it's the way you remember your birth family. It's a fact from an eon ago. Today I love him the same way I love you, and Teddie, and you two, Heather and Imani. I love you because you've become part of me, because when I am around these people, parts of me feel more complete. That's motherhood."

"I'm starting to hear you," Sara said, her voice small.

"Sara, when I regained consciousness and I could see the hate and the intent on that man's face, I didn't see red or lose control, I simply saw that for us both to survive, he needed to die. Immediately. And in that moment, nothing else mattered. I didn't care if I didn't survive the attempt, I just needed to make the attempt."

Images of the man approaching her replayed in Sara's mind, the hate, the intent, and she knew that if Crina hadn't intervened, she would have had to fight for her life, and the end result would have been that she killed the man herself. But she couldn't shake her anger at Crina's willingness to endanger Teddie and Silas.

"Then maybe you should have really made your point," she said. "Why didn't you let me fight him, let me find out the hard way whether I'd kill to save myself?"

"Because, my love, you're so stubborn, you'd have tried to save him somehow and in that moment of hesitation, he would have smashed your head open."

Giving in, agreeing with Crina, felt impossible to Sara, and she saw her stubbornness in a new light. She had always seen her self-defense skills as something that would protect her and her family, her friends, but the end of a long fight isn't always surrender, and she'd never thought beyond that point, living safely distant from that reality. Raising her head slowly, she looked at Crina, surprised to see tears streaking her face.

"You're right," she said quietly. Crina's eyes widened. "I need to stop pretending that peace can make everything alright. If anything, I've made this situation worse. I've had opportunities to kill Desdemona, and if I'd taken them, nothing would have changed, except our little world would be safe."

"Killing is something we should never become accustomed to," Crina said. "But sometimes it's necessary, and sometimes-"

Imani interrupted Crina by pouring Old Fashioned into her empty wine glass, and Heather's.

"Because," Imani said with a laugh, "sometimes a fucking bitch just needs to die."

Chapter Sixteen

The sounds of someone shuffling around woke Sara to the now familiar feeling of not knowing exactly where she was. The pillow against her cheek was textured and a little rough, and the light covering over her body wasn't really keeping her warm. The couch. She was on the couch. In her apartment. Opening one eye, she saw Silas and Teddie in the kitchen, and heard them whispering to each other, then Teddie glanced in her direction.

"The jig is up, mom," she said.

"What jig? You guys woke me up with all your banging around."

"I told you we couldn't win," Teddie said to Silas.

"But now that you're up," Silas bounced over and kissed her on the forehead, "can you please come help us make coffee and blood?"

"I'm not up," Sara mumbled, her brain a few seconds slow in realizing that both of them had injuries to their right hands. Groaning she pushed herself upright, glancing around the room for any sign of the time, confused by the night sky outside her windows.

"It's five thirty," Teddie called out. "We just woke up too."

"Isn't that a bit late for coffee?" she asked, slowly crossing the small space between the couch and the kitchen.

"You do you, bitch," Teddie laughed, and Sara smiled, then, registering her arm in a sling and Silas's bandaged hand, the smile faded.

"How are you both feeling?"

"It's weird," Silas began.

"It is, right?" Teddie jumped in, as they both moved out of the way of the coffee maker, the banter confirming that Sara did need a coffee or she'd just be irritable.

"The healing," Silas continued. "I haven't ever had a wound like this and I can feel it healing."

"So itchy," Teddie said.

"*So* itchy," Silas agreed.

"Listen you two, this weird twinsy nonsense needs to stop," Sara said as she flicked switches on the espresso machine and got the coffee and milk out of the fridge as Teddie and Silas took their act over to the couch.

"I told you she'd wake up grumpy," Teddie said, and Sara shot her a look.

"Sara," Silas said, his voice comically grave as a smile played at the corner of his mouth, "we heard a little about your night, but we're both glad you're okay. Can you come tell us all about it?"

Sara decided that silence was her best defense until she got some blood in her system so she quickly prepared three jars of blood, and set them in the warming oven.

"I thought I heard Crina here," Teddie said. "But I was so high, it could have been a dream."

"Nope, she was here," Sara said. "Heather and Imani too."

"Sorry I slept through it," Silas said earnestly, rising from the couch and encircling her in a hug from behind. "I hope it wasn't too rough."

Shrugging, Sara wriggled her way around to face him and kissed him on the lips.

"It was a bit gnarly but I'm glad it happened," Sara said.

"Wait," Teddie said breathlessly, "is there peace in old lady vampire land?"

Thankfully, the ding of the warming oven saved Sara from having to answer. Pushing Silas gently away, she grabbed the three jars deftly between her two hands and carried them to the coffee table. Returning to the coffee maker she took the first two shots and put them beside the jars, and returned to make one for herself.

"Why aren't you answering meeeee?" Teddie would not let up.

"Girl, mama needs her juice before she can deal with your bullshit," Sara said with a laugh, wondering why she took her own blood to the living room, before nipping over and snatching it up while theatrically ignoring Teddie, causing her to break into laughter.

"Mom, no it still hurts when I laugh," she spluttered.

"Drink your blood, girl," Sara finally smiled, then downed her blood in one long gulp. Once her coffee was ready, she returned to the living room, this time sitting on the floor and facing them, the sight of their bandages actually causing her heart to ache.

"Before you ask, I'll tell," she began. "Crina came and explained herself in terms that worked for me. And I've definitely not been taking care of Heather in the way she needs. So it's a time for growth and acceptance for all of us."

On the couch, Silas and Teddie glanced at each other, their expressions serious.

"This is why I don't want to talk about this with you," Sara said, wishing her coffee would cool down faster. "Look, I'll just have Crina give you her mom-centric talk on murder, she'll do a much better job than I would."

"But..." Teddie began and Silas placed his good palm on her thigh.

"She's been through a lot," he said. "Do you want to tell us about your night?"

"Also no," Sara said. "I need some time with it, I'll tell you eventually. And Silas, I apologize in advance for the nightmares."

"More nightmares?" he laughed before turning serious. "All in a day's work my love. I got you."

Teddie began to protest when a furious knocking sounded at the door.

"It's me, Yukari."

Sara leapt to her feet, something in Yukari's tone making the hair raise on her neck and arms. Yanking the door open, she saw Yukari, a stricken expression on her face, clutching a tablet.

"Have you seen the news?" she asked, as she pushed past Sara.

"No, I just woke up, what's going on?"

"It was just on NY1," Yukari said. "Oh, hi Silas, hi Teddie, how are you feeling?"

"Don't worry about them," Sara said panicked. "What are you talking about."

Sara sat between Silas and Teddie while Yukari flicked at her iPad then turned it to face them, revealing a male newscaster, frozen. Yukari hit the pause button.

"And now we have breaking news from Harlem," the man said. "A homeless man is dead after he attacked two police officers with arrows. In a grisly twist, he attempted to suck the blood from their wounds."

Sara felt panic as the newscast continued. The screen cut to an assortment of handheld videos from various social media platforms, all showing a crowd surrounding a slight man with black hair, brandishing a crossbow in one hand and an arrow in the other. Suddenly two policemen pushed through the crowd, one Black and husky, the other Latino, tall and slender. Over the sound of the crowd's yelling, she could barely hear them try to reason with the man and he advanced on them, causing the Latino to draw his gun.

"Put down the arrow," yelled the Black officer. "We don't want to hurt you. We're here to help you."

Suddenly the footage cut to a closeup of the man's face, confusion and pain morphing into fear and anger, but it was the dark, dark circles below his eyes that caused Sara to gasp. She recognized the glaze that was overcoming his eyes. Whatever differences the variants of their virus had, she hoped that he wouldn't black out into nothing but instinct.

"We want to advise viewers that the next scenes are particularly violent," the newscaster said in voiceover. "If you are sensitive, or have younger viewers in the room, please change the channel now."

On the screen the action continued. The man dropped the bow to the sidewalk almost absently, and the Black officer stepped closer to him. Sara's heart was racing. Out of nowhere, the man switched his attention to the other cop, who was screaming for the people surrounding them to clear out. Unable to take the shot, he holstered his weapon, and both officers advanced on the man, and Sara watched in horror as he began to windmill his one arm, the arrow turning into a swirling blur that struck the Latino officer in the arm, and when he tried to help his partner, the Black officer was stabbed in the leg. As the Latino came around from behind to restrain him, the man dropped the arrow and threw his arms around the other officer's thigh, and pressed his face against the bleeding wounds.

"What the fuck?" the officer screamed out, TV bleeping him. "Get him off me. Fuck, he's biting me."

The Latino officer tried to get his arms around the attacker's neck, presumably to choke him out, but as soon as the man smelled the blood pouring from the wound in the officer's hand, he released his grip on the man's thigh and snatched the bleeding hand to his mouth, sucking hungrily on the back of it while the officer screamed and yanked at his arm. Suddenly, a man in the crowd stepped forward, gun in hand, and the scene went black and a gunshot sounded. The scene cut to ambulance workers and additional police officers clearing the scene as the man's body and the two officers were loaded onto gurneys and loaded into ambulances before fading back to the newscaster in the studio.

"Both police officers are now in a stable condition at Columbia Hospital. Police have not been able to confirm the identity of the deceased."

Yukari turned the tablet back towards herself and switched it off, then began talking before anyone else could.

"I've already sent Liz to work at Columbia, she's going to see what she can find out, we need to find out if the men are infected. She said it will be pretty tricky to find out but she will do her best."

"Fuck," Teddie said from the couch. "I'm sorry you guys. Desdemona has made it impossible for me to go back there. Liz isn't as crafty as I was, and she doesn't network between the different labs the way I did."

"I know that," Yukari said. "But I need to tell you something, Sara. It's okay for you guys to hear it too. I.." she paused, taking a deep breath. "I might need to go public."

"I'm sorry, Yukari," Sara said. "What do you mean?"

"We need to stop this," she said. "I might need to take my current persona public."

"Oh, okay," Sara said, relieved. "That's not a problem, we can set you up in an apartment and a lab pretty quickly, offsite, wherever you want. When it's all done, you can just go into hiding for fifty years."

"That's not what I mean," Yukari said. "Please, I'm sorry to be so dramatic, but this has been on my mind for a while and I think that it's the right thing to do."

"What is, Yuka?" Alarm was creeping into Teddie's voice.

"We need someone working outside of our circles, working in the public sphere, because this virus, it's out there. Whether Desdemona brought it to America or whether someone gets it in Romania, we need it vaccinated and eradicated before any time passes, before a strain like ours comes along."

"I don't understand," Teddie said.

"Before the world finds out that it grants eternity," Silas said, and Yukari nodded.

"Exactly," she said quietly. "Sara, I have been thinking about this a lot in recent years, and obviously more so in the recent weeks. I think that it is my duty, as a scientist, to keep the human race safe from the consequences of what would happen if anyone, you know, discovered us, what we are, what a virus has done for us. It's what I need to do."

Sara sat in stunned silence, staring into Yukari's beautiful fearless eyes.

"Well, we don't need to do anything super dramatic, not right now," she began, and Yukari cut her off.

"Sara, I need to be a part of that world, full time, to protect it. I can't continue to dip in and out lightly, and if I am to continue to have the desired effect in the scientific community, I need to be visible and accountable and present."

"And you need to age," Silas said, making Teddie and Sara gasp.

"Yes, right again Silas."

"Are you going to take a vaccine?" Teddie's voice was horrified.

"It's the only solution," Yukari said, tears welling in her eyes. "And I would not be able to return here, there can be nothing linking me to any of..." she paused, waving her arm in a wide circle, "...any of this, this life, this building. But don't cry for me-"

"Yukari, you cried first," Teddie's voice was breaking.

"Yes, but also, I feel peace," she said. "I have been discussing it with Fan and Ama, and they agree that it is a noble and valiant thing to do. It's also something that literally has to happen."

"It doesn't though," Sara said. "You said yourself, this new variant, you don't think it grants any life extension."

"I said that after some very rushed and primitive experiments," Yukari said. "But at some point, way back before our time, nobody knew this virus gave us a longer life, that only became apparent in the decades after infection, in those men. We don't know what changes this version will bring. And our version, I don't know how come Desdemona is decaying so rapidly, I targeted a protein that should only be present in our unique strain, the protein is slightly different in this new version, only slightly, but that difference seems to be what makes us live a long time. I have already vaccinated Andrei, and his need for blood is gone, the idea of consuming blood nauseates him. I refused to have him become part of Desdemona's plan."

Sara took it all in silently, marveling at Yukari's strength and also her tenacity. She hadn't told anyone that she was planning to vaccinate the kid. Good for her, she thought.

"You're amazing, Yukari," Silas said. "You're so brave, on top of being a genius and all."

Yukari gave a tiny laugh and blushed. "You need to stop," she said. "But here's the bad news, on top of the bad news I already delivered. I can't reverse Desdemona's vaccine. She will always be immune to our strand of the virus, and I talked to Stefanya, and she says that these days, all of the surviving Cursed women were made by her, or made by someone that she made, so we don't have any different strains. The only hope she had was if there were different strains within our community. As it stands, I cannot help her."

"Boo fucking hoo," Teddie said.

"Indeed," Yukari said with a smile. "But, Sara, I know that you won't want to hear this, but the smartest thing for us to do is to find her and kill her. The words feel like vomit in my mouth, I hate that I have to say them, but it is not how I feel, it is a necessity."

"I agree with you, entirely," Sara said, and once again, Silas and Teddie exchanged worried glances. "We will meet with Fan and Ama later tonight or tomorrow and figure out the best way to set a trap, to lure her to New York and kill her. It's the only way, and I deeply regret my decision to spare her, because if I'd been more aggressive-"

"More man-like, you mean," Teddie whispered.

"Enough from you," Sara said. "If I'd just killed her three months ago, you wouldn't be in this position, Yuka, and that breaks my heart."

"I was in this position then," Yukari said. "I've been in this position for several years, since mRNA vaccines were proven effective and I had breakthroughs. I wish I'd had the vaccine ready, for the women of the Locks who she killed. They could have just chosen to age, living their lives, experience old age, and you know what? They could have experienced death like no Cursed woman ever has before them. To live four or five hundred years, then finally cross over to whatever is next. Maybe nothing, maybe something, but imagine if our purpose here is to absorb and give love and then take that love with us when we pass? Those women would have had a front row to a mystery I can only dream of."

"That's beautiful," Sara said, "I wish you'd been able to talk to me about this, it's fascinating. Yukari, are you scared?"

"Not one bit," she replied. "Life and death are the way of existence, everything is temporary, we understand so little. That has always frustrated me, but what has always appealed to me is the life of service, the way the Buddhists view it. No matter what happens when we die, I have always felt that it is better to spend a life in service, this is how I've managed to live so long and still greet every day as a miracle."

On the couch, Teddie began to cry, punctuating the bigger sobs with an "ouch" as the bones in her shoulder moved against the damage from the arrow, and Sara and Silas exchanged sad glances, their eyes filling with tears.

"You guys, no," Yukari said firmly. "This isn't a sad thing, this is a fantastic thing. This is me doing something that I've wanted to do for a very long time, only now I also have the science to actually be of use, to actually, potentially save the whole planet, or at least protect it from the greed of men, the same thing we've been fighting against since the formation of our order."

"But we can never see you again?" Teddie managed through her tears.

"Theodora," Yukari said gently. "You and I both know that love will always find a way, and I will always manage to somehow sit beside you at a Starbucks when you least expect it. I love you all more than you'll ever know, and this love will keep me going until I die as an old woman, hopefully surrounded by all of you."

Chapter Seventeen

Pausing before knocking at the rear door to Heather's apartment, Sara took a minute to do a new thing: to ask herself what she wanted from the situation. Three days ago, she'd banished Crina and Heather, alongside Fan and Ama, for being parties to murder, a move that felt powerful and right in the moment, but felt hysterical and a bit embarrassing a day later. And now she was meeting with them to talk about defeating and most likely killing Desdemona. Such is war, she joked to herself before forcing herself back to the topic at hand. What did she want and how was she going to make sure she got it, after centuries of bouncing from crisis to crisis with other people's happiness as her priority?

She wanted peace, she wanted to be able to know that her people were safe and that they could all enjoy New York City for another century, if they wanted to. As the thought played in her mind, she realized what she wanted. She wanted to save New York, for herself, for everyone. It was vague and amorphous but it was enough to put some guardrails on the meeting. She also wanted Crina to leave the city, at least for now, she realized. Sara wanted to find herself without a constant stream of criticism, passed off as motherly care.

Satisfied, she knocked on the door, hearing footsteps immediately.

"Hello love," Crina said, wrapping her in a hug that she returned halfheartedly.

"Hey," Sara said, pushing past her. "Am I late? Heather's text was a bit vague."

"No," Crina said, unperturbed by her behavior. "You know what it's like getting them all on a call at once. Now that you're here, we'll text them and then we wait for the delays."

"Do you need any blood?" Heather called out.

"No, I'm good thanks," Sara replied as she entered the living room and saw Heather curled up on her crocheted blanket. Bending, she kissed her on the top of the head before sitting next to her, happy to see a little smile spread across her face.

"That's good to hear," Heather said. "So, I was meaning to ask you-"

"Before we get lost in small talk," Crina interrupted, plonking herself at the other end of the couch, "we need to decide who we want to do the favors we need."

"What favors?" Sara asked.

"Who do we want here, alongside us fighting? And who do we want to ask to accompany the men back to Romania?"

"We're sending them back?" Sara was shocked, she'd slept restlessly convinced that the men would be killed without consultation.

"Yes, pet," Heather said. "You're right, they're innocent."

"But you said they've seen too much..."

"Everyone has a price," Heather said enigmatically.

"So, what I was thinking," Crina continued, "Is that we can ask Yfke and Skye to stay and fight, and maybe Christine and Lindsey can chaperone the men back to their cities?"

"It sounds like you've decided already," Sara said. "And like a wise woman once said, it's better to ask an open question than seek a predetermined answer."

"Who said that?" Crina snapped.

"I believe it was me," Heather laughed, taking Sara's hand as her phone dinged several times in her lap and she looked at it. "Well this is a first, they're all ready now."

Silently, Crina began tapping at her phone and the TV screen divided into four squares, which materialized into the faces of four women who Sara had known forever, but not seen in person for longer than she could recall.

"Hi guys," waved Yfke, her sunshine blond hair bouncing around her bright eyes. "We can't see you."

"Oh sorry," Crina got up and rested her phone against the base of the TV, and the three New York women appeared in a little box in the top corner of the screen.

"That's better," said Skye, the only Indigenous Australian Cursed woman, one of Teddie's best friends after their shared decade in Paris. "How are we all?"

"Nevermind us," said Lindsey, a Londoner whose hair was never the same color, presently it was pink. "How the fuck are you all holding up?"

"Yes," said Christine, feisty, Irish, her bright blue eyes full of concern. "It's been terrible being so far away while all this is happening."

"It's not like you've not been busy," Heather said. "Weeding out the rats."

"It wasn't that hard," Skye said seriously. "They identified themselves pretty readily by fucking off as soon as Desdemona called. We think that they're all on their way to New York right now."

"They might be there already," Yfke said. "Can't be sure. I've been working with Fran. How are you after the scene in the Park?"

"We're all hanging in there," Sara said. "Couple of war wounds but it could have been so much worse. We have three men in custody, in the building, and the rest are dead."

"We talked to Yukari earlier," Skye said, immediately blinking away tears. "What a brave woman."

"She's doing what needs to be done," Yfke said. "And she's doing it for us. But I'm not here for small talk. I have to know. Are you calling to ask us to come and fight beside you?"

Rolling her eyes, Sara nodded and smiled at Yfke's predictably Viking response. As much as she was known as the party girl of their crew, Sara had seen her fight in the final days of the purge, as a baby Cursed, alongside Fan and Ama. She was strong before she got Cursed, and there was an elegant brutality to her fighting.

"We need some muscle," Crina said. "And we need some chaperones."

"We need all four of you, and maybe more," Heather said, and on the screen, Lindsey and Christine dropped their heads. "What? Is there a problem?"

"Well," Christine began, "me and Lindsey have just had a victory in a lawsuit against Desdemona's stupid church takeover, and we have court dates, full nun nonsense, from Wednesday next week."

"Fine," Crina said. "Can you come tomorrow, just overnight, and take the men back with you?"

They waited as Lindsey and Christine picked up their phones and texted each other quickly before nodding.

"We're bringing them to London?" Christine asked.

"TBD for now," Heather said. "We're going to talk to them after this call and offer them a buyout. We'll see how it shakes out and I'll call you back."

"No problem," Lindsey said. "As long as we're back in London for Wednesday, we're good. Happy to help."

"Thank you," Crina said. "Yfke, Skye, we need to warn you, it's dangerous, she's operating without any conscience."

"She always did," Skye said. "But she's stealthier than we ever knew."

"She's not that good at it though," Lindsey said. "We've found a bunch of screwups in the property takeovers, she did them as transfers without proper forms, you guys need to look into the process of what she took from you."

"Yeah, I'm all over it," Heather said. "I've found a few things, but I do need to run through it again. Thanks for the reminder."

"You've had a lot on your mind, Heather," Sara wrapped her arms around her old friend.

"We need to get down there and talk to the men now," Heather said. "And you four need to get on a plane."

"Or two planes," Yfke said. "Me and Skye will get there as soon as we can."

"Yeah, we need to leave like right now," Skye said, looking at her phone. "I just bought us tickets on a flight that leaves in three hours. First class via London."

"Oooh," Christine said. "Send us your flight info and we can fly together."

"We don't have time," Lindsey interrupted. "There's a flight we can do this afternoon, we'll beat you there. We'll see you when you land."

"Okay, fine," Yfke mugged.

"I saw that," Lindsey said with a smile.

"You were meant to," Yfke replied. "Anyways, it's been an age since I had to pack for a battle, I need to go."

"Bye mateys," Skye said. "Hang in there, we'll be there soon."

Heather waited until all four squares had gone black, then ended the call.

"Okay, let's go see how much it's gonna cost us to buy out these blokes. It already cost a fortune for their new passports, let's put them to good use."

In a weird, almost formal, silence, the three of them left Heather's and made their way through the rear hallways down to the rooms where the younger man and the recent capture were being held. Sara wanted to discuss, to strategize, but the silence told her this job had already been handled and she was just going to be a witness to something preordained. The feeling sat with a new comfort on her shoulders, and she felt a tingle of satisfaction. She was adjusting to the new order, but she also wondered why people were still including her in everything. Suddenly, she wished she was back in her bed with Silas, doing nothing while they could, in the middle of this maelstrom.

When they arrived at the door to the apartment where Andrei, the younger one, was being held, Heather paused.

"Be vigilant," she cautioned, "he doesn't seem like a threat, but you never know."

"The only thing he could beat us at is video games," Crina said with a chuckle. "Let's go in, I'll do the talking."

After knocking, Heather unlocked the door via the fingerprint scanner. As the door opened, they heard tinny gunshots and crackly dialog, clearly from a shooter game.

"Andrei?" Crina called out.

"Yeah, come in," the boy said, and they walked in, immediately seeing Andrei, his back to them, engrossed in the game on the television. "What now? What's going on today?"

"We've come to talk to you about going home," Crina said, and almost instantly, the action on the TV paused and the boy swiveled to face them, distrust on his face.

"Why does it take three women to have this discussion?"

"Don't be paranoid," Crina said. "I just need to know, if you could live anywhere in the world, where would you want to go?"

Shrugging, the boy looked into each of their eyes.

"This feels like a trick," he said.

"It's not," Crina said, her palms raised to placate him. "You've been pulled into something that doesn't concern you, by a very sick woman. We are a group of women who operate in the shadows, we help people less fortunate than ourselves. But we value our privacy very highly, which is why we have come to you with an offer?"

"Right," Andrei spat. "And if I don't accept the offer?"

"Oh, I can't see why you wouldn't accept it," Crina said jovially. "In exchange for your silence, we will buy you a house in the city of your choice, with a monthly stipend of ten thousand American dollars. For the rest of your life." Crina paused as the man's eyes widened. "That's it. That's the offer. But if we ever hear that you've shared any details about this, about us, then the money will stop."

"And you'll kill me?"

Chuckling, Crina shook her head. "No. The money will just stop. That's it. I also want to add, that because you've already seen enough to compromise us, this building is going to be sold, we will not be here by the time you arrive home. Your story, your information, will not be of use to anyone."

"Then why are you doing this, the money, the house?"

"Because we are good women and we deeply regret that you were dragged into this mess by a crazy woman."

"Do I have to stay in the place that I choose?"

Crina shook her head.

"No, Andrei, once we place you in a home, you're free to do as you wish with it, it will be legally yours. Keep it, sell it, rent it out. We just want you to be happy."

Crina was speaking in soothing tones, sounding maternal in a way that was too familiar to Sara. She wondered if this was authentic or if Crina was just really adept at motherly manipulation.

"Germany," Andrei said. "I want to live in Berlin."

"That's a good choice," Crina said. "We need a day to set up the logistics, and tomorrow one of us will accompany you to Berlin. You'll be in a hotel until you find a house, you can discuss the details on the plane."

"You're serious?"

"Completely," Crina said with a benevolent nod. "We just want to make things right for you and set you up for a good life."

"Are you... are you...?"

"What is it, Andrei? You can ask us anything."

Sara quickly panicked, wondering if Desdemona had told him that they were vampires.

"Are you the Illuminati?"

All three of them burst into laughter, and the boy appeared crestfallen.

"I wish," Crina said. "But if that were true, the world would be in much better shape. Anyway, Andrei, thanks for listening and being so kind. We wish you well and hope that you have a magical life in Berlin. I'll be back to see you later tonight to walk you through how things will work and once again, we apologize for the crazy lady bringing you into her problems."

Clearly confused and overwhelmed, Andrei bowed his head and pressed his palms together, and automatically, the three of them responded by doing the same thing, and they exited the apartment in silence.

"Bless you, my child," Heather said as they left the room.

"That shit is so ingrained," Heather whispered after she locked the door. "If we never have to be nuns ever again, I don't think I'll ever stop responding that way."

"It's harmless," Crina said. "Okay, next is Gabriel, Liz told me that he's pretty thorny, but he's been vaccinated and sedated, I just need to grab something from the meeting room."

Without another word, Crina turned and bolted down the hallway, vanishing around a corner.

"I guess that means we wait for her outside the guy's door?" Sara said, and Heather shrugged. Turning to face her, Sara wrapped Heather in a hug, clearly surprising her.

"You need a holiday," she said into Heather's hair, feeling relief as her old friend relaxed against her.

"We all do," she replied. "When all of this is all over..."

"Iceland?"

"Fuck no," Heather laughed, breaking the hug. "Somewhere sunny, crystal clear water, sexy, optimistic men, no tall buildings and even less drama."

"Count me in," Sara said, taking a strand of Heather's hair and placing it behind her ear. "Where are we sending Toma?"

"Bloody nowhere," Heather said irritably. "Imani says she will take responsibility for him, in the short term."

"Huh," was all Sara could muster in response, as her mind kicked into overdrive imagining Crina's reaction to that news.

In silence, they turned and walked along the stone corridor, their footsteps crunching softly, as if they were walking on dry snow. When they turned the corner, they saw Crina leaning against the wall outside the room where Gabriel was being held, a satchel slung from her shoulder.

"She's so fast," Heather said.

"She's about to complain," Sara whispered.

"Come on you two," Crina yelled. "I don't have all day."

"Told ya," Sara said as they sped up their pace.

"Let me do the talking," Crina said as she pressed a finger against the lock.

"Like we have a choice," Heather giggled as the door swung open.

"Gabriel?" Crina called out before continuing in Romanian. "We come in peace. Are you decent?"

"I am awake," came a surly male voice and the three women fell into a triangle formation, Crina at the front, and they made their way through the small antechamber into the main room where Gabriel sat on the thin mattress on the floor. "What now?"

"It's time for you to leave us," Crina said ominously, and the man's head jerked up, his dirty blonde curls whipping back, alarm in his eyes. "On an airplane," she added and his body relaxed, but his eyes remained narrowed.

"I don't believe you," he said.

"I don't care," Crina said. "It's either that, or the police, and I show them this."

Removing a tablet from her satchel, Crina turned it on, tapped at the screen and turned it to face him.

"Gabriel, this is you, with a gun, hunting human beings in Central Park. You were doing this why? Because a crazy lady injected you with poison that made you drink blood and want to kill people. How do you think the police will react to that story? Do you think they'll believe you? No, they won't. They hear stories like this every day, and they will lock you up in a psych ward until they ship you back to

Bucharest. So," Crina paused, flipping the tablet over, switching it off and sliding it back into her satchel, "that's one option."

"Is there another?"

Crina nodded. "Yes, you fly back to Bucharest tomorrow. One of us will escort you. When you get there, we will give you somewhere to live, and you will receive two thousand dollars a month, for the rest of your life, in exchange for your silence. This woman, she is dangerous and she will want to kill you, and we will protect you as part of this deal."

"But why? Why are you so generous, after I tried to kill you?"

"We do good," Crina said. "We help people. This is what drives her crazy. We don't know why."

"I accept, but I have one worry," Gabriel said. "The blood, I drank the blood, what did she do to me?"

"She hypnotized you," Crina said matter of factly. "I have some blood here, let me show you."

Reaching back into her satchel, Crina withdrew a very small mason jar with a silicon lid. She twisted off the lid and held it out to Gabriel, who shuddered in revulsion.

"But, but, she had me drinking it," he whispered. "She said I would die without it."

"She lies," Crina said, screwing the lid back onto the jar. "You were hypnotized. She is cruel and she destroys people. She is insane, she wants to start a cult."

Gabriel's shoulders slumped.

"I was in a cult," he moaned. "How does this happen?"

"It doesn't matter," Crina said gently. "You'll be going home tomorrow. Before we leave you, is there anything you can tell us about where they kept you?"

Suddenly, Gabriel's face turned to the floor.

"I too have lied," he said quietly. "We were in a warehouse building, and there are more men. We had to come into New York over a bridge, from the south. But my lie is this. That evil woman, she is here."

Chapter Eighteen

Kicking her shoes in the small puddles on the ground of the rooftop, left behind by overnight rain, Sara watched as the splashes sent droplets flying through the air until they landed in other puddles. Ripples circled out, eddies ringing in the shallow pools, as her anxiety did the same thing in her heart, her thoughts a churning mess of strands of plans, fears and a growing desire to simply flee. With all the benches wet, Sara had nowhere to sit and think; instead she meandered around the raised garden beds and the water tower, pausing to stare down a light shaft all the way to the bottom, five stories below, the frigid air helping to clear her mind.

Somewhere in the complex beneath her, Crina was introducing her son to Christine and Lindsey, who'd arrived late the night before, and Skye, who'd only just arrived with Yfke. Sara smiled at the memory of her dinner with Silas and Teddie, where he'd revealed that he now had to tell Crina that he and Yfke had been friends for centuries, unbeknownst to anyone, and yes, they'd dated, off and on, but, as Silas confessed with a laugh, "not since electricity." Instead of jealousy, Sara found herself happy that Silas had put himself first in ways that she'd never known were available to her. She also hated how the information had fed her curiosity over other secrets Silas was keeping.

Right now, Sara wanted to get downstairs and reunite with her sisters, hear their laughter, their stories, but she also had a strong feeling that she needed to go into that room with something, a strategy? A way forward? Nobody was expecting her to be a leader, not officially, but the conversations she'd had with various sisters the night before left her feeling like there was a vacuum that only she could fill, an answer dancing just beyond her fingertips. A light rain began to fall, the puddles shattering into chaos, and she looked up, taking in the day. In her pocket, her phone rang.

A blocked number. She sighed.

"Hello."

"Guess who." It was Desdemona.

"Not in the mood for games, Des," Sara said, making her way to her loft door. "What do you want?"

"I just wanted to compliment you on your nice outfit," she said. Sara froze. "Oooh, that got you."

Tensing her legs and focusing solely on her door, twenty yards ahead of her, Sara burst into a run, her phone in her hand, slicing through the air as the door drew closer and she anticipated the feel of a bullet tearing into her skin. Slamming against the wet door, she pressed her fingertip into the lock, too hard, her heart pounding as she lifted it briefly before placing it gently against the circular reader which flashed green instantly. Twisting the knob so hard she thought it might break, she pulled the door open then slipped inside, slamming the door closed, then falling to the floor, out of sight of anyone who might be looking through the thin band of windows along the wall.

With her heartbeat hammering in her ears, she returned the phone to her ear.

"Darling sister, if I wanted to shoot you, you'd be dead already," Desdemona said playfully. "Guns are so distasteful, don't you think?

"Didn't stop you from arming your men with them in the park though."

"My options were so limited," Desdemona continued. "And you know, *men*. They only understand simple things. Guns. Pussy. Violence."

"What the fuck is wrong with you?" Sara spat. "You're acting like a psychopath. Oh wait..."

"I just wanted to commend you on calling in the cavalry," Desdemona said. "I see you have a full house, with Skye and Lindsey and Christine, even that awful Yfke in town."

"You really should get a television," Sara said. "Much more entertaining than watching us."

"Not really," Desdemona sniffed. "It's just surprising, the way you're putting all your eggs in one basket."

"Not sure I follow. Maybe you're just speaking in cliches."

"I could blow that building to smithereens," Desdemona said, her voice now flat. "Take you all out at once."

"Right, yes, solid brick buildings are so flimsy," Sara snapped. "Look, okay, you've made your point, you're able to see us. Congratulations. Was there anything else you wanted?"

"I wanted to check on my men," Desdemona said. "How are they doing?"

"Some better than others."

"Oh?"

"Most are dead, and the survivors are vaccinated and will be relocating to their best lives."

"So much for no kill," Desdemona said sarcastically. "I knew your morals would crumble."

"I'm not the boss here, remember? These days, every girl is a slayer."

"What the hell does that mean?"

"Like I said, it's time you got a television," Sara said. "Before I hang up on you, can I just confirm our appointment for this Friday in the North Woods? Will there be another delivery?"

Desdemona yawned, long and languidly, before answering.

"I haven't decided," she said. "These men are proving as disappointing as they are expendable. Why? Would you like some more? I have plenty."

Shaking her head, Sara weighed her words, not wanting to anger Desdemona into another delivery of multiple men.

"No, Des, what I'd like is for you to accept that Yukari is working herself to exhaustion to come up with a solution for you, and your skirmishes just set us back."

In the silence that followed, Sara thought of the discussion she'd had with Yukari the night before, and decided to try Yukari's idea.

"Actually, Des, if we can be reasonable for a moment," Sara kept her voice level. "Yukari is devastated, she blames herself for all of this, and she can't take it anymore. She's talking about taking Surrender."

Desdemona gasped.

"I know. It's awful, but she thinks that because she's the only one who can help you, if she takes herself out of the picture, then you have no chance."

"She'd never."

"Oh you're so wrong, dear sister. And also, this version of the virus that you're spreading, we can now confirm it doesn't offer longevity."

"Don't you think I don't know that?" Desdemona's voice finally broke.

"I don't know what you do or don't know, but I know that Yukari is cracking under the pressure. So, I'll leave the decision of whether to send us more men up to you."

"Okay, no men this week," Desdemona whispered. "But don't get complacent, Sara. There are other ways to encourage you."

"Des, we couldn't be more encouraged, you'll get your eternal life back, I promise. Maybe go get a facial or a collagen treatment? I hear they're great for wrinkles."

The line went dead. Sara flipped her phone from one hand to the other, a wicked grin on her face, then she did a group text calling an immediate all-hands in the basement meeting room.

Since she didn't stop to change or even look in the mirror, Sara was the first to arrive in the meeting room. As usual, she busied herself with arranging chairs and doing a mental headcount before grabbing some more seating from the storage room, arranging it in a deliberately haphazard pattern, and now, she was pacing nervously in front of the dais, unsure if she should be leading the meeting, or contributing from equal footing on the floor.

Hearing voices, she looked up. Heather. Why was Heather always the first to arrive?

"What's wrong, pet?"

"I don't know how to not be a Lock mother, it seems."

"Then fucking be one," Heather tutted, not liking the position of her throne and hauling it unceremoniously to the front. "If you're gonna reclaim your crown, I want a front row seat."

"Us too," said Teddie and Fran, arriving arm in arm. "Us too."

"Wait," Fran paused. "A front row seat for what?"

"Sara's gonna be Lock mother again," Heather quipped, winking at Sara, who was growing frustrated.

"Told you," Teddie said.

"How much do I owe ya?" Fran reached into her pockets, then pulled out her hands, middle fingers extended. "Nah, just fucking with ya, Sara. What's going on?"

Sara was about to reply when a loud bustling sound came from the hall, and in swept a large group, Silas at the center, flanked by the Europeans and Crina.

"Hey girls," she called out. "I'll hug you all later, and I see you've met my boyfriend."

"I trained him for you!" Yfke called out, flopping into Eleanor's old throne, then patting the seat beside her for Silas, who took the seat, a blush creeping up his cheeks.

"You done good," Sara called out, relieved to see Yukari, Embla, Imani and April Veronica filing in slowly. Liz, as usual, was last. Sara sighed away her anger at Liz's constant micro-aggressions.

"Grab a seat, girls, this won't be a long meeting," Sara said.

"Girls and boy," Yfke corrected her with a cackle.

"Yes, that," Sara said, stepping up onto the small stage. As she turned to speak, she was interrupted by Heather, who began to clap her hands together, and before long the entire room followed along, and it was Sara's turn to blush.

"Okay, fuck you all, I'm just up here so you can see me, it doesn't mean anything," she said as the applause subsided. "I just spoke to Desdemona."

Instant silence fell.

"Yep. She's here. And she's watching us. So no more roof garden. No more outside. No more nothing. She could see me on the roof. And I have her assurance that there will be no man or men being delivered this week."

A rustling in the hallway turned into Liz skulking into the room and taking a seat in the rear row, never making eye contact with Sara.

"So, I told Desdemona that all the men were dead with the exception of Toma, Gabriel and Andrei. I also told her that you, Yukari, would take Surrender if she didn't back off."

"It worked?" Yukari asked with a smile. Sara had never seen her look so tired.

"Yes, it seems to have worked," Sara said. "So, this is where I need you all to pitch in, we need ideas. As far as we know, she has more men, she has all the Madrid sisters, also potentially some acolytes from other Locks, which is what now Heather? How many?"

"Around ten are unaccounted for. Doesn't mean they're here," Heather said. "I don't think they're as fight-trained as we are, but we can't be sure."

"Some of them are," Christine said.

"Obviously, this is all very problematic," Sara said. "She's frozen us in. We can't trust any delivery service, we can't open the doors for anyone. Silas, what's our blood stockpile like?"

"I prepared for this scenario," he said. "We have enough for almost a month, and that's without any rationing. I'll work with my people to continue a secure method that keeps the delivery guys safe."

"I think the safest thing we can do is take some of us off-site," Sara said. "April, Embla, that means you. Teddie, you too. Unless you'd be able to do five minutes against Fan or Ama, you'll get picked off. Liz, how confident do you feel?"

"I'll go, it's fine," she replied listlessly, not even looking up.

"So," Fran said, "then what? We just sit here like prisoners until she makes her next move?"

"You tell me, Frances," Sara said. "You're the hacker. Can't you just do that thing they do in movies where you put the face into some software and then you're like, I found her?"

"It's more complicated than that but maybe."

"Do you need to be in the city for it to work?"

Fran shrugged. "Not really, I guess. I haven't left the city in decades. Feels weird to think about."

"Oh my fuck," Heather said suddenly. "How could I be so bloody stupid."

"What?"

"The warehouse down in Red Hook," she said angrily. "The property I let Rosa take so that she got the confirmation. Desdemona has a bloody warehouse."

"Can I get the address?"

Heather nodded.

"Send it to Fan and Ama," Sara said. "I doubt she's still there but there might be some clues. If she's revealing that she's here, she's not anywhere that we could trace to her. But I was on the roof and she was watching me, so she's either rented or bought something in a building adjacent to us."

"Only two buildings are tall enough for that clear of a view," Heather said. "We can get cameras on them right now."

"Nope," Skye said, standing. "This is Desdemona, she did that to draw you off the scent of where she really is. She could have just talked her way in, called you, and left. She will want you to waste time and resources on another red herring."

"Then what do we do?" Imani said. "We need to follow leads, we need to find the bitch. If we sit here, she'll kill us."

"I just texted the address to Ama and Fan," Heather said. "So, in the first instance, we need to check that out."

"You all need to get out of this building immediately," Skye said. "There's no easier target than everybody in this building, unable to leave."

At that, everyone started talking, some yelling out, some speaking quietly to the person next to them. Sara locked eyes with Skye and shrugged. There was nothing to do but wait.

"Everybody shut the fuck up," Skye yelled, and silence landed like a thunderclap. Sara gave her an approving nod.

"I understand it's not easy, but it has to happen," she continued in her thick Australian accent. "She's got this place fully surveilled, every time any of us leaves, we could be walking into a trap."

"Do you know how many computers I need to keep our security running?" Fran's voice was desperate.

"You'd be amazed how much you can get done from a phone, Frannie mate," Skye smiled. "We can load your stuff into a truck in ten minutes. It's not forever, it's just for now. What are our options?"

"I have a place," Silas said, without hesitation. "West Village."

"Me too," Heather said, with obvious reluctance. "Upper East." Several heads turned in her direction but Heather ignored them, picking at imaginary lint on her skirt.

"Nope," Skye continued. "We need to travel light. First instance, we all leave when Chrissie and Lynds take the boys to the airport. Let's all spend a night at an airport hotel, two or three of us in one room. Tomorrow, we regroup, we can start doing short term rentals until the problem is eradicated."

"And of course," Yfke nodded, "this might be all a big fat nothing if Fan and Ama find her today."

Silas rose to his feet and walked up to the stage.

"Yukari," he said turning to face the room ."Is your lab at my upstate place still functional?" Yukari nodded but said nothing. "Then this is what I propose. We all move out as soon as we can. We take the bare minimum. Fran, are you backed up to a cloud?" Another nod. "I have a lot of tech up there in one of the barns, and we can order anything else you need overnight. But Skye is right. We need to move before she can get anything planned. Right now, Des knows we're all rattled, so she'll expect something tonight. You all leave with backpacks only. Christine and Lindsey, sorry to boot you out but you can take taxis and be gone and safe. Imani, you and Toma will travel with us, because I don't trust him alone. Everyone else, go to the subway, one stop down to 96th and then take a 2 up to the Bronx, on the way, find your nearest car rental place and go rent a car, in pairs. Text me once you're in your car and driving and I'll give you the address."

"Oh great," Liz sneered from the back row. "Now the man is in charge. And we're all okay with it."

"I'm okay with it," Crina said, her voice threatening. "And we need to get the hell out of here five minutes ago, so unless you've got a better idea."

"Yeah, I've got a better idea," Liz said. "I'm going with Lindsey. Fuck this place and fuck this shit."

The shock on Lindsey's face morphed into horror, but she remained quiet.

On the stage, Silas blew Liz a kiss.

"Bye bitch," he said effeminately. "Give my love to my motherland."

"Wait," Liz sputtered, "Aren't you going back to London?"

Lindsey shook her head. "Nope, you're coming to Bucharest."

"I've changed my mind," Liz said.

"Too late," Crina said. "Raise your hand if you support the transfer of Sister Elizabeth to the London Lock – or any Lock that will take her?"

All the New York sisters raised their hands.

"Romania is lovely this time of year," Crina said. "Now, I suggest you get packing. You're leaving in about an hour."

With a huff, Liz stormed out of the room.

"Oh no," Imani cackled. "That was the last time I'll see Liz storm out of a meeting."

"Fuck you, Imani," Liz called from the hallway.

"Thanks a ton, you lot," Lindsey said with a chuckle. "Now I have two brats to take care of."

"I heard that too you bitch," yelled Liz.

"Let's focus," Sara said, taking Silas's hand. "Pack enough to stay warm on the journey, not much more. Two bags of blood in your pack, just in case. Wear face masks and use separate exits. Heather and Fran, you're the last to leave, because we need you watching the cameras to make sure there's nobody around."

A strange silence settled on the room as everyone considered the haunting concept of the compound, empty for the first time in over two hundred years.

Chapter Nineteen

Almost a hundred years ago, when the Upper West Side was beginning to "cement up" as Teddie called it at the time, and the North Woods were crowded, Sara would take a taxi across the George Washington Bridge, to Englewood Cliffs. Sometimes, she'd pay the cabbie to wait, other times she'd offer a handsome reward if he would return several hours later. Then, she'd get lost in the forest, ridding herself of the malaise that she felt when civilization became too much. From the small, muddy parking lot at the side of the road, she would hike over boulders, down to the bank of the Hudson River, spending the day scrabbling in the earth, searching for nothing in particular, finding nature in the shape of little crabs, smooth stones or sunbleached shells as above her, oaks and maples provided a canopy so green it fed her soul.

When they left the city earlier that morning, frost in the air, Sara remembered those excursions with a twist of melancholy, as Silas turned onto the Palisades Parkway. The trees were bare, jagged black silhouettes against the gray unforgiving sky. In silence, she peered across the river, catching flashes of The Cloisters between the passing trees. In the back of the car, Imani and Toma shared her silence, and Sara was glad that Silas focused on the road ahead of him, did not turn on the stereo, letting their silence be a farewell to the city. She glanced at his hand, almost already healed, a band-aid now replacing the bandages. In the silence, Sara wondered when she would return, and also, what would she be returning to? Gradually, as they drove further north, the doubts receded and by the time they stopped in Kingston for pizza, a light snow began to fall, and her thoughts turned to the future.

The snow got heavier as they drove on, and by the time they arrived at Silas's property, the ground was a blinding white. After hours of near-silence, Silas opened up, telling them about the various buildings on the land, including a building that had once been the winter home of the chickens of the farm, informing them that he'd converted it into rooms and that would be where Imani and Toma would be staying, along with the Europeans. Entering via a locked gate at the end of a driveway Sara had not seen on her previous visit, the car bounced along a gravel road until they arrived at a large gray barn, yellow electric light emanating from the windows, snow swirling in the warm glow. After depositing their passengers in the care of Yfke and Skye, Silas drove back to the main road, and they circled the property for minutes before arriving at the long driveway that Sara recognized, but they turned left after the security gate, and in the failing light, Sara finally saw the lake, a frozen dark mirror surrounded by bare trees, the reflection of the stormy sky creating the illusion of a vortex drawing the heavens down into the earth

Now, with their luggage inside the warm Hobbit House, as Silas called the small home built into a hill, Sara sat beside a crackling fire in the fireplace, her fingers twirling absently in the waves of warmth, her melancholy proving difficult to dislodge. The last time she was in this home, her mind had been awash with the possibilities of a new life, free from Lock responsibilities and care. Hours later, that dream had been destroyed in an ugly night that Sara still could not recall without shuddering. She had died that night. Shit, she laughed to herself, how many times had she died since?

"Is it talking time yet?" Silas appeared beside her on the hearth, his fingers light on her shoulder.

"Sure, pull up a cushion," Sara said.

"Nah," Silas plopped down almost on top of her. "I'll share yours."

"Well, okay then," Sara mock grumbled, repositioning herself on the oversized pillow as Silas wrapped his arms around her waist and kissed her cheek.

"I know today was hard," Silas began, and she cut him off.

"No, fuck that," Sara said, before kissing him on the lips. With a mumbled agreement, Silas kissed her back, his arms holding her up, his palms flat against her spine, the heat of the fire on her cheek, and for a minute she considered letting it go on this course, but the moment needed something else. She broke the kiss.

"I meant I had something to say," she said, relieved to see happy expectation on his face instead of disappointment.

"Sure," he said with a lopsided grin. "Fire away."

"What if we just... you know... ran away?"

"We have a dozen pizzas to deliver to the main house in an hour," Silas said with comic urgency.

"Okay, after that."

"Where do you wanna go?"

"Don't know, don't care," Sara said.

"Are we taking Teddie?"

Sara nodded, her eyes locked on his.

"Can you tell me why? Like why now?"

Wriggling around to face him, Sara wrapped her arms around his waist, threading her fingers together, and they laid back, each secure in the arms of the other, their eyes never breaking contact.

"Because none of this matters," Sara said. "We're acting like this is world war three and at most, it's a minor skirmish that will burn itself out in fifty years. Desdemona is going to die, and the ridiculous hold that she's had over these women, it will dissipate. I just want to raise our sights and take in the big picture, you know, like everyone is saying. Let it all go, and just enjoy ourselves."

"I am listening," Silas said. "But why now?"

"Because the stakes are so high."

"That's the opposite of what you just said."

"It's not, from where I'm standing. Silas, she could have shot me this morning. She didn't, but she had me in her sights and she could have. And you know what I can't shake? I can't shake the what if of it all. What if you'd gone up to the roof? What if it was Teddie, going up to pick some rosemary? She wants to hurt me. Losing either of you would destroy me. And the whole drive, I've been thinking that we probably got very lucky, that she was probably sitting there with a rifle, ready to take you out."

"I thought of that too," he said.

"And you didn't say anything?"

"You have enough on your mind, my love."

"We all have the same amount of a lot on our minds," she said, kissing his nose. "Any suspicions that you have, please tell me, in case it's something I'm missing."

"Nothing is escaping you," Silas shook his head admiringly. "The way you pivoted today, the way you organized moving your entire Lock up here even though your heart was breaking."

"It was," Sara said quietly. "It felt like giving in."

"Giving in gets such a bad rep," Silas smiled. "I don't know why. It's usually the best option, at least when it's an emotional matter. Principles are when you don't give in. That's fine. But this whole thing? Clinging to a city because losing it to stupid old Desdemona is too hard to imagine? Nah. You'll get over it. We will all get over it. Also, we can go back as soon as she's gone."

"That's the thing," Sara said. "I don't want to go back. Today was the day that the spell broke, I don't know how else to say it. The enchantment that New York has had over me, almost since the day I arrived, it's gone. I mean, no shade," she paused, laughing, "it's still the greatest city in the world, but it's time for us to go our separate ways. I want to just throw a dart at a map and you and me and Teddie, we go see what it's like. Whether it's Copenhagen or Johannesburg or, I don't know, let's just go."

"So the whole world is our oyster?"

Sara nodded and then kissed him, taking her time.

"Silas, where have you always wanted to spend a lot of time?"

"By your side," he said.

Sara froze, and for a second it felt like her heart did too, and she stared into Silas's eyes, the firelight adding orange flecks. Hoping he'd add something, Sara remained silent as his arms pulled her closer until their chests were touching.

"Sorry not sorry," he said eventually. "Cheesy or not, it's the truth. I've wanted this for so long, with you, that I don't care where we are because you know what? It doesn't matter. Any new city will be magic with you, finding new places, new routines. Traveling light. Reuniting with the others whenever chance or desire dictates it. Fifty years flying by beside a river or a beach or a bustling market in the south of France, just dipping lightly into the fabric of a place and moving on before people notice us. As long as I get to share the world with you, the actual location isn't too important to me."

"Oh, okay, I was hoping you'd say Sydney," Sara joked. "I've always wanted to go to Sydney."

"Jerk," Silas smiled, kissing her. "Sure, we can go to Sydney. It's summer there now, it would be the exact opposite of this."

"And the exact opposite of Iceland and New York and London and Paris and Bucharest, all the places I've lived," she said. "Silas, imagine all that space, all that ocean."

"All those sharks and spiders," he added.

"Don't tell me big old you is afraid of eensy weensy spiders?"

"Two things," Silas said, his voice stern. "One: Phobia shaming is not cool, and two: Have you seen those things? They're not exactly teensy weensy or whatever your pejorative term for small was. They're fucking huge."

"And we don't even know if their venom would work against our virus."

"And I don't want to be the guinea pig that finds out."

"So when can we leave?"

Inhaling deeply, Silas squeezed his eyes shut.

"Do you want fantasy answer or honest real life answer?"

"Can't they be the same?"

"I wish but no," he said.

"I'll take the truth please."

"I can't just leave," he said. "Not right now. Soon, sure, but not like tomorrow. It just feels too... irresponsible?"

"But that's exactly what I'm talking about," Sara said. "If we all just ghost Desdemona, if we leave her just yelling into the void like an old woman with dementia, what will she do? She's toying with us because we are responding."

"Sure, but you're only taking Teddie with you, which would mean leaving strong, responsible people like Yukari and Fran to pick up the slack and I love them too much for that. She'd eat them for lunch. I can't do that to them."

Now it was Sara's turn to inhale deeply, as the familiar disappointment of responsibility crept into her fantasy, but she wasn't ready to give up just yet.

"Do you remember last time we were here, in this strange house that you built on a whim?"

He nodded. "Of course I do, those memories, that weekend, they are special to me for so many reasons."

"It was the end of our fantasy period," Sara said.

"Yep, it's like that weekend is dusted in fine gold, I don't know if it was the light or it's just my stupid heart embellishing the memories but it all seems innocent and perfect and..."

"Optimistic," Sara said. "You wore me down. You made me feel optimistic. Silas, you got me to finally decided to go Scholar and live in this little house."

"Wait, you actually decided to take me up on the offer?"

"Yeah, I thought about it that whole drive home, I just never got the chance to tell you."

Sara watched as his chin quivered slightly, but Silas corrected himself before the tears got him.

"I... uh... Sara, I've felt so guilty, this whole year, I was blaming myself for all the shit, I thought I made you move too fast, I threw too much at you right off the bat, and then, what happened happened, and you've just had such a hard time of it. I really never even suspected that you might have been ready to..."

"To move in on the second date?"

"To go scholar, here, with or without me, as I believe the original offer stood."

"Oh it was entirely with, I can assure you of that."

Silas's phone began to ring in the small kitchen.

"Ah shit," he spat. "That's Fan's ringtone."

Sara released her hands behind Silas and he lurched backward, dragging her with him until he released his arms from around her and caught his fall.

"You better get it," she said. "I've been trying not to think about them all day."

"I've been texting them," Silas said as he walked to the kitchen. "They were staked out but they saw nothing."

Sara heard Silas answer the phone from the other room, then watched as he walked back and sat beside her, Fan's voice crackling indecipherably from his phone.

"She's right here," he said. "Okay." Moving the phone from his ear, he put it on speaker.

"Hey Fan," Sara called out.

"No need to yell," said Ama with a laugh. "It's both of us."

"Hi Sara," Fan said. "How's life in Hobbit House?"

"Pretty great so far," Sara said. "How's the stakeout going?"

"We have a body count," Fan said proudly, and Sara's heart leapt.

"Desdemona?" she asked.

"No, sorry," Ama said. "We should have opened with that. I told you Fan."

"Well, if we'd killed Des I think we *would* have opened with it," Fan said. "But here's what we got. We killed three Madrid sisters, captured two and there were four men, so we knocked them out, vaccinated them and dropped them off at JFK with their passports and enough cash to get home and then some. We're back at the warehouse now. The Madrid girls ain't saying nothing so we don't have any intel for you, sorry."

"Sounds like you've done plenty," Silas said.

"i'm pissed," Ama said. "If Heather had remembered about this place earlier, we might have killed the queen."

"No blame game," Silas said. "She's been struggling since Edinburgh."

"We all have, Silas," said Fan tersely. "Those women were my friends too. We are at war."

Silas looked at Sara and rolled his eyes.

"Roger copy over," Silas said with a cheeky grin.

"Stop being a baby," Fan snapped. "We have a long night ahead of us. Not all of us get to cuddle by the fire with their honey and do nothing. Some of us have to dispose of three bodies, perform a brutal interrogation and then do a bunch of cyberhacking on the devices that we've found here."

"Why don't you call Fran?" Sara said.

"You weren't our first call," Fan said, still pissed. "She's waiting for us to unlock the computers now."

"Yes," giggled Ama. "I don't think Apple ever figured out how much easier fingerprints made it for murderers to unlock a computer."

"Of course, we haven't mentioned that to the two that are still alive," laughed Fan. "They think that we will be cutting their fingers off next time we see them."

"I have a pocket full of index fingers," Ama said. "So far I haven't found a computer or phone that they won't unlock."

"What are you going to do with the surviving sisters?" Silas's tone was serious.

"Oh relax Si," Fan said. "That's really up to them. If they want to go back to Madrid, well, that's a no, but if they want to go to Bucharest, I've talked to everyone there and they'll take them on and see if they can rehab them."

"Do you think they know where Desdemona is?" Sara's voice was taut.

"Finally" Fan crowed. "An intelligent question. The truth is, I don't think they do. They've been pretty forthcoming about the fact that she left with one of the men and three sisters earlier this morning. I guess they have a van that they travel in. Also, we did find out that Des never slept here, but nobody seems to know where she's actually been staying."

A shiver ran down Sara's spine at the thought of Desdemona actually living in an apartment near the compound, watching them scamper carelessly across the roof for weeks.

"I know what you're going to ask, Sara," Ama said. "And we're going to try to have Fran and Embla triangulate the phones that we got today, see if we can get a ping near the compound."

"Anyway," Fan said, cutting her off. "Any day that involves a drive to JFK is a bad day and I'm tired and we have a long night ahead of us, so we're going to go now."

"Please keep your phones on all night," Ama said. "We will call if and when we have any breakthroughs. We will be here, waiting, in case they return, but if they're not here by like three, we will get on with our cleanup date at the Compound furnace."

"Thank you," Sara said. "You guys have done an amazing job."

"I told you she wouldn't be pissed we killed em," Fan said.

"I'm right here," Sara said with a chuckle.

"I don't like being on the receiving end of your anger, Sara," Ama said.

"You're kidding, right?"

"She's not," Fan said. "She's fucking terrified of you. Honestly, I am too, a little bit."

"Anyways," Ama leapt in. "That's enough oversharing for one day. Keep your phones beside you. Talk soon. Love youse."

The line went dead.

"That's a lot to unpack," Silas said, turning to face Sara.

"So much to unpack."

"Okay, well I do have an unrelated question. We have all those pizzas to deliver. Would you like to do it on foot, or would you like to drive?"

Sara pondered the walk around the lake, the wide trail, probably less than half a mile, and a smile spread on her face.

"We're gonna walk it," she declared. "And dress warm. Lots and lots of layers."

"Yeah," Silas said, a curious expression on his face. "I mean, it's a snowstorm, why wouldn't I?"

"Oh, I wasn't talking about that," Sara smiled. "We're just going to need something to lay on on the way home when you fuck me in the middle of a snowstorm."

Silas's face screwed up in prudish disgust for a moment, then a hungry smile lit his orange eyes as he nodded slowly.

Chapter Twenty

The following morning, the pre-dawn darkness in the Hobbit house was rattled by the ringing of Sara's phone. The sound cut through Sara's dream like a knife, the tinny electronic sound bouncing off the walls. Silas bounced naked from the bed and dashed to the kitchen, Sara right behind him.

"It's Imani," he said as he answered, putting the phone on speaker.

"What's up?" he asked. "You've got us both on speaker."

"It's Toma," Imani said, her voice shaking. "He's gone."

"What do you mean gone?" Sara tried to keep her voice light.

"He's gone and he left a note. It just says that he's sorry but he had no choice."

"Did he hurt you?" Silas asked, while frantically gesturing for Sara to start getting dressed.

"No, he got up to pee, probably an hour ago, I heard him get up and go into the bathroom, but then I fell back asleep. I just woke up. The note was by the sink. I am so sorry, you guys I-"

"No time for that right now," Silas said, his voice now flat, military. "Lock all the doors. Don't turn on any lights. Close all the curtains."

"Silas I-"

"Imani, I just need you to hold tight for me, right now, I'll check the security cameras," Silas said, flicking at his phone. Sara stood beside him, watching as he located the camera pointing out from the front door of the barn, then rewound it until they saw Toma walking into the frame. "Yep, got him leaving. 4:42am. Hang on."

Silas flicked at his phone again, and the screen was replaced with an aerial view of the gate they'd driven through the day before. Silas rewound until a car pulled up, kept going as Toma exited it and walked backwards, reverse jumped the fence and exited the frame.

"He got into an SUV, a Porsche Cayenne, at 4:45am. They're gone."

"Fuck me," Imani said raspily. "Silas, I'm sorry."

"Don't be, Imani. We can play the blame game later. We don't have time. Right now, I need you to wake everyone and get them into the panic room."

"There's a panic room?"

"It's downstairs. Pull hard on the painting of the flowers beside the bathroom, it'll reveal the door handle behind it. Get everyone in there. Take a few bloodbags. Also take the cushions from the couch. Once it's open, push the painting back into place until it clicks, then get inside and pull it closed. Lock it. Turn on the monitors, you'll connect to the surveillance cameras."

"Got it."

"Don't leave the house, no matter what happens, until you hear from us."

"Yes, boss."

"Okay, Imani, thank you."

He hung up and spun to face Sara.

"Dress as warmly as you can," he said. "Fuck, I have all weather stuff at the main house but not here."

"We have good socks and shoes, and jackets," Sara said. "Is this an on-foot thing?"

"Could be," Silas said, holding the phone to his ear. "Teddie? Hi, it's me, how's everything there?"

Silas moved the phone from his ear and put the call to speaker.

"Morning," Teddie said groggily.

"Okay, we have a problem, I need you to pay attention and get moving."

"What's up?"

"Toma has taken off, and he left a note saying he's sorry but he had to do it. That's all we know. Right now, I need you to secure all the doors. I'm going to activate all the locks via remote. The cameras are all connected to the computer in the security room at the end of the downstairs hall, behind the kitchen. There are weapons in that room too. Get everyone in there. I'll text you the password for the computer. Lock the door from the inside."

"Got it," Teddie said, and Sara was proud of the steel in her voice. "Let me get everyone safe and I'll be back in touch."

"Yes. Once you're locked in that room, nothing can get in. Please message Fan and Ama, tell them that we assume that somehow Desdemona has tracked us here."

"Somehow? It has to be Toma."

"Yep," Silas said, anger finally arriving in his voice. "It has to be."

"Okay, gimme five I'll call you back."

And she was gone.

"I didn't check him thoroughly," Silas spat as he hauled on the heavy canvas jeans he'd worn on the drive north. "Sara, he fucking played us. I went through his bag but who fucking knows if the guy had an AirTag up his ass?"

"First time I'm thinking of that," Sara said. "But we don't have time for the blame game right now."

"You're right," he said, his voice calmer. "We need to figure it out though, so we can respond the right way. If it's just an AirTag or some sort of locator, it needs bluetooth."

"You sure have a lot of panic rooms," Sara said, pulling a second sweater out of her duffel bag and dragging it over the one she was already wearing.

"I had nothing to do with that one," Silas said, hurriedly dressing, layer upon layer. "That's what happens when you let Fan and Ama live here for a couple years after that stupid movie."

"What movie?"

"Panic Room with Jodie Foster, of course," Silas said. "Sorry, you're new to the eccentric lesbian aunts thing. They were obsessed with that movie."

Chuckling, Sara sat to lace her boots. A glance at her phone told her it was almost six.

"So what's the plan, my love?"

Silas was bent over, peering out the window by moving the curtains aside just a touch. "Visibility is terrible," he said. "It's really foggy, and it's still snowing lightly. Once everyone is in the panic rooms, they're safe. She can burn the houses down and they'll be fine. Imani and Toma were at the main house last night, so if they're tracking him they would have seen them go there and return. They don't know about this house. We are safe. We just need to figure out a strategy."

"Toma knows we didn't stay at the main house, so he'll tell her there are more houses on the land."

"Right, but there are... seven other houses."

"Unoccupied?"

Silas nodded. "Yes, but they are all lit by timers. A couple of them will be lit already. And once again, I have cameras on all the gates."

"What about perimeter fences?"

Silas shook his head. "No, just the gates and all the buildings."

"So, here's the question. What would Desdemona want the most?"

"To hurt you."

"Right. So if you're hard to find, she will go for Teddie."

"Likely."

"So let's head to the main house on foot," Sara said, and Silas nodded. In silence he went to the linen cupboard and pulled out two white sheets, flapping them in the air to unfold them, letting one drop and placing the other one over Sara, tying two ends below her chin.

"Camouflage," he said.

"I feel like Snow White," Sara said. "I'm also freaking out a lot and doing everything I can to keep my shit together."

"I hate this question," he said. "But can you shoot a gun?"

"I hate this answer," Sara replied. "Yes."

Without a word, Silas walked to the wood paneled wall in the bedroom and punched it with the side of his fist. A cupboard popped open with a click, the door blocking Sara's view of what was inside. Stepping back, Sara was shocked to see two pistols gripped in each of his hands. Setting them on the corner of the bed, he returned to the closet, bent and lifted a heavy bag that he set beside the guns on the bed.

"Two pistols each," he said, avoiding her eyes. "A knife sheathed on your right calf. I'll carry a rifle. We don't need two."

Lifting a heavy gray-silver gun from the bed, he held it in front of her, flicking at a switch.

"Safety off. Safety on. Keep the safety on til you need it."

"Always."

"Same with this one," he lifted a smaller black pistol. "Keep this one in your waistband, we will carry the others." He set the pistol on the bed beside her, then returned to the bag, handing her a thick-bladed eight inch knife in a black metal holster.

"Clip that to your left calf, inside," he said, before turning and withdrawing a larger sheathed blade for himself. In silence, he bent and belted it to his outer right calf. Sara followed suit.

Sara's phone rang. Teddie.

"We have visual!" Teddie spoke as soon as the call answered. "Three women, approaching on the driveway."

"That's so brazen," Silas said. "Teddie, stand tight. They cannot get into where you are."

"They're calling out, but we can't hear what they're saying. They're trying to lure us out."

Silas's phone rang, and he glanced at Sara before answering it.

"Silas, I think Toma is back," Imani said. "Two figures just jumped the fence."

"Got it," Silas said. "Do not leave that room."

"We won't. Skye and Yfke took off, it's just me and Fran here now," Imani said. "Silas, he stole my AirPods."

"That's weird," Silas said. "Stay secure. Don't leave. I'll call as soon as it's safe."

"Thank you." He ended the call.

"Why wouldn't they wait until tonight?" Sara asked.

"They can't," Silas said. "They know we know they're coming."

"That's why he left the note," Sara said. "He wasn't supposed to do that. He's given us a head start."

"Maybe," Silas said. "My question in, do we wait them out? This building isn't on any county property map. Right now, Desdemona is probably watching the other houses."

"How? Via drone?"

Silas nodded. "Maybe but it's so foggy, she'd have to fly close and you'd hear it. Either way, this is a numbers game and she has what? At most five other people?"

Sara snatched up her phone and called Fan, who of course answered immediately.

"I heard you have company," Fan said.

"We do," Sara said. "But I need you to get an answer out of one of those Madrid bitches literally five minutes ago. We need a confirm on numbers, you said Des plus three women, and a man, now two men including Toma. We need to know weapons, intel, anything."

"Why are you talking to me and not killing them?"

"Because we are half a mile from them, and we don't want to walk into a trap, which is clearly what this is."

"Perfect answer," Fan said. "Hey Ama, we got some torturing to do."

The line went dead.

"They're so extra," Silas said.

"Right now, I'll take it," Sara said, reaching across and resting her hand on top of his.

"I considered going to Desdemona, myself, but now, I know it wouldn't be enough," Silas confessed, and Sara spun, anger on her face. "Relax, after my trip to Bucharest, I knew I'd have to tell you and you'd stop me. Also, I now know that it wouldn't stop her. She'd kill me and keep on coming for you."

Sara's pulse echoed in her ears in the silence that followed. Silas pulled his hand away from hers and began flicking at his phone, which he turned to show her. On the screen, three figures skirted the rear of the lake house, guns drawn. Despite Silas's assurances of security, Sara felt sick to her stomach that Teddie was inside, and worse, she was being hunted by sisters. At least she had Heather and Crina with her. Turning the phone back to himself, Silas clicked for a moment before turning the phone back to her. A pair of male black-clad figures were kicking in doors on the upper floor of the barn building, and looking behind every wardrobe. Sara watched avidly until they finished exploring the final room a the far end from the camera, emerging, shrugging their shoulders and returning to the staircase. Silas switched cameras to the lower level only to catch them leaving by the front door. Another switch and they saw them outside, walking right, back to where they'd left the car.

"We need to get moving," Sara said. "They're going to think that everyone is inside that house, and we don't know if they have grenades."

"We need that info from Ama and Fan," Silas said, his voice pained. "We won't be any use to them if we walk into an ambush."

"Well we can't just sit and watch," Sara pushed herself up to standing, the walls suddenly feeling like they were closing in around her. "If you want to sit here and wait for permission from your aunties, go right ahead but I have to help Teddie."

With a simple nod, Silas stood, walked to her and wrapped her in a hug.

"Okay, we will head out," he said quietly. "Just give me two minutes. Imani can be our eyes via the cams, I'll have her text us any updates."

"Thanks," Sara said, unwrapping herself from his embrace and stalking to the kitchen on legs that felt rubbery and unreliable. Taking a pitcher of coffee from he fridge, she poured two mugs full, taking one to Silas in the other room, then returning to the darkened kitchen and running one wrist and then the other under warm water from the faucet while she used her free hand to bring the coffee to her lips. The warm water centered her, as she fought to regulate her racing mind, deliberately slowing her breathing. She let go of anger at Desdemona, and fear for Teddie. Neither of these would help her now.

She closed her eyes and focused. She needed to think like Desdemona, or right now, she needed to *be* Desdemona. She came up short. The Desdemona that she knew, the Desdemona that she could predict, was an ancient version, a model superseded by jealousy and hate and desperation. This Desdemona was ruthless and brutal and cruel in a way she could hardly imagine.

"We can go," Silas appeared beside her at the sink. "Thanks for the coffee. I heard from Fan. The estimate is six including Des. That's the number that they got from the sisters they have in Brooklyn. Des. One man. Three sisters. Toma. No explosives that they know of."

"Thank you," Sara said. "We know where they all are, right?."

"We don't have a location on Des. The men got into the Porsche and drove away again, I'd assume they'll go to the main house," Silas said, and Sara's anxiety ratcheted up several levels. "Don't worry about Teddie, Embla is one hell of a bare knuckle fighter."

Not much use against a gun, Sara thought to herself.

"So," Silas moved to the door. "We will move around the lake, the way we went last time you were here. Keep your sheet covering as much of you as you can, the light is terrible, it's almost a white out, they won't be able to see us. There's a couple of downed trees we can hide behind that would put us in shot range of the house."

"I remember," Sara said. "I climbed one when I had my freakout."

"Yes, that exact one," Silas said. "It's gonna get chilly, but we will be fine. I'll be behind you, I think my rear guard training is probably a bit better than yours."

"Probably," Sara said, shutting off the water and turning to face him. "I love you, Silas. I love you with all I am, and it's terrifying."

Surprised, Silas paused, staring into her eyes, then he wrapped her in his arms and squeezed.

"You're my world," he said. "Let's just get through this little hiccup and we will be on a beach in Sydney in a month."

Sara burrowed her face into his down jacket.

"Deal," Sara said, then pointed at the door. "Let's go."

"Stealthy as a fox," he said with a smile.

"I should have worn my fur," Sara joked and Silas chuckled.

"Next time we're in Reykjavik you can wear it someplace fancy," he said, taking her hand, picked up his gun with the other hand and led her to the door. As it opened, all sound died around them, absorbed by the falling snow, flakes so large that Sara could see their intricate cross-stitch patterns briefly as they fluttered past her eyes. Silas pushed her forward, then fell in behind her, as she followed the cobblestones, visible as irregular lumps in the snow, down to the slushy path around the lake. They continued without a word, Sara focusing on the comforting sound of Silas's breathing, until they rounded a corner and she could finally see across the lake, to the dock in front of the house, and behind it, the house itself, its shingled roof now white with snow. On any other day, it could be a postcard, but today, it was giving horror movie.

Sudden movement caught her eye, and Sara saw three figures appear on the dock, moving warily, signaling to each other as they moved along the windows, looking for a way into the building. Silas tapped her on the shoulder, then bounded past her as the trail curved, leading her to the fallen tree that she had climbed the last time she was here. Silas raised a clenched fist, then stopped.

"We have a perfect viewpoint from here," he said.

"Are we going to shoot them?"

"I'd prefer not to," he said. "Let's just see what happens. The only person I plan to shoot is Desdemona. Here, I'll give you a leg up, keep low."

Bending, he made a saddle with his hands and she stepped into it with her muddy boot. Silas lifted her onto the rough trunk, her view blocked by some trees. Sara crawled along the tree several feet, until she could see the house again, relaxing when she felt Silas pull up behind her. On the dock, one figure pulled a phone from her pocket, tapping at it angrily, then staring at it, waiting for a response. Suddenly, three figures came tearing around from the side of the house, and Sara instantly identified one as Crina solely from the way she moved, startling the pair on the dock. In a blink, Crina felled one interloper with a single punch, while the other two focused on the remaining pair, who fell into defense positions that did not defend them. Both were grabbed from behind, their arms snapped upwards and back. Sara watched their mouths open in screams of pain that were swallowed by the falling snow.

"Good job, mom," Silas said behind her, and they watched as Crina wrapped the other woman in a headlock, deftly avoiding her kicking legs until they slowed and stopped. Yfke, her blonde hair bright against her black clothing, removed a loop of rope from her jacket and bound the woman's legs from ankle to thigh in a quick string of knots, and Crina stepped back. The woman fell to the deck in an awkward collapse, legs folding, then head first forward before tumbling onto her side. More women appeared on the deck, and Sara easily spotted Teddie, standing beside Skye.

"Teddie, no," Sara whispered.

"Those women never do as they're told," Silas replied.

"No," said a voice behind them. "They never do."

Sara froze.

It was Desdemona.

Chapter Twenty-One

"But you'll do as you're told," Desdemona cooed malevolently. "You're going to do exactly as I tell you. Starting with, drop those little guns, right now. or the last thing you'll feel is one bullet passing through both of you."

"Do it," Silas whispered, and Sara opened her palm, releasing the pistol, hearing it clatter along wood before it splashed into the lake. She felt Silas move his arm, then heard more clattering and another splash.

"What else you packing?"

Neither of them said anything.

"Unless you want me to strip you naked and search you, I'd answer."

"We each have a gun in our waistband," Sara said. "And a knife on our leg."

"I have a rifle," Silas added.

"Get it all," Desdemona commanded, and Sara heard footsteps, then boots scratching on bark. Behind her, Silas's body jerked violently several times, then someone tugged at her sheet covering. She felt hands unbuckling the knife sheath, then a frigid hand slid against her lower back and pulled out the gun.

"Are you sure that's all you have?"

"Yes, Des," Sara called out.

"Get their ankles," Desdemona said. "And, don't move or I'll shoot."

Sara listened to the metallic grinding sound of Silas having his legs cuffed, then she felt pressure around the top of her left boot, then her right.

"Bring them down," Desdemona said. "Him first."

Sara heard Silas thump to the ground, then hands gripped her legs and she slid painfully backwards, the rough bark scraping at her chin and cheek before the support of the tree vanished and she fell briefly, steeling her legs for impact, fighting to stay upright when she landed.

"Turn, slowly," Desdemona said, and Sara obliged, blinking in disbelief when she finally saw Desdemona, her goading face floating in the cloud of a white fur coat, her head crowned by a matching white fur cap. The floor-length coat was almost identical to her own, presently stuffed into a box somewhere in Iceland. She briefly made eye contact with Silas, mouthing "WTF?" He made a comical face, and Sara barely suppressed a laugh. Desdemona's arms, outstretched, held a gun so impractically large that Sara didn't think it could be real.

Only after she'd taken in Desdemona's bizarre appearance was Sara able to focus on her face. Her hair, sharp curls below the hat, was an artificial blue-black, which was jarring enough, but the lines at the corners of her mouth and eyes were deep and cruel, and the skin of her face sagged with the weight of age.

"Hi Des," she said. "Nice camouflage."

"Gracias," Des said, wrinkling her nose. "Bit better than, what is that? A bedsheet?"

"Desperate measures and all that," Sara said. "I hope you bought your copycat fur on Depop."

Desdemona sneered, her new wrinkles deepening noticeably.

"I owned this before you bought yours," she said petulantly. "You copied me, sister."

Sara turned to see the two men helping Silas to his feet. Despite their face coverings, she could tell that one of them was Toma, and he was taking care to not hurt Silas as he lifted him to standing. Turning back to Desdemona, Sara noticed that she seemed shaky, the gun wavering in her hands, her finger definitely exerting pressure on the trigger. Sara decided to play nice, because that would only kill her figuratively.

"I'm sorry," she said. "It looks great on you. And I'm sorry, in general. I hate this, I hate how things are. Des?"

"Put the jackets on them," Desdemona said, ignoring her. The men dropped the backpacks they were wearing. In silence, they pulled out a tangle of gray canvas, belts and buckles. It wasn't until they stood upright that Sara realized that each man was holding a straightjacket. Her stomach sank.

Desdemona was going to execute them.

"Arms out," Desdemona said, pointing the barrel of the gun at Silas, then Sara. "Don't give me an excuse to pull the trigger."

Obediently, they raised their arms, and the men slid the long sleeves onto them before buckling the jackets in back. Then, they painfully pulled the arms, crossing them in front of their stomachs, jerking Sara violently from side to side as more straps were buckled.

"Now the cuffs and we are good," Desdemona said.

The men took heavy silver wrist cuffs from a backpack. Sara felt their weight immediately as one end was locked around her left wrist, then the hasp ground around her right wrist, the chain linking the cuffs tight against her back.

She stole another look at Silas. He was glaring at Desdemona with a hateful intensity that she had never seen. His defiant bravery tugged at her heart.

"Do me a favor, *por favor*," Desdemona said. "Try and wriggle out of your cuffs. We have chains back in the car but I think this is sufficient."

Angrily Sara pulled and flexed her shoulders and arms against the restraint but the straightjacket only tightened with each movement, and she could not get any leverage against the cuffs. Her only way out would be to tear off her hands, but the jacket didn't even give her enough strength for that.

"I can't escape, and you have a gun," Sara said. "Even if we got our arms out, we'd just fall over."

"You have your mother's eyes," Desdemona let the gun drop to her side and stepped closer to Silas, inspecting him hungrily. Pulling up just inches from his chest, Desdemona lifted the barrel of the gun to move a lock of curly hair away from Silas's eyes. He didn't flinch. "Sara, wasn't it weird falling for someone who looks so much like the person you call mother?"

"This conversation would have been so much more pleasant beside a fireplace," Sara said. "If you're going to kill us, why didn't you just shoot us?"

"Who said anything about killing?" Desdemona took another step closer to Silas. "You know what? It's not just the eyes. You're familiar to me. Tell me, *hermano*, have we met before?"

"Yes," Silas said. "I met you in Cadíz, when we first arrived in Spain, before you were made."

"Did we speak?"

"Yes, we spoke, my Spanish wasn't good."

"No, I mean more recently."

"I have seen you, but I don't know if you've seen me."

"So you are one of the watchers, the rumors are true."

"No, I am alone, there are no more."

"I don't believe you."

"I don't care."

"You will."

Stepping back, Desdemona turned to face Sara.

"Welcome to the beginning of your end."

"Please, Desdemona," Sara's voice was even. "If you're going to kill us, just do it."

"I'm not going to kill you," Desdemona said. "That would be too... kind. I'm going to destroy your whole world."

"That's better than *the* whole world," Silas said.

"If you say so," Desdemona said bitterly. "I wasted too much time on destroying you, Sara. Sending women to all the Locks, making your stupid lives shittier. Just so you could be the queen of New York. It's all gone now. What else do you have to defend?"

"Absolutely nothing, Des," Sara said. "Our time as Cursed women is ending. The world is too vigilant. And you? You're dying, I can see it. Look at you. Was it terrifying, getting wrinkles? When I died, I wasn't scared."

"I fear nothing," Desdemona said. "I just refuse to be beaten by you. That's why I'm going to burn the whole thing down."

"There's nothing left to burn," Sara said. "What do we have? A bunch of money? Some old buildings? We are nothing, Desdemona, nothing. We should have ended with the men, five centuries ago. What exactly are you threatening?"

A bitter smile lifted Desdemona's cheeks but didn't touch her dark eyes. "I'm not just talking about us, I'm talking about it all."

"You'll need to be a bit more specific," Sara needled her.

"I despise the whole world," Desdemona said. "The world has become a disgusting place. It's shallow, angry and ignorant. It's time to see what would happen if our secret went public."

Sara froze.

"We all know what would happen," Sara whispered. "Men will happen. The greed of men, the weakness of men. The one thing that I always thought you and I were united against."

"Until this one came along," Desdemona kicked her foot into the mud, sending a dirty spray over Silas's pants, "A man knows our secret, which means the world is about to end. And instead of killing him. you welcome him. So, this means that the doomsday clock is already ticking. We've always known that a man would destroy our lives if we let it happen."

"Can't you see your own hypocrisy?" Sara's voice strained. "You've murdered how many people now? Broken how many rules? Infected how many innocent people? This man here has never broken a rule. All generalizations are dangerous, Desdemona. There are always exceptions."

"Spare me the sermon," Desdemona said, before turning to the two men standing behind her on the path. "Have you had any contact with the others?"

They both shook their heads and Sara squinted through the snow, trying to see their eyes, the only part of their face visible in a narrow slit in their balaclavas.

"Toma?" she called out, and they both jerked their heads up.

"I am not Toma," said the one on the left.

"No, the other one is my wonderful spy," Desdemona said, jerking her thumb at the other one, who dropped his head.

"We were good to you, Toma," Silas called out.

"You were good to *me*," Desdemona said. "You welcomed an infected man, my Trojan horse."

"We do not have much time, miss," said the man who wasn't Toma. "Nobody is answering, and people will come searching for these two."

Theatrically, Desdemona whirled around, the silver gun limp in her hand, the hem of her white fur now spattered with mud.

"You're right," she said. "I'll cut to the chase. I have a little present for you."

Sara stretched against the restraints, testing their limits, but there was nowhere she could get any sort of muscular momentum. She was trapped.

"Even if you managed to escape, I'd shoot you like a dog," Desdemona said. "In fact, it's kind of hard not to, but that would be a mercy you don't deserve."

"Can you get on with it then," Sara snapped. "It's fucking freezing."

Without warning, Desdemona spun, raising her free hand and smashing it into Silas's jaw, throwing him back against the fallen tree. Off balance, he slammed to the ground. Handing her gun to one of the men, Desdemona strode over to where Silas was twisting face down in the muddy snow. Sara's heart pounded in her chest and she fought to control the adrenaline freakout that definitely would not work out in her favor.

On the ground, Silas writhed onto his back, blood scent from his split lip filling the frozen air. Desdemona bent and grabbed a handful of his hair, lifting him off the ground with one hand as he groaned in agony. She hauled off, smashing a brutal blow to the other side of his face, releasing his hair at the moment of impact. The meaty recoil of the punch melded with the splash as he collapsed to the muddy ground, his eyes closed, his legs bent beneath him.

"You know what I missed most about the end of the Purge? When we hunted down the last of the Cursed men?" Desdemona said to Sara as she wiped her bloody fist across the white fur of her coat, leaving a disgusting scarlet smear. "I miss torturing the men, don't you?"

Sara couldn't take her eyes off Silas.

"I never tortured anyone," she said.

"The rest of us did," Desdemona hissed. "Ama. Fan...." she paused and turned to Silas. "Crina, your perfect mother, she delighted in it. And I won't lie. It was fun. And I'll tell you something else. I knew that what we were doing made us no better than them. We did to them what they'd done to others, yes, but tell me, do you still believe women are not as brutal as men? Because..."

Desdemona kicked Silas in the stomach with all her might, an explosion of blood and spittle spraying from his mouth, scarlet splattering her coat.

"...because we are." Desdemona whipped her leg back and kicked Silas again, this time in the side. Slowly, Desdemona kneeled on his chest, pressed a hand over his mouth and pinched his nose with her other hand.

"NO!" Sara screamed. "Stop. Please, Desdemona, stop."

"Relax, mija" Desdemona said sweetly, not at all perturbed by Silas thrashing about beneath her. "I'm just putting baby to sleep."'

Bile rose in Sara's throat and she swallowed it down, fear gnawing at her heart, her pulse racing noisily in her eardrums. If she let her adrenaline take her, she would tear her hands from her wrists, but that felt better than doing nothing. Her body began to tremble, electricity popping inside her muscles. She welcomed it.

Silas fell limp, and Desdemona pushed herself up from his still body. His battered face lolled to one side, and Sara saw that his top lip was completely torn open, white teeth showing through the gap. His cheek was beginning to swell.

"There, there, brother," Desdemona cooed, bending and wiping the blood from his face with the sleeve of her fur coat. "We need to clean you up for your little surprise."

Sara's heart sank and she willed herself to start fighting, to start pulling against the cuffs but something, the horror, her sadness, was derailing her entire nervous system. She had never felt this desolately sad. She felt a tendon pop in her shoulder but nothing more. Her wrestling slowed and she raised her face to meet Desdemona's gaze.

"Please, Des, we can stop all of this," she said, her voice broken. "What's done is done but we can save what's left and make a new future."

"Oh so now you're bargaining," Desdemona said. "I already made this offer. You turned it down."

She turned to the men.

"Masks off," she commanded, and they removed their hats and pulled up their balaclavas and Sara blinked.

"Toma?" she said to the first one.

"No, I am Rad," the man, the spitting image of Toma said.

The other man removed his balaclava.

"I am Toma," he said. "He is my twin."

"Remember what I told you back in Spain?" Desdemona cackled at Sara. "Never trust a twin. I told you we should have put it in the rules."

"I am sorry," Toma said, looking directly into Sara's eyes. He raised a finger to his ear, and tapped it twice. Desdemona spun to face him.

"Shut your filthy mouth," she yelled. "You're going to regret that."

"Stop killing innocent people," Sara screamed at her, and Des turned slowly back to face her.

"You're right, let me get back to killing those who deserve it."

"Knife," she said to the twins. Rad pulled Silas's knife from a backpack. Removing it from its sheath, he handed it to her.

"*Mulțumesc!*" Desdemona thanked them in Romanian, walking back to where Silas lay prone, snow gathering on his long eyelashes. She passed the knife from one had to another, its blade shining cold silver fire in the gray morning light. The horror inside Sara grew so overwhelming that she felt she might black out.

"Please, Desdemona, no," she whispered desperately.

"You're three hundred years too late to ask for favors," Desdemona said, raising the knife and bringing it down across her own wrist. A violent jet of red blood arced through the air, splashing off the tree trunk. Slowly, Desdemona flicked the fur coat out behind her and crouched beside Silas. Even though he was unconscious, as soon as Silas smelled the blood, he began to twitch, his eyes darting around beneath his eyelids, spine arching, heels digging into the mud. With inexorable slowness, Desdemona brought her wrist to within an inch of his mouth, and as the first drops of blood hit his tongue, Silas's head snapped up, his lips clamping onto the wound, his cheeks hollowing with the power of his suction.

"Whoa," Desdemona said, trying to pull her arm back. "He's a hungry one."

Silas made disgusting slurping sounds as blood foamed and bubbled around the edges of his mouth. With her other hand, Desdemona brought the knife to the side of Silas's face and she drew it three times across his cheek, Silas so lost in feeding that he didn't even notice. Desdemona tossed the knife back towards Toma and Rad, where it landed in the mud.

Placing her free hand on Silas's forehead, Desdemona yanked her wounded arm free of his mouth. Rising slowly, she turned to the twins.

"Get me the bandage," she said quietly. "We need to leave."

On the ground, Silas's tongue darted in and out of his mouth, searching for any more blood, and a sickening animal moan rose from his throat. Slowly Desdemona pulled herself up standing, her white coat now saturated with blood and smeared with mud, satisfaction on her face. After a quick glance at Sara, she pointed her wrist at Silas and sprayed blood all over his face. Then, with a wink, she bent and rubbed it into the gashes left by his own knife.

"So that's my gift to you, sister dear. Now you get to watch the love of your life die slowly. He will be as immune as I am."

Sara couldn't speak. Her world was turning black. It felt like her heart was collapsing inside her chest, agony unlike anything she'd ever known.

"If you don't freeze to death, and this is the kick in the ass that Yukari needs, then call me."

Desdemona turned to the twins.

"Get me out of here, now," she barked. They threw the backpacks over one arm each, and then Desdemona ran straight into the woods with them behind her, until they vanished behind some fir trees. Collapsing to the ground beside Silas's lifeless body, Sara kept her eyes open as long as she could, her world nothing but Silas until the darkness claimed her.

Chapter Twenty-Two

Flashing images. Weightlessness. Rising. Dropping. Screaming. Being carried. Being stripped. A scalding shower that might have been cold water and still too hot. Darkness. Yellow light. Screaming for him. Where was he? Why can't I see him? Flailing. Hitting something or someone. Hands. Always hands. Helping holding restraining, never soothing. A cold washcloth moving gently across her forehead. Light, somewhere distant, she needed to get to it. In her chest, Sara's heart accelerated, each thump a painful drum beat. Writhing, she still felt restraints holding her.

"Sara," said a voice that she recognized as Embla's after a slight delay. "Sara, you're safe. You're safe. No need to panic. Silas is safe. You're safe. There is no threat, you're in bed in the main house."

"My arms," Sara croaked. "I can't move them."

"We had to restrain you," Embla said. "You came out swinging. That's why I need you to breathe."

She felt hands grip her own, gently, their warmth reassuring her.

"Breathe with me," Embla said, inhaling deeply. Sara followed suit, exhaling along with her.

"Where is Silas?" Sara asked between breaths.

"He's downstairs," Embla said. "He needed some stitches so we have him doped up."

"I need to see him," Sara tried to sit forward, only to discover a strong band of something across her chest, restraining her completely.

"Yep," Embla said. "Now that you're awake, that's the plan. We just need to make sure you're not going to spike again."

Sara's eyes felt like they were gummed closed, so she lifted her eyebrows. One eye and then the other popped open, revealing Embla with one eye swollen almost shut, the yellow remains of a decent bruise beneath it.

"Did I do that?"

"Yeah," Embla chuckled. "Quite a right hook you got there."

"I'm disgusted with myself," Sara said. "I'm sorry."

"Don't be," Embla's voice went quiet. "I'm sorry we took so long to find you."

"How long have I been out?"

"An hourish? Maybe more?"

"Can you untie me?"

"Yeah," Embla released her hands and untied the knots in the canvas sheet that held her to the bed. Feeling the pressure release, Sara sat up too quickly and her vision swam.

"What the fuck is wrong with me?"

"We had to sedate you a little, m'dear," Embla popped back up beside her. "You're gonna be spacey for the next little while. I'll help you get downstairs. After we get you dressed."

It was only then that Sara realized she was naked and all her clothing, what little she had packed, was back in the hobbit house.

"Were my clothes wrecked?"

"Not so much wrecked as just muddy and bloody," Embla said. "You're going to be modeling the latest in April Veronica wear."

Turning, Embla lifted a pile of folded clothing from a chair in the corner of the room, and Sara swung her legs off the bed. With a mother's tenderness, Embla slipped Sara's feet through a pair of soft gray sweatpants, pulling them up to her knees, then lifting her to standing and pulling them the rest of the way up.

"Arms up," Embla said, and Sara complied, enjoying the feel of the equally soft jersey sweater that fell down over her body with a comforting warmth. Once her head popped through the neckhole, she found herself staring into Embla's eyes, filled with tears.

"Sara," Embla said. "I love you so much, I'm sorry we weren't there for you."

"Nothing to apologize for," Sara said, leaning her head against Embla's chest. "Do we know if Silas is... did she... did it work, what she did?"

"Yukari says we won't know for a while," Embla said softly. "But she says that it's likely that it will be effective."

All the air in Sara's lungs evaporated and she couldn't remember how to inflate them again. Her whole body began to shake, and from a million miles away, she felt Embla's arms encircle her and begin to squeeze, until her breathing started again.

"I'm sorry, I should have lied," Embla said. "You know I'm not very good at lying. But what I am good at is getting through things. And Sara, no matter what happens we will get through it."

They held hands in silence for a moment.

"I'm afraid I have a bit more bad news," Embla continued. "The men grabbed Imani and Fran while we were searching for you. They've taken them."

Sara froze, nausea constricting her throat.

"Are they alive?"

"We don't know," Embla said eventually. "We just don't know."

"Can you help me downstairs please?"

"Of course."

Strong arms supported her first faltering steps, motor skills taking a backseat to the panic that was racing through her system like a rat trapped in a burning house.

"I'm just gonna carry you," Embla said, and suddenly she was scooped up and moving, bouncing as they descended, step by step, to the living room.

"Here she is," Silas's voice floated across the room. "My queen."

Sara wriggled herself free from Embla's arms, turning to see Silas on the couch, bandages covering his left cheek and stitches extending up from the left side of his lip. His right eye was swollen shut, much darker than Embla's. Extending her arms rigidly, Sara took tottering steps to him, barely noticing Teddie and Yukari getting out of her way, her eyes locked on Silas's one open eye, its chocolate pupil flecked with the brightest orange shards she'd ever seen.

"Can I hug you?" Sara asked, and Silas shook his head slightly.

"Probably a bit tricky right now," he said. "Just come sit here," he patted the couch cushion beside his hip, and extended his arms, wincing at the movement.

Taking his hands in hers, Sara sat beside him, her eyes taking in the damage that Desdemona had done to her man, both the visible, on his face, the stitches, the black eye, probably more stitches beneath the bandages, and cracked ribs beneath the blanket. She hoped that was all there was. She rubbed a thumb over the indent in his hand, left by the arrow blade, now almost healed. Hopefully his face would prove as resilient.

"I'm so happy to see you," he said, his speech fuzzy, "but smiling hurts like a motherfucker, so if it's okay can you just be a little less delightful?"

"That's pretty easy right now," Sara said. "Silas, I'm so glad you're alive."

"Me too," he said. "And I'm even gladder than she didn't hurt you."

Sara heard footsteps behind her then felt a kiss on her hair.

"It's me, April Veronica."

"Hey my love," Sara said, not taking her eyes off Silas.

"We have so many guardian angels," Silas said, winking at April Veronica with his good eye.

"Not enough, apparently," Sara said, as she began to cry. She felt like her body contained nothing but sadness, deeper than the universe. She sat frozen, while tears poured from her eyes, too broken to move.

"Could you guys give us a minute?" Silas asked, and Sara heard shuffling as the room's other occupants all went elsewhere and suddenly the room was empty, except for her and Silas and her sadness.

"I'm sorry," she managed through the tears. "I can't stop."

"You don't have to," Silas whispered. "We had a rough morning."

"A rough morning?" Sara chuckled through the tears. "That's all it was?"

"It's all I'm going to let it be," Silas let go of one of her hands, and she felt his rough fingers wipe tears from her cheeks. "I'm not going to let Desdemona take my hope."

"What if she's stolen mine?"

"Nope," Silas's voice grew emphatic. "She can't touch us. Sara, in your darkest days, you fought for hope, remember? I was there. No matter how grim it got, you always looked for a tendril of hope, something to pull you out of the darkness. She could have killed us both dead, right there, in that stinking, freezing mud. Our story could have ended. And it didn't. So, I'm choosing gratitude, for this moment, for the million moments to come, because we still have them. You are thinking that Desdemona won, but I'm thinking that she made a grave mistake. She let us live. She gave us more time."

Sara felt her emotions even out slightly, and she blinked away the last of her tears and gazed into Silas's eye, seeing honest happiness there.

"When I was blacking out," Silas whispered, "I was convinced that it was the end for me, and I couldn't help you and I couldn't save you and the world was going dark and I thought I was dying, hopelessly. When I woke up, and you were there, breathing but unconscious, Sara, I've never felt such joy. I started hooting and hollering like an idiot and that's how the they found us."

"I couldn't save you."

"There's not much anyone can do at gunpoint," Silas said. "She's a fucking monster, that one. But, and Sara, I really can't stop thinking about it, she had that gun pointed at you most of the time, it was a Magnum, one slip, you would have been gone. And she's so fucking erratic, I just kept on waiting for her to snap and blow you away, but it didn't happen. We're alive. It's enough silver lining for me."

"I wanted forever with you," Sara said. "What if she took that away from us?"

"Time doesn't matter," Silas said, taking her hand again. "Being together does. The rest of it, it's already written, we just get to make the most of what we have, the time we have together, I'm not going to sit here and cry over something that we don't understand. I want a million days with you, but I'll take one more day after what we just went through. Sara, now I understand why you were so dark in Iceland, you went to your death, I just went to mine, it's fucking deep and terrifying but now that I'm on the other side, and I'm holding you and you're completely fine, then all my needs are met."

"Going to your own death sure does fuck you up, huh?"

"Damn straight," Silas said, almost smiling and wincing immediately. "Can you please be less charming and funny? Laughing hurts."

"Sorry," Sara said with a smile. "I'm sure that uncontrollable tears are just a breath away, if you'd prefer."

"Is there a happy medium?"

"I'll try to find it," Sara pulled his hands to her lips, kissing his fingertips and the backs of both hands, inhaling his salty musk. "Do they know where Desdemona is?"

Silas shook his head. "She took off in her car. Mom, Yfke, Skye and Heather are out patrolling the perimeter in cars. They lost their tire tracks in a residential neighborhood not too far away but it's not likely she'll hole up too close to us."

"Did anyone try calling her?"

Silas nodded. "Only on Signal or via chats. We don't have the number she's using. She's not answering, of course."

"I just can't get over how insane she looked," Sara said. "Yes, she looked older, but her eyes were vacant, haunted, and somehow, crazy, like actually insane."

"Yeah, I thought that too," Silas said. "And the coat, she was wearing your coat. She's your stalker, you've driven her crazy for so long, it was terrifying to see her so fixated on you. Not to go on and on about it, but I'm still surprised that she didn't just blow us both away. It tells me that she's lost sight on her long game."

"She doesn't have a long game any more," Sara said. "She's scorched earth or nothing at this point. And what she... this thing she's possibly done to you... I mean, how was Crina when you told her."

"You don't want to know," Silas looked away finally. "I thought we were going to have to sedate her, but she's good, she got herself under control, then grabbed the elders and left. Search party or bust, at least she's focused on something, because I saw her heart break, Sara."

"I know the feeling," Sara said, and the tears returned.

"Nope," Silas repeated himself. "We are not giving that to her. We're not doing sadness. We're not giving that insane monster one single thing that she wants. Me and you? I'm putting us first. As soon as I'm better, we can go to Sydney. The elders can take care of this mess. We've done enough."

"Really?"

"Yeah, fuck it. Sara, we don't get paid enough to care this much."

Squeezing his hands against her chest, Sara felt a slice of happiness pierce the ashen desolation inside her.

"Desdemona has nothing," Silas continued. "She has no assets, no support. We have the last of her women in custody and from what I hear, they're all relieved to be free from her. We don't trust them, of course not, but mom said that they all told her that they have been terrified of her for years and the only way to survive was to play along."

"I hope that's the truth," Sara said. "I don't want any more people to die."

"Except Desdemona."

"Well yes, but she must know she's in her end game. Even if Yukari is able to reinfect her or extend her life, Crina won't let her live. I could pull her apart with my bare hands and not think twice about it..." Sara paused, remembering Crina describing this exact feeling to her just days before. "She's crossed a line and sealed her fate."

"She's terrified of dying," Silas said.

"Don't," Sara said quietly. "I can't talk like that, not until we know whether she... you know..."

"It's gonna be what it's gonna be, my love," Silas squeezed her hands. "A year ago, you were ready for the end of your life."

"But I wasn't though," Sara said. "I know that now. I was ready for a new something, anything, and you came along."

"And we've had this amazing adventure, for a year."

"It's been a bit busy," Sara said, rolling her eyes.

"That's how the world is now," Silas said. "Haven't you noticed that everyone online is always talking about how this is the hardest year ever, and we just wish we could go back to some other earlier year? Things were always easier before now, it seems. Before the pandemic, before the rise of authoritarianism, before transgender people existed."

"But that time never existed," Sara said. "There have always been third spirit people, we had them in our village in Romania, I've always known people who didn't fit the binary."

"Of course that's all true," Silas said. "But that's my point, everybody is hungry for a past that didn't exist, for a time of familiar predictability. That's how we remember the past. But it's never how it really was. Of course the world is a massive dumpster fire, if all you focus on is the bad news that the media spreads, or the sad nonsense on social media. But every day that I get to spend focusing on you, and our love, is a perfect day. So, if Desdemona's stupid trick has worked, and all of a sudden, I start to age, then sure, I'll get selfish, I'll want as much of you as you can give me, but I won't let misery cloud those perfect days."

"I literally just found you," Sara said. "And she knows exactly how much you mean to me..."

"Because it's something she never had for herself," Silas said.

"So she stole it from me."

"We won't let her," Silas said. "And like I said, we don't know if what she did will work. As soon as we got here, Crina ripped open her wrist and bled into all of my cuts and forced me to drink her blood, hoping that, you know, it might override."

Sara cocked her head.

"Why didn't you start with that?"

"Because I didn't want to trigger you with memories of your patient, and also, because it was fucking disgusting," Silas said. "Just
between you and I, you know that my mother loves to be theatrical.
It was pretty annoying to watch her do it, I think she was trying to
impress Skye and Yfke."

"Did it work?"

"Judging from the serious eye rolling I got from Yfke, I'd say no,"
Silas chuckled. "Either way, everyone's had a shot at fixing me, and all
I wanted was to go upstairs and lay beside you."

"You're going to use this as an excuse for unbridled schmaltziness,
aren't you?"

"Have you met me? I want to be your full time Hallmark card. I
want to bring you flowers, I want to do every single corny thing that
we can do at any minute of the day. I want you to sleep in my arms. I
want to shower with you and massage you and kiss you constantly. I
want to inhale your breath just so I can feel closer to you. I want you
to feel surrounded and protected by my love. Sara, this is the apex of
my life, loving you, being by your side, even if it's for a shorter period
of time, I'm hungry for every moment and grateful for the same."

"Like I said," Sara pulled a hand from his and pinched his nose.
"Non stop schmaltz."

"I'm pretty tired," Silas wriggled deeper into the couch. "Snuggle
up?"

In silence, Sara lifted the comforter and slipped in alongside Silas's
warm body, feeling his strong arm wrap around her from behind and
pull her close to him, wincing from the pressure against his ribs but
not letting her escape. Turning her face into the hair on his chest, she
felt his heart beating against her cheek, the same muscle that had been
pumping life to him for half a millennia. Threading her spare arm up
over his chest, she let it rest on his shoulder, avoiding the bandages.

Within seconds, his breathing deepened, and his arm slackened against her back, but it didn't fall away. It never did. Silas could hold her gently all night while he slept, as if somehow, even subconsciously, he could never fully let her go. Listening to his heart, she felt tears begin to slip from her eyes, as she beseeched his heart muscle to keep up its drum beat forever.

Chapter Twenty-Three

"Knock knock!"

Yukari's quiet voice startled Sara.

"Come in," Silas said, before Sara could respond. Rushing to sit upright, Sara bumped Silas.

"Ouch," he said, moving her arm away from his bandaged shoulder. "Here, let me pull myself upright and then we can organize you."

"I'll just sit beside you," Sara swung her feet from the sofa and rapidly arranged the comforter as she heard the door open. Looking up, she saw Yukari, followed by April Veronica and Embla.

"Do you feel like some company?"

"I always feel like your company," Silas said. "Come on in, everybody, sorry we're hogging the couch."

Sara watched as the women, normally so garrulous, entered the room, their sadness and concern palpable. She knew Silas would step up and defuse it, and she didn't have to wait long.

"Sadness is forbidden in the patient's room," he said, his voice booming. "Patient will only entertain guests who bring good humor, glad tidings or," he paused, pointing a finger at Embla, "juicy gossip."

"I don't have any gossip," Embla said. "Not technically. But we have information."

"We're piecing together what we found in Imani's room," April Veronica said. "Her phone was still there, I'm sure they made her leave it behind. And next to it was an AirTag."

"Fucking Toma," Sara spat. "He's showing us that we missed it when we searched him."

"Men," Silas said with mock severity. "Can't train 'em, can't kill 'em."

"And you sure as hell can't trust them," Sara said.

"Or so we thought," April Veronica said. "Until we started getting the notifications."

"Yeah," Embla said. "It seems like Imani's Airpods are presently heading to Pittsburgh."

Suddenly remembering Toma's strange behavior at Desdemona's side, the earnest apology and the weird tapping of his ear, Sara sat upright.

"He did it on purpose," Sara blurted. "Silas, did you see when he tapped his ear after he apologized?"

"Nope, sorry, was busy being in agony right then. Missed it somehow."

"He what now?" Embla was confused.

"She had his twin," Sara said.

"Yeah, I told them that part," Silas said.

"Right, of course. Anyway, when it looked like she was going to kill us, Toma apologized, and it made Des furious, and then he caught my eye and he quickly tapped his ear. I thought he meant that he heard someone coming, but maybe he was telling me to track the Airpods."

"That makes sense," Embla said. "He left the AirTag on the shelf by the phone."

"Huh," Sara said. "So maybe he wasn't all bad?"

"It's twins," Yukari said. "It should have been in the original rules. It should have said never make a twin, because that's as strong of a bond as mother and child. Desdemona used that bond to get him to hurt Imani, now he's trying to help."

"That's literally what Desdemona said this morning," Silas said.

"Twins creep me out," April Veronica said, making them all laugh.

"Ouch," Silas gasped. "I can always count on you, Peanut."

"So," Yukari said, her voice tiny, "I have news."

"It's bad, right?" Silas's voice was upbeat. "I knew it would be bad."

"It's not that bad," Yukari said. "It does appear that you have the vaccine in your system, yes."

Sara's heart actually hurt at the news.

"But one of the things that I've been working on is maybe slowing down the advancement in Desdemona, and I think that's our best bet. I will shift all focus to developing that."

"Thank you, Yuka," Silas said. "I wasn't worried, I know you've got my back."

Yukari bowed her head deeply, then raised it, staring into Silas's eyes.

"I am doing my best," she said.

"How much can you slow the process?" Silas asked.

"I am pretty sure I can slow it down enough that it would mirror the natural aging process," Yukari said. "I'm just running a bunch of tests before I finalize the new mRNA formula. I'll need to return to New York to get it done."

"When do you think you'll be ready?" Sara's voice was sharper than she intended, and Yukari actually flinched. "I'm sorry, Yuka."

"A week? Two? I need to actually work with humans in the epidemiology world," Yukari said. "In the meantime, I'm just using AI to stay on top of everyone else's research."

"Are you still thinking of giving yourself the vaccine?"

Yukari nodded. "Yeah, I need to fully inhabit that world, publicly, to ensure that the research steers away from our secret."

"But that doesn't really require you to become immune," Embla said. "You can do it for a decade and then vanish."

"I need a guinea pig," Yukari said bluntly. Silas raised his arm to volunteer, wincing at the pain. "No, I wouldn't be comfortable testing on anyone but myself. I'm gonna go get you some blood, Sara, you're a full-on panda with those black eyes. Silas, should I bring you some?"

"I don't feel the thirst," he said honestly. "Maybe a little, but it's not like it would be normally."

"I think it's a good idea to try," Yukari said. "If there's any virus still working in your system, the best thing would be to feed it."

"Whatever you say, boss," Silas said, and Yukari left the room.

"It is such a difficult day," Embla said. "I am deeply sorry for all of this. I hate it. I hate it all so much. A group of women being torn apart by one woman who knows better."

"Women can fuck up too," April Veronica said. "Look at the women leading far-right politics, the women advocating for less rights for other women. Gender doesn't make you immune to selfishness, it doesn't stop you from doing whatever you can to impose your will on everybody else."

"But it should," Embla said. "Women have watched as men have destroyed everything they've touched. From government to whaling to I don't know, even basic reproduction. I don't know if it's gender or just a need to feel superior, in control."

"Ding ding ding," Sara said. "That's Desdemona right there. A fucking lifetime loser who wants to be the boss, the leader, the fucking cherry on top. She's just like all those women that are fighting against our own needs."

"She will destroy everything that you and the elders built, this peaceful utopia, for what? For what, Sara? To be in charge of a few women?"

"She's already destroyed it," Sara said. "No matter how this ends, she's changed the fabric of our little world."

"No," Yukari said, appearing with a mug of blood in each hand. "We have a future. Bucharest will endure as a Lock, and if there's just one Lock on the planet, and we all use it as a base, that is enough while we build new foundations."

Silas's phone dinged and he glanced at it.

"Fan and Ama will be here in an hour," he said. "Brace yourselves."

"It's not us I'm worried about," Embla said. "They're going to want to kill the prisoners."

"I won't let them," Sara said. "We will send them to Bucharest."

Sara could smell the coppery notes of warm blood and began to salivate. She extended a hand to Yukari and took the overfull mug with a slow grace, bringing it to her lips without waiting for any toast. In between sips, she kept an eye on Silas, who first sniffed his blood, catlike, and then took a tentative mouthful. She could see that he was having trouble getting it down.

"You okay there, Si?" Yukari asked.

"Fifty fifty," he said. "I can get the whole thing down, it'll just take some time."

"Thank you," Yukari said. "Then I'll need you to pay attention in the bathroom next time. If the virus stops absorbing the blood from your stomach, your stool will be black."

"I love a bathroom surprise," Silas said with a childish cackle.

"You're the world's oldest ten year old boy," Embla said from the couch. Glancing at her, Sara noticed that she was sipping from April Veronica's glass of blood.

"Embla," Sara asked. "Is that synthetic?"

Embla shook her head. "Busted," she whispered. "I was going to tell everyone. You all know I've been aging, and now I'm a test subject for our future. I need to transition onto a blood diet then back to synthetic, to see if we can identify what causes what."

"Also, I want her to live forever," April Veronica threw her arms around her girlfriend.

"I know the feeling," Sara said, tears pricking her eyes.

"Foul ball," Silas yelled, setting his empty mug on the floor with a wince. "No sad talking. Only good vibes here."

"God you're ridiculous," Sara said, taking his hand and kissing it.

In her pocket, her phone vibrated. Sara released Silas's hand and yanked her phone out.

"Oh shit you guys, blocked number," Sara called out.

"Put it on speaker," April Veronica said, and Sara obeyed.

"Hello?" she said.

"Sara, love, it's Imani."

At the sound of her friend's voice, Sara's head began to spin.

"You're okay?"

"I am, for now, but madam here wants me to be her messenger."

"Hi Des," Sara said perkily. "I know you're there. You don't need to be scared. I'm just sitting here having a mug of blood with my boyfriend."

"Sara, don't," Imani said, fear in her voice. "Please. Don't. Yes. Desdemona is here. Fran is okay too. She's in our room. I... uh... what were the words? Oh yes, ground rules. I'm here to tell you the ground rules for this next phase."

"Go ahead, Imani."

"Firstly, we know that Crina and Skye and them are out looking for us, I need you to call them off immediately."

"Easier said than done," Sara said. "There's a reason we say never pick a mother."

After some muffled sounds, Imani returned.

"Sara, if you don't do as I say right now, me and Fran, she's going to starve us."

Sara was aghast. Blood starvation was the cruelest torture.

"Well we don't want that then, do we?" Sara's tone was deliberately light.

"No guv, I'd say we don't," Imani chuckled. "So, I'm gonna give you the number of a burner and you'll be able to use that to get ahold of me whenever you have news."

"News about?"

"About Yukari's progress."

"She's here, do you want me to put her on?"

More muffled sounds.

"No, just have her on speaker. The second thing is that there's a hard deadline on this. Two weeks. In two weeks, if not sooner, we will return, for the vaccine that you've created. And any vaccine that is for Desdemona will need to also be given to Silas, from the same needle, at the same time."

"That's unsafe behavior," Sara said. "Sharing needles."

In the background, she heard Desdemona whispering angrily.

"Yes, Desdemona, I'll tell her that too," Imani said. "She says that she'd rather risk catching a disease from Silas than having Crina murder her outright."

"Fair," Sara said. "Now tell me, if we are good little girls, will you get the blood you need?"

After some rustling, Imani replied.

"Half rations," she said, her voice suddenly dry. "No heems. Don't worry about us, mate, I need to go on a diet."

The joke fell flat and silence fell. The call was still connected, Sara guessed that Desdemona had muted it. When the mute was lifted, Desdemona spoke.

"Hello sister," she said, "miss me yet?"

"Don't be silly, I just saw you this morning," Sara refused to let any pain or anger into her voice.

"Just once, you should try honesty," Desdemona said. "Has someone called Crina to get her to return to your base? I will need photographic evidence texted to this number as soon as she gets back. Once I receive that text, I will allow Imani and Fran to feed."

"Consider it done," Sara said. "Speaking of feeding people, you've left us with some extra mouths. Would you like them back?"

"Not really, maybe you should put an ad in the paper. Free to good home. Immortal Spanish women, easily led, not too bright. I hear it's the in thing in America these days."

"So that's a no, then?"

"Before I go," Desdemona ignored her. "There's been something I've wanted to tell you, for a century. An entire century. Do you have any idea, dear sister, what it's like to not be able to share delicious gossip for that long?"

"No, because I'm not a psycho," Sara said. "Unlike you."

"Sara, what I'm about to tell you is the truth."

"If you're going to tell me, then tell me."

"Your most trusted person has been making a fool of you."

"I mean, who hasn't?"

"Be serious," Desdemona erupted in fury. "I am about to tell you truth, I wish there was something I cherished that I could swear upon, but there is not. I tried to start this discussion when you had me locked up in that stinking cell, but you're too smug to ever listen to me. And here we are, because of this person our entire way of life is destroyed."

"Is this information about yourself, Des? Because that's who has ruined our world."

"You simple idiot," Desdemona snarled. "Crina has been using you, exploiting your pathetic loyalty, while she traveled the world, convincing elders to take Surrender, or outright killing sisters that displeased her."

"Des, this is literally a description of your last six months," Sara said angrily.

"Talk to Crina," Desdemona continued. "She's been murdering women way longer than I have."

Sara could feel Silas's eyes boring into her but she kept her own eyes fixed on the rug on the floor, her mind racing for the perfect questions to counter the madness spilling from Desdemona's mouth.

"She and I have talked about this already," Sara said finally.

"Did she tell you she always played us against each other? That she promised New York to me?"

"You're lying."

"Did she ever tell you about the months she spent with me at the Madrid Lock?"

Sara glanced at Silas, who shrugged and shook his head.

"I mean," Sara replied, "if you say so, then I guess it must be true."

"Just listen, and stop being a smart ass," Desdemona hissed. "She has spent the last century meddling in all our Locks, always telling sisters not to reveal her whereabouts to you. And at the end of every visit, someone died. Coincidence? I think not."

"Des," Sara said wearily, "I see your game, it's the same as it ever was. Sow suspicion in our minds. Pull us apart."

"Not one word out of my mouth on this call has been untrue," Desdemona said.

"Sure, I'll double check when mom gets back," Sara said.

"You absolutely can, *hermana*, but remember, she has lied to you for so long, you see her dishonesty as truth. I'll tell you something else. Rosa switched out your heems, that's why you fed on that poor woman. You were starving."

Sara didn't know what to think for a moment before remembering that Desdemona was an expert manipulator.

"Now isn't the time for conspiracy theories," Sara said finally.

"It's not a conspiracy, Crina kept her son from you."

"This is not what happened," Silas yelled.

"Oh there you are, hows the patient?" Desdemona was not fazed. "Right. So was your mother supportive of your return to New York? Did she want you seeing Sara as a patient?"

Sara watched Silas's face carefully, but he was stone.

"No," he said finally. "She did not want me anywhere near New York at that time."

"Like I said," Desdemona said snottily. "I'm going to go now, but I do want you to consider that your life has been a lie. More than once, Crina promised me that I would become Mother of New York once you were out of the way. And Crina has more secrets than you know."

"Sounds like pretty generic mother in law drama," Sara managed. "I thought you said you were going."

The line went dead.

Sara leapt to her feet.

"No time for hysterics," she said, turning to face them all in turn. "When they get back, we say nothing about this. Please. Silas and I will talk to them all, separately, and see if this hangs together."

"She's just trying to get to you," Embla said.

"No," Silas said. "Nobody knew that my mom didn't want me to return to New York, she kept me busy in other parts of the world, but I'd heard her talking about Sara burning out in New York, and I wanted to get back to save you."

"Did Heather know about this?"

"I doubt it," Silas said. "If anyone knew, it would be Fan and Ama."

"Well great, they'll be here in half an hour. Let's get to work."

Chapter Twenty-Four

"Okay," Silas said, now dressed in jeans and a bizarrely patterned black, pink, yellow and blue sweater that screamed 80s, his arm in a sling. "Fan and Ama are finally five minutes away."

"You guys understand the assignment?" Sara turned to April Veronica and Embla. "Let them talk. Don't tell them about the Desdemona phone call. Not til I give the signal."

Both women nodded sagely.

"Are you coping, Sara?" April Veronica asked as she squeezed her arm.

"I'm numb," Sara said quietly. The deepening mystery of Crina was still ricocheting around inside her, an ugly puzzle that fell into place all too easily the more she thought about it.

"Come sit by me," Silas patted the couch cushion beside him, and Sara nestled in against him.

"This sweater is a lot," she said, making Embla laugh out loud.

"What do you mean?" Silas chuckled. "It's vintage."

"It's garish," Sara said. "I hated that eighties palette, the bright pinks and blues and yellows."

"But it's got a kangaroo and a koala," Silas protested. "It was from a shop called Koala Blue."

"I gather they went out of business," Embla said, and the three women all laughed while Silas harumphed broadly, making them laugh harder. As the laughter faded, Sara heard car doors closing.

"They're here," she said, and all four of them fell into the universal habit of silence and small adjustments to clothing and seating that happened when humans were waiting for other humans to enter a room.

"Don't all get up at once," Fan called as she shouldered the door open, stepping into the living room with her arms loaded with shopping bags. Mr Handsome scampered in behind her and began scouring the floor for scraps.

"We've had a rough day, auntie," Silas called from the couch, and Sara watched as concern and happiness fought for control of Fan's face as she dropped the bags to the floor and rushed to Silas's side.

"That witch done fucked you up," Fan whispered as she trailed her fingers along the slices on Silas's cheek. "You still pretty though."

Another clattering from the doorway turned out to be Ama, carrying a large box that she quickly shoved onto the table before hurrying over to Silas.

"Awwwww, my beautiful prince," she said, kissing his forehead. "You're sad huh? You even broke out the sad sweater."

"See?" Embla said. "Even Ama thinks your sweater is terrible."

"No, I don't," Ama straightened and flipped off Embla. "I love this sweater but I know that Silas only gets it out of mothballs when he's really sad. I haven't seen you wear this since..."

"Since JuanMa died?" Fan asked.

"Yeah, probably," Silas said. "Anyways..."

"Hold up," April Veronica said, raising a hand. "Who the fuck is JuanMa?"

Sara, feeling terrible for making fun of the garish sweater that clearly meant a lot to him, now also felt guilty for just how interested she was in his answer. She knew that Silas's last love was a guy but he'd always been cagy with the details.

"Uh oh," Fan said theatrically. "Did we out you?"

"Juan Manuel Obrador," Silas said loudly, "was the love of my life, until I met this fine woman at my side. He was the closest I ever came to breaking any of our rules. He shoplifted this sweater for me."

"Oh why didn't you stop me, Silas?" Embla was stricken. "I was ridiculing your queer history?"

"No, you were ridiculing something that gives me a lot of comfort, but that's okay, it's also kind of loud and over the top."

"Like me!" Fan danced around, waving her arms. Shaking her head, Ama knelt by Silas.

"JuanMa has been on my mind a lot on the drive up here," she said. "As soon as I saw you wearing that sweater, it told me everything I need to know."

"Yep," Silas said. "I'm afraid that it's Deathland for me too."

"What the fuck?" Sara said angrily. "Please don't say that."

"When JuanMa got sick," Silas's voice was quieter than she'd ever heard it, "we didn't know what to call the end of it all, so he'd just say that at some point he was going to go live in Deathland. He made up this whole place, this land, I guess you'd call it. It was kind of an anti-heaven but it was so nice. He'd tell me about the houses, they were all designed by Gaudi, and the best thing was that every animal that ever lived was there, so you could go to the zoo and see dinosaurs, plus all your childhood pets. So... sorry I went deep on that, I haven't thought much about Deathland until..."

"Until today," Fan finished for him. "So Desdemona made you mortal?"

"We're not sure yet," Sara snapped.

"I'm pretty sure," Silas said, tightening his grip on her shoulders. "That glass of blood is sitting in my stomach like a rock, it's never felt like that before. But Yukari says she can slow the process down to like you know, natural aging or maybe even slower."

"Yeah, we know," Ama said. "We've been talking to her about this for some time."

"About what?" Silas asked.

"Deathland," Fan said. "I'm not kidding."

"She's not," Ama stood up, searching for somewhere to sit before jumping onto the couch beside Sara. "We've been deep in this discussion for..."

"Fifty years?" Fan leapt onto the arm of the couch beside Ama, perching there like a raven.

"You guys, I'm confused," Silas said.

"Death," they both said at once.

"Right," Silas smiled. "That clears it all up."

"Enlighten them, my love," Ama said. Fan leaned down and kissed her long and hard, then sat cross-legged on the floor.

"Haven't you guys ever wondered if death is a part of life?" she paused, turning, making eye contact with each of them. "What if, by choosing to live for as long as we have, we've interfered with something that is actually an important part of our own life?"

"This is the age old dilemma," Sara said. "And it's an all or nothing bet on finding out."

"True," said Fan. "But it's the finding out that has gotten more and more interesting as time goes by, at least to us. Since we got back together again, it's basically all we talk about. We've been all over the world investigating this stuff, we've lived in silence in Buddhist retreats in Nepal, we've taken weird ass cactus with Navajo shamans in New Mexico, we've gone to university to study with the greatest thinkers on consciousness and the process of death, and literally, the only answer is, there's just one way to find out."

Watching Fan talk, Sara reacted to her words viscerally. They reminded her of the frisson she used to get as a therapist when a depressed patient would talk about death as an attractive option, and she felt shallow, for only seeing death as an ending, not as something potentially greater, something perhaps essential to life.

"Sara, Silas," Fan continued, "haven't you ever wondered if the purpose of life was to put our souls through physical sensation? To give our emotional cores something tactile? We exist to feel, we exist to experience, but what happens to all of this magic? All of these memories, all of these emotions, all of these insanely complicated sensations, the sun on our faces, the softness of cotton against our skin, our tongues touching when we kiss. And we were in Costa Rica just after Lockdown, remember Ama? We were watching those butterflies, just these huge gorgeous things with wings of orange and black and yellow, just flying, kind of clumsily, the wind directing them, but they were just sailing in the sunlight, looking for some pollen, and Ama turned to me and said that she was ready to go to Deathland."

"I did," Ama said. "I still am."

"So that's why we rushed up here, Silas," Fan walked over to him and took the hand that extended from his sling, kneeling before him. "We don't want our beautiful prince to go through this alone, so we are going to ask Yukari to vaccinate us with what you have."

"No," Silas said firmly. "I can't have that on my conscience."

"There's nothing for your conscience to bear," Fan said, tousling his hair. "This is something we've wanted to do forever."

"Can you imagine us as an old lesbian couple?" Ama said with a grin. "We might even open a guesthouse in Maine with like a yoga retreat and vegan food?"

Fan turned to Sara.

"I want to feel my skin wrinkling," Fan said gently. "I want to see what I look like at ninety. I want to feel the privilege that getting old is, you've lived long enough and now your body is beginning its journey back to the earth. I want the whole damn experience of life."

Sara didn't know what to say, certain that the only response that they'd approve of was that she would also ask Yukari to vaccinate her.

"I still want to live forever," Embla said.

"Fuck yeah," April Veronica chimed in. "I just got here, dammit."

"Yes please," Ama said, turning to them. "Watching you two find love was another thing that made us decide that we want to do this. We see so much of us in you, young us, and that showed us that everything is a cycle. As Cursed women, we have stepped out of that cycle. We want to jump back in and ride it to the end. We can hand over our title to you baby dykes, you will have to outlast us."

"That's a tall order," Embla said. "But I am honored that you think of us as the younger you."

"I don't know what to say," Sara said quietly. "I can't process this. I've never known a world that didn't have you in it. You guys taught me literally everything I know. You taught me to fight, to think, you two taught me about women and power and love, I just owe everything to you both."

"And whatever we are," Ama pinched at her chest, "whatever this is or was will live on in you, in your memories and in your actions."

"But we're not looking for immortality or legacy or anything," Fan said sternly. "We know that everything is temporary, nothing lasts, and nothing *should* last forever. I'd literally rather be remembered for an act of kindness than any huge battle move."

"You guys came here when JuanMa died," Silas said. "Remember?"

"Yeah," Fan waved her arm, pointing at the room. "This cabin was just a tiny log home, there were just a bunch of tin sheds and that stinky chicken farm."

"I loved those chickens," Ama said. "Remember we tried to make them into wild chickens?"

"That's right," Silas laughed. "You built all those nest boxes and put them up in the trees."

"The foxes took care of those birds in seconds," Fan said.

"Right, but owls moved into the boxes," Silas said. "I still love hearing them at night."

"Me too," said Ama, resting her head on Sara's shoulder. "I loved those years that we spent here, building this house."

"Going to all those AIDS marches in Washington DC," Fan said. "Organizing for ACT UP, trying to stop that monster Reagan."

"You mobilized all of Northern New York," Silas said. "I'm so grateful still that you guys took that time for me."

"What about your mom?" Sara asked, as innocently as possible.

"She wasn't around much," Ama said. "And we love our little prince, so we were happy to hang out until his pain was gone."

"That surprises me," Embla chimed in. "I always saw Crina as the world's most overprotective mother. Why wasn't she here too?"

"I actually don't remember where she was," Silas said. "Do you guys? I remember she had to leave New York just before things got bad for JuanMa, but wow, I absolutely don't remember what dragged her away."

Fan and Ama exchanged glances, then shrugged in unison.

"She always had her own priorities," Ama said.

"Oh absolutely," Fan agreed. "Nothing stands in the way of our Crina."

"Right," Sara decided to gamble. "It was like when I found out she was waiting for me to burn out in New York."

"I bet that's why you stayed so long as Lock Mother," Fan said. "You knew what she was up to and you stayed to spite her. Amazing, Sara. You're so strong. I love you."

"No, actually," Sara said, and Ama's head jerked up off her shoulder. "I didn't know for sure until right now, but thank you for your honesty, I hope it can continue."

"I knew it was a trap," Ama said tersely to Fan. "I was making the stop talking face at you."

"Well your stop talking face looks a lot like your keep talking face I guess," Fan said. "Anyways, who let the cat out of the bag?"

"Desdemona," Silas said. "She called just before you arrived."

"Wait," Fan said. "So this whole thing was a set-up? You let us pour out our hearts about our decision to go to Deathland with you and the whole time you were just buttering us up to find out if Desdemona was telling the truth?"

"In a nutshell," Silas said.

"Cold," Fan said. "Ice cold and I have to say, you've made me proud."

Ama wriggled around on the couch until she was facing Sara.

"That must have been hard to hear, I'm sorry."

"I mean, it's not been great," Sara said. "But can I ask you guys something? Do you guys know that she spent months at a time in Madrid? Is that something you were aware of?"

"We weren't," Fan said. "She knows that we love you and hate Des. She feels responsible for Des. She never mentioned spending much time in Madrid, she did admit to swinging by in between visits to Bucharest or Warsaw."

"But she told you she went to Madrid?"

"Of course not," Ama said. "We heard it from Stefanya, and you'll never believe it, but we did the same thing to her. We could tell something was wrong so we pretended that we knew already."

"I don't know how that woman led a revolution," Fan said. "If she's on her second bottle of wine and her third episode of The Real Housewives of Somewhere, she'll tell you anything."

"I'll keep that in mind," Sara said. "But back to me, because this is all about me, what do you think I should do?"

"In terms of your mother slash mother in law slash evil overlord?" Fan chuckled at her own joke.

"Sure."

"It's the same for any kid when they realize that their parent is just a regular human," Ama said. "You'll feel disheartened for a while but when you look at her motivations, you can decide if you support them or not. Sara, she's not a bad person, she just..." Ama paused, and pointed at Silas, "...she's a lone wolf who loves keeping a secret."

"Ouch," Silas said. "So what do you think her motivations are? Have you judged them?"

"We try not to judge," Ama said.

"Oh shut up," Fan laughed. "Of course we judge. It's fun. We know that Crina always lied to you guys about being at her upstate place. She was usually in Iceland, sure, but often, she'd leave and visit a Lock, and it was always 'don't tell Sara.' She didn't stay with the Lock, she'd get a hotel or something. Stefanya said that she was just monitoring the security, watching for watchers, which made sense."

"Desdemona implied that she would stay at the Madrid compound," Ama said.

"You need to understand," Fan said. "There's no solid communication network between us old girls. I know everyone thinks we are like some cabal of frozen senior citizen vampires, but most of us are just skipping school. Once someone goes scholar, they just get to do whatever they want. Nobody checks. And for some reason, Crina sees the security of our entire kind as her responsibility. Desdemona is just fucking with you, I trust Crina almost as much as I trust Ama."

"We've tried to uh... modernize her way of thinking," Ama said. "We also tried to get her to let us help her. She's fully committed to doing this by herself. Sara, I doubt she would ever hurt you."

"Desdemona said that women would take Surrender after her visit," Sara said.

"Oh yeah," Ama said. "She definitely sees herself in a counselor role. She'd hear of a sister in an existential crisis and she'd go sit with them. It's a noble thing to do. Typical of Desdemona to try to see it as evil."

"But if you guys were considering mortality," Silas said, "wouldn't that have been something to include you in?"

"I mean, sure," Fan said. "But you're forgetting that your mother is a one-woman show."

"That's not something I forget," Silas said. "Ever. But I'm asking if you asked to go with her, to visit these women?"

"Of course we did," Ama said. "They were our friends too. But she never let us into that side of her life. It was disappointing."

"Does she know she disappointed you?" Silas asked, surprised to hear of dissension between his aunts and mother.

"She knows how we feel," Fan said. "But it doesn't matter. None of us old bitches are good at compromise. It's another reason we are choosing mortality. The last gasp of the vampire matriarchy has gotten so ugly."

"I thought you two were part of it," Sara said. "The way you acted in Iceland, you absolutely wanted to kill all the halflings and anyone else who got in your way."

"That was just simple security talking" Ama said. "Any leak must be eradicated. We are softer now than we've ever been."

"Okay, so final question," Sara said. "And again, full honesty is appreciated."

"Fire away," Fan and Ama said at once.

"Was the end game to finally install Desdemona as Lock mother in New York?"

Fan and Ama exploded into laughter.

"Fuck no," Ama said. "That's just so obviously Crina fucking with Desdemona. She was just baiting the hook. She was probably spending time with Des to manipulate her."

"I tried to talk to Crina after Helsinki took Surrender," Fan said. "I wanted to kill Des. Because I loved those women. I was angry, and I wanted to avenge it. She insisted that I stay out of it, she created Des, and she wanted to be the one to end her."

"So why didn't she do it" Embla asked.

"Exactly," Silas said. "Could ask a favor of you two?"

"Anything," Fan and Ama said at once.

"I can't be around her right now, and I don't think Sara is ready to see her either. Can you guys fabricate something that needs to be done in New York and send her and the others to the City for a while?"

"Sure," Ama said brightly. "We were only coming for the night, because we have those women locked up in the Compound but we can ask for her help."

"I'm texting now," Fan said, her fingers dancing over her phone's screen. "I'm gonna buy us all some time do deal with our mommy issues."

Chapter Twenty-Five

The ding of the warming oven echoed around the kitchen of the hobbit house, and Sara grimaced. In the week since Yukari confirmed that Silas was no longer Cursed, Sara's blood intake became something shameful that she only did in private. Silas was in the bathroom, and she doubted that he heard the ding, but it bothered her nonetheless. Her mind already miles away, she watched as someone else's hands, autopilot, opened the oven and retrieved the mug of blood, bringing it to her lips. Outside the little window, snow was falling, each flake drifting left then right and over again until it hit the ground, no wind to interrupt its dance with gravity.

A noise from behind the bathroom door caused her to panic-gulp the remaining blood, snapping her back into the instant. Hurriedly, she rinsed the mug in the sink, using a scrubbing brush to dislodge the stubborn blood cells from the inside rim. Behind her the bathroom door opened and Silas's heavy footsteps padded up behind her, warm arms wrapping around her waist as a bristly chin parted the hair on her neck.

"Whatcha doin?" Silas purred in her ear.

"Nothing, just cleaning up the sink," she lied, setting the mug upside down on the drying rack while she licked her lips to get rid of any tell-tale droplets.

"Looks pretty clean to me," Silas said, and his hands gripped her hips, spinning Sara around to face him as his kisses moved to her cheeks and his hands moving her hair back from her face. Stepping back a little, he lifted her chin to face him. His stitches had been removed and his beard was growing back in the areas that Yukari had shaved after the attack. His lip had healed slowly, like a normal person's, and a jagged scar pulled his lip crookedly. They stared into each other's eyes for an instant until he leaned in and kissed her lips. Opening her mouth to kiss him back, Sara was horrified as a wet blood burp erupted from deep inside her.

"Oh, shit, I'm so sorry," she said, turning her face away as Silas began to laugh.

"Better an empty house than a bad tenant," Silas said, pulling her against him. "Sara, you don't have to hide your feeding from me."

"I know," she said, still not certain there weren't any more burps coming. "But it feels weird and doing it privately feels a bit more... respectful?"

"I appreciate it," Silas smiled his new, lopsided smile. "But Sara, it's not necessary. The smell of it doesn't bother me, not one bit."

"I'm sure it smells like bad breath," she said, trying to not exhale into his nostrils.

"It doesn't," he said quietly. "I love your breath smell."

"Gross," she whispered.

"It's not," he said, nuzzling her neck again. "It's sexy. Every scent you have drives me wild. We got the pheromone match like crazy."

"Someone else's blood on my breath is not *my* pheromones," Sara placed both palms on his bare chest, pushing him back slightly. "It's just you being weird."

"Weird for you," he smiled, letting go of her and returning to the living room where he plonked naked onto the couch, his arms behind his head.

"Are you gonna get dressed?"

"Nope," he said. "Do you not love being naked inside a warm house and watching snow fall outside?"

"That's one kink that I do not share," Sara sat beside him, leaning her head into his armpit, his musk intoxicating her, reminding her that their pheromone match was just as strong for her. Outside the big windows of the living room, the snow was falling so heavily that it obscured the lake almost completely. "But I get it. This is pretty nice."

"Why don't you lose your sexy tracksuit combo and see if I'm right?"

"I need to ask you something, and I don't think nudity is the appropriate wardrobe."

"Is it something you've asked before?"

She nodded slowly.

"Then I veto your question and encourage your nudity." He kissed the top of her head, his lips lingering on her hair.

"Or, answer me and I'll get naked. Carrot. Stick."

"I have both for you right here," Silas joked, grabbing his junk and flapping it at her.

"I'm gonna need five hundred year old Silas, not fifteen year old Silas."

"Sara, please don't ask again," he said, letting go of his genitals and taking her hand . "It's the only thing I can't cope with right now."

"That makes two of us," she said. "Hence the urgency."

"Can we make a deal that this is the last time we discuss it, regardless of the outcome?"

"I can promise to try," she said.

"Fire away."

"Silas, I want the vaccine," she said, her voice flat. "It's the only solution that makes sense for me."

Silas went to speak, and Sara put a finger to his lips.

"Let me say all my things, and then you can say your things. I think my things make more sense when delivered in a clump. If we keep on interrupting, I know you'll be able to pick my motives apart."

"I'm sorry, go ahead."

"Silas, I am not afraid to die," she said quietly, staring deep into his eyes. "What I am afraid of is us taking different paths."

"But we cheersed to taking different paths at our first date."

"We did, but those paths were voluntary, they were roads we wanted to travel together. This path," she paused, placing her palm against his heart, his chest hair wiry against her palm, "this path has forked. It's you aging, at whatever pace, and me staying like this."

"*Dragosta chinuită*," he whispered in Romanian. The tortured love. That was how the original Cursed women referred to watching their loved ones age while they did not.

"Yes," Sara said. "It's unfair for you to make me go through that."

"But then I'd always have a hot young wife!" Silas joked. "I'd be living the dream."

"Hardy har har," Sara flicked the end of his nose. "Like I said, I need five hundred year old Silas now. I need the man who understands *dragosta chinuită*."

"Okay, You got him."

"What would you do in this situation? If I was the one headed for old age and you were the immortal?"

"If I was in your situation, I would insist on getting the vaccine," he said. "But I'm not in your situation. I'm in the actual position of losing my immortality. It's not hypothetical for me. And I know if the tables were turned, you wouldn't let me get the vaccine either. And for that reason, I am fully opposed to you giving up the most wonderful gift on this planet just so you and I can get AARP cards and wrinkles together."

"So you'd make me endure the tortured love?"

"It will be different, because this will be the first time ever that both parties are aware of what's really happening. It won't be you hiding behind a bush a hundred yards from your aging mother and spying on her. As far as I'm concerned, our future will be just one more unique thing that only we get to do."

"I want to share all of that with you," Sara said, tears welling in her eyes.

"Crying will end this conversation," Silas cautioned, and Sara caught herself. "Thanks. And Sara, I respect you so much for what you're asking to do, for me. So can I offer a truce?"

Sara nodded.

"Can we revisit this in a year? Nothing much will change, I might have a few gray hairs, but we will have some distance from that nightmare scene in the forest with Des? Everything has been in turmoil since that day. I need to figure out my mom stuff, fuck, we still haven't even gotten to the bottom of her mysteries."

Sara turned her head and kissed Silas on the soft skin of his ribs.

"I'm trying to talk to you," his voice was hoarse. "You can't kiss me there unless you want the talking to stop."

"I was just trying to find an undamaged place to kiss you," she protested.

She watched as his penis predictably began to swell between his legs.

"You know there's nothing sexier than offering me a compromise," she whispered, her hand snaking down to his groin. "Thank you, we can revisit this in one year."

"My penis?"

"No, we'll be revisiting that right now."

An hour later, tangled in bedsheets, comfortable silence surrounding them, Sara's thoughts returned to Crina. Dispatching her and Heather to New York with the three captives, and making them responsible for all the remaining Spaniards had been a genius move. But even from a distance, Crina was overpowering and annoying, calling Silas hourly, at least, wanting to know of any changes to his health. She'd never once asked how Sara was doing, and now, in the lens of Desdemona's words, Sara realized that wasn't unusual. Looking back over her life, Sara saw that Crina had never really mothered her, Sara had just placed her in a familiar role.

Beside her on the bed, Silas snored gently. Like she'd done countless times in the past week, she watched his chest rise and fall, the machine of him whirring along like it had done for so long, perfectly tuned but now less impervious to time. As he relaxed, his snoring became longer and lower, and his lips parted, the lower one glinting in the gray light pouring in the door from the living room, the top one marked by a new, shiny scar. She wanted to kiss him, but not wake him. Who am I kidding? she asked herself. I want to take care of him forever. At that thought, her breath caught in her throat, and Sara wondered if she could let herself cry quietly enough to not wake him.

A rap at the door settled that. Silas woke instantly, sitting bolt upright.

"What's going on?" he asked, his eyes confused and blinking. "Who's here?"

"Stay there," Sara said, sliding off the bed and quickly hauling on her tracksuit from before. Entering the living room, she was pleased to see Teddie waving through the window.

"Bitch," she called out. "Let a sister in before she freezes to death."

"Get dressed Silas," Sara called out as she went to open the door. "We got company."

"Yes boss," Silas called out and Sara heard the bedroom door close behind her as she pulled open the front door, sending swirls of snowflakes around her as Teddie picked up a large foil-covered dish from the ground.

"Get out of my way, woman" she said as she pushed past Sara, stamped her feet on the little mat and continued into the kitchen. "Oh that's right you idiots don't even have a microwave."

"We have an oven," Sara appeared beside her. "Did you just invite yourself to lunch?"

"By the time this is ready, it will be dinner," Teddie sniffed. "I wanted to make something for you guys."

"What is it?" Silas appeared in the kitchen doorway wearing black sweats and a Black Lives Matter jersey that Teddie had gifted him.

"Hey loverboy," Teddie cooed. "Glad to see you're out of the misery sweater. I made you my short rib lasagna."

As if on cue, Silas's stomach rumbled.

Teddie went over and hugged him gently then patted his tummy.

"Sorry little guy you're gonna have to wait for your food," she said in a baby voice. "Your parents don't have a microwave."

"Fine by me," Silas said. "I don't like microwaved anything, good things come to those who wait."

"So I hear," Teddie said, turning to the small oven. "I can't work this thing. Silas? Three fifty please."

Sara stood back, watching the easy familiarity between the two people she loved most in the whole world.

And then it hit her.

"I figured it out," she blurted, startling them both. "Silas, I figured out what I did to make Crina hate me!"

"Crina hates you?" Teddie was aghast.

"Hate's probably a bit strong," Silas said, his brows knitted curiously.

"This is already a three-bottle dramurgency," Teddie said, lunging for the cluster of bottles of wine at the end of the counter. Grabbing two with one hand and one with the other, she turned to Sara.

"Three glasses and a corkscrew, mom," she said before dancing off into the living room.

"I've been obsessed with Desdemona's truth bomb last week-"

Silas appeared with glasses and began opening all three bottles of wine at once.

"Oh shit, it's that bad?" Teddie laughed

"So, anyway," Sara continued, accepting a glass of wine without a break in her talking, "all week I've been wracking my brain. Was there something I missed? Why would she want to watch me burn out? And I think I just figured it out."

She paused, looking expectantly at both of them.

"Are we supposed to guess?" Silas asked. "Because I am not willing to play that game."

"It's you, Teddie. It was when I decided to make you. I... uh never told you this but she did not want me to make you. Wait, before you get all hurt, you would have been very well taken care of. She wanted us to send you off with a bunch of money and a house and just you know, all the protections that we could offer. But I couldn't let it happen, and Crina and I fought about it. I loved you so deeply, and bringing you with me along on this long, charmed life, that was all I could see. In my heart, it had to happen."

"Thanks, mom. I'm glad you did."

"Right, me too, but I had entirely forgotten about the fights. I had credits, I needed one credit to make you and I had more than that.

And Crina flat-out said I wasn't permitted to make you but she could never tell me why, in any way that made sense. But... wait, holy fuck you guys, she was speaking as a mother, Silas. She was speaking as *your* mother. Fucking hell. This is a lot, and I'm wracking my brain for all the reasons she gave me. She said I was too close to you, Ted, she said that I'd worry forever, I'd never know peace again, that my love for you would make me vulnerable."

"These are all good things," Silas said. "It sucks that she saw them negatively."

"It made no sense at the time because I didn't know she was a mother," Sara said. "Even though she was Lock mother, she became scarce pretty quickly. She started making trips back to Europe. And when she stepped down, she bought the property up here. I rarely saw her after that."

"Her place is like ninety minutes away," Silas said. "I deliberately didn't want her too close to me."

"Right but it wasn't just traveling upstate. She admitted to taking a steamer back to London a couple times. Nobody ever really knew where she was or what she was doing."

"Do you think she actually was in Madrid with Des?"

"It's possible," Sara answered. "I don't think she liked Des, ever. But we never really certain that she was definitely here in New York. She could have been anywhere."

"I was allowed to be around you, and all the women in New York," Silas said. "I was allowed to walk the streets around the compound, although if she ever saw me I'd catch hell afterwards. But she always told me that I was forbidden from talking to or seeing Desdemona. Madrid, the entire city, was off limits."

"This is a lot," Teddie said, draining her wine. "So wait, is Crina a good guy or a villain?"

"It's not that clear cut," Sara said. "She's off on her own trip, and she's using us as what? Lab rats? Entertainment? Either way it's pretty callous."

"She's a fake-ass bitch," Teddie said. "Mom, you know I've always had my suspicions about that one. Blowing into town every year or two, making us all kiss her ass. Sorry, I know it's your mom, Silas..."

"Oh, don't be," Silas said. "This whole me being her priority thing, that's the one thing that I wouldn't have predicted. She's always been fixated on the Locks and you Cursed women. She's always been bitter that Stefanya did more in the Purge, and that Fan and Ama, who trained alongside her, they got the big kills, they were the ones who turned the tide. They already had martial arts training, so they were able to do a lot more. Hasn't she ever talked about this stuff with you?"

"Not in those terms," Sara said. "I'm now mainly concerned about finding out who I can trust? You guys, I'm kind of shutdown and cold over the Crina stuff, but I'll be gutted if Heather has been helping her."

"Heather is the most inscrutable person I know," Silas said.

"No, no, no no," Teddie sat her glass on the floor and waved her arms theatrically. "Nope. Heather? I am not playing this game. We are calling her now." Teddie pulled her phone out of her jacket.

"Wait," Silas said, before proceeding to fill all their glasses to the brim. "Now call her."

Teddie hit dial, and Heather answered immediately.

"Teddie m'dear, what a wonderful surprise," Heather said, "wait, you've got me on speaker. Who's there? Is it bad news?" How's Silas?"

"I'm right here, Heather," Silas said. "No additional bad news from me."

"Good lad," Heather said.

"I'm here too," Sara said.

"I'd expect nothing less," Heather said. "Things are busy here in the city but I'll tell you one thing, this pile o' bricks feels empty and creepy without you lot running riot. But wait, you called me, what's up?"

"Are you alone?" Teddie asked.

"At the moment, yes," Heather said. "Crina's left me in charge while she's off on some errand, so I've got a bunch of irate Spanish women crammed into Marguerite's old apartment and I need to take them their blood and some food here in a bit. I'm just gonna order pizza. They seem to like pizza."

"Heather," Sara's voice was firm. "I need to ask you a question, and if our relationship is as real as I think, I'd really love you to answer me honestly."

"I'm always honest with you pet," Heather didn't even sound worried. "What is it?"

"How long have you known about Crina's plan to let me implode in New York?"

"Sara, I don't think that was her plan at all, she was always talking about us all moving to Iceland in the future."

"Heather, I'm talking about a plan over the last century, the plan that involved bringing in Marguerite to try to get me to crack."

"Well, firstly, Sara, love. I don't believe it at all. Who's your source?"

"It's Desdemona," Sara said, continuing before Heather could react. "And Fan and Ama corroborated it. They didn't know much but they have confirmed it. I still need to talk to Stefanya."

"Well you've managed to shock an old woman," Heather said. "This is the first I'm hearing it. But I have to say, I don't understand what I'm hearing. I'm sure there's another side to the story."

"I'll tell you everything when I see you," Sara said. "But it seems that Stefanya isn't the only elder who is willing to let us all die out so they can start again."

"I... I.." Heather was lost for words. "I'll need my poker face when I see her. She's back tomorrow."

"Where the fuck is she now?" Silas's voice was angry.

"Taking care of something," Heather said. "That's what she always tells me when she takes off, that she's just taking care of something."

"Fuck," Silas said angrily. "We can't even have Fran ping her phone."

"She's not the only techie we have," Teddie said. "I'll give it a shot, and if not I can contact Fran's hacker girl in Ukraine. Is Desdemona still in Pennsylvania?"

"Yeah," Heather said. "They just drive back and forth every day. Different towns, different hotels every night. She knows we're not following them any more. She FaceTimes me and Crina every night, to prove we are in the City."

"You've been talking to her?" Sara couldn't keep the shock out of her voice.

"Yes, there was no point telling you because you're already going through enough," Heather said matter of factly. "If she says anything of note you'll be the first to hear."

A knock sounded at the front door, making them all jump.

"Heather, someone's here," Teddie said.

"I heard."

"Before we go, Heath," Sara's voice was pleading. "Can you swear on the memory of our lost sisters that you didn't know about Crina's plan."

"I can," Heather said. "You can trust me, Sara. You always could and you always can."

"Okay, my friend," Sara's tone was heavy. "I love you and I am so relieved that I wasn't wrong about you. You're a perfect old thing, you are."

"Enough with the old," Heather smiled. "Now answer your damn door while I go feed these miserable Madrid witches."

The phone went dead, and Silas straightened up and pulled the door open, revealing Yukari in a fur-lined bright yellow down jacket, her bright eyes beaming in the cold.

"Hi you guys," she said, stepping inside and shaking snowflakes from her hood. "I had to come straight away. I just got back from the City. I have a good vaccine to slow down the aging."

Chapter Twenty-Six

"I love a party," Yukari said, twirling beneath a spray of fairy lights.

"Well, normally, so do I," Sara deadpanned, gazing around the living space of the main house. "But this will be my first Mortality Party, and I'm not okay with it."

"You would be if you were getting your own mortality shot," Yukari stopped spinning and took Sara's hands, for support initially, and then for balance as the room continued to twirl without her.

"I don't even know if that would help," Sara said, pointing her chin at the definitely excessive party makeover that the living room had received courtesy of the Christmas department of a nearby Walgreens; Strands of holiday lights in bright whites or alternating rainbow colors crisscrossed the ceiling and draped down every wall. "This feels somehow wrong, like we're lying to ourselves about what is actually happening tonight."

"It's what Fan and Ama wanted," Yukari said. "And you know they do everything their own way. This is the first party of its kind in history, and I guess they don't want it to be all solemn and sad."

Sara flopped onto the sofa. Solemn and sad had been her constant companions for the better part of the last century and she knew that a few thousand tiny twinkling lights would do nothing to dispel them.

But the party was going to take place regardless of her feelings around it, so Sara decided to face her sour mood head on. Without a word, she made her way to the upstairs bathroom, the same one she'd gotten ready in over a year ago, ahead of her big dinner with Silas, out on the deck. Closing the door behind her, she stared at the woman in the mirror. Of course there were no physical changes, but there was something different about her face. She moved closer, trying to figure out the change. It was defeat. The face looking back at her had no vitality, no spark.

Staring into her own brown eyes, the mirror reflected back nothing but sadness. This new version of her had lost all fight. She was less. The potential of a centuries-long love affair was now gone, replaced by a nightmare scenario where she would be nursing Silas through all the stages of human frailty, and the fact that he'd have Fan and Ama as adventure buddies did nothing to budge her depression.

A knock at the door startled her.

"Sara?" It was April Veronica's voice.

"Yes?"

"Are you okay in there?"

Sara unlocked the door and opened it, revealing the youngest Cursed woman, a worried look on her face, her arms behind her back.

"I was looking everywhere for you," April Veronica said. "And when I didn't hear any noises from in here-"

"Oh, gross," Sara said, stepping out into the hallway.

"Oh come on," April Veronica said. "This old place is so not sound-proof, I kept on thinking of your first date here. I would never have been able to use the bathroom, you can hear everything."

"Well, for most of its life, there was only one person living here," Sara said. "So what's up? Why were you looking for me?"

Still keeping her arms behind her back, April Veronica pushed Sara with her chest, back into the room she was sharing with Embla, the same room Sara had awoken in after Desdemona's attack.

"I got you a present, obviously," April Veronica said, kicking the door closed behind her, then turning and presenting a gift, a large lumpy object in a brown paper shopping bag. "I figured you might need some cheering up."

Sara's heart twinged, as it always did when April Veronica took care of her, and she looked at the young woman, wiser than her years. She would make a formidable Cursed woman. Hell, she already did.

"I know you're not good with gifts," April Veronica laughed as she thrust the present into Sara's hands. "And I'm guessing you're not good with Mortality Parties, so I wanted to help out."

"You're too good to me," Sara said as she tore into the package, confused by glimpses of bright yellow fur.

"It's a new onesie," April Veronica said proudly. "They didn't have Care Bears, I made Embla go to four different places, so you have to be Pikachu!"

The onesie made Sara happier than all the lights in the living room. The love and care from April Veronica crashed into a memory of the end of her beloved Care Bears onesie, probably now a moldy pile of blue fake fur in the woods outside the Akureyri guesthouse. Clutching it in one hand, she threw her free arm around April Veronica and squeezed her tight.

"I do not know where I'd be without you," she said. "I mean it, kid."

"Ditto," April Veronica said before extricating herself from the hug and lunging beneath her bed and grabbing a Walgreens bag. "I hope you don't mind matchy matchy."

A short while later, naked and warm inside a cocoon of neon yellow nylon fur, Sara stood at the top of the stairs, her arm around April

Veronica's shoulders. The weed elixir that she'd chugged before getting changed hit her system, cloaking the room in a a fuzzy glow, each tiny blinking light now haloed, a sea of sparkling bubbles.

"The cosplay party has arrived," Embla called out from below them, and Sara blinked her eyes into focus, finding Embla standing beside Silas, over by the table.

"I'll help you with the stairs," April Veronica, now dressed in a sea-blue Snorlax onesie, whispered in her ear. "I think you went a bit hard on the weed drink."

"You shouldn't make it so delicious," Sara giggled, willing her feet to step down to the next riser until she felt April Veronica's arm around her back, guiding her forward and down, over and over until her feet felt the difference between the bounce of the stairs and the solidity of the floor. "Hey, why isn't there any music playing?"

"Because we just got here," Embla said, "and I don't think anyone remembered to pair their phone to the speakers."

"That's a me problem," Silas darted over to the credenza against the back wall. "Hey, sexy Pikachu, I've got your iPod connected to it, what's your happiest playlist?"

"Have you met me?" Sara burst out laughing. "All of my playlists are soundtracks for sadness."

"Ignore her," Embla said. "Search by genre. Disco."

"Young people are geniuses," Sara cooed, blowing Embla a kiss as a familiar disco beat filled the room.

"You're playing Sylvester?" Teddie appeared from the bedroom at the far end of the living room. "Mom! Remember all the times we went to see Sylvester?"

Letting the beat move her feet, Sara danced over to Teddie, wrapping her in a hug.

"Of course I remember," she said loudly. "They were so incredible, we thought we'd all be dancing to their music for decades."

"Do you remember we talked to them that one night?" Teddie began to dance around Sara, breaking out ancient disco moves.

"Oh, that's right," Sara laughed. "I told them I thought they were better than David Bowie."

"And they loved to hear it."

"I can't believe you two met Mother Sylvester," Embla said, joining their dance circle.

"There will be more mothers to come," Sara said. "And... I'd like to add... you're pretty Mother yourself, blazing your own trail like a motherfucking comet."

"How high are you?"

"She's pretty high," April Veronica appeared beside them, as the music got louder and the bass echoed deliciously in her chest and she felt Silas's rough, large hand grip one of hers and pull her to him.

"Oh, you're gonna dance with me?"

"I don't have a choice," Silas whispered into her ear. "But I promise you nothing."

He moved with the rhythm as she lay against him, content to feel his heart beating against her cheek, vaguely aware of Teddie, Embla and April Veronica all dancing around them. Squinting her eyes until the fairylights became her entire universe, Sara threw her arms around Silas's shoulders and buried her face against his neck, inhaling his aroma so deeply that it made her woozy and her dancing suffered a misstep, her foot landing on top of Silas's.

"Keep it there," he whispered, his foot carrying hers. "Now the other one."

Sara placed her other foot atop Silas's, as his arms pulling her tight while her feet danced without her, and her lips kissed the skin where

Silas's shoulder met his neck, tasting salt. Sara didn't know if it was the weed or just pure fact, but a wave of something more than contentment washed over her and through her, love for Silas and the women dancing beside them, to a song she had loved for half a century. She wanted the moment to last forever.

But now it couldn't.

The thought sobered her, bursting the balloon of weed intoxication and leaving Sara adrift. Suddenly, she felt like a scarecrow, a puppet being animated by someone else, and she stepped off Silas's feet.

"Uh oh," he said quietly in her ear. "What happened?"

"Oh nothing," she said into his neck. "You know me. Things get too good and as soon as you acknowledge how good they are, they aren't good any more."

"That's never been scientifically proven," Silas said, his dancing slowing. "Wanna get back on my feet for another spin?"

"I'd love a cocktail, actually," Sara said, "I suddenly feel altogether too California-sober for a Mortality Party."

"I hear you," Silas said, his arms releasing her. "Be right back."

After Silas went over to the kitchen, Sara dance-walked her way to the sofa and sat down, her eyes never leaving the young women dancing, their eyes closed, their bodies moving, smiles on their faces, her good mood returning as a contact high. Fran came swirling onto the dance floor, beckoning Sara to join her, her pupils wildly dilated. Sara mouthed "later" at her as she felt weight beside her on the couch, the cushions moving her up and down. Expecting it to be Silas, she was surprised when she heard Fan's voice in her ear.

"I believe the children are our future," Fan sang.

"Were you always this corny?"

"Was corny even a thing in the fifteen hundreds?"

"You're right, corny is a new thing," Sara said. "For you, and the world in general."

"I like being corny," Fan said. "I like being dumb. I like being things that you don't have time to develop when you're under constant stress. The first century of my life was pretty stressful."

"But what if there's something else that you might enjoy being, but you'll die before you discover it?"

"Nice try," Fan said. "But that, in a nutshell, is the human experience. Dying before you figure everything out. You're just struggling because you're currently in a figure shit out phase."

Laughing involuntarily at Fan's statement, Sara turned to face her. Fan's hair was pulled back into short pigtails, and messy glitter makeup surrounded her eyes, and she was wearing what looked like a girl's private school uniform, perfectly tailored black, white and red tartan.

"Girl," Sara laughed. "I'm actually in an I don't know anything at all phase. But you look amazing, what is this?"

"I had it made in New York," Fan said. "This is the official tartan of Scottish witches!"

"How much of that material did Heather buy?"

"I think she bought all of it," Fan said. "There were quite a few bolts of it in her spare bedroom."

"Well, it suits you," Sara said, spying Silas and Ama entering the room with drinks on trays. Ama, in a very tight romper also made of witch tartan, headed their way, instructing them to take a tumbler of blood from her. Sara chugged hers as soon as she got it, not wanting to drink blood in front of Silas, stashing her empty mug on the floor a split second before he appeared in front of her.

"Choose your poison," he said with a wink. "I whipped up French 75s and margaritas."

Pausing to consider her options, Sara decided on the French 75, leaving the margarita for him. She loved the taste of tequila on his breath.

"What did I miss?" he asked as he squeezed close to Sara.

"Fan being cheesy," Sara said, cheersing him.

"I believe the term you used was corny," Fan said, double fisting her blood and cocktail.

"I stand corrected," Sara said. "And I'm also staying quiet because I don't want to say anything else that will piss her off."

"I'm a five hundred year old woman," Fan smiled. "Everything pisses me off."

"Now that," Sara raised her glass, "I can cheers to."

As their three glasses clinked in the air, the music volume lowered dramatically, and Ama's voice rang out.

"I hereby declare the first ever, and I mean, literal first ever, Mortality Party, a resounding success!"

"My love," Fan matched her volume. "You're making an awful big deal out of a party for less than ten people."

"For everyone here who I'm not in a relationship with, I'd like to share the secret to a long, happy relationship," Ama moved to stand beside her girlfriend. "Don't ever react. No matter what they say, no matter how hard they try to push your buttons, just never react. Thank you for coming to my Lesbian Love Lesson."

A light round of applause sounded, and Ama bowed to each of them in turn.

"Thank you, thank you," she said. "And I know we are making light of a very serious thing tonight, but I also appreciate you all so much for bringing the joy, not just tonight, but always, because that's the other key to any life at all, long or short. Joy. It's a bottomless resource, if you just remind yourself of that fact, you can be happy forever."

"So," Sara heard herself speaking before she even knew she was going to say anything, "why are you guys choosing to limit that forever? Can't you just whip up some joy and figure out a way to hang around?"

Silas's warm hand took hers, and she loved him for not shushing her or telling her to be quiet.

"Sara," Fan's voice was quiet, "we love you and we are holding so much space for you, but Ama and I really want you to understand where we are on this whole mortality thing." Pausing, Fan glanced at Ama, who immediately understood, gliding over to Sara's iPod and stopping the music. In the silence that followed, everyone took seats around Sara, either on the couch beside her or on the floor facing her, and she felt self-conscious, a narc whose misery had derailed yet another good time. Awkwardly, Sara tried to chug her cocktail, but the bubbles caught in her throat, making her cough.

"I'm fine," she sputtered. "Don't let me ruin your party."

"No, no, no," Ama, on the arm of the sofa, leaned over and rubbed Sara's back. "This is why we wanted this party, we want you all to be part of our decision, sure, but we also want you all to understand it, and to support us, and Sara," Ama kept her tone neutral. "We realize that we are giving up the one thing you wish for Silas, but the other side of that coin is that he will not be alone on his journey."

For a split-second Sara weighed up being supportive versus being honest. Honesty won.

"He's already not alone on the journey," she said, fighting to keep her voice sweet. "Every person on this planet is on that journey."

Another hand squeeze from Silas, but no recrimination, only served to embolden Sara.

"Our numbers are down," she continued. "There are less than sixty of us left on this earth. We are a manageable group and it just seems a bit... I don't know... I don't know the word... okay, so we are just now ditching the rules and routines of half a millenium, we are at the start of our first new chapter in forever, literal forever, and you guys want to shuffle off what? Fifty years into it?"

Fan and Ama exchanged knowing smiles, and Ama continued rubbing her back.

"I'll take this one, love," she said, and Fan gave her a thumbs up. "Sara, I'm a Buddhist. I know that we're not supposed to be religious, but I don't see Buddhism as religion, even though it is. I see it as philosophy, and I've had the unprecedented opportunity of being able to apply the wisdom of Buddhism to the longest life of any Buddhist ever. But about what? Fan? A hundred years ago?"

Fan nodded in agreement.

"Yeah, over a hundred now, well over."

"I started to get deeply depressed," Ama continued. "There are so many questions that I can't answer, and they're questions that nobody can answer for me. I need to know what happens when we die."

"But what if it's nothing?" Sara's voice was plaintive.

"Then it's nothing," Ama's voice didn't change. "But time is also nothing, and we've had so much of it, more than anyone we know of, and what do we have to show for it? We all have those memories, those ancient ones, they don't feel like things that actually happened. Sara, do you remember the day we met?"

"Of course I do," she said. "I came to that bunker that Stefanya had set up in the forest, in the abandoned church."

"How did it smell?" Fan joined in. "What were you wearing? What did you do earlier that day?"

Sara wracked her brain, all too aware that such details were long lost, overwritten by her brain.

"Ancient memories just become facts," Ama said. "We know things happened but the actual memory has degraded, it's gone. And that's what got me started on pondering our entire existence. What if we are energy, and we get made into these human shapes, and our purpose is to experience things and then we return to the energy armed with love and visions of the beauty we saw on this planet?"

"Then it's our duty to amass as much love and experience and beauty as we can," Sara said.

"I can't speak for you, Sara, or anyone here," Ama's voice was so gentle. "But I've forgotten more love and beauty than most humans ever get to experience. I want the ticking clock. I need my time to be special because it's limited, because the moments won't be infinite any more. I want to see the love of my life with gray hair, I want to feel my body do what it's meant to do, to age and to mature and weaken, because there will be beauty in those experiences. I'm not afraid of any part of the human experience. Our immortality has made us complacent, and I am hungry for the things that we've denied ourselves."

"I've had this discussion with Imani," Sara said. "Literally thousands of times."

"And it doesn't make you curious?" Fan turned her sparkly face to Sara. "You don't want to find out if the Bardo is real?"

"I mean, sure, yes, I do, and I hope it is," Sara said. "But you two have been off having one hell of a grand adventure. My life was finally about to start, and just a week ago, it was torn away from me, so it's a lot for you to ask of me, to have me at your party tipping out my forty for your immortality. If I could say anything, anything at all, that could change your minds or at least delay your... vaccination, then it would be this. I want everything to stop changing. I want to be surrounded by the women – and man – that I love in this new age. I haven't had the wild adventures that you've had, exploring the world with a lover who gets you completely, knowing that they'll always be there for you, for centuries, not decades."

"We know, Sara," Ama's hand finally stopped rubbing Sara's back. "But this is something we were always going to do, what has happened with Silas just kind of forced our hand. We want to demystify the whole thing. Nobody knows the future, but now that I can see the rest of my life mapped out like this, me and my old lady traveling until we're too old, then settling someplace beautiful for our final years, sounds like the truest, clearest decision I've ever made."

"Same here," Fan said. "But once again, I do think, Ama, that we've kind of overreacted and we're being too... us. Right, April Veronica?"

Sara, confused, looked at April Veronica, sitting on the floor with Mr Handsome on her lap, who gave Fan a wan smile and shrugged.

"I know what you're saying," April Veronica said. "And yeah, you guys are excited about something and you want us all to get excited too but it's not where Sara is, and you didn't factor that into your..."

"Party planning?" Ama groaned. "You're right of course, and Sara, I apologize. Ladies and gentleman, I think we need to adjust our planned activities."

"You're nixing the ceremonial vaccination?" Fan's voice was serious.

"Only the ceremonial part," Ama said. "Yukari, we will do that part later, in private."

"Okay," Yukari said, clearly relieved. "Let me know when you're planning it."

"Well," Fan said, clearly a little irritated that her party was going sideways, "can we at least hit Silas with his slowdown serum?"

"No," Yukari's voice was stern. "I told you already. I have to use the same needle, same dosage, on him and Desdemona, that's her condition for the safe return of Fran and Imani."

"Well," Fan repeated herself. "What are we waiting for? Let's call that bitch and plan the world's first Delaying Mortality Party."

Chapter Twenty-Seven

After parking the car down by Riverside Park, Sara got out and paused, looking over the Hudson, normally hidden by a thick carpet of green leaves, the vista now interrupted by nothing but sticks, bare branches pointing to a million galaxies, the river flowing, gray and eternal, behind them.

Behind her, she heard the trunk slam closed and turned to see Silas, his arm out of the sling, struggling with their luggage.

"Here, give me some of that, you're not a pack mule."

With a groan, Silas handed two heavy duffel bags to her, and they walked in silence uphill on 104th Street, a chill wind whistling in their ears. At the corner of West End Avenue, Sara stopped, gazing up at the windows to her apartment, darkly reflecting the sky. She felt oddly nervous about entering the compound, which was presently, for the first time in its existence, completely empty.

Sensing her reticence, Silas dropped his luggage to the sidewalk.

"Wanna go to a hotel?"

Sara shook her head.

"No, but let's just drop the bags inside and walk around some. The grand old lady feels a bit haunted today."

"Are you talking about the building or yourself?"

"Bit of both, actually," Sara said, relieved that the light changed, allowing her to cross and escape Silas's questioning. After they'd deposited their bags inside the entry lobby, they went back out to the street, and Silas slipped his hand inside hers. She she led him slowly around the compound perimeter, just another couple out for a wintry stroll. A late night phone call to Desdemona had led to vague plans to meet in New York, in the vicinity of the compound. Desdemona's one requirement was that Crina be out of the city, so Silas had summoned his mother to his upstate property using Desdemona as bait. Predictably, Crina rejoiced at the news that Des was headed to the Hobbit House, and she and Heather left New York immediately, revenge on Crina's mind.

"What do you think your mom will do when she gets to your place and we aren't there?"

"Don't know, don't care," Silas said. "All I know is that she will kill Des on sight, and we need to get Imani and Fran back safely. Once we get them back, I don't care what she does."

"Right, but then what?" Sara said, pausing at the corner of Broadway and looking north and south at the nearly deserted sidewalks and the sparse traffic. It felt like the entire City was empty, and a chill ran deep through her bones. "Actually, table that, I want to get inside, I'm freezing."

"Noted," Silas smiled. "First, one thing."

Leaving her to survey the intersection, Silas stepped into the corner bodega. Sara returned her attention to the life passing her by, taxis and cars and pedestrians, and she tried to lose herself imagining their lives, but nothing came to her. Darkness surrounded her, an emptiness that scared her deeply, a certainty that the meeting with Desdemona would be an ending, but of what she didn't know.

She was worried sick. And every time she looked at Silas, she imagined him elderly, struggling... and dying.

Silas reappeared beside her, his arms clutching bunches of flowers, a red and white Thank You bag containing several bottles of wine hanging from his wrist. The friendly, expectant look on his face broke her heart a little.

"Your place or ours?" he asked with a grin.

"Let's go to mine," Sara said, turning back to where they came from. "Ours still looks like a tornado hit it."

"But ours is closer," Silas said. "And I'm gonna drop these flowers."

Sara hurried ahead and unlocked the door to the building that she and Silas had lived in briefly, holding it open for Silas and a gust of frozen wind. They trudged up five flights in silence. Sara used her finger to unlock the door, then they were inside the ruin of their apartment, stuff still strewn everywhere.

"It looks like we have squatters," she said as she surveyed the mess.

"I hope they didn't steal my vases," Silas said, carefully laying the bouquets on the small countertop, then standing the wine beside them. As she watched, Sara felt the first burn of thirst in her throat. Fuck. Her heems and her blood bags were in the luggage. Reading her mind, Silas turned to her.

"Hey, I'm gonna go grab the bags real quick," he said. "If you like, can you snip the stems of the flowers? I'll arrange them when I get back."

And he was gone, out the secret rear door. New York was eerily silent. No sirens. No yelling. No hip hop blasting out of a passing car. Sara opened the cutlery drawer, finding it similarly bare. No scissors! Every other drawer? Empty. There weren't even any sharp knives to trim the flowers' stems. With a dejected sigh, Sara wandered out of the tiny kitchen and circled the coffee table, looking at the bare brick walls, every brick representing an atom of her being. This building was as much Sara as her hair, her skin. She had birthed this building and guarded its occupants like a wolf. Now, like a diseased body part, she could feel that something was wrong. Something was cracking the foundation, but she couldn't tell if the damage was structural or spiritual. Aware that her thirst was worsening the depression, she returned to the kitchen and opened the hot water faucet, testing the frosty water with a fingertip until it warmed and she pressed her wrists together beneath the flowing water, marveling at how much effect such a simple act could have over her moods. Her phone rang, and she hurriedly dried her hands on the front of her jacket. It was Yukari.

"Hey Yuka."

"Just checking in from the road, Sara. I have you on speaker with Teddie and the teenagers."

A chorus of hellos rang out inside the car.

"I'm driving in America," Embla called out. "It's kind of freaky."

"Well keep it safe freaky please," Sara said. "What's your ETA?

"We'll be in the city by noon," Yukari said.

"And I will have the location locked in by then," said Teddie. "I mean it won't be a problem, I'm just making sure we will be alone. It's Tuesday, I think I have a solution."

"Speaking of alone," Sara said, "I think that this is the first time this entire complex has been empty. Me and Silas are the only people here."

"Where are the Spaniards?" Teddie asked.

"They're with Yfke and Skye in Red Hook," Sara said. "It's just us here."

"Oh hell," April Veronica yelled. "You guys are empty nesters! Don't turn my old room into a sewing room."

"Never would," Sara laughed, grateful again for the young woman's energy and outlook. "But I have to say, I don't like it, so hurry up and get here... safely."

"I guess that means we don't have time to stop at the Pancake House," Embla said.

"If today goes well, we can celebrate there tonight," Sara said.

"Today will go well, mom," Teddie said. "We have what she needs, and we can get our girls back."

"It's the after part that I'm worried about," Sara said. "Desdemona isn't known for going quietly."

"So," Teddie wheedled. "Weapons, yes? No?"

"Ugh, I think we have to," Sara said. "I just don't know whether we go old school or trad?"

"It's not gauche to bring a gun to a Slicer fight," Embla said. "We need to be prepared. She had guns last week."

"And we are all going," April Veronica said. "I'm exercising my free will. I want to be there to help get Franny and Manny back."

"That's what you call them?" Sara laughed out loud.

"Don't encourage her," Embla said. "She came up with it last week, thinks it's hilarious, she does."

"I sure does," April Veronica said. "And Sara, why don't you just do nothing for the next couple hours? You have a whole city block to yourself. Why don't you and your man friend try to have sex in every building?"

"Yeah," Teddie jumped in. "And I bet it's been a long while since the roof deck saw any action."

"You lot are weird," Sara chuckled. "I'm distracted and it's freezing."

"We had sex on the roof deck a couple of weeks back," Embla said. "So maybe go christen the big conference room."

"Actually," Teddie interrupted, "where is your sexual partner?"

At that moment, Sara heard the rear door unlock, turning to see Silas carrying one duffel and kicking the other along the hall, a smile on his face.

"He's playing porter," Sara said, putting the call on speaker. "He just brought our bags up to our room."

"Wait," Teddie continued. "Where you all staying at? U-Haul Couple Realness or Mama's Mental Breakdown?"

"We're back in the U-Haul suite," Silas yelled out. "Am I speaking with Clown Car Number 2?"

"You better not be trying to claim that you were Clown Car Number 1," Embla's voice was indignant. "You two are definitely not serving clown."

"Get off the phone and go serve some D," April Veronica cracked herself up.

"Peanut!" Silas yelled as he let the bag fall to the floor. "Is that any way to speak to your elders?"

"D is off the menu," Sara said, winking at Silas. "Get back to driving. But first, I do need to ask an unnecessary question."

"Yes," Yukari said. "I definitely have the vaccine with me in the car, I didn't forget it."

"You know me too well," Sara laughed.

"And I know you haven't asked, but I did administer it to myself, Fan and Ama last night."

Sara's heart sank, but she swallowed pushed ahead.

"Good to know," she said. "And they're coming to the City too?"

"Yes," Embla said. "They will also be upset to be denied Pancake House."

"They'll get there just before we do," Teddie said. "So, if you do throw down, make sure you wrap it all up by like 11:30."

"And look at the time," Sara said. "I really need to go. I have an appointment at the beauty parlor in ten minutes."

"Do you really mom?"

"No, Ted, I just want this phone call to be over. So bye, love you, bye, love you."

She hung up.

"Why is everyone so determined to get you laid?" Silas, now kneeling at the bags, asked with a wicked smile.

"They're more interested in embarrassing me," Sara said, her eyes widening when she saw Silas retrieve the insulated lunch box that held the blood.

"Take a seat, my love," Silas said, pointing at a stack of cushions in the corner. The addiction was making Sara irritable and she wanted nothing more than to snatch the lunchbox from Silas's hands and run into the bedroom. Salivating, Sara perched on the cushions, watching intently as Silas opened the shunt on the tube and took it between his lips.

"Still warm," he said, a ruby droplet on his lower lip capturing her attention fully as her addiction clawed painfully within her. Fighting to keep her motions steady, Sara took the bag, still warm to the touch, and put the little tube between her lips, counting to five between sips.

"No need for manners," Silas said, and her anger flared. She did not want him watching her feed, it felt strangely invasive and improper. Keeping her gaze fixed on the floor, she finished the entire bag, refusing to swoon once it was done, yet only partially successful, her relaxing fingers dropping the bag. Silas picked it up and took it to the kitchen, and Sara watched him walk away, her love for him so inextricably mixed with sadness.

"What do you need?" Silas appeared beside her again.

"Let's take a walk," Sara said. "I haven't walked all the back corridors since we built the place, I... for some reason, that feels like freedom right now."

Silas extended a hand and helped Sara up, kissed her on the lips, his bristles tickling her. Hand in hand, they wandered the perimeter hallway on their level, five stories above the street. The buildings on Broadway did not have rear hallways, so once they reached the end of that level, they went down, past the doors to Heather's place and later on, to Fran's. As they descended, the air grew colder and more still, and by the time they hit the basement level, Sara was unable to shake the feeling that the building, her home for so long, was little more than a glorified crypt.

"Is that blood on the floor?" Silas's voice startled her, and Sara looked at the stone floor, at what definitely looked like a long smear of blood, now dried.

"Yes," she said, her eyes following it along the hall to where it curved beneath a locked door.

"Is this where they were holding the Madrid sisters," Silas said. "What happened?"

Sara gingerly pushed the door open and gasped. Just inside the door, the wide blood streak broadened into a wild, irregular pool, still wet in some places, the scent still fresh enough to spike her hunger.

"Fucking hell," Silas whispered behind her. "What did they do to them?"

Sara flicked the light switch and a dull yellow light flooded the space They both surveyed the room, the walls streaked with bloody handprints. Silas stepped around the puddle into the other room, and gasped.

"Stay out there, Sara," he said, his voice shaky. "Whatever happened in here, the mattress is soaked in blood."

"Come with me," Sara barked, turning and running out of the room, following the trail, evidence that a body had been dragged along the hall. Unlocking the door to the furnace room, Sara was once again surprised by silence. The furnace should have been running, but it was not. She hauled open the heavy metal door and looked inside, gagging immediately at the sight of the twisted corpses of three dark-haired women, their arms and faces lacerated with deep gashes, their eyes open, dull and dead.

"Looks like someone left without finishing what they were doing," Silas said angrily.

"We need to figure out how they died," Sara said, emotion choking her voice.

"I need you to go clean up," Silas said, pointing his chin at her hands, now covered in blood from the furnace cover. Without protest, Sara pushed around him and went down the hall to the conference room, leaving a bloody fingerprint on the security pad. Inside, she went to the small bathroom at the rear and ran her hands under icy water, the blood stubbornly clinging to the lines in her palms. In the mirror, she saw a woman who looked even worse than she had at the Mortality Party, two days earlier, a woman rocked by worry, horror and disgust. Drying her hands on her jacket, she called Skye,

"G'day mate," the Aussie answered immediately.

"Hey, Skye. You in Red Hook with the Spaniards?"

"I'm fine thanks mate, thanks for asking. And yep, me and Yfke are stuck here with the two less sour ones. Crina and Heather are babysitting Team Desdemona back in the city. Why? What's up?"

Sara scrambled to find a reply, unsure whether she could trust Skye, or Yfke for that matter.

"Oh nothing," she said eventually. "I'm just updating a map so we know where everyone is."

"Well I'd like to update your map with us taking these bitches back to Bucharest," Skye said. "Yfke is completely stir-crazy and she isn't doing well in captivity."

"You guys can go out," Sara said.

"Nope, Crina has ordered us to basically never leave. We've been shut inside for a week."

"When was the last time you talked to Crina?"

"About ten minutes ago, why?"

"Typical," Sara lied. "She won't pick up when I call but she's talking to everyone else."

"Between you and me, mate," Skye's tone was conspiratorial, "something's up with her. She's been acting like a complete psychopath. I told her I wanted to take these women home and she fuckin' flipped. Told me I had to keep them safe until she came to take them back to Romania. She wants to do it for some reason."

"Weird," Sara said. "Did Crina tell you where she was?"

"Hang on," Skye said. "Isn't she headed to meet you? Sara, what's going on?"

Knowing she was cornered, Sara scrambled for something strategic.

"Sara, don't lie to me." Skye's voice was alarmed. "Me and Yffie have been stuck here like mushrooms, kept in the dark and fed a lot of bullshit. Come clean with me, mate!"

"Can I trust you, one hundred per cent?"

"Course you bloody can."

"Okay, this will be a lot, I came here to meet Desdemona, Yukari has a vaccine for her, and we will get Imani and Fran back. I lied to Crina that the meeting was happening at the upstate house because I know she will kill Des on sight. She can kill her tomorrow, after we have our friends back."

"What the fuck? They just left the Spanish women unattended? That's bullshit. We were told that at least one of us needs to be here at all times."

"Skye, I really need to know that I can trust you."

"For fuck's sake, Sara mate, I already said yes. I'm good as me word."

"The Spanish women are dead," Sara said. "It's recent."

"What? Sara, are you sure Desdemona's not in the building? She would kill those women."

"It's not Des," Sara said. "We have her chipped. She's driving east on 80. I think Crina left in a hurry because the bodies are still in the furnace and they're not burned."

"And they were murdered?"

"Silas is in there figuring it out," Sara said. "Too much blood, I was starting to black out."

"Fucking hell, we will be right over."

"No, please, both of you, stay there," Sara said, urgent to get off the phone. "I'll call you tonight after we see Desdemona and we will come help you get the women over here to the compound."

"Fuck that," Skye spat. "We are sitting fucking ducks in this place. Desdemona knows this location, fuck me, we might as well put a fucking neon sign out the front telling everyone where we are."

"Look, I have to go," Sara said. "If you need to feel safe, go check into a hotel, I'll call you as soon as we're done with Des."

"Yep fine," Skye said, her voice bristling with anger. "Yfke is out at a Dispensary, as soon as she's back we will move out and wait for your call. And Sara? Please. Do not underestimate Desdemona."

"I won't, I promise."

"And Sara? Thanks for trusting me. I got you."

"Thanks, and you guys be careful too."

The line went dead and Sara let herself out of the bathroom, jumping when she saw Silas hunched over in Teddie's throne.

"I'm burning them," he said hoarsely. "I lit the fire. I didn't want you to see what I saw."

"Were they murdered?"

Silas raised his head, nodding.

"Yes, I guess," he said. "Slicers to the spine, and more. I guess they fought back, they're pretty torn up."

"Let's get this Desdemona thing over and done with," Sara said, moving for the door. "Because I have a mother in law to deal with."

Chapter Twenty-Eight

Heavy flakes of snow were falling as Sara stepped out into the courtyard of The Cloisters, Silas on one side of her, Yukari on the other.

"Where should we do this?" Yukari asked, and they stopped, taking in the walled, open quadrangle inside the main building. Four bare trees, one in each corner, snow catching in their branches, and one small pergola building in the center, small bushes almost buried in snow pebbling the ground.

"I don't care," Silas said. "It doesn't matter, she's not going to try anything with Fan and Ama here."

"She's always been scared of them," Sara said. "She will definitely be on edge."

"Let's just stand in front of the little house," Yukari said. "If we stand under a tree, we might get covered in falling snow."

Nodding, Sara walked to the small wooden building in the center of the square, her feet vanishing into the fresh snow before landing with a satisfying crunch. Reaching it, she turned and took in their surroundings. Covered walkways surrounded the square, icicles hanging from the gutters, darkness engulfing the paths behind them. Somewhere in the walkway, April Veronica and Embla were armed and waiting. A walkie talking crackled to life in the pocket of Sara's floor-length North Face, and she pulled it out.

"Desdemona is here," Fan said. "I repeat, she's here."

"She's almost half an hour early," Sara said. "Never mind. Is she alone?"

"She's in the passenger seat," Fan said. "One twin is driving, I guess the others are in the back. I can't see."

"Well, we are ready, I guess," Sara said. "Bring her through."

"Do we have permission to neutralize the men?"

"For the billionth time, no," Sara said.

"I know boss," Fan laughed. "Just fuckin with ya."

Irritably, Sara clicked the walkie off and turned to Silas.

"Here we go," she said. "And if things go south, I love you both very much."

Instead of replying, each of her companions took one of her hands and squeezed it, and they all turned to face the spot where Desdemona would be entering. Time slowed unbearably, and Sara strained her ears for any sound of conflict, hearing only the tinsel sound of snowflakes landing on her shoulders. Movement in the dark caught her attention, and in seconds, Desdemona emerged from the darkness. To Sara's horror, she was still wearing the white fur coat, now the yellowed color of a Polar bear, the fur matted. Sara wondered briefly if she'd just cleaned it in a laundromat. The dye had washed out of Desdemona's black hair, leaving it shot through with gray, pulled back into a severe ponytail. Her flint eyes were rimmed in eyeliner, black kohl clumping among the wrinkles.

"Sister dear," she called out as Toma and Rad appeared beside her, both carrying pistols.

"Nope," Sara yelled. "Not today. No games, no niceties. Let's get this over so we can move on to the never seeing each other again portion of our lives."

"I wasn't about to be nice," Desdemona took two steps forward before stopping and taking in her surroundings, the men pointing their guns at Sara and Silas, their expressions cold. "I was going to point that anything would have been less theatrical than the Cloisters."

"What? You requested neutral territory at short notice, this is the best I could come up with."

"You're always so ridiculous, I just-"

"Shut your fucking mouth," Sara spat. "If you didn't have two armed men behind you, I'd be tearing your throat out with my bare teeth."

"Finally, a spine," Desdemona smiled, and Sara took in the crow's feet that appeared at the corners of her eyes.

"Yeah yeah," Sara looked around. "Where are Fran and Imani?"

"Come out, girls." Desdemona turned and waved her arms imperiously, and slowly, four figures emerged from the shadows. First, Fran and Imani, and then behind them, Fan and Ama, holding them upright. As they moved into the light, a shudder of revulsion shook Sara to her core. They'd been starved. Fran's dark circles made her look like she'd been in a fight, and even beneath Imani's midnight complexion, Sara could see the deep bruising. Both women's cheeks were sunken but their eyes burned as brightly as ever. Imani raised an arm to wave, lost her balance and stumbled. Ama caught her.

"Hey you two," Sara called out. "Bring them to me."

"Not until the deal is done," Desdemona said, taking another step into the courtyard. "They can wait another few minutes."

"Alright then, bitch," Sara called out. "Come get your shot."

Desdemona went to speak, and Sara raised a hand.

"Save it," she said. "We have your instructions. Firstly, you and Silas will attempt to drink some blood, each from our own source. Once you're certain that Silas is immune to our virus, you'll both be vaccinated from the same needle."

"Which I admit is a risk, considering he's been fucking a whore like you," Desdemona said.

In another life, the words would have punctured Sara. Finally, she was immune to Desdemona, who was clearly expecting a comeback.

"Whatever," Desdemona said eventually. "Anyway, let's drink some blood."

Reaching into a pocket in the fur, she pulled out a very small blood bag, holding it aloft.

"Yukari, would you care to inspect this?"

Yukari, carrying a much larger blood bag, walked over to her, sniffed, and then tasted, the blood from Desdemona's bag before proffering her own for inspection.

"That's blood alright," Desdemona said. "Okay, so on the count of three, eh Silas?"

Sara turned to look at Silas for the first time since Desdemona's arrival. His jaw was clenched so tightly that the sides of his face flared out, and he was swallowing compulsively. Sara had never seen him this transformed by anger. He took the blood bag from Yukari.

"*Arriba, abajo, al centro y pa'dentro,*" Desdemona called out with a mocking smile, "*Tres, dos, uno!*"

They both began to drink. Desdemona gagged first, pulling the bag away from her mouth.

"All of it," Sara called out. Desdemona flipped her off and resumed drinking from the bag. Beside her, Silas finished the whole bag, then threw it at the ground at Desdemona's feet, before emitting a long, awful groan. Sara watched in horror as he fell to his knees and began to vomit streams of shocking red blood over the white snow. Her attention was diverted by a similar noise from Desdemona, who struggled to remain upright as blood jetted from her mouth. Barely bending, Desdemona heaved most of her blood onto a small snow-covered bush.

"Yay, we both passed," she mumbled when she was done, dragging a sleeve across her mouth, leaving a new gory streak on the cuff.

"Wait there," Sara instructed, turning to Silas. "You okay?" she whispered. He nodded, extending a hand. Gripping it, Sara pulled him to his feet. She pulled a bandana from her pocket and wiped his mouth.

"I'm good," Silas said, dodging a kiss. "Now it's my turn to have bad breath. No kissing til later."

"Can we get this done?" Desdemona took a step forward and Sara raised a palm.

"Fran? Imani? Are you guys strong enough to come out here?"

Shapes emerged from the darkness, and Sara's heart swelled to see Teddie, Embla and April Veronica guiding Fran and Imani into the light of the courtyard while Fan and Ama moved across the courtyard, stationing themselves behind Sara.

"Ello guvna," Imani mugged, her voice raw. "Top up yer drink?"

"We're fine, Sara," Fran said. "Nothing a decade in a padded cell won't fix."

"How about we drop some acid and go to a jam band?" Silas said, and Fran's face cracked into a smile.

"Sounds good to me, Si," Fran said. Sara watched as Fran's eyes met Silas's, her face full of concern.

Sara gestured for Desdemona to move forward. Cautiously, Des moved closer to Yukari, the men staying close behind her.

"Are you ready, Yukari?"

"Sara, I'm always ready," Yukari said, reaching into her purse for a small blue plastic case. "Can you both expose one shoulder?"

Beside her, Silas unzipped his parka and shrugged it off one shoulder, pushing his t-shirt up to reveal a muscly shoulder cap. Desdemona threw her fur open to reveal ugly mom jeans and a plain striped button blouse, a combination so out of sync with the fur that Sara laughed involuntarily.

"What's so funny?" Desdemona was livid and a blush crept up her cheeks.

"It's not funny exactly," Sara said. "But if you're gonna copy someone's fur coat to make a point, you need to you know, stick the landing. Beneath your jealousy, you're just a basic bitch with mommy issues."

"I liked it better when we weren't talking," Desdemona said. "I've been living in a car for a fucking week. What do you want me to do?"

"Fuck off and die," Sara said. "Not necessarily in that order."

"I'm ready when you're done being silly," Yukari said. "Sorry, my fingers are freezing."

While they'd been talking, Yukari had ripped open two alcohol swabs. She wiped Silas's arm first, then Desdemona's.

"So I'm doing Silas first, correct?"

Desdemona nodded. In silence, Yukari opened the little plastic case and took out a syringe. She handed the case to Sara, then held the needle up so that they could all see the contents.

"This is a twenty milliliter syringe," Yukari said. "As you can see it is completely full. I will administer ten milliliters to Silas, and then immediately administer the remainder to Desdemona."

"Hurry up, I'm freezing," Desdemona said. "And shake that syringe, mix it up well."

Wordlessly, Yukari shook the syringe vigorously then turned to Silas. After flicking the syringe twice she plunged it into his arm, slowly depressing the plunger until it reached the halfway mark, then she withdrew it from his flesh.

"Sara, if you can just press down on the injection site until I'm done here," Yukari said, turning to face Desdemona. "Do you want me to wipe the needle with alcohol?"

"Yeah right," Desdemona scoffed. "As if. Hold that syringe where I can see it until you stick it in my arm. Now."

With considerably more force than she used on Silas, Yukari stuck the needle into Desdemona's pale, exposed shoulder, her thumb hitting the plunger hard, the entire injection over in a third of the time she'd taken with Silas.

"There, you're done," Yukari said, disgust in her voice. "*Baka wa shina-nake-ya nao-ra-nai.*"

Beside her, Silas laughed, and Desdemona glared at him.

"Now now," she said patronizingly. "I have some questions. How much will this slow down the aging process?"

"A lot," Yukari said. "I can't be precise because you're the first two humans to receive it. Answer is complicated by how long you've been immune. Is it four months?"

"Almost five," Desdemona said. "As if you don't remember."

"I only commit important things to memory," Yukari said, and Sara filled with pride. She'd never seen Yukari go hard on someone before.

"Well, it's not a magical youth elixir," Yukari continued, waving a finger in Desdemona's face. "So you're gonna be stuck with those wrinkles and gray hairs, but I'm guessing you will have at least another eighty years?"

"And what about side effects?"

"Are you serious?" Yukari's voice was almost loud. "When you put insane pressure on a scientist, you miss out on the whole research thing. I don't know what your side effects will be. Probably upset stomach, headache."

"Whatever," Desdemona said, pulling her coat up over her shoulder and wrapping it closed around her.

"That's it then," Sara said. "How about you get the fuck out of here before Crina gets here."

Desdemona's eyes narrowed.

"You swore she wouldn't be here," she whispered.

"And she's not... yet..."

"Before I leave," Desdemona took a step closer, and Sara felt Silas tense up beside her, "I want to say this. Didn't any of what I said sink into your feeble brain?"

"I never said it didn't bother me," Sara said firmly. "Unlike you, Des, I can cope with hardship. I can accept difficult information. I don't need to brainwash women into obeying me."

"Funny," Desdemona sniffed. "Because that's exactly what Crina did to you, to all of you."

"She never brainwashed me," Silas said. "I always knew who and what she is. It's only you, Des, who seems surprised."

"Shut up, you disgusting aberration," Desdemona said, puffing up her chest.

"Time to go, Des." Sara stepped forward, a fist raised. "You got what you came for. Now get back to what's left of your Lock."

"Speaking of my Lock, what have you done with the prisoners? Will they be returning to Madrid with me?"

Surprised by the turn in conversation, Sara and Silas glanced at each other, and Desdemona's face grew angrier.

"Did Crina already kill them?" Desdemona said dramatically. "Shocker. And nobody will give a shit and mommy Crina will get away with it again."

"Well, I guess if they broke the rules," Sara said. "That makes it okay, then doesn't it? Conversely, you've broken a lot of rules, and you're still alive."

"What *pinche* rules?" Desdemona yelled. "The Lock world is dead and I won't miss it. Nobody vanishes quite as well as an incredibly wealthy vampire. Our paths will never cross again. I'll be too busy enjoying whatever time I have left, the last thing on my mind will be this stupid Lock world."

"No," came a voice from the covered walkway. "The last thing on your mind will be me. I will be the last thing you see. I will be the last breath you take."

Her face contorting in shock, Desdemona spun to face Crina, a Slicer in each palm, walking down the steps at the other side of the courtyard. As she stepped out into the snow, Skye, Yfke and Heather appeared behind her.

"So, Desdemona, what were you saying again?"

Chapter Twenty-Nine

Sara watched the blood drain from Desdemona's face, the red anger on her cheeks fading, her mouth slackening, a glimmer of fear in her eyes before she snapped back to herself, turning to Sara, fury replacing fear.

"You swore to me that she would not be here," Desdemona seethed.

"I did my best," Sara said. "Mom, aren't you supposed to be at the upstate house?"

Across the courtyard, Skye stepped forward, standing beside Crina. Smiling amiably, she waved at Sara.

"Uh yeah, sorry mate, that's my fault," Skye yelled. "Crina and I have a no secrets policy."

"I'm not surprised," Sara yelled back. "Just disappointed."

"I'll get over it," Skye said, blowing Sara a kiss, possibly the most annoying thing she could have done. Deciding to bring focus back to Desdemona, Sara turned to her.

"I did everything you told me to do. Do not hurt any of my people on your way out the door."

"Which door were you planning to exit through?" Crina took another step forward.

Sara watched intently as Desdemona, just steps in front of her, fought to retain her composure. Her eyes darted around the courtyard, walled on all four sides, with the only open door, one that led back into the museum, behind where Teddie was standing, If Desdemona ran now, she stood a fair chance of making it that far. If nobody stopped her.

Frantically, Desdemona waved her hands at Toma and Rad, summoning them to her side. Shaking their heads in unison, they switched on the safety on their guns, pocketed them and took several steps away from their captor. Once again, Sara saw Desdemona's mask slip briefly before she turned her attention back to Crina.

"So, the great Crina, warrior of history, legend of the Purge, you brought how many of your warriors to face me today?"

"Technically, I just brought Heather with me, because she was already in the car." Crina took another step forward. She was now out from beneath the covered walkway, and snowflakes were catching in her thick black hair. "Yfke and Skye took the subway. We met out front. Don't worry, you'll only be facing me."

To Sara's surprise, Desdemona took two steps in Crina's direction.

"It's never been only you," she said. "You've been pitting sister against sister for centuries. Anyone who disagrees with you instantly becomes your enemy. You are a cancer, corrupting us against our own."

Crina scoffed and wagged a circling finger at Desdemona.

"I don't know why you're wearing Sara's fur coat, but dear daughter, you look a fucking wreck, Des. For once, your words and your wardrobe match."

"Insults?" Desdemona took another step. "That's what you're going to do? Insults?"

"They're as effective as a Slicer on a bitch as thin-skinned as you," Crina said, also taking a step forward. Behind her, Skye, Heather and

Yfke took the same step, and Crina waved them back. They retreated obediently.

"You're gonna have to dirty your blade," Desdemona said. "I told them all about you, the truth."

"Oh, this will be good," Crina said. "Okay, crazy, hit me with your truth."

A nervous tic on Crina's face, twitching beside her right eye, alerted Sara. For five centuries, that had been the sole indicator that Crina was stressed. Sara was suddenly very interested in what was said next. As she stared, the snow stopped falling and everything became still and hyperfocused.

"Can you confirm or deny that you set Sara and I up to fail?"

"What the hell are you talking about?"

"Oh, so when you had me send Marguerite and then Rosa to New York, you didn't tell me to do it to see if we could break Sara?"

"I had nothing to do with those transfers."

"And you never told me that you saw me as Lock mother, in New York but not just of New York, but of all Cursed women?"

"Oh, that I'll cop to," Crina said. "I was lying to you. I offered you the one thing you wanted, just to mess with you. I watched you go absolutely crazy. No real motives other than just fucking with you."

"Actually, Crina," Fan said, her voice echoing loudly, "That's not the entire truth."

A cloud of anger passed briefly across Crina's face.

"What do you mean, dear Fan?"

"Look, Crina," Fan said, clearly trying to deescalate, "this is probably the last big gathering of Cursed women. No matter what happens today, we all go our own ways, survive as best we can. So, as someone who's been there since the beginning, who helped write the rules, let's bring that integrity here today. I think we all deserve to know the truth."

Behind Fan, Ama held up her phone.

"Yes," Ama said. "I have Stefanya, Toni, Courtney, Lindsey, Christine and everyone in Bucharest on via video. Say hi to everyone?"

Crina's shoulders slumped.

"Can we not, Ama?"

"This is history," Ama shook her head. "It's a shame we can't record it."

"You all need to stop," Crina said. "I have done nothing but devote my entire life to our sisterhood. Please don't do this."

"Perhaps," Sara said. Crina turned to face her and shot her a look so withering that it would have destroyed her, once, but not now. "But I'd like to ask you again. Did you deliberately set me on a course of self-destruction in New York?"

Bristling with anger, Crina remained silent. Sara's mind felt like it was imploding inside a jumble of memories, a waterfall of difficult times, endless stress, loneliness, countless times she'd begged Crina to come into the City to help with a problem, and the equally countless excuses.

"Your strength was a part of an experiment, but not in the way you think," Crina said, her voice softer. "I've kept secrets. And now," she paused, glancing at Desdemona, "is not the time for me to reveal all."

"Your secrets are lethal to me!" Sara's voice cracked. "You sabotaged me daily until my friends, my family, tried to put me to death! Another one of your secrets saved my life."

Before Crina could answer, Teddie strode out into the courtyard and made her way to Crina, a trail of footprints in virgin snow appearing faster than the eye could see. Without a word, she hauled off and slapped Crina hard across the face, causing her to drop one of the Slicers, the thin metal scything through the snow as it vanished.

"You monster," Teddie wailed. "You made me put my own mother to death for a motherfuckin' experiment?"

Rubbing her cheek, Crina raised her eyes to Teddie's.

"Back the fuck up, buttercup," she whispered, and Sara saw the arm still holding a Slicer tense up. "I don't want to hurt you, but I will defend myself."

Teddie stood her ground, and Sara coiled her body like a spring, ready to take out Crina.

"I am not afraid of you, Theodora," Crina said. "You've never killed, you've never fought, and you've never done one single thing to help our kind."

"Try me, bitch," Teddie said. "Move that Slicer one fucking inch and you'll find out if I can fight or not."

"Move it half an inch and you'll be dead," Sara yelled.

"Can we all stop being so dramatic?" Crina said. "Yes, I've had a secret agenda. But no, it's not a selfish one. I'm not a selfish person."

"Hey mom," Silas turned to face her. Sara noticed that he'd been crying. "I think I am entitled to disagree with you there."

Finally, Crina's facade broke. Apprehensively, she met Silas's gaze.

"I have devoted my entire life to you, Silas," Crina said. "All of it. This secret of mine? It grew out of my protection of you."

"Nice try," he said. "Do you have any idea what happens when you leave a child in a monastery? And you move that child to a new monastery every year? Do you know how it feels to be so lonely that you want Surrender but you can't quite get it to work? Do you re-member how many times I begged you to let me join a Lock, any Lock? Mom, every time we told someone about me, they welcomed me. And now I see how hard you worked to keep me and Sara apart. Was I an experiment too?"

"Enough!" Crina stepped down into the main square, just feet from Desdemona. "E-fucking-nough." Turning, she made eye contact with each person, her eyes burning red, her lips trembling. "Fine. Fucking fine. There's one thing that has driven me. One thing. And I have never told anyone except Stefanya, because it absolutely destroys everything we've built, every thing we've done, as women. If I share this information now, it will ruin each and every one of us. It will undermine our lives."

"*Dios mio,*" Desdemona fanned herself theatrically. "I see where Sara gets it from."

"You fucked with my son," Crina hissed. "You won't walk out of here alive."

"Mija," Desdemona remained unruffled. "It's not looking so good for you either."

"What is it?" Fan walked up to Crina. "If you have something to share, something that might explain your... whatever is happening now?"

"Okay," Crina said, spinning so they could all see her face. "Do you want to know what is going to happen to us? To all of us?"

Nobody replied. Nobody blinked. The phone in Skye's hand began to squawk. Stefanya's voice, her words unintelligible.

"What is she saying? Teddie called out.

"It's Stef," Skye said. "She says we should believe Crina, and Crina, she is asking you to not say it."

Silence fell as everyone turned, making eye contact with each other before returning their attention to Crina, who was standing alone, her face forlorn.

"Secrets got us here," Fran said, pushing herself to standing. "Whatever your secret is, Crina, it has hurt Sara, and we all know that secrets corrode over time. Truth is always better."

"We will all feed," Crina said, her voice dead. "On a human. That's the thing I've tried to keep secret. It's not just men. It's the virus. Eventually, it turns everyone into a killer."

"That's it?" Fan shrugged. "We've known the risk for centuries." Stefanya's chattering from Skye's phone reached a new intensity.

"No, Fan," Crina whirled to face her. "You're not listening. The virus, it eventually takes us over completely. And once it's that strong, the blackouts become more frequent. The next step is waking up next to a dead human."

"Impossible," Fan said. "Why hasn't it happened to any of us?"

"*Yet*," Crina said. "Hasn't happened *yet*. It *will* happen. And here's one thing that you don't know. Every sister, literally every sister, who has taken Surrender, knew this. Most of them had come close to killing. A couple of them succeeded. The rest got lucky, their prey escaped."

"Pic or no proof," Embla called out.

"You'll have to take my word for it, I'm afraid," Crina said. "The whole nothing can be written thing, you know. But here's an example. Dear Francesca, haven't you ever wondered why your maker took Surrender so quickly after she made you? Frances, she almost fucking *ate* you."

"Nope," Fran pushed herself upright and out of April Veronica's arms. "Don't bring her into this."

"Fran, you're the oldest sister ever made. How old were you?"

"I was forty eight when I converted," Fran said. "We had been close for almost a decade, she made me rather than vanish from my life."

"And do you remember a night at your place when things got weird?"

Fran's head bowed.

"Yes, she attacked me."

"Why?"

"I don't know," Fran said. "Well, I do now, I broke a glass in the sink, I gashed my hand open, and she went crazy. We wrestled and I choked her out. When she came to, she left."

"She called me," Crina said. "But once that happens, once the virus is strong enough to control you, it's time to die."

The words shattered like bombs inside Sara's mind. She thought of how her thirst had grown since she fed on Laura, how she needed so much more blood to control the thirst.

"So," Desdemona said. "You took it upon yourself to keep this a secret while you did social experiments on us?"

"Sara is the strongest Cursed woman I've ever met," Crina said. "I monitored her closely, under extreme pressure, and she never cracked."

"Until you had Rosa switch out my Heems," Sara said.

"Even then, we didn't know if that would have any impact on you," Crina said. "You showed no signs of danger. Sara, my love, my child, I thought you were going to be the answer to the mystery. I just wanted to make our lives easier, to figure out a way to change our destiny."

"But you didn't make anyone's life actually easier," April Veronica called out. "You nearly killed Sara."

"You're too young, too idealistic, to understand," Crina said. "Call me in five hundred years after you've eaten your best friend. We can talk then. And don't be offended, you're literally the type of sister we need for the future. I love it that you don't need to fight or kill or feed on strangers. That's wonderful. But I alone chose to shoulder this truth, so that everyone could live without fear. I helped women die before they became mass murderers. In every utopia, there has to be someone who shovels out the sewer. Stefanya and I chose to be those people."

"Choosing to be an executioner isn't too far from being a murderer," Embla said. "Crina, why didn't you tell me? You know how terrified I am of this virus."

"Same here, mom," Silas said. "How can we ever avoid a destiny if we don't know it exists in the first place?"

"Can we take this back to the compound?" Crina glanced at each of them. "I'm fucking freezing and there's a ton more to this. Sara, you're stronger than any sister I've ever met. Your soul, your resolve, they're enormous. I wanted to pull you out of this Lock in the sixties. In my mind, the experiment was done. You showed no signs of burnout. But you wanted to stay in New York. You were happy here."

"You switched out my heems," Sara said. "To prove your point, you starved me until I fed. On a human. Do you have any idea of the shame I felt?"

"Yes, my love. I have seen it on every sister that I accompanied to Surrender," Crina said. "Yukari, answer me honestly. What direction have I always pushed your research in?"

"It's true," Yukari said. "She always wants me to find a way to stop the dark control from happening."

"Did you know that it was inevitable?" Fran yelled out. "Did she tell you?"

Yukari shook her head.

"Look, you guys, I'm sorry," Crina said, projecting her voice. "I did what I thought was right. I have lived with that fear for centuries. It is considerable."

"It still seems like you're getting away with something shitty," Teddie said, and Crina cut her off before she could continue.

"Why am I getting crucified while this bitch here," she paused, pointing her chin at Desdemona, "murders innocent people and you just extended her life. I had so many opportunities to kill her when we had her in custody. I didn't. I played along. Same with these other men here, one of them refused to be vaccinated and next thing you know, he's helping Desdemona kidnap our kind. You guys keep on making big mistakes instead of doing the difficult thing. Those men were dead when they met Des, and you are all offended that I think they should have been killed."

Now it was Imani who pushed herself upright.

"These two men kept us alive," she said, taking a wobbly step forward. "You guys, all of you, no, wait, Toma, pull up your sleeve."

Toma raised an arm, then pulled his sleeve back, revealing a neat gash surrounded by heavy bruising.

"They let me and Frannie here feed from them," Imani said. "It was their idea."

"Big deal," Crina yelled. "Of course they wanted to help you, they want eternal life, in the long term, and in the short term, they know you're their only chance of escaping this deranged fucking Muppet."

"That's not true," Toma said, turning to face Imani. "I didn't want to cause suffering. She had my twin. That's why I told Sara I took your Airpods. I was never on this bitch's side."

"It's true," Sara said. "I didn't understand it at first, but yes, Des, we saw your movements for the past week thanks to Toma."

"Whatever," Desdemona said sarcastically. "Crina, you've been a disappointment to everyone who ever loved you-"

"Stop!" Yfke yelled, shutting Desdemona up instantly, before turning to Crina. "What the actual hell are you talking about? Crina, I've known you as long as anyone here. Have you fed on another human? Have you? Because I have not. I'm not lying. Fan? Ama?"

They both shook their heads.

"I nearly did," Stefanya's voice crackled out of Ama's phone. "Thirty years ago. The thing happened. but I controlled it. Then I made Embla and switched to vegan and I've been okay."

"Come on, Stef," Crina said. "You're on shaky ground and borrowed time, and you know it. That's why you keep yourself holed up in the middle of nowhere. No temptation, huh Stef? Also, you're not being entirely honest, Stef. You've fed before."

"We all have," Christine's voice came from the phone. "We've all found ways to do it. All of us elders know the feelings, we know the symptoms, we deal with it. Why didn't you just talk to us about this?"

"How did this whole thing become about me?" Crina turned, suddenly pleading. "I came here to kill Desdemona for fucking with my son, and somehow I'm getting a tribunal? This bitch wiped out Edinburgh, she wiped out Helsinki and Warsaw. That wasn't me."

"No," Sara said. "But you just said it yourself. You came here to kill Desdemona. You killed the Spaniards in the compound." A round of gasps did not stop Sara. "You're just too comfortable with killing."

"You think I did that?" Crina's was shocked. "Nope, they killed themselves last night. Desdemona, they were so ashamed of what they'd done, they literally bit their wrists open and bled out."

"She's telling the truth," Heather called out.

"I've told nothing but the truth since I walked in here," Crina said. "I love our world so much, I've tried to let you all dream, and live, and love, without the horrible truth hanging above your every day. I haven't done any damage, I've only tried to help."

"No," Yukari broke her silence. "No. Science needs information to function, and you've withheld valuable information. If you'd been honest about this... this inevitable strengthening of the virus – I could research it. We could weed it out or make an antidote or figure out dosage. Whatever the virus needs from a living person, I can locate that. Why did you keep this to yourself?"

Above them, a gap opened in the clouds and a shaft of sunlight broke through. Suddenly, all the icicles sparkled and the fresh snow turned to glitter.

"Can I go now?" Desdemona asked. "I've heard enough."

"You really expect to be allowed to live after what you did to my son?" Crina growled. "We aren't going to make this same mistake twice, are we?"

Crina slowly surveyed the crowd.

Confusion ran rampant inside Sara. She'd arrived at the Cloisters fully prepared to let Desdemona walk out, but was that only because she knew Crina would find her and kill her at some point, but Sara's hands would be clean. And if what Crina said was true, her virus had tasted living human blood, and it was a matter of time before she blacked out again. What if she fed on Silas? She urgently wanted to be alone with Crina, to know every secret she had learned about their virus.

"We don't kill," Teddie said. "I for one don't feel like watching you murder someone."

"I'm with Teddie," Silas raised a fist.

Slowly, hands raised around the perimeter of the courtyard.

"Well, if you are still a democracy," Desdemona said, "it looks like I'm free to go."

Silently, Fan and Ama walked over to Crina and whispered in her ear. Sara was certain they were telling her to stand down, that they would find Desdemona later. When they separated, Crina nodded at Desdemona.

"Get the hell out of my sight," Crina said. "And Des? Always be aware that if I see you again, you will die by my hand."

Raising one finger aloft, Desdemona turned to face her path out of the Cloisters. Gesturing with her hand, she waved Imani, Fan, Embla and April Veronica to clear the way. They obliged, hobbling back along the passageway, and slowly, Desdemona walked towards the door, pausing every two steps to make sure nobody was following her.

"I'd like my security guards back," she said when she reached the top of the steps. "You guys, you know they'll kill you as soon as I'm gone."

"I'll take my chances here," Toma yelled. "Nobody should trust a witch."

"My sentiments exactly," Desdemona said

Turning, she appeared to slip on a patch of ice, falling to one knee. As Desdemona pushed herself upright with one arm, Sara noticed that her other arm crossed her body strangely, instead of supporting her.

Toma's voice sliced through the silence.

"Shit she's got a gun," he yelled.

Desdemona snapped to her feet, her fur coat flying wide open as she rose, a small pistol in her hand.

A split second of confusion fractured Sara's vision, and her reflexes flew into action before she took in the scene. Spinning, she slammed palms into Silas and Yukari, sending them backwards to the ground. In her peripheral vision, she saw women leaping, crouching, moving fast. At any second, Sara anticipated a simultaneous gunshot, agony and the blackness of death, as she continued her spinning sweep, pausing when she got to Desdemona, her arm now stretched straight out, pointing not at Sara.

Following the angle of her arm and the gun, Sara's eyes landed on Crina.

A single pop rang out in the air, and a tiny hole appeared in the center of Crina's forehead, a look of uncomprehending surprise on her face, briefly, before she fell in a crumpled heap in the snow, her fingers releasing the Slicer before she landed.

The blank illogic of shock hit Sara's mind and she fought to stay in control. She turned back to Desdemona and found herself staring deep into the blackness inside the barrel of the tiny pistol. Calmness flooded her and she felt like she was made of viscous light. Pulling her focus back, she saw Desdemona taking her time to get her centered in the pistol's crosshairs.

This is gonna hurt, Sara thought.

And she faced it. Deep inside an endless moment, Sara recognized her ending, as inevitable as feeding, as inevitable as love, and she wondered if the bullet, when it left the chamber in a flash of gunpowder and spark, would travel in slow motion? At what point would she cease?

Instead, the black hole in the barrel of the pistol dropped clumsily. Sound returned to her ears as Sara pulled her focus back in time to watch Desdemona fall to the snow, landing on her side in the puddle of blood that Silas had puked up earlier. Where Des had been standing now stood Heather, a bloody Slicer in her hand.

Sara switched from frozen to frantic and she vaulted over the space between them, skidding to a stop beside Desdemona's prone body. Kneeling down, she saw Desdemona's chest rising and falling and looked up at Heather, who had tears streaming from her eyes. Heather bowed and spat in Desdemona's face.

"That was for Edinburgh, bitch."

Ghastly sounds escaped from Desdemona and her head moved from side to side. To Sara's horror, she spoke.

"Just fucking do it," Desdemona slurred.

Sara extended her arm.

"Give me the Slicer, Heather, I'll do it."

"No fucking way," Heather said. "I'm gonna take my time with this bitch."

Chapter Thirty

Six Months Later

T he first thing Sara noticed as the plane descended through the clouds was the abundance of greenery, even in such an industrial space as the far Rockaways. New foliage on trees still sported the neon green of early summer, and the grassy verges around the serpentine freeways sparkled emerald. It must have rained. Either way, the shimmering pockets of vegetation were a tonic to her eyes, accustomed as they were to nothing but pristine white and deep volcanic blacks of an Icelandic winter. Gazing out the window at endless clouds, Sara thought about the last time she did this, not even a year ago, and how different it felt this time around.

Then, her only worries had been whether or not she would clear customs, and if she could save Teddie. She remembered seeing New York from the plane, and the feeling of seeing your home after an absence. This time, she viewed the city almost as an adversary, one that had nearly beaten her, not once, but twice. A gap in the clouds showed her a flash of endless blue ocean, a respite from the monotone view, reminiscent of the winter she had just endured. The clouds closed and the ocean disappeared as quickly as it arrived, leaving her to her swirling memories.

Her stomach knotted as she recalled her last few days in New York, in the aftermath of the events at The Cloisters. She had spent six months avoiding these memories, but as if her subconscious sensed the City drawing closer, they suddenly became painfully fresh and vibrant. In slow motion, she replayed the horror movie of clearing the scene at The Cloisters. As long as she lived, she knew she'd have nightmares of helping Fan and Ama to lift Crina's lifeless body into a moving box. Or the sight of Fran and April Veronica using so many cups of coffee from a nearby Dunkin to wash all the blood down to the earth before covering it in snow. Sometimes, the worst of all was watching Skye and Yfke carrying Desdemona up to Silas's car, the most disgusting insults pouring from her mouth every time she regained consciousness, while everyone wept around her. No, she corrected herself, the worst was the soulless look on Silas's face for the rest of that day, his eyes vacant, his mouth hanging open unless she closed it with a finger under his chin. That night, she had pressed her naked body against his, under every blanket she owned, but nothing could stop his shivering. Two days later, they had departed for Reykjavik.

Turbulence jostled the plane, and Silas took her hand. Turning to face him, Sara gave him a smile, Silas returned the smile, then closed his eyes and let his head fall back. Every day in the house outside Reykjavik, they had been close, physically, and barely communicative, emotionally. They'd shared a bedroom, but their days were usually separate and silent, as each of them struggled to reconcile their losses. After some initial arguments around Sara still wanting the vaccine, she had not brought it up, but she also knew that was why Silas had been so adamant about coming to New York with her. He wanted to ensure that she didn't get vaccinated by Yukari.

After centuries of close-proximity living with the women of her Lock, the solitude of Iceland had been a blessing for Sara as she grieved

Crina. The complicated strands of their relationship made the anger and denial stages of her grief longer and weirder, compounded by being with the only other person on Earth who felt the same way, and yet, his issues were so much deeper. Surprisingly, the rest of the world left them alone, as if sensing that what they were going through was so great, so terrible, that it was best to leave them be. Weeks had passed without speaking to another human being, while winter storms whipped snow and ice against the windows. At night, she and Silas would curl up in their bedroom, secure in each other's arms, gazing silently at their skylight, hoping for the Northern Lights.

The rumbling of the landing gear brought Sara back to the present, along with a strong feeling that she did not want to be here, did not wish to go back to the Compound. The familiar ghosts she sensed in every dusty corner of the building now felt like specters of terrible grief. It was no longer her home. Nowhere was. The women she loved had largely scattered to new callings around the globe. Heather and Imani were in Edinburgh, with Toma in tow, deciding the future of that building. Fan and Ama were at the upstate property. Yukari was living in the Murray Hill apartment building and working with crews of virologists around the world. Like last time, the real reason she was returning was Teddie.

It had been decided that the Compound would be turned into housing for female refugees, the queer and trans communities, women of color, and anyone who needed it. Teddie, Embla, Fran, Rad and April Veronica had spent the past winter bricking up all the back entrances, hiding all traces of the original nature of the building. Later today, Heather would arrive, and together, they would begin the arduous process of signing over all the holdings from the old religious order to the new foundation that would run the compound. Sara begged Teddie to accompany her to Iceland at the end of this visit, but once

Teddie had declined that offer, Sara's interest in being in New York had dwindled to the point where she had booked their return tickets for just three days from now. She wanted to get in and out, to get back to doing nothing with Silas in Iceland.

The bump of the wheels hitting the earth surprised her, and she gave Silas another smile.

"Here goes nothing," he said to her. About to reply, a beam of reflected light hit Silas's face, highlighting several gray hairs in the stubble around his chin and his crooked, scarred upper lip, reminding Sara that he, unlike her, was aging. In silence, she rested her head on his chest and stayed like that until the plane was at the gate.

An hour later, still in silence, the taxi pulled up outside the West End Avenue entrance. Silas got out and went to the trunk to retrieve their single suitcase. Sara felt frozen in place.

"You okay ma'am?" the cabbie asked.

"Sorry," Sara said, opening her door. "Just got lost in a daydream."

"Sounds nice," the cabbie said. "Have a good rest of your day."

The door at the top of the stairs burst open, and Teddie, April Veronica and Embla spilled out, surrounding them. Behind them came a tall, dark man and it took Sara's mind a second to place him. Rad, Toma's gay twin. Now a full Cursed man, he was part of what Teddie called the Glampire Coalition. Sara had not been in favor of his conversion, nor that of his brother, but her depression had taken precedence, and now the deed was done. As the group of youngsters crowded them, Sara felt herself dissociating and she was grateful that Silas was able to animate himself and return the hugs and smile appreciatively.

Suddenly, Teddie was standing in front of her, brown-orange eyes boring into her own.

"Mom," she said, loudly. "MOM! Snap out of it. Earth to Sara! Earth to Sara!"

"Sorry my love," Sara wrapped her arms around Teddie and buried her face in her neck. "It's all a bit overwhelming."

"I got you," Teddie said, and Sara felt the arms encircling her move strangely, as Teddie gave hand signals to the rest of the group. "We're gonna go straight up to the roof, if that's okay?"

Sara nodded before breaking the hug, even though all she wanted was to be left alone in her old apartment, as if its energy could heal her and prepare her for the days ahead.

"We have to go through your flat," Teddie said. "We haven't touched it since you left. I aired it out the past few days."

"Did you put the espresso machine back?" Sara asked as she pulled away.

"Yes, mom," Teddie said, taking her hand and leading her up the stairs and into the lobby. Immediately the scent of the building filled her nose, the bouquet of old cement and ghosts that always told her she was home. Teddie nattered on as they climbed the stairs, but Sara focused on the feeling of the banister as it trailed past her fingertips, the ancient polished wood cold and smooth, her eyes lighting on every small detail as she searched for changes on each floor they passed, as if six months was a significant absence.

"Wanna unlock your old door?" Teddie asked, and slowly Sara pressed her fingertip against the pad beside the doorknob. Teddie bustled her directly up the spiral staircase, across the little loft and out onto the roof deck. Sara squinted her eyes against the bright early afternoon sunshine. As they adjusted, she saw a long table set in the center of the vast space, between garden beds that were bursting with flowers. She saw olives on the olive trees, and in one of the raised beds, a wall of sunflowers swayed in the breeze. The cement floor of the deck was still wet from the morning rains, and the whole area looked clean and alive and beautiful.

Behind her, Sara heard the others emerge from the doorway, turning to see Silas sandwiched between Embla and April Veronica, his head thrown back in laughter, and behind them, Fran, waving, and Rad carrying a very large red cooler.

"It looks incredible up here," she said to Teddie, finally.

"There she is," Teddie replied. "I knew Sara was in their somewhere."

"Girl, I've been in here for six months," Sara said, pointing to her head. "It's getting out there that's hard."

"I hear ya," Teddie said. "Well, I just heard from Heather, she's landed, she'll be here shortly, and I figured that we should have a party."

"I don't need a party," Sara sniffed.

"It's not for you," Teddie said, taking the cooler from Rad and setting it on the long table. "It's a party because it's not raining and the sun's out. Have you forgotten what New York is like in the summer?"

"No, but I just did an Icelandic winter, and this feels like a hot summer's day."

Teddie took Sara by the upper arm, and pointed at something on the opposite side of the roof, leading her away from the crowd.

"Oh here it comes," Sara said. "The inquisition."

"Damn straight here it comes," Teddie said. "I've been worried beyond worrying, sister."

"We had a lot to deal with."

"And how'd that work out for you?"

"You're not going to like this too much, Ted, but I don't have much to tell you. We existed in comfortable silence. We had good days and bad days. We cried a lot but we were numb a whole lot more."

Sara remembered how it felt when the house began to feel like her whole world, a cocoon that enveloped them both, a winter that she hoped would transform them into something with wings, something that could fly away from the messy grief they were both mired in. Silas took a very masculine approach, focusing on repairs to the house and vanishing for days on end into the greenhouse, nurturing everything from their daily lettuces and wheatgrass to a newfound interest in bonsai. Sara withdrew into a heavy blood haze during the first month, her feeding compounded by so much shame that she still consumed blood in private, despite Silas's insistence that it did not bother him.

"But you guys are fine?"

A half-hearted shrug/nod caused Teddie to take Sara by the shoulders.

"Tell me what the fuck is going on, mom."

"Teddie, my love, I just did," Sara's voice was calm, but still sounded tired. "It's a big house, we rattled around in it. We love each other, very much. I think we are both still waiting for everything to be magically okay."

"That doesn't ever really happen," Teddie said cautiously.

"Oh, I know," Sara said. "And you and I both know that time heals everything, but it's just hard because his time is now..."

"Shorter," Teddie finished her sentence, and Sara nodded.

"So, can I ask how you're doing?"

"Sure," Sara took Teddie's hands from her shoulders and held them. "But I don't know the answer. With Crina, it's been hard. It's been like getting a new lens over your entire life, so you have all these questions, but the only person who knows the answer is dead. I think that's a lot of it for Silas too. It's a little easier for me because Crina wasn't actually my mother. I guess."

"Now I understand the silence," Teddie said, wrapping Sara in a hug.

"I missed you so much," Sara whispered.

"So stay." Teddie didn't miss a beat.

"Or you can come to Iceland," Sara said.

"What? And miss out on the opening of our queer trans housing development?"

"You can't even be seen by them," Sara said.

"I can in my burka," Teddie said. "I am so used to wearing it these days."

"You've switched the religions that mask you," Sara chuckled.

"Yep, for the same reasons," Teddie kissed her cheek. "Nobody questions it and I have my anonymity again. I just can't go to Brooklyn any more. Which is fine. We've been finding some clubs in Jersey City and it's been a trip."

"Embla told me," Sara began, only to be interrupted by noise from the other side of the roof deck. Glancing across, Sara saw Heather, and beside her, Yfke, Fan, Ama and Yukari. Her stomach sank as her anxiety rose.

"Wait, why is Yfke here?"

Teddie took her hand.

"You'll be okay," she said, leading her back over to the crowd. "I promise."

"Why can't we have a party where I don't know everybody?" Sara asked.

As they drew closer, Sara heard her name being called by a cacophony of voices before she was engulfed in a succession of hugs, all of them back-crackingly intense, even Yukari's.

"I am so glad you are home," Yukari whispered. "We've been very busy."

"Everyone take your seats," April Veronica yelled out, and Sara instead made her way to Silas, taking his hand, needing the comfort of him as she watched the seats fill, trying to figure out the best place for them to sit until there were only two seats remaining, facing each other in the center of the table. Reluctantly releasing Silas's hand, Sara made her way to a seat between Fan and Ama, and Silas sat across from her, between Yukari and Yfke. A weird silence fell over the table, making Sara suspicious, or maybe a little bit paranoid. She wasn't sure which but she'd never been to a party so solemn. She looked up and down the table, and nobody met her gaze, kicking her anxiety into overdrive.

"Oh sorry," April Veronica leapt to her feet. "We are supposed to be toasting."

Embla leaned beneath the table and grabbed two large thermoses, handing one to April Veronica. Silently, they moved around the table, filling silver goblets with blood. Sara noticed with a pang that Embla skipped the goblets in front of Yukari and Silas, but Silas grinned and thanked her as if she'd poured for him, and she kissed the top of his head before moving on. Sara was irritated that a goblet had been put in front of Silas at all, but she let it go. Once everyone was served, they returned to their seats. Sara wondered if there'd be a benediction, and who would even give it. To her left, Heather stood.

"They say that you always know your true home by how your heart feels when you return to it," she said, raising her goblet. "And looking around this table, my heart is happy. I didn't feel this way when I came back to this building, but now I do. It's you, you wonderful, beautiful humans, who are my home, and I have to say, it feels great to be where my heart belongs. I love you all, and cheers."

A chorus of cheers rang out around the table and everyone brought their goblets to their lips, except Yukari and Silas, who did his cheers with an empty hand. Sara stopped watching him as she drank her blood, keeping her head bowed as she waited for the cloudy intoxication to pass. When she raised her head again, she watched as Silas smiled beatifically while everyone else wiped their mouths with napkins or sleeves, and chatter began to burble around her. Once again Sara was hounded by a feeling that something wasn't right, but she couldn't identify it, as she kept on looking from person to person around the table. It wasn't until she returned her gaze to Silas that she realized that Fan and Ama had taken the toast.

Both of them were immune.

She looked from Fan to Ama and back again as smiles broke out on their faces and they leaned forward and winked at each other.

"Are you going to ask," Fan asked, turning to her. "Or are we just going to have to blurt it out?"

A silence fell, so potent that it insulated them from the sounds of the city. Panic scattered through Sara's body, and she glanced around the table, weirded out by the same happy expression on everyone's face.

"You're all freaking me out," was all she could manage, her voice thin and constricted.

"Wait," Silas said. "Fan and Ama, you took the toast! Shit, was I supposed to just do it too? Is this some new ritual? You guys," Silas roared with laughter. "Did I just commit a vampire faux pas?"

"No," Ama reached across the table and took Silas's hands. "This is why we called you all here. We have something rather important to tell you."

Sara locked eyes with Teddie who mouthed "don't worry" before standing and coming over to stand behind Sara, her hands massaging her shoulders.

"Please," Sara pleaded. "I don't have much bandwidth and I'm gonna puke if my anxiety goes up one single notch."

"The vaccine didn't work on me," Fan said. Sara pressed her spine against the back of her chair, staring at Silas, watching the smile dwindle on his face as confusion took hold. "Sara, did you hear me?"

"I heard you."

Sara turned her head slowly, her eyes locking on Fan's. She couldn't look at Silas. She was suddenly furious that the vaccine worked on Silas and not other people.

"I'm sorry we didn't tell you," Yukari said. "That's on me, I was full science nerd for the winter. It was a mystery. I couldn't figure out how Fan's virus had mutated away from the rest of ours."

"Which is where I come in," Yfke, on Silas's other side, took his free hand. "I mean, seriously, I don't know why nobody tells me anything."

"Because you're a huge gossip?" Silas said, with a weak, nervous laugh.

"No, dummy," Yfke said, her light tone irritating Sara. "Well, maybe."

"It was my mistake," Yukari interjected. "I have always thought that we were all descended from Stefanya."

"We are," Sara said.

"Nuh-uh," Yfke said. "Even these bitches forgot." She jabbed a finger at Ama, then Fan. "I mean, this is literally the first time it's been proved, it's not like we had science when we got made."

"I'm sorry," Sara's head was spinning. "I don't understand."

"Remember my origin story?" Yfke asked, "Remember? I was being held in that castle, and these bitches came in one night and raised hell, they let us all go, they killed the guards, and we were making our way out and we got cornered by these two huge bastards."

"It was the first time we saw you fight," Ama said admirably. "You guys, all the other prisoners just fucked off, but this bitch here, she jumped right in."

"Anyway," Yfke continued, "it was dark and chaotic and there was a lot of blood and we all got torn up pretty bad before we managed to dispatch them."

"I took the head clean off one of them," Fan boasted.

"Anyway, for the second time," Yfke said, "back then, we thought you need to get bitten to get converted. We weren't converted yet."

"Yeah," Ama said. "We weren't sure we wanted this devilish curse. We just wanted to be warriors."

"But then," Yfke said, "a few days later, Fan and I started to feel the thirst. We must have gotten their blood in our wounds."

"We panicked," Ama said. "We didn't know what was going on, but we knew we needed a coverup. We didn't want Stefanya or Crina to know we'd gotten infected by a man."

"We asked Stefanya to convert us that night," Fan said. "We never told anyone that we thought we had already been infected."

"And then," Ama said, "we simply forgot."

"I didn't forget," Yfke said. "I always felt different. I have never swooned from the blood toast."

"Now we know why the synthetic was never strong enough for me or Yfke," Fan said.

Blinking furiously to clear her mind, Sara raised a palm.

"What, precisely, does this mean?"

"I'll take it from here," Yukari said. "It meant that I had a second strain of our virus to work with. And I'm not going to torture you any further. You guys, I was able to reinfect Ama. The vaccine worked on her. But she now has the other virus, and we think that..."

Sara stopped listening, a rushing sound in her ears blocking out everything else. Staring straight ahead, she locked eyes with Silas, blinking nervously as he went to speak.

"Will it work on me?" he whispered, and beside him, both Yfke and Yukari began to nod, then Yukari reached behind her, hauling up a black backpack. Setting it in her lap, she rummaged inside, then produced a familiar rolled piece of black leather.

At the head of the table, Heather rose and walked to Yukari, who handed the leather scroll to her.

"Silas," Heather said. "Welcome to your reinfection party."

The collision of emotions inside Sara was more than she could handle, nausea and a wickedly untrustworthy surge of hope wrestling around her hammering heart as she watched Heather unroll the leather, revealing the same silver syringe that they'd used to convert April Veronica.

His eyes wide, his mouth opening and closing like a fish's as he searched for words that wouldn't come, Silas laid his arm out across the table and Yukari took the spool of rubber tubing from its pocket in the leather binding and tied him off. Heather held the syringe aloft and went to speak. Sara cut her off.

"Just do it," she whispered, "please."

With a nod, Heather flicked at Silas's inner elbow until she found a good vein. Sara watched intently as the needle tip pinched Silas's skin gently before it pierced it, the shiny metal spike sliding into him. After pulling the stopper back, Heather pressed down, the contents emptying into Silas. Within seconds, Heather withdrew the needle, and pressed her thumb over the pin prick of blood that appeared.

"Welcome back to the club, Si," she said, taking his hand and guiding his thumb to replace hers. "Just keep that pressure up for a minute while I get you a bandaid."

Finally, Sara was able to let her eyes move upwards, to Silas's face. His chin began to waver, and a tear spilled from each eye as he mouthed "I love you" and Sara felt herself begin to lose it, and she inhaled sharply, determined to voice the question that was eating her alive.

"How long..." she faltered, the words almost too hard to speak. "How long until we know if it... it worked?"

"It will work," Yukari said. "I had your blood sample, so I reinfected it. I just used your own blood to reinfect you."

Surrendering to her tears, Sara collapsed forward, her forehead on the table as she wept. A strong hand, Silas's, slid between the table and her cheek, and she pressed against it, the exchange of heat from his skin grounding her in the moment, connecting them, and she felt him lift her face and she let it happen, until their eyes locked and she saw the pure joy in Silas's face, his grin wider than she'd ever seen. A wild, unfamiliar happiness began in the soles of her feet and rocketed up her legs, exploding in her chest, filling her with a golden lightness as she threw herself across the table, pressing her lips against his, tasting salty tears before she felt his hands grip the back of her head, pulling her tighter and tighter, as a weightless, pure love lit them from within.

"I think you need to change our tickets," Silas whispered to her. "It's time to go to Sydney."

Hours later, the wreckage of dinner was scattered across the table. Above it all, an endless sunset spun out, dragging violet clouds across an indigo sky streaked with hot pink and orange. People had decamped to the couches around the raised garden beds, beside the entrance to Sara's apartment. Since they'd left the table, Sara and Silas had been glued together, finding ways to have as much skin touching as possible, her hand clamped inside of his, as people talked to them, telling them of things that had happened while they were away. Sara had half-listened at best, her mind focused solely on Silas, and the wide-open road of their unlimited future.

"Penny for your thoughts."

Heather appeared beside them, soon joined by Teddie.

"You know what I'm thinking," Sara said.

"And I'm still not thinking," Silas said. "I can't let myself believe in any of it."

"Okay, you doubting Thomas," scoffed Heather. "We won't celebrate until you down your first pint of blood. Let's just be miserable until then, insulting Yukari and the tests she ran before we invited you to come back."

"I can't deal with this twice," Silas said. "I hope you understand."

"Course I do, pet," Heather rubbed his knee. "Can I tell you a story to brighten up your day?"

Sara, whose day was already bright enough because she knew Yukari wouldn't have gone ahead with anything in public that wasn't guaranteed to work, nodded enthusiastically.

"It's about Desdemona," Teddie said.

"A name that has never brightened any of my days," Sara groaned. "Wait, did she die? That would make me happy."

"Oh no," Heather waved a hand. "Death would be too good for her."

"I visited her last week," Teddie said, causing Sara's head to whip around.

"What?"

"I love to visit her," Teddie said. "Sit and tell her about life."

Sara groaned. "I thought she was in a nursing home."

"Worse than that," Teddie said. "She's in a psych ward, she doesn't even have her own room. It's so awful. They just wheel her in front of the TV every morning then put her back in her bed at night. She's diagnosed as paranoid, delusional, narcissistic and bipolar schizophrenic, with violent tendencies. I faked her doctor's letters myself."

"Tell them the best part," Heather said, with a titter.

"She has a sign around her neck," Teddie said. "It says BITE RISK."

Sara and Silas burst out laughing, and Sara felt the lightness again, running through her body and her soul, and she knew Silas was going to be okay.

Surrounded by people that she loved, Sara felt her heart swell and she leaned back against Silas's chest.

"How you feeling my love?" she asked, and Silas wrapped his arms around her, pulling her tight to him.

"I feel a little cheated," he said, and she saw consternation pass across Teddie's and Heather's faces.

"Huh?"

"I went to hell and back and all I have to show for it are these gray hairs."

Craning her head back, she watched as Silas ran his hand over his stubbly chin, silver hairs shining amongst the sea of black ones.

Rolling her eyes dramatically at his dad joke, Sara planted a kiss on his jawline.

"I'll take it."

Above them, the last rays of sunset left the sky, and Sara waited expectantly for the silvery night sky of New York City to spread, dripping down from the rising moon until it surrounded her whole world, wrapping her in the familiar cloak of moonlight that she'd worn for ages, and would wear forever more.

Chapter Thirty-One

August, 2064

While Sara waited for Silas on a bathroom break, she walked around Selfoss, the tiny Icelandic town she once knew now replaced by a generic metropolis. Disappointed by the rampant globalization, she wandered past chain restaurants and stores, looking for a pub she and Silas had visited habitually, forty years earlier. When she saw it in the distance, she wished she hadn't bothered. It was now a Starbucks. She returned to the car, happy to see Silas leaning against it, his hair glinting in the sun while he gazed unbothered at the clouds. Without a word, they climbed inside the car and it set off.

"I'm starting to think the gift we got for Embla isn't sufficient," she said eventually.

"What does Miss Manners recommend for a vampire's hundredth birthday?' Silas asked, making himself chuckle.

"Well I don't think it's a vintage eighties sweater like yours," Sara said.

"You watch, she'll love it," Silas said, and they lapsed into comfortable silence as the car sped on. Sara wondered if it was time for them to talk about moving here. After four decades in Australia, the heat was getting to be too much for her. They'd already relocated to Tasmania, the island to the south of the continent, but this year's fire season had been brutal. For a minute she'd investigated moving them to the new cities in Antarctica, but Silas, now accustomed to the dry heat of Australia, had shut that down quickly.

Despite the thirty two hours of travel to Reykjavik, the excitement at seeing old friends grew as the hydrogen car drove itself along the new, widened highway towards Vik. Relentless summer sunlight gave the green hillsides a vibrant green hue, the color so saturated that it looked fake. As they drove in silence, they took in the changes to the countryside, the green fields now dotted with trees that had sprung up alongside the warmer temperatures and heavy rainfall that marked the summer months, trees that were able to survive the milder winters and now housed birds that migrated from Ireland and Scotland every summer.

After stopping several times to pet Icelandic horses, they arrived in Vik, now the third largest town in Iceland, wending their way up a hill behind the city until the road ended, at the gate to Fan and Ama's farm. The metal boom raised as they approached and they rattled over the cattle grid and made their way down into the valley, finally reaching the fairytale stone home beside a broad, shallow stream.

Before the car could release their seatbelt locks, Ama and Fan came racing out of the house, their long gray hair still surprising Sara even though it had been that way for over a decade. Dressed in matching wool sweaters and utility pants, they rushed to each side of the car, ripping the doors open.

"Get out," Fan yelled happily. "We need to squeeze you."

Sara wasn't even fully out of the car before she was wrapped in a bear hug. It was the same every year. Even though they'd both taken Yukari's updated vaccine in the 2040s, they hadn't started to age for a long time. It was only in recent years that they had started to look like old ladies, a role they were both relishing. Unlike Yukari, who'd changed her mind a decade ago, and was now Cursed again with Yfke's virus. Like Fran, she'd be a gloriously gray-haired woman for centuries to come.

As they hugged, Kath and Kim, a pair of Aussie cattledogs, came hurtling down the hillside, joining in the melee. Since Fan and Ama adopted Mister Handsome back in the dark New York days, they'd never been without dogs. Silas had gifted them the Aussies a few years back, and Fan and Ama both admitted they'd finally met their match in a pair of dogs as effervescent and tireless as themselves.

As the barking and the hugging subsided, they moved inside, where the dining table was already set. Before they'd even sat down, Ama was ladling steaming soup into the bowls and Fan was pouring shots of aquavit. Familiar with the chaos, Sara knew she just had to ride it out, let the girls talk over the top of each other and just wait for the excitement to die down, so she tasted the soup.

"Unless you're starving to death," Fan cackled. "hold the fuck up." She raised her shot glass, then banged it on the table and downed it, with everyone following suit. "Skøl," she said. "Now, eat your damn soup."

"It's lamb," Silas said. "You guys are eating meat again?"

"Yeah yeah yeah," Ama said. "After five hundred years of vegetarianism, this is the only way I can keep my muscles up."

"Getting old is weird," Fan said. "We need meat and I have developed one hell of a sweet tooth."

Sara looked at their faces, so girlish despite the wrinkles, still beaming with love and energy. The soup was delicious, and Sara was hungrier than she realized, enjoying the food almost as much as she enjoyed being mothered by Fan and Ama. They brought her a second bowl of soup, and another helping of home-made bread, toasted over fire. Once they were done eating, she raised her newly refreshed glass of aquavit.

"Cheers, you two. It's always magic to be with you." she said. "When you asked us to come early for Embla's party, I thought something was wrong. Wait – is anything wrong?"

"She cuts right to the chase," Ama clucked as the four of them sipped the potent liquor.

"Some things never change," Fan smiled. "Silas, I don't know how you put up with it."

"Let me stop you right there," Sara said. "I didn't travel for two full days to listen to your anti-Sara schtick."

"But it's our thing," Ama said. "We're the aunties who think nobody could ever be good enough for our nephew."

"We're just joking," Fan said. "You know that."

Nodding, Sara looked them over. There was something different about their energy, and concern gnawed at her. Fan caught her staring.

"Don't give me that look," she said. "Don't. Fine. *God*. Okay. We'll just say it. Yes, we asked you here for a reason because..."

"Because something has come up," Ama finished for her. "And we don't want to panic you, so we won't drag it out."

"We need you to move here," Fan blurted. "To take care of us."

"Is something wrong?" Silas's voice was panicked. "Are you sick?"

"No, Si, we're just old," Ama said. "All our vampire strength is gone."

"We need help around the farm," Fan said. "And let's face it, Australia's too damn hot."

Silas and Sara both nodded knowingly. They knew this day would come, they just thought it would be further in the future.

"Wait, so that's a yes?" Fan looked at Ama incredulously. "It was that easy?"

Silas narrowed his eyes at Sara, waiting expectantly for her to confirm the move, relaxing when she nodded eagerly in agreement.

"I mean," she smiled. "We've been talking about it. We knew it was coming."

"But we still need to sweeten the deal," Ama said.

"There's no need to sweeten any deal," Silas said.

"We always planned to come back at some point," Sara said. "We have just been really busy down there, but all the stuff we've been doing can be run from here."

"We built you your own house," Ama blurted. "Just like the one you had in upstate New York, a smaller version of the Reykjavik compound house. It's about a mile down the road."

"We built eight houses back there," Fan said. "We've invited your old Lock."

"You already asked them?" Silas shook his head. "Oh I get it. They all said no and that's why you're asking us?"

Fan cuffed him across the skull.

"No, you little jerk," she said. "Everyone said yes."

"Even Fran?"

Fan and Ama nodded.

"You guys, that's the sweetener," Ama said. "The New York crew is already here!"

"Follow me," Fan yelled, bounding for the door. By the time they got outside, she was at the steering wheel of a beat-up old four-wheeler. "Let's go!"

Silas gripped Sara's hand as Fan sped the little vehicle along a deeply rutted gravel road that rose up to the mountains behind the house, slowing for the occasional cow, sheep or horse. Cresting a rise, Sara gasped. Below them, in a bowl-shaped valley, was a row of eight front doors, and beside each door, one long glass window, the houses behind them built into the hillside, their roofs covered in grass. A herd of sheep was grazing atop the houses in the center.

Scouring the countryside for anyone from New York and seeing no one, Sara took in the magical landscape that was going to be their new home. In the high distance, a pair of waterfalls tumbled into a stream that careened down the hillside until it passed in front of the updated hobbit houses. Fan steered them across a metal grill bridge over the stream to a circular gravel drive where the road ended.

"It's okay, everyone, she said yes," Fan called out, her voice deafening as always, and as Sara watched, one of the doors opened, and Fran, Embla, April Veronica, Rad and Teddie came spilling out, rushing towards them. Leaping from the vehicle, Sara raced into Teddie's arms, picking her up and spinning them in circles until she got dizzy.

"Howdy, neighbor," Teddie said into her ear as she set her on the ground and they both just swayed, hugging tightly, feeling their hearts beating fast inside their bone cages, their rhythms almost in sync.

Over Teddie's shoulder, Sara watched as Embla, Fran and April Veronica smothered Silas in a group hug, and Rad ran in circles around them, creating holofilms of the reunion with his communicator.

"You've been keeping secrets again," Sara said, and Teddie slowed their spinning.

"Or," she said with a cheeky grin, "I finally had the chance to do something great for you, and I took it."

"Thank you, Theodora," Sara said, kissing Teddie on the tip of her nose. "I hope we get to be neighbors."

"Yep," Teddie released Sara from the hug and took her hand, leading her to the door on the far left. "Hey, Silas, wanna come see your new love nest?"

"I'll be there in a minute," he called out, still engulfed in his love circle. "You start without me."

As they approached the door, it opened with a soft click.

"It's programmed to my biometrics," Teddie said. "We'll get yours added asap. Come on in."

Stepping inside, Sara's heart melted at the resemblance to the house by the lake at Silas's property in New York, the circular living room with the bedroom, bathroom and kitchen spoking off in the rear. Unable to contain her excitement, Teddie walked her through all the rooms, substantially larger than they were in New York, and a show-stopper bathroom complete with a soaking tub and a sauna.

"But wait," Teddie said. "There's more."

Pressing on a wall panel beside the front door revealed the entry to a hallway that extended back into the mountain. The gray concrete floor and walls all emanated heat, and they followed the hallway until it ended at a small antechamber with three doors.

"We're behind the main house now," Teddie said. "These rooms are empty, you can do whatever you want with them."

"Silas will want a greenhouse," Sara said.

"I was about to say that," came a male voice from behind them, then Sara felt familiar arms around her waist.

"Welcome to Fan and Ama's Vampire Retirement Village," Teddie said.

"Do you love it?" Fran appeared in the hallway. "You guys, I hope you love it."

"If it got you to leave New York, it must be alright," Sara said, pushing off Silas and wrapping Fran in a hug.

"It was time," Fran said. "If anything, I forced everyone to stay longer than we should. The youngsters wanted to leave in the fifties, after the superstorm wiped out Lower Manhattan, but to me, that felt like quitting. But now with all the flooding and the disease, it's starting to feel like living on the Titanic."

"Why didn't you tell us?" Sara whispered.

"Because we planned to come build this and it was a surprise," Fran whispered back. "I'm glad you're staying."

"Speaking of surprises," Teddie said, "we need to go to Embla's place."

"Uh oh," Silas said. "The kids have something else planned?"

"I say nothing," Fran said, grabbing Sara's hand and heading out along the hallway, Silas and Teddie in tow. When they emerged into the golden sunlight, there was nobody to be seen.

"All the doors look the same," Sara said.

"You're in number one, the kids are in number eight," Fran said, pointing to the door on the other side from Sara's.

"It's like we're living in The Prisoner," Silas said with a chuckle, and Fran high-fived him.

"I knew you'd say that," she said.

When they got near Embla's door, it swung open, and the youngsters, arm in arm, waved them in.

"Price of admission, one hug," Embla said to Sara, who obliged, nuzzling the women on her way past. In the main room, Fan and Ama were already seated on a wide, curving couch that faced the window wall. Ama patted the couch between them and Sara and Silas sat. Teddie took a floor cushion, and Rad and Fran went to the rear of the room, whispering to each other. Suddenly, the glass wall darkened to black, shutting off the outside and plunging them into darkness.

"Sorry you guys," Rad said. "Give me a minute."

Ghostly ambient lighting emanated from panels in the cement walls, and Sara and Silas exchanged nervous glances.

"Wait," Sara said. "Where is everybody else?"

"Big storm up in Akureyri," Ama said. "Imani, Toma, Heather and Yuka will come down as soon as the road reopens. Stef is at her place, she's just late."

"Stefanya is going to live here?" Silas's voice was incredulous.

"Of course not," Ama said. "Princess has a private mansion on the property next door."

"She's going to be the Real Housewife Of Vik," Embla said. "Not joking."

"Okay, April Veronica," Fran said. "We are ready."

Embla and April Veronica walked hand in hand into the center of the room.

"So," Embla said, "we wanted to welcome you to your new home with something that we only recently discovered. Silas, did you know that Crina had a house down here in Vik?"

Silas shook his head, and Sara began to worry that they were in store for another ugly Crina surprise. In the four decades since her death, she and Silas had spent hours talking about her and her complicated legacy, but those conversations had become increasingly rare, and Sara liked it that way.

"The house had been rented out for many years," Embla continued, "until recently, the tenant passed and we went in to clean it out."

"We found Crina's secret hiding place," April Veronica said.

"It was an attic," Embla corrected.

"I didn't want to freak them out."

"We're already freaked out," Silas said.

"Don't be," Fran said. "Raddy, you ready?"

"I'm ready," he said. "Say the word, Embers."

"Let me just say," Embla said, "before we start, this is just a fraction of what we found."

"Oh no," Sara said. "What did you find?"

"Photos," April Veronica said. "That's the word, Raddy. Photos."

A royal blue rectangle the size of a bedsheet appeared on the darkened glass, fading to a black title card.

Crina's Secret Photo Album.

"Hooo boy," Silas said, taking Sara's hand in his as the title card dissolved into a photograph of Silas, black hair slicked back with pomade, striding along Sixth Avenue in a pin striped suit, probably late 1930s. He looks like a movie star, Sara thought. The image faded out, replaced by one of Sara, her hair curled tightly, in her Chanel black dress and straw hat, walking in Times Square.

"Oh wow," Silas said.

"Remember those people that just took your photo on the street?" Sara said. "I can't believe she bought these photos. I used to tell her I didn't want to pose for them, waste their time."

"You didn't waste their time," Embla said. "As you'll see, she probably bought every photo you posed for. There are so many of these photos, of both of you. We've grouped the best ones, so you can see what you looked like at different times over the past two hundred years."

The show continued, one photo after another, of Sara or Silas, sometimes with Crina, in the clothing of different eras. Glancing at Silas, Sara saw his chin begin to quiver, and that was enough to set her off too, happy tears streaming down her face.

"I'd hold onto your tears," Teddie said. "We've saved the best for last."

"Spoiler alert," Raddy called out. "We still have half an hour of photos first."

The next photo was in color, of Silas in the sixties, his hair a curly mop, his clothing a crazy patchwork of colors and patterns and various fabrics.

"No shit, Sara," Fran called out, "You're lucky I didn't find him first."

"Hubba hubba," said Rad, making everyone laugh.

The photos rolled on, now all in color, many of them taken without the subjects' knowledge. Crina, the greatest observer of their rules, had broken a core tenet. For love. Sara could tell that this was as overwhelming for Silas as it was for her. They watched the rest of the slideshow in silence, surprised by the final shot, Sara and Silas, backs to the camera, cuddling beneath the Northern Lights during Sara's first visit to Iceland. The image faded to black, and then the screen went blue again.

"That last one was on her phone," April Veronica said. "I included it because it was the most recent one."

"That was so beautiful," Sara said, her voice thick with emotion.

"Aye, aye," Silas said, coughing to clear his throat.

"Well, we also found these," Teddie said as the lights came on in the room, and Fran brought them a leather bound portfolio. She set it gently on Silas's lap. The ancient red leather had darkened to brown around the edges and along the stitching, and the embossed gold letters had faded with time. They spelled out one word: FAMILY.

"Are you okay?" Sara asked, and Silas nodded before opening the heavy cover. When she saw the first image, Sara's heart melted. It was an ancient charcoal sketch portrait, the paper thick and yellowing, of a very young boy, instantly recognizable as Silas, shoulder length curly hair, probably six years old.

"Oh my heart," Sara said.

"I remember this," Silas said. "A man came to the farm, he did these sketches of all of us, he came a couple times."

Turning the page, they saw another sketch, a slightly older Silas, this time his hair choppy and short, a dour expression on his face.

"I hated sitting still for this guy," Silas said. "Wow, I haven't thought of this in nearly six hundred years, this is insane."

Turning the pages, the charcoal sketches gave way to small watercolors and then, Silas froze. The next image was a sketch portrait of a very young Sara.

"Oh," she said quietly. "That's me, but I'm young. That would have been when Crina started to visit my village. Look at me, what a little urchin I was."

Indeed, in the sketch, tomboy Sara was wearing a leather vest over a simple shirt or dress.

"Keep going," Silas said. "I want more baby photos of you."

Instead, when they turned the page, Sara was shocked to see a chalk and charcoal portrait of Teddie as a tiny child. Sara burst into tears, and Silas waited patiently before turning to the final page, revealing another portrait of Teddie, this time, she was seated on her mother's lap.

"Oh Teddie," Sara sobbed, "I'm seeing your mother's face all over again, this is beautiful."

Teddie stood and rested her hands on Sara's shoulders, squeezing them tight.

"Well, then you're going to love the rest of Crina's stash. You guys, there are paintings and daguerreotypes and just so much stuff. There's a daguerreotype of me and my mom, and as soon as I saw it, I remembered Crina taking us to the photographer's studio, and how uncomfortable momma was with sitting for so long. Sara, these photos are as much of a gift for me as they are for you."

On the couch beside her, Silas gently folded the book closed, and pulled it against his chest as sobs rocked his body.

Around them, people rose and moved away, but Sara paid them no mind. She let her head fall onto Silas's shoulder and he pressed his cheek against her hair. The windows lightened, flooding the room with day, and Sara heard corks popping in another room and then Teddie was pressing a flute of champagne into her hand.

"To love, you guys," Teddie said, and Sara looked around the room at the faces of people whose lives she'd built, and whose effect on her own life was inestimable. For once in her life, she was lost for words.

"To acceptance," Silas said loudly beside her, rising to his feet and pulling her up with him.

"To the future," Sara said. "I'm so grateful that this is my future."

"And to Crina," Teddie said, "for being the mother we all needed."

"And doing what needed to be done," said April Veronica and Embla in unison.

When they were all done drinking, an awkward silence fell over the room, the enormity of Crina's truth still too raw to process, small talk too obvious to endure.

Fan and Ama circulated, gathering the empty champagne flutes and taking them to the kitchen.

"Okay, you bloodsuckers," Fan yelled, "there's no such thing as a free ride. Let's get the animals fed so we can relax for the rest of the day."

Hours later, her skin itching like crazy from the straw, Sara hoisted herself onto a bale and watched as Silas, Rad and Fran loaded the last of the bales onto a small trailer hitched to a quad, and Rad zoomed off to feed the horses in the upper paddock. Their work was done. Sara followed Rad's ascent up the mountain, little flowers dotting the grass, horses and sheep grazing or resting in the shade below young trees, the dip of the little valley they'd all be living in. She knew she was looking at her future, very clearly. She saw the vision and dedication of Fan and Ama, their refusal to extend their lives any further, the way they were embracing mortality, with the same pure sense of adventure they'd brought to six centuries of love.

Looking out over the rolling green and yellow hills, the ocean sparkling in the distance, Sara realized what Fan and Ama had done. They had created their own Deathland, a happy place for them to age in, to eventually die in. And now they had peopled it with people that they loved, to finally create the utopia they'd fought for, forever.

Then Sara took in Silas, as he and Fran lost themselves in gossip and feeding handfuls of grass to some visiting horses, the sunlight hitting the errant curls in Silas's black hair. She was happy that he was reunited with Fran, they had a similar humor and now he had someone to talk music with. He threw his head back in laughter, at something Fran had said, and in that moment, Sara saw the farm in a second way, as something Fan and Ama built out of love for Silas, a gift for the man they loved as if he were their own child. A man blessed by many mothers.

She drank in the vista before her, a land that would be good for her man, the perfect world for his good nature, his wild, accepting heart and his insatiable curiosity, and she felt a great peace. With it came the knowledge that at some point, no time soon but eventually, they might tire of living, and this could become their Deathland too. They could tend this land as they aged. She imagined seeing Silas get wrinkles, laughlines marking his face, while his eyes, his beautiful brown and orange pupils, stayed the same. She knew he'd always look at her with love, a love that had saved her life, more than once. This place was their home, until they both decided it was time for that next adventure, beyond this world.

A crackling in the grass behind her startled Sara, making her gasp as she spun around to see Stefanya, almost unrecognizable in gray overalls, her black hair pulled back into two tight braids.

"Sorry, my child," she said with a warm smile. "I didn't mean to make you jump. Hope it was a good reverie."

Sara was never sure if she should hug Stefanya, so she stood still, her arms limp, until the woman reached her and threw her arms around her shoulders.

"Hey Stef," Sara whispered. "I was lost in, you know, the usual."

"Sex and death?" Stefanya released the hug and stepped back.

"Love and death," Sara said with a shrug.

"So much worse," Stefanya chuckled.

"I almost didn't recognize you in... what did you used to call it?"

"Icelandic GAP," Stefanya laughed. "Damn you for remembering. Also, I'm dressed like this because I'm decorating my new home. I'm hosting our dinner tonight and I can't wait for you to see my house. It contains many hidden surprises for you, specifically."

"I'm not sure if I like the sound of that," Sara said. "But I'm down to find out. I need a shower first, after, you know, the longest flight on earth, making a life-changing decision and then feeding the menagerie."

"I love all of this for you," Stefanya leaned forward and sniffed at Sara's armpit. "And for all of us, But first, if you don't mind, I'd like to show you something."

Without another word, Stefanya took Sara's hand and led her along a worn path through the yellow-green grass. As they walked, Sara craned her head backwards and watched as Silas and Fran sped off in an ATV. When she turned her attention back to the direction Stef was taking her, she was surprised to see a small grassy knoll topped by a wild, circular garden, at least thirty feet across. Rose bushes bloomed in riots of red, yellow, pink and white, and between them she saw familiar herbs, sage, lavender, and thyme, as well as plants she could not identify, small, scruffy Icelandic natives, flowering in spikes of tiny white and purple flowers. The path that they were on led into the heart of the garden. When they neared the center, Stefanya pulled her forward until they stood level in front of a a low cement pedestal topped with a rough-hewn block of black granite, an engraved metal plate facing them.

CRINA ATANASE

MOTHER

WARRIOR

PROTECTOR

A wave of powerful, complex emotions washed over Sara, and she smiled as tears rimmed her eyes.

"Ama and Fan did this," Stefanya explained, squeezing Sara's hand, her voice low. "They brought her ashes here, to her home. This is the first grave of any Cursed woman, as far as I know."

"It's beautiful," was all that Sara could manage, and they stood in silence, their eyes locked on the gravestone until Sara could continue. "Stef, I still can't think about her, about that day, without feeling like I let her down, like we all let her down."

Stefanya took Sara's other hand and pulled her around to face her.

"Please, child, stop that nonsense," Stefanya's chocolate eyes were full of compassion. "Even more than me, Crina was a warrior. Unlike me, she never took breaks, she never took her eye off the prize. And do you know why?"

Sara shook her head, wincing as if she expected a blow.

"She loved you and Silas so much and she felt that it weakened her. No matter how fierce she was in battle, she carried a vulnerability that no other sister had. And so she overcompensated. Sara, she overcompensated for being a mother."

"I just hate that she did this alone," Sara said.

"She didn't," Stefanya said. "She always told me what she was doing. I helped her when she needed it or when I wanted to, but even then, this was her private crusade. Once she discovered that eventually the virus would turn us all into killers, protecting us became her strength. She let her love for all of us transform her into our greatest protector. She loved watching us all dance along merrily, believing our ideal could last forever."

"I have spent forty years believing that I let her down," Sara spoke words she hadn't even been able to say to Silas.

"Sara, my love. She was in awe of you. Many of us were. She didn't throw you to the wolves in New York. She honestly believed that you were the exception to the rule. Your strength, your resilience, and your astonishing ability to never let the virus control you. She believed that you were the one who could save us all."

"And look how that turned out," Sara began.

"I'm looking at it," Stefanya said. "And I couldn't be more proud. Sara, you're exactly the person that Crina knew you were. The ideal that Crina died to protect is alive in you, and Silas. Because of you, I see it in all the women here."

"And men," Sara whispered.

"They're honorary women to me," Stefanya laughed. "I need to get back to my place and get ready for your visit. Why don't you wait here, and I'll send Silas up."

"Thank you, for this and for that," Sara smiled, for she had been feeling guilt over seeing Silas's mother's grave without him. Releasing her hands, Stefanya bent to pick a hot pink rose from a bush.

"Ouch," she muttered, raising her hand to show Sara a vibrant red pearl of blood on her finger tip. In Sara's nostrils, the scent of the blood mixed with the heady fragrance of the rose. "A snack," Stefanya joked as she popped her finger into her mouth, and then turned and walked off along the path, leaving Sara alone, the wind whistling in her ears as she turned back to face Crina's headstone. Golden sunlight sparkled from a million facets in the granite, and Sara's heart swelled as

Stefanya's words settled into the dark places where she had harbored shame, bringing her peace.

More than a gravestone, she felt Crina's presence on this land as an anchor and a talisman, and it reassured her. She turned slowly, spending time examining the tiny flowers, each one a miniature masterpiece, life bursting through hostile soil. She inhaled deeply, the cleanest air she'd ever breathed, scented with rose and sage. She hoped that she would be able to remember Stefanya's words for Silas, to explain Crina in a way that would bring him to this feeling of finally understanding.

A motor in the distance caused her to turn. Silas was speeding her way on an ATV, his open shirt flapping behind him. Their eyes met and he grinned, raising a hand and waving. Watching his approach, Sara's heart was full, her head swimming with the beautiful reality of her life, and she felt profound gratitude. She was even grateful to herself, for pushing ahead even though life is always a mystery, always a gamble, always a heartbreak.

Her future was hurtling towards her, the way future always does. She saw endless peace, love and camaraderie. Every day bringing another waterfall, a new rainbow.

Sara sighed and closed her eyes. She finally knew the truth she'd been seeking for so long, the pursuit of which had driven her to the brink of ruin back in the 2020s.

There was no meaning to life except love.

And eternity was nothing without it.

The End

Acknowledgements

Firstly, if you've followed Sara's story through to its end, I thank you wholeheartedly. I hope you're happy with where she ended up. I started writing this book just after the 2024 election, and the process kept me afloat during the aftermath: the human rights attacks, the siege on my hometown, and the general darkness of neonazism that has enshrouded the globe. Art and creativity remain our greatest solace, our greatest defense and our greatest gift. I hope that I was able to brighten your time with these books. While it's time to say goodbye to Sara, I will stay in the Vampire State world. The next books will surprise you. I promise.

This book is dedicated to Heather Taylor, my dearest friend since I was eighteen. When I started thinking about Sara's life, I couldn't imagine it without a Heather of her own: A friend of immense integrity, a heart the size of the ocean, a wicked dry sense of humor. Someone that she could always talk to and trust. Even though my Heather is in Australia and I'm not, we talk constantly, and at the end of a two hour phone call, we invariably text each other things we forgot to talk about. I needed Sara to have that friend, because I know that having Heather in my life has made it immeasurably better. I love you Heather. So much.

I'd be lost without my husband, George Castro, he's my everything. He's also a brutally honesty story editor. His help on this book was huge. Te amo, bubbass.

My phenomenal sister/cousin Skye Pyman edited this book, and also did some supportive heavy lifting when things got hard. Skye, I love you more.

We lost Miss Tuna during the writing of this book, making it my first book not completed with her asleep at my feet. Olivia and Graciela took over the job of delivering puppy kisses. Dogs make everything better.

Once again, my ultra-talented lifelong friend Steve Gidlow helped with headshots, practical magic and cover design.

We finally visited Spain! Thanks and love to our incredible hosts, Emily Thompson & Felix Schliebitz. Tintos de verano forever.

I am grateful for these books because they brought Jane Estes into my life. Jane is a champion of writers and readers, as well as one hell of an inspiring human. I'm honored to call her a friend.

As usual, Lindsey Kelk was my sanity saver, and I hope I was hers. We will always have Kamala cake, LK. Always.

I'm insanely lucky to have a circle of incredible friends who delight me with a million things while I'm writing. In no particular order, thanks and buckets of love to Tammy Germani, Christine Weiss, Patricia, Matt, Benicio & Felipe Stone, Liz Tooley, Yfke Van Berckelaer & Hugues Barbier (I never knew singing in a French castle was on my wish list...), Christine Linardon, Valentina America, Paul Amirault, Adriane & Tom Boat, Larry Hardy, Nichole Fifield, Yukari Fujimoto, Rosa & Hector Castro, Bhava Sangita, Barbara Binstein, Joan Oexmann, Heather Long and Kim Kahl. You're all amazing and your friendship is a blessing to me.

Art brings light to darkness. We fight for what's right. And we try to leave the planet in better shape than we found it.

Humbly,

KJD

About the author

Kevin Dickson is an Australian-American author who lives in the hills on the edge of Los Angeles with his husband George, their two dogs, Graciela and Olivia, and a vicious parrot named Chapulín. When he's not writing, Dickson likes to play records, tend his garden, hike, travel and tirelessly consume movies, books and music.

The author does not endorse or enjoy social media. Any official accounts will be poorly and sporadically managed, at best.

To contact the author, please email vampirestatebooks@gmail.com

Other books by Kevin Dickson

From Him To Eternity: Vampire State book one
Seasons Of Blood: Vampire State book two
Deathland: Vampire State book three
The Winter Forever: Vampire State book four (Fall 2026)
Blind Item (co-author)
Guilty Pleasure (co-author)